PRAISE FO...

Colonel Brandon...

"The hero of *Colonel Brandon's Diary* has more tragedy ... his life than any three or four bodice-ripping Regency rakes. Elopements! Duels! Adultery! Love children! *This is Jane Austen?* the skeptic might ask; we reply, it sure is! It's all in *Sense and Sensibility*, cunningly hidden in the backstory, but Amanda Grange has brought this dramatic tale to full life in the best book yet in her series of heroes' diaries."

—*AustenBlog*

"In her fifth novel in the Austen Heroes series, Amanda Grange has actually succeeded in improving upon Austen's character Colonel Brandon . . . As always, Grange is one of the most gifted writers in the Austen subgenre, giving us a touching inside story that is hard to put down."

—*Austenprose*

Edmund Bertram's Diary

"Amanda Grange has hit upon a winning formula and retells the familiar story with great verve."

—*Historical Novels Review*

"Once again, Amanda Grange has provided a highly entertaining retelling of a classic Jane Austen novel, as seen through the hero's eyes . . . Pure fun, with the story told in a diary format that makes the reader feel like she's taking a peek into Edmund's innermost thoughts . . . I enjoyed every moment of it."

—*Romance Reader at Heart*

"A sympathetic portrait of a young man struggling with the difficult choices that life throws at us all."

—*AustenBlog*

continued . . .

Captain Wentworth's Diary

"Amanda Grange has taken on the challenge of reworking a much-loved romance and succeeds brilliantly."

—Historical Novels Review (Editor's Choice)

"In this retelling of *Persuasion* we are given a real treat . . . Like the other books in Ms. Grange's series, scrupulous attention is paid to the original, even while interpreting what is not explicitly shown, and some well-known scenes are fleshed out while others are condensed, nicely complementing the original." *—AustenBlog*

"Amanda Grange's retellings of Jane Austen's novels from the point of view of the heroes are hugely popular and deservedly so . . . *Captain Wentworth's Diary*, a retelling of Austen's *Persuasion*, will entrance and enthrall old and new fans alike." *—Single Titles*

"One of those wonderful historicals that makes the reader feel as if they're right in the front parlor with the characters . . . this book held me captive. It is well written and I very much hope to read more by this author. Amanda Grange is a writer who tells an engaging, thoroughly enjoyable story!" *—Romance Reader at Heart*

Mr. Knightley's Diary

"Sticks close to the plot of Austen's *Emma*, mixing [Knightley's] initially censorious view of Miss Woodhouse with his notes on managing the hereditary seat at Donwell Abbey and affectionate asides on his collection of young nieces and nephews." *—The Washington Post*

"A lighthearted and sparkling rendition of the classic love story."

—Historical Novels Review

"Charming . . . knowing the outcome of the story doesn't lessen the romantic tension and expectation for the reader. Grange hits the Regency language and tone on the head." —*Library Journal*

"Ms. Grange manages the tricky balancing act of satisfying the reader and remaining respectful of Jane Austen's original at the same time, and like Miss Woodhouse herself, we are given the privilege of falling for Mr. Knightley all over again." —*AustenBlog*

"Readers familiar with *Emma* should enjoy revisiting the county and its people and welcome the expansion of Mr. Knightley's role. Others will find an entertaining introduction to a classic." —*Romance Reviews Today*

"Well written with a realistic eye to the rustic lifestyle of the aristocracy, fans of Ms. Austen will appreciate this interesting perspective." —*Genre Go Round Reviews*

"A very enjoyable read and an amusing tale." —*Fresh Fiction*

Berkley titles by Amanda Grange

MR. KNIGHTLEY'S DIARY

CAPTAIN WENTWORTH'S DIARY

EDMUND BERTRAM'S DIARY

COLONEL BRANDON'S DIARY

HENRY TILNEY'S DIARY

DEAR MR. DARCY

LORD DEVERILL'S SECRET

HARSTAIRS HOUSE

Dear Mr. Darcy

A RETELLING OF *PRIDE AND PREJUDICE*

Amanda Grange

BERKLEY BOOKS, NEW YORK

THE BERKLEY PUBLISHING GROUP
Published by the Penguin Group
Penguin Group (USA) Inc.
375 Hudson Street, New York, New York 10014, USA

Penguin Group (Canada), 90 Eglinton Avenue East, Suite 700, Toronto, Ontario M4P 2Y3, Canada
(a division of Pearson Penguin Canada Inc.) • Penguin Books Ltd., 80 Strand, London WC2R 0RL,
England • Penguin Group Ireland, 25 St. Stephen's Green, Dublin 2, Ireland (a division of Penguin
Books Ltd.) • Penguin Group (Australia), 250 Camberwell Road, Camberwell, Victoria 3124, Australia
(a division of Pearson Australia Group Pty. Ltd.) • Penguin Books India Pvt. Ltd., 11 Community
Centre, Panchsheel Park, New Delhi—110 017, India • Penguin Group (NZ), 67 Apollo Drive,
Rosedale, Auckland 0632, New Zealand (a division of Pearson New Zealand Ltd.) • Penguin Books
(South Africa) (Pty.) Ltd., 24 Sturdee Avenue, Rosebank, Johannesburg 2196, South Africa

Penguin Books Ltd., Registered Offices: 80 Strand, London WC2R 0RL, England

This book is an original publication of The Berkley Publishing Group.

This is a work of fiction. Names, characters, places, and incidents either are the product of the author's
imagination or are used fictitiously, and any resemblance to actual persons, living or dead, business
establishments, events, or locales is entirely coincidental. The publisher does not have any control over
and does not assume responsibility for author or third-party websites or their content.

PUBLISHING HISTORY
Berkley trade paperback edition / August 2012

Library of Congress Cataloging-in-Publication Data

Grange, Amanda.
Dear Mr. Darcy : a retelling of Pride and prejudice / Amanda Grange.—Berkley trade paperback ed.
p. cm.
ISBN 978-0-425-24781-5
1. Darcy, Fitzwilliam (Fictitious character)—Fiction.   2. Bennet, Elizabeth (Fictitious character)—
Fiction.   3. Life change events—Fiction.   4. Upper class—England—Fiction.   5. Social classes—
England—Fiction.   6. Young women—England—Fiction.   7. England—Social life and
customs—Fiction.   I. Austen, Jane, 1775–1817. Pride and prejudice.   II. Title.
PR6107.R35D43 2012
823'.92—dc23
2011051898

PRINTED IN THE UNITED STATES OF AMERICA

10 9 8 7 6 5 4 3 2 1

AUTHOR'S NOTE

I've always been fascinated by Jane Austen's novels, and by *Pride and Prejudice* in particular. It was started in 1796–97 and then revised a great deal before being published in 1813. It seems likely that it was originally written in epistolary form since *Sense and Sensibility*, started at around the same time, was first drafted in this way.

Over the years I have asked myself what new characters would be necessary to reveal the plot if the epistolary form were used, and what interesting insights those letters would reveal. I imagined the feelings of the social climbing Caroline Bingley on first discovering that her brother knew Mr Darcy of Pemberley, and Louisa Bingley's feelings towards Mr Hurst. I imagined the family who lived at Netherfield and their reasons for vacating the house, so that it was fortuitously available for Mr Bingley to rent. I imagined letters between Elizabeth and her sensible Aunt Gardiner, and letters between Elizabeth and Jane. I imagined Mr Darcy's letters to his family when his father died and his feelings when he shouldered his responsibilities to his younger sister and the Pemberley estate. And I imagined his feelings for Elizabeth, revealed in his letters to his family and friends.

When other people want to explore their ideas about Jane Austen's books, they chat with fellow Janeites or write learned articles. When I want to explore my ideas, I write novels.

I have taken the opportunity to include the futures that Jane Austen herself planned for Mary and Kitty Bennet, revealed to her family members when they asked her what became of the other Bennet girls.

So here it is, my vision of how *Pride and Prejudice* might have looked in its earliest incarnation, written to entertain anyone who is in love with Jane Austen and *Dear Mr Darcy*.

Amanda Grange

1795

❧ MAY ❧

Pemberley, Derbyshire,
May 25

Dear Mr Darcy,

I hope I am not doing wrong by writing to you, being only the housekeeper, but your father is very ill and I thought you would want to know. The physician says it is nothing to worry about, just his old complaint, but I think it is different this time. I am taking it upon myself to write to you, so that you may come home and see for yourself if you wish.

Respectfully yours,
Mrs Reynolds

Cambridge, May 26

Mrs Reynolds, you have done me a great kindness. I have been worried about my father ever since I left him at Easter and I am exceedingly grateful to you for your concern. I shall set out at once and I hope to be with you the day after tomorrow.

Fitzwilliam Darcy

Mr Darcy Senior to Mr Darcy

Pemberley, Derbyshire, May 26

My dearest son,

I have discovered that Mrs Reynolds has written to you and I cannot find it in myself to condemn her since I believe she is right in her fears. I hope I will live to see you again but, in case you arrive too late, I will leave you this letter, so that I may say everything I wish to say.

I will begin by saying that I am very proud of you. You are everything I ever wanted in a son, for you are a true Darcy, and I can think of no higher praise than that. Remember at all times who you are and maintain a superiority of demeanour as you have a superiority of birth. Do not encourage the familiarity of the vulgar, for be warned, they will seek to bring themselves to your notice; but only assume the proper bearing and it will be enough to discourage their pretensions.

Take care of your sister, protect her from those who would ingratiate themselves with her and, as she grows older, keep her safe from fortune hunters. When the time comes, arrange a good marriage for her; a marriage to one of her equals but also to a man she loves. It is the dearest wish of my heart that she should be happy.

By that time, no doubt you will be married. Remember that the woman you favour with your hand will not only be a wife to you, she will also be a sister to Georgiana and the mistress of Pemberley.

She will need to command the respect of the servants and the love of your family; she must reflect the greatness of the Darcys; she must be a gracious hostess and a model of feminine virtue; she must be a modest lady; and she must be possessed of a refined taste and true decorum. And she must be a woman you can admire, respect and esteem, as well as love.

For advice on matters of this nature I refer you to my brother's son, your cousin Philip. He, too, bears the name of Darcy, and on his shoulders, as well as on yours, will fall the responsibility of upholding the Darcy traditions and continuing the Darcy name. It is a noble calling, and one in which I know you will excel.

Be affable to the poor, be kind to those in need, be a good landlord and a fair master. When anyone serves you with particular devotion, then repay it, as I have repaid the faithful stewardship of Mr Wickham. It was a delight to me to send his son to university, so that George might rise in the world and make his mark as a man of standing. I must now leave it to you to assist George in any way you think will be of benefit to him in the future; in particular, consider appointing him to the living of Kympton if he should go into the church. It is a valuable living with a good rectory and it will provide him with a respectable livelihood.

And now I can write no more, for I grow too weak to hold the pen. I hope that I will be spared long enough to see you again, but if not, I give you my blessing, my son, and I leave you with these words: be a good friend, be a fair man, be a tender brother, but at all times remember who you are: Fitzwilliam Darcy of Pemberley.

Your loving father,
George Darcy

～ JUNE ～

Mr Darcy to Mr Philip Darcy

Pemberley, Derbyshire, June 1

Philip, I write to you with terrible news. My father is dead. I arrived home, alerted by Mrs Reynolds, to find that he was very ill. I ran across the hall and as I climbed the staircase I thought it would never end. I reached the door of his room at last and I stopped for a moment to compose myself. The physician, hearing me, came out looking very grave. He shook his head and I had an awful moment when I thought that I was too late and that my father was already dead, so I steeled myself for the worst and went in. The room was dim and I could see nothing at first but then I made out his form on the bed. His chest was not rising and falling and as I went forward, my feet were as heavy as lead. But he turned his head and saw me and I fell to my knees at his side, taking his hand in mine, thanking God that I had returned home in time. He smiled and returned the pressure of my hand, and had time to give me his blessing before he closed his eyes and was gone.

How long I stayed there I do not know. Mrs Reynolds found me at last and helped me below. I sat in the dining parlour until the light faded and only stirred when the candles were brought in. The light falling on the miniatures over the mantelpiece roused me, and I thought how much my father had loved to see them there, often turning to the portraits of Georgiana and myself and looking at them with pride.

I cannot believe he will never see them again.

I feel empty and alone. And yet, in this empty state, I have more to do than ever before. The servants are looking to me to guide them, and not just the servants, but the tenants and the villagers, all those who rely on me and Pemberley and the Darcy name to shelter and protect them, and ensure their prosperity and well-being. They are all waiting for me to take the lead and I do not know where I am going to find the strength to do it. But I must find it, and soon, for everyone is depending on me, not least of all Georgiana.

She was very pale, poor little girl, when she heard the news. It went to my heart to see her so wan. I did what I could to comfort her but although I did my best, she needed a mother to help her, yet her mother is now long dead. To be an orphan at only eleven years old. Poor child! She is as lost as I am.

I thank God for my aunt Adelaide. She set out from Cumbria as soon as she heard the news and she has now taken Georgiana back to Cumbria, where our Fitzwilliam cousins will pet her and spoil her and do everything in their power to cheer her. I saw her depart with a pang, but I can rest in the knowledge that I have done what is best for her.

My cousin Henry came with my aunt and remained here when my aunt returned to Cumbria. You remember Henry Fitzwilliam, my military cousin on my mother's side, I am sure. He will be with me for the funeral but I would value your support as well. I must be dignified and give a lead to the other mourners, but at present I do not know how I am to survive it. Will you come?

Darcy

Mr Philip Darcy to Mr Darcy

Wiltshire, June 2

I will come at once.

PD

Lady Adelaide Fitzwilliam to Mr Darcy

Fitzwater Park, Cumbria,
June 3

My dear Fitzwilliam,

You will want to know how we are all getting on in Cumbria. Georgiana is very quiet and your uncle is shocked to see how altered she is, being so thin and pale, but we are all determined to help her out of her grief. Thank goodness it is summer and so she can go out of doors. Maud means to take her out riding this afternoon. It is a fine day and we hope the fresh air will put some colour in her cheeks. Peter has promised her one of Sheba's puppies, and although she did not appear to pay much attention to him at the time, she later asked me how many puppies there were and so I am sure the sight of them will do her good. We will take care of her and keep her with us until she is restored to her former animation.

We are all so proud of you and the way you are bearing your bereavement. Your father would be very proud of you, too. It gives you some comfort, I hope, to know that your family are all thinking of you.

Your loving aunt,
Adelaide

Mr Darcy to Lady Adelaide Fitzwilliam

Pemberley, Derbyshire, June 4

You will never know what a help your letter has been to me. To know that Georgiana is safely with her cousins and looking forward to choosing a new puppy helps me to bear what has to be borne.

The funeral is now over, thank God. Henry and Philip were with me and were a great support to me, walking one on either side of me as we set out on our melancholy journey behind the coffin.

As we set off down the drive I thought of nothing but my father: the day he set me on my first pony; the day he taught me to fish; the look of pride on his face when I started school; the advice he gave me when I came of age; and the last sad but treasured memory of him taking my hand and giving me his blessing as he died.

As we left the grounds and turned onto the road, I was comforted by the sight which met my eyes, for the road was lined with people, their heads bowed and hats removed, all gathered to pay their last respects. They fell in quietly behind us as we passed, and, as we walked, more and more people joined the procession—all silent, but giving me strength by their presence and by the obvious love they had felt for Papa.

By the time we reached the church, the procession stretched back as far as the eye could see. The church was soon full, and those who could not find room inside waited peacefully outside. I heard their voices murmuring the responses, coming through the open door with quiet feeling. Mr Light gave an inspiring sermon and my father was finally laid to rest with all the dignity of his position, and all the love of his family, and all the regard of his fellow men. And as the earth fell on the coffin, I said good-bye.

We turned away, and as we did so, I felt an unexpected lightening of my gloom. For the first time I felt that I could bear the loss and that I could take my father's place as the master of Pemberley.

In some way I feel his spirit is still with me. I have his words to guide me, and the letter he left me to sustain me, and I know that I am fortunate to have them, and that I was fortunate to have him as my father.

By the time we returned to Pemberley, Mrs Reynolds had prepared a hot meal for all the mourners. Our neighbours gave me their condolences and remembered the many happy times they had had with my father, whilst the kitchens and stables overflowed with everyone from the neighbouring villages who had followed my father to his last resting place, and who each had a tale to tell of his kindness and generosity.

And now it is over and life must go on. Henry is to return to his regiment but Philip has agreed to stay with me until the end of the month and help me with all the affairs that need to be set in order. And when I have seen to the most pressing business, I will be ready to bring Georgiana back to Pemberley.

Your affectionate nephew,
Fitzwilliam

Lady Adelaide Fitzwilliam to Mr Darcy

Fitzwater Park, Cumbria,
June 20

My dear Fitzwilliam,

We have been thinking of you constantly over the last few weeks and we were all glad to hear you speak so movingly of the funeral, and to learn of your own dignified part in the affair. It is never easy to lose a parent and it is even harder when you are only two and twenty. I am glad Philip is with you. Having lost his own father when he was young, he will be able to help you through this difficult time.

I am sure that Philip will be able to help you with all your matters of business, too, but should you need any further help with your affairs, your uncle has commanded me to say that you may call upon him at any time.

Georgiana's spirits are much improved and she has lost her sad, pinched look. We took her to Ullswater a few days ago and had a picnic by the lake, which she must have enjoyed, because when Peter gave her a puppy—a beautiful golden bitch—she named it Ullswater. Her reason was that the puppy's eyes were like liquid, which reminded her of the lake. But Sam the groom set her giggling by saying that it was a very good name, as the puppy was "ullus watering" something! She tried to stifle her giggles, of course, thinking them not very ladylike, especially at such a time, but we were all so happy to see her laughing that we did not mind in the least. She is blossoming in our fresh Cumbrian air, and—thank goodness!—our Cumbrian sunshine. Your uncle was remarking only the other day that Georgiana must have brought it with her, for we have never seen such a summer and our usual rain has been held at bay.

Your cousin Maud is taking Georgiana riding again tomorrow and if the weather continues fine, we are going on another picnic on Saturday.

Your loving aunt,
Adelaide

Mr Darcy to Lady Adelaide Fitzwilliam

Darcy House, London, June 26

Ullswater! How I would love to see Georgiana laughing again; even hearing about it does me good! I must confess, though, that I am concerned about her future; not the next few weeks or even months, but the next few years. I cannot always be at Pemberley and I do not want her to be alone in such a great house. I am thinking of sending her to school, so that she will have constant company and other girls of her own age to mix with. Let me know what you think of the idea; I would value a woman's opinion. Ullswater would have the run of the estate whilst she was away, with the other Pemberley dogs, and be there to welcome her on every return.

Please thank my uncle for his offer of assistance but I believe we have things well in hand. The only matter that troubled me was the matter of my father's godson, George Wickham—I dare say you will remember him—because, in my father's will, he spoke of me giving the living of Kympton to George when the present incumbent dies. This I would willingly do, were it not for the fact that George is not suited to the church. My father saw George's charm and his ease of manner, because that is what George took care to show him, but George has a darker side and I have had ample opportunity to see it during our time at university together.

I have spoken to the family solicitors about the matter and they have reassured me that my father's will only *requested* that George be given the living, rather than stipulating that it should be so. It has set my mind at rest on the subject, particularly since I now think more poorly of George than ever. I invited him to the funeral but I had no reply until this morning, when he claimed my letter had gone astray. Since his own letter was clearly a thinly veiled request for money, I told him that my father had left him the sum of one thousand pounds, and I arranged for the amount to be sent to him at once, but I cannot forgive him for not attending the funeral.

He thinks no more of his own father than he did of mine. Old Mr Wickham has been ill for some time and is not likely to live for more than a few months, and yet George never visits him, even though I have repeatedly asked him to. It will be a sad day for the Darcy family and a sad day for Pemberley when old Mr Wickham dies.

I will join you at Fitzwater Park as soon as I have finished with business in London, and then I must take Georgiana home to Pemberley. I cannot thank you enough for taking care of her, and for restoring her to health and happiness.

Your affectionate nephew,
Fitzwilliam

⤙ JULY ⤚

Fitzwater Park, Cumbria, July 3

School is a good idea; I will write to all my friends and find out which they think the best for her. She will not need to go at once, however, and we are hoping you will leave her here with us until the end of August at least. When you have finished with your business affairs, then why not spend a few weeks in Cumbria with us before taking Georgiana back to Pemberley?

You need not worry about her education in the meantime, for we are not neglecting it, I assure you. She is playing the pianoforte every day, she sings and dances with her cousins, she sketches and paints and sews, and when she is not doing any of these things she is training Ullswater, who is eager to please and who follows her everywhere. It is charming to see the two of them together.

Your uncle and cousins send their best wishes, and I am

Your loving aunt,
Adelaide

～ AUGUST ～

Darcy House, London, August 1

Thank you for your list of schools; I mean to visit them all. I will be glad of the occupation, for it will help to banish the low moods that come over me from time to time as I think of my father and everything I have lost. But Philip has been a great help to me, and so have all my friends and acquaintances—the ladies in particular.

When they knew I was visiting schools in order to choose one for Georgiana, they all had something to say on the matter; indeed, they all expressed themselves ready and willing to help with Georgiana in any way they could. I never knew that such noble sentiments lurked beneath the surface of so many beauties, for it seems they are all longing to have a sister! If I were inclined to vanity I should think it was my fine person that attracted them, for I hear myself described so everywhere I go, but I suspect that if my fortune dwindled to ten pounds a year, instead of ten thousand a year, my figure would be held to be nothing out of the ordinary.

However, I have been thinking of matrimony, I must admit. I never intended to marry until I was thirty, but now that I am the last of my line I think I owe it to Pemberley not to wait so long, for I find myself worrying about what will happen if I were to die without a child.

The estate is not entailed and so I can leave it where I will, and I have left it to Georgiana. If anything happens to me, I know that she will be well provided for and that she will not have to leave her family home. But the estate would be a heavy burden to her, being so young, and would have to be left in the care of a steward. If Mr Wickham were healthy, then I would not be so concerned: he served my father well, and the estate would be safe in his hands. But his health is precarious and I fear he will not live much longer. Besides, when Georgiana marries she will take her husband's name and the Darcy name in Derbyshire will die out. And so if I can find a suitable wife I believe I will wed.

I have been looking about me but no one satisfies me. My aunt Lady Catherine has often said that she and my mother betrothed Anne and myself when we were in our cradles, but that is a long time ago and I am persuaded that Anne likes the idea no more than I do. I cannot believe that Lady Catherine is serious in expecting us to carry out the wishes of our mothers, which were formed when we were no more than a few months old.

My father gave a lot of thought to the matter of my marriage and wrote about it at length in his final letter to me, and I owe it to myself, as well as to Pemberley, to take his words to heart. My wife will not only have to be my companion for life, she will also have to be the mistress of Pemberley and a sister to Georgiana, and I have found no one worthy of any of those roles.

Philip understands. As the head of his household he has similar duties, although even he is not in such a precarious situation. He has brothers who are only a few years younger than himself to inherit if he should die without a son, and they would be fully able to run the estate, whereas I do not have such a luxury.

Perhaps you can introduce me to some young ladies in Cumbria. I am sure you must know someone you think might suit me and I hope to join you there next week. Henry intends to travel with me. Now that Spain has made peace with France, he has a brief period of leave. I hope it is not a signal that the coalition is going to collapse. I do not want to see Europe ravaged by more wars, but I fear it is inevitable. We expect to be with you by Wednesday. I am looking forward to seeing you all again, particularly Georgiana. I have missed her.

I am enclosing a note for Georgiana with this letter.

Your affectionate nephew,
Fitzwilliam

Mr Darcy to Georgiana Darcy

Darcy House, London, August 1

Dearest Georgiana,

I will be joining you in Cumbria next week and I will be staying with you for the summer and then bringing you home with me. Your bedroom has been newly decorated with a blue paper and there is a basket for Ullswater, though I hope you have trained her not to water everything! I have missed you and I am looking forward to seeing you again.

Your affectionate brother,
Fitzwilliam

Colonel Fitzwilliam to Mr Darcy

Fitzwilliam House, London,
August 5

A note in haste. I am sending this by hand as I will not be able to travel to Cumbria with you after all. I have been called back to my regiment and by the time you receive this I will already be on the Continent. I will not conceal from you that things look bleak. There are rumours that more countries are set to make peace with France, and if that happens, I believe that only England will have the stomach, and the purse, for further opposition. Give my love to my family and tell Georgiana that I am looking forward to seeing her when I return to England.

By the way, I saw your friend George Wickham this morning. He was rolling out of a tavern at ten o'clock, drunk. He presented a sorry spectacle, lurching from one side of the road to the other. He is young yet, and there is a chance he will mend his ways before he is very much older, but it is lucky your father left it to you to decide if George should hold the living, for otherwise he would bring the church, the neighbourhood and the living—as well as himself—into disrepute.

Your cousin,
Henry

～ SEPTEMBER ～

Darcy House, London,
September 25

I am sending this letter in care of your regiment and I hope it finds you, wherever you might be. I am beginning to wonder whether we will ever see peace on the Continent again. I thank God we are protected by the English Channel and that our navy keeps us safe, although I hear that the government are intending to repair and strengthen our coastal defences as a precaution against invasion.

Georgiana is now at school, where she is happily established. She was sorry not to see you and is looking forward to your next meeting. She will be much grown by the time you return. She has lost the sad, pinched look she had when Papa passed away, largely thanks to your mother. I am exceedingly grateful for it. I thought at one time that she would never recover, but all things pass and she is happy again.

I am not surprised by what you tell me of George Wickham. I have seen him several times in London myself. On the first occasion he tried to speak to me, but as he was under the impression there were three of me, he did not know which one to address and so he contented himself with falling over instead. On the last occasion, he was too busy with his women to notice me. Unless he changes, I doubt if he will even want the living. He has not shown any interest in the church, and I do not think he has any intention of becoming ordained.

You will be welcome at Pemberley when you return. Send a letter to announce your arrival if there is time or, if not, come anyway.

Your cousin,
Darcy

⤞ NOVEMBER ⤝

Mr Wickham to Mr Darcy

The Red Lion Inn, London,
November 6

My dear Darcy,

I owe you a letter! It must be nearly six months since I received your last. I neglected to thank you for the one thousand pounds, for which I must apologise. I would have done so when I saw you in London, but you did not see me and I could not get away from my friends, so I am repairing the omission now. I must thank you, too, for paying for my father's funeral expenses and settling the small debts I had at the time. I hear you have appointed a new estate manager. I only hope he may be half the man my father was, God rest his soul.

I have been giving some thought to my future and I have decided not to go into the church, and so I have decided to relinquish all claim to the living your father so generously promised me. I hope you will now be able to bestow it elsewhere.

You will not think it unreasonable of me to ask for some kind of pecuniary advantage instead of the living. I mean to go into the law, and as you are aware, the interest on one thousand pounds—the sum your father generously left me—does not go very far. Your honoured father, I am sure, would have wanted me to have something in lieu of the living, and a further sum of money would be useful to me. Three thousand pounds should pay for my studies.

Your very great friend,
George

Mr Darcy to Mr Wickham

Pemberley, Derbyshire,
November 8

I am very pleased you have decided not to go into the church. I am also pleased you have decided to study for the law. I will send you three thousand pounds as soon as you resign all claims to the living.

Yours,
Darcy

Mr Wickham to Mr Darcy

The Red Lion Inn, London,
November 17

Thank you for the three thousand pounds in return for my forfeit of the living. You may be certain I will put it to good use. I will make your revered father proud of me.

Your very great friend,
George

1798

⤙ MAY ⤚

Longbourn, Hertfordshire,
May 6

Dear Aunt,

I am writing to thank you for the bonnet you sent me for my birthday, which I think is adorable and which is the envy of my friends. I have already worn it, you will be pleased to know. It adorned my head this morning on a walk into Meryton, where it was much admired. How lucky I am to have an aunt who lives in the capital and who can send me the latest styles! Thank you again for such a welcome gift.

I am being very much spoilt and I am having an enjoyable day. Jane has given me a new fan, which she painted herself, and Mary copied an extract from Fordyce's Sermons in her best handwriting and then framed it. She presented it to me 'with the hope that it would guide me through the Torrents and Turmoils of a Woman's Life'; Kitty gave me a handkerchief, and Lydia said that she would have given me a new pair of dancing slippers, but she had already spent her allowance. I had a new pair of boots from Papa, for my others were worn through. Mama gave me a new gown, in the hope it would help me to catch a husband, and said, sighing, 'Eighteen years old and still unwed! It is a sad day, Lizzy, a very sad day indeed.'

We are going to my aunt Philips's this evening for a celebratory game of lottery tickets. Charlotte Lucas will be there and Susan Sotherton, so I will have some congenial company. There is a rumour abroad that Charlotte's father means to give up his business and move out of Meryton now that he has been given a knighthood. I hope to hear more about it from Charlotte tonight.

Susan is not so fortunate in her papa. He is still drinking a great deal more than is good for him, and his gambling is causing the family some unease. They have already had to sell two of the carriage horses and more economies look certain to follow—if Mr Sotherton can be persuaded to make them.

It is fortunate that Netherfield Park is entailed on Frederick, so that at least Mr Sotherton cannot gamble the roof from over their heads, as he does not own it but only holds it in trust for his son.

An entail is a strange thing, is it not? Here are we, bemoaning the fact that our estate is entailed, so that Papa cannot leave it to Mama (or anyone else he pleases) when he dies, but must leave it to Mr Collins, meaning that we will no longer have a home.

But with Susan's family it is quite the reverse. They are relieved that Netherfield Park is entailed, for otherwise their papa could sell it and then they would no longer have anywhere to live. Mama hopes that one of us will marry Frederick, but as he appears to be quite as fond of drinking and gambling as his papa, we are none of us inclined to have him. We will not marry until we find men we like, admire, love and respect. Or, at least, Jane and I will not, though I cannot answer for my younger sisters, who seem to think that marriage to anyone is an object, just so long as they can do it by the age of sixteen.

Thank you again for my bonnet. It will have a second outing this evening, where I hope to astonish everyone with my finery.

Your loving niece,
Lizzy

Mrs Bennet to Mrs Gardiner

Longbourn, Hertfordshire, May 6

Ah! Sister, it is a sad day, a sad day indeed. To think I now have two daughters of eighteen years old or more and neither of them is married, nor in a way to being so. It is hard on a mother, very hard indeed. You know nothing of it yet, your children are still too young to be a worry to you, but it is a sore trial, it is a very sore trial indeed. And it plays havoc with my nerves. I have such palpitations when I think about it, such beatings of my heart, but no one here cares about it and no one pities me.

I did think, when Jane visited you a few years ago, and she met that nice young man in London who wrote her some poems, that she would soon be married, but it all came to nothing. You must ask her to visit you again. She can come to London at any time and Lizzy, too, can come at a moment's notice. There will be more young men for them in London than there are in Meryton.

Indeed, I do not know who there is for them to marry here. There is only Frederick Sotherton, a handsome young man to be sure, and the heir to Netherfield Park, but wild, sister, very wild.

If the Lucas boys were older ... But then, the Lucases never had any compassion, and their sons are too young even for Lydia. Do you not know anyone in London? We could all pay you a visit. We have not seen you or my brother for ever such a long time. You have only to say the word and we will be there in a trice, even though it is not pleasant for me to go out and about at my time of life. But no sacrifice is too great for my girls.

Your poor sister,
Janet

Mrs Gardiner to Miss Elizabeth Bennet

Gracechurch Street, London,
May 7

My dear Lizzy,

I am very glad that the bonnet was to your liking. I hope your day was enjoyable and that your mama did not bemoan your single state for too long. I am relieved that neither you nor Jane is inclined to have Frederick Sotherton. I remember him from my last visit—a young man who will get worse before he gets better, I dare say. I am sorry for Susan and her sisters. Their situation is far worse than yours; for, if your mama could only see it, there is very little danger of your papa dying for thirty years or more, by which time it is reasonable to assume that one of you will be settled in life and can help the others if need be. And if not, you can always come and live with us here.

But in this particular I agree with her: there are very few suitable young men in Meryton and so I have written to your mama, inviting you all to stay for a few weeks.

Your father, I dare say, will not feel he can join you, but we hope that your mama and sisters will stay with us until the end of June. You have not seen the children since Christmas and if you do not come soon, you will hardly recognise them when next you see them. Try to persuade your father to make one of the party. It will do him good to leave his library for a short while.

Give my love to your sisters,
Your fond Aunt Gardiner

Mrs Bennet to Mrs Gardiner

Longbourn, Hertfordshire,
May 9

Sister! You are so good to us! A few weeks in London is just what I need to set me up, and Jane will find someone, I am sure of it. All that beauty cannot be for nothing! We will have her married before the end of the summer, I am certain!

Your sister,
Janet

Miss Elizabeth Bennet to Miss Charlotte Lucas

Gracechurch Street, London,
May 20

Dearest Charlotte,

How welcome it is to be in London and with my aunt once again. To be sure, Jane and I have to suffer Mama's constant hints about finding husbands, but we have an ally in our aunt, who is full of sympathy and calm good sense. She, at least, does not want us to catch the attention of every man between the ages of twenty and sixty, and can talk about other things than fortunes, expectations and handsome faces. She even refrains from talking about bridal bouquets if we should happen to dance twice with the same young man. And yet, if anything were to persuade me to marry, it would be my aunt's example, because between her and my uncle there is love and understanding, with a great deal of mutual admiration and respect.

The house is a happy one and I must confess, if I could find the same, I would be willing to enter into the married state.

But for now I am enjoying being unencumbered and delighting in the sights of London. We have been to the Lyceum Theatre and been well entertained with *The Hypocrite*, a play taken from Molière's *Tartuffe*; we have been shopping and have bought some very fine muslin and a serviceable sarsenet from Grafton House; we have visited the museum and the British Gallery; we have walked in the parks and eaten ices at Gunter's; in short, we have been devoting ourselves to pleasure!

The little children are thriving and are all benefiting from Jane's company. She plays with them constantly and is always patient with them, and it is not difficult, for they are all of them well behaved.

The only person not very happy is my uncle. The war is bad for trade and he wishes it to end as soon as possible. We have met a number of émigrés here in London and they have seen horrors in their native France. It makes me very glad for what we have: a country where we might live out our lives in safety.

Does your brother still dream of going into the army? I hope not, or your mama will not know one easy day, worrying whether or not he is safe. Persuade him he would be better off joining the church, or following your papa into trade.

We will be here for another six weeks at least and we rely on you for news of home. Papa has promised to write but his letters are few and far between.

Your dear friend,
Lizzy

Miss Charlotte Lucas to Miss Elizabeth Bennet

Meryton, Hertfordshire,
May 22

Dearest Eliza,

What a time you are having, to be sure. I envy you your convivial entertainments and convivial company. With you and Jane gone from the neighbourhood, there is hardly anyone sensible for me to talk to. My mama is quite as eager as yours to see a daughter married, and continues to invite every promising young man to the house, but she is constantly disappointed. She invited an acquaintance of my papa's last week and contrived to leave me alone with him for half an hour, but it did not answer. He talked to me about the weather for five minutes and then buried himself in a newspaper. I was not altogether surprised, as he was a very handsome young man and evidently thought well of himself. But I do not despair of ever finding a husband, though I would be happy to know that one would be forthcoming in the next two or three years. I am not yet an old maid, but that time is not far off.

I do not hope for much in marriage. I am not romantic and I know that such felicity as your aunt enjoys is not to be expected, though no doubt it is welcome if it should come about. But if a respectable man should offer for me, I dare say I would take him, regardless of my expectations of future happiness.

My brother is still eager to go into the army, but as he is yet too young to enlist there is time for him to change his mind.

And now I must go. We are having some friends to supper and there will be an impromptu dance afterwards. Mama has hopes of Mr Williams and is showering him with hospitality, but I think he comes only for the table. He is a man who very much likes to eat.

Give my best wishes to your friends and family in London.

Charlotte

 JULY

Colonel Fitzwilliam to Mr Darcy

July 5

My dear Darcy,

At last I have time to write. I am not at liberty to divulge my position so reply to me at Fitzwilliam House and I will find your letter next month when I will, God willing, be home on leave. The army has been keeping me busy. You will have heard by now that the French have their sights set on Egypt and that General Bonaparte has landed in Alexandria. His aim is to disrupt our trade routes, but he is mistaken if he thinks Admiral Nelson will let him have all his own way. The French are no match for the British at sea.

I will call upon you at Pemberley on my way up to Cumbria. I hope to be there in the middle of August and I will be able to tell you much I am not at liberty to put in a letter. I know you are interested in the progress of the war and what it will mean for Pemberley, as well as our nation as a whole.

I am looking forward to seeing both you and Georgiana again.

I intend to thank her in person for the pipe case she embroidered for me; it was very prettily done. I have seen much worse work from girls of sixteen, and Georgiana is only fourteen. You must be very proud of her accomplishments.

Your cousin,
Henry

Mr Darcy to Colonel Fitzwilliam

Darcy House, London, July 12

You are welcome at Pemberley anytime, you know that. You must stay with us for as long as you can. Georgiana will be delighted to see you and so will I. I am in London at present, but I will be taking Georgiana back to Pemberley in a few days' time. I will be very glad to hear the truth about the war; we hear only a part of it here, and even that small part comes a long time after the event.

As for Georgiana, I am partial, but I agree with you. School has done her good and she is becoming very accomplished. I am very proud of her, as you will imagine, and I am persuaded my mother and father would have been proud of her, too.

I was worried, after my father died, that I would not be able to raise Georgiana, that I would not know how to take care of her, or how to make her happy; but the last three years have shown me that I am equal to the task. It has given me a great deal of pleasure, as well as a great deal of relief, to see her grow into such a happy . . . I was going to say, *girl*, but when I called her a little girl last week, she gave me a withering look and reminded me that she is fourteen. So you see, I am not a perfect brother, for all I flatter myself that I have done well!

You, it seems, *are* a perfect brother, if your sister Maud's comments are to be believed. I saw her in town yesterday, with your mama. They were buying Maud's wedding clothes. Maud spoke very highly of your good sense in liking her betrothed. I hear that he is a good man and likely to do well.

I had another chance encounter yesterday evening, for I came across Charles Bingley. Do you remember him? We were at school together. He was a few years younger than me, but I saved him once from a bout of bullying and his generous nature has liked me for it ever since. He has changed very little. He is still friendly and trusting. He reminds me of Georgiana in that way. Though he is some years older than her, being now at university, he has an innocence about him that is not often met with. I like it. Unfortunately, it makes him a target for every rogue in the city. I had to rescue him from the men who were fleecing him at cards and I suggested that, if he wished to play in future, he should join a reputable club. He confessed that he would like nothing better, but said he had no one to propose him, or to second him, either.

'If that is all,' I said, 'I will propose you myself.'

He thanked me unaffectedly and I liked him even more.

I mean to make sure he is elected to the club. His open temper is agreeable and a good foil for my reserve. I will never rid myself of it, I fear, as it is a Darcy family trait and unavoidable. My father had it and, as you know only too well, my cousin Philip has it, too. It is fortunate that your side of the family suffers from no such difficulty. My mother was forthright, your father, too, and our aunt, Lady Catherine, cannot be accused of being reticent, or backward in giving her opinions!

We will look forward to welcoming you at Pemberley. Philip will be here. It is a long time since you have seen him and I know he is looking forward to meeting you again. I have to warn you, however, that he will probably try to find you a wife. He is always encouraging me to marry and reminding me that I am the last of my line. Fortunately, I have outgrown the morbid fancies that plagued me following my father's death and I am content to take my time. A wife of mine must be beautiful, but in my experience, beauties are all too often conceited and I have no fancy for a conceited wife. Then, too, they rely on their beauty for their attraction and I must have an intelligent wife. All the bluestockings of my acquaintance are dull, however. Besides, they never want to leave town, and as I spend much of my time at Pemberley, that would not do.

I have looked about me in Derbyshire but I demand a great deal from a woman I could call Mrs Darcy, and as I have never met anyone who satisfies me I am content to remain a bachelor, at least for the time being.

If there is one thing I am looking forward to when I marry, it is that I will no longer be the target of every woman between the ages of sixteen and sixty. They follow me everywhere, and I grow tired of them flattering and praising me. How refreshing it would be to find someone who did not like me! But unless Pemberley should fall down, or I should lose my fortune, I believe I will search for such a woman in vain.

Darcy

Mr Charles Bingley to the Bingley family

London, July 15

Dear Mama, Papa, Caroline, Louisa, Ned, Harry, Amelia and Sue,

I should have written sooner, but upon my honour I have been very busy these last three weeks. I never knew it would be so difficult to engage a set of rooms! However, it is done now and I am very comfortable. My lodgings are in a good part of town and you will be pleased to know, Mama, that I have been invited to a number of par-

ties. I met one of my old schoolfellows, Darcy, at the Carmichaels'.
You have heard me speak of Darcy before: he saved me once at
school, when some of the older boys were making sport of me. He
performed a similar office for me two weeks ago and, though the bul-
lies wanted my gold this time and not my hide, the upshot is that he
has done me the great kindness of proposing me for White's. There
are many people who find him proud, but I have seen nothing of it.
He is taciturn and reserved with those he does not know, but he is
talkative enough with his friends, and I count myself lucky to be one
of their number.

Caroline, I have bought the satin you asked for, and Louisa, I
have bought you your music. They should reach you in Yorkshire in
the next few days.

My love to you all,

Your affectionate son and brother,
Charles

Mr Frederick Bingley to Mr Charles Bingley

Yorkshire, July 16

Well, my boy, your ma has been pestering me to write so I suppose
I had better get on with it. We were all very pleased to hear about
your friend Darcy helping you out. I said to your ma, 'Ma,' I said,
'there'll be no good comes of all this fancy schooling,' but she would
have you go to university, and I was afraid what would become of it.
But this Darcy sounds like the right sort and I'm glad you've made
friends with him. I don't know I hold with you joining a club, but
your mother says of course you must, it's what all the gentlemen do.

Just be careful, my boy, there's plenty of sharks in the water, in business and in the fine world, too.

Your brother Ned has destroyed all your mother's plans for him by saying he wants to take over the running of the shops. It won't happen for a while, not till I'm dead, or at least so old I can't manage, but I'm glad he's taking an interest—as glad as I was when you didn't. You're a good lad, Charles, and I'm proud of you, but you never did have a head for business. You'd have been robbed and cheated by everyone you had to deal with, and we'd have ended up bankrupt.

Your mother and sisters are dancing about, saying I'm to ask you more about this Mr Darcy, but I've told 'em if they want to know more they'll have to ask you themselves; I've work to do.

Your sister Caroline says she'll put a note in with my letter.

Well, my boy, take care, and write again soon, your mother looks forward to your letters.

Your proud Pa

Miss Caroline Bingley to Mr Charles Bingley

Yorkshire, July 16

Greetings and felicitations, dearest brother.

Louisa and I are longing to hear more about your friend Darcy. He is not . . . but no, I do not suppose so . . . and yet, perhaps . . . your Darcy is not *Mr* Darcy? Mr *Fitzwilliam* Darcy? Of *Pemberley*? If so, you must invite me to town *at once*. He is one of the most eligible men in England. He is just the sort of man I would like to marry. He has ten thousand a year besides his estate, and all my friends from the seminary would be green with envy if I became his wife. And why should I not? I am sure I am good enough for anyone. Let me know by return if it is he.

Your loving sister,
Caroline
    P.S. Thank you for the satin; it arrived this morning.

Mr Charles Bingley to Miss Caroline Bingley

London, July 18

Yes, Caroline, I mean *Mr* Darcy, Mr *Fitzwilliam* Darcy of *Pemberley*. Tell me, are we always to write of him in italics? If so, I must buy some new pens, for it is playing havoc with my nib. As for inviting you to town, it would do no good, for Darcy has returned to Pemberley and he means to remain there for the summer.
    I am glad the satin arrived.

Your loving brother,
Charles

Mr Frederick Bingley to Mr Charles Bingley

Yorkshire, July 20

Well, my boy, you weren't expecting another letter so soon, I'll be bound, but your ma's been pestering me to tell you to help your sisters and introduce them to some fine gentlemen. I believe we were a lot happier before all this tomfoolery, but your ma said as how we must have it now that the shop is doing well. She's got me dressed up in a cravat and a tailcoat and I can't get comfortable in 'em. Caroline and

Louisa are spoilt by their schooling and they don't want to have anything to do with the local lads. There's my clerk, now, he's been sweet
on Caroline for years, but she must have a fine house and a carriage
and all manner of things, and where is a lad like that to get 'em? I said
as much to your ma, but your ma mistook my meaning and said, 'Then
Charles must find our Caroline someone who can. This Mr Darcy's
left town but there are plenty of other fine gentlemen to be had.'

She says I'm to ask you to invite Caroline and Louisa to stay, but
don't do it if you don't want to, my boy.

Your proud Pa

Mrs Bingley to Mr Charles Bingley

Yorkshire, July 20

Now don't you go listening to your pa, Charles, of course you'll have
your sisters to stay. They'll be setting off tomorrow so you can
expect them on Thursday.

Your doting Ma

Mr Darcy to Mr Bingley

Pemberley, Derbyshire, July 23

I was glad to hear you had been accepted at White's. I am sure you
will find it useful to have a club in town. White's is the best, and of
course St. James's Street is a convenient location. If you will allow me,
I will give you a word or two of advice. Avoid the seats in the bow
window as they are jealously guarded by those who set value on such

things. Avoid, too, the betting book. You will find men there who will try to entice you into betting on any trivial thing, such as which raindrop will reach the bottom of the window first, but you should ignore their blandishments. They will soon realise you mean what you say if you hold true to your resolve, and then they will not trouble you anymore. If you have any difficulties of any kind, just mention my name. And a final word: business is never spoken of at the club.

The weather here is very good. Would you care to join me at Pemberley? The countryside is very fine and you would be welcome to spend the rest of summer with Georgiana and myself. You will not lack for other company, as we are hosting a house party here. You will meet some of your old schoolfellows, as well as two of my cousins, and I am persuaded you will enjoy yourself.

Yours,
Darcy

Mr Bingley to Mr Darcy

London, July 25

My dear Darcy,

Upon my word, it is very good of you to invite me, I would like nothing better than to come and stay with you. I have heard a lot about Pemberley and I would like to see it. I have never seen Derbyshire, either, and I am already looking forward to it. My sisters are with me at present, but they will be returning to Yorkshire on Wednesday and then I will be happy to join you in Derbyshire.

Sincerely yours,
Bingley

Mr Darcy to Mr Bingley

Pemberley, Derbyshire, July 27

Good, then it is settled. Since your sisters must pass through Derbyshire on their way up to Yorkshire, I suggest they join us at Pemberley for a sennight to break their journey. They will be most welcome. There are plenty of good walks about, and there is good riding, too. I can supply them both with horses if they are horsewomen; if not, they will find plenty to do in the house and gardens. My sister has a pianoforte and a harp, and she often sketches and paints out of doors. Though some years younger than your sisters, she is looking forward to welcoming them, as I am. Mrs Reynolds has prepared rooms for you all and we will expect you later this week.

Yours,
Darcy

Miss Caroline Bingley to Mrs Bingley

London, July 28

Mama,

Louisa and I are going to Pemberley! *Pemberley!* One of the finest estates in England. How green all my friends will be. I am sure Miss Darcy will be just as delightful as her brother. She is some years younger than Mr Darcy, Charles says, but so much the better. Louisa and I are sure we will dote on her. She plays the pianoforte and the harp, which means we will have plenty of opportunities to play duets with her and sing whilst she plays; and of course we will play whilst she sings, too. How wonderful it will be, spending the summer in Derbyshire! The invitation is only for a sennight, but you must not expect us back in Yorkshire very soon, for I am sure we can make ourselves indispensable to Mr Darcy and his sister and then they will both be begging us to stay.

By the bye, we have been shopping, as you might imagine, for we are both determined to look our best. Just think, by this time next year I might be Mrs Darcy, and you might be visiting me at Pemberley. I will be sure to write to you often and let you know all about it.

Your dutiful daughter,
Caroline

Mrs Bingley to Miss Caroline Bingley

Yorkshire, July 30

My dear girl,

I knew that all that schooling would pay off in the end. I told your pa so, but would he listen? Not he! I had to put my foot down sharp and make him send you to the seminary, and see where it's taken us! Now, don't you stint at the dressmakers'; you need plenty of finery to keep up with all the lords and ladies. I'm not going to have them saying as how you look like you came from trade; and no need to mention it—these grand folks look down on things like that. I'm sure you're just as good as any of them, and if you don't catch yourself a rich husband, then my name's not Bingley. Everyone says how you're the most accomplished girl they've ever seen, with your French and your Italian and your goodness knows what. And elegant! The neighbourhood's never seen anything like it. You can walk the length and breadth of a room with a book on your head, and I've never seen anyone do anything like that in my life. You make the most of your chances, my girl. Catch this Mr Darcy and then invite your old ma to Pemberley. What times we'll have! And don't you go counting the cost! Buy all the latest fashions and folde-rols and send the bills to your pa.

Your doting Ma

Miss Louisa Bingley to Mrs Bingley

London, July 31

Mama,

Will you speak to Caroline most seriously? She keeps saying that I must not try to attract Mr Darcy's attention, nor engage his affec-tions, when we go to Pemberley. She says that she is destined for Mr Darcy, she feels it most strongly, but this is absurd, she has never even met him. I am the eldest and I am the one with the strongest claim and I am sure I do not know why I should neglect a chance of fixing Mr Darcy. From what Charles says he is very rich and very handsome. Caroline will keep saying that I am as good as engaged to Mr Hurst, but Mr Hurst has not yet proposed, and he is so indo-lent that he might never summon up the energy to do so.

Do, pray, write to her, Mama, and do it by return.

Your loving daughter,
Louisa

⌒ AUGUST ⌒

Mrs Bingley to Miss Caroline Bingley

Yorkshire, August 1

My dear girl,

Now I know you have your heart set on this Mr Darcy, and small wonder if he is as rich and handsome as you say he is, but if he should happen to take a fancy to Louisa, then let him have her. We'll all be visitors at Pemberley, just the same.

Your doting Ma

Miss Louisa Bingley to Mrs Bingley

London, August 2

Dear Mama,

I hope your letter has done some good. I am sure I wish Caroline every success, but I believe Mr Darcy will prefer me. Caroline and I have been shopping as you instructed and we have bought two new bonnets apiece. Caroline has bought a new string of pearls and a fan, and I have bought three new pairs of shoes and a new reticule, as well as a brooch. We would have bought new dresses but there was no time to have them made. There is no time for anything, we are off in half an hour!

Your loving daughter,
Louisa

Miss Caroline Bingley to Miss Violet Cranmore

London, August 2

My dear, sweet, most amiable friend,

How long it seems since we were at the seminary together, and how I miss our conversations! What a joy it was to have such congenial company. It seems an age since I saw you. Have you seen any of our friends since we left the seminary? I hope they have weathered the years better than Maria Roberts. I saw her in town yesterday and I could not believe how ill she appeared. She was very thin and had neglected her looks entirely. Her face was covered in freckles. You would have been horrified to see her and I did not know where to look. It was truly mortifying.

But of course you do not know that I am in London. Louisa and I are presently staying here with my brother Charles. However, when you reply, I beg you will address your letter to Miss Caroline Bingley, Pemberley, Derbyshire, for we are on our way there to spend the summer with Charles's dearest friend, Fitzwilliam Darcy.

You will be pleased to know that my mama and papa are both well, as are my brothers and sisters. Do write to me at once, my fairest friend; I am anxious to hear that your family are well, and to hear all your news.

Caroline Bingley

Miss Violet Cranmore to Miss Caroline Bingley

Devon, August 4

My dearest, most adored friend,

How good it was to hear from you after such a long time, and how flattering to know that your communication was prompted by nothing more than a wish to be assured that my family and I are well. You will be relieved to know that they are all flourishing. My eldest sister is lately betrothed, and I am about to be betrothed as well. Papa thinks I am rather young, but Mama knows that it is True Love and so she does not stand in my way. You, of course, have plenty of time in which to find a husband. You are not so very old. Why, even Louisa, who is older than you, is not to be pitied, and when Sally Carpenter ventured to say that Louisa was becoming an old maid, I set her right at once.

I am very sorry you have to visit Mr Darcy. He is an ill-favoured man, I hear, and his park is very small.

Your eternally faithful friend,
Violet

Miss Caroline Bingley to Mrs Bingley

Pemberley, Derbyshire, August 4

Greetings and felicitations, dearest Mama.

You have never seen anything like Pemberley! It is the largest estate I have ever seen. There are woods and streams, and the drive is so long it took us ten minutes to reach the house. And what a house! The hall alone is larger than our morning room and dining room put together.

We were shown into the drawing room, where the furniture is the most handsome in the world. Almost as handsome as the master of the house! I never thought Charles would know anyone half so fine as Mr Darcy. He is tall, and even more handsome than his reputation, for you know the world is like to call a man handsome just because he is rich. He has dark hair and dark eyes, a fine figure and an air of being somebody. I would be very happy to live here all my days.

Write to Charles and tell him he must not speak of our leaving. I have told him so myself but he says that we must not outstay our welcome, but I am sure Mr Darcy will be just as glad to have us here for a fortnight as a sennight, particularly if we make ourselves agreeable to his sister. Pemberley is so large that two more visitors will not make any difference. And tell Papa he must buy an estate so that we might return Mr Darcy's hospitality at once.

Your dutiful daughter,
Caroline

Mr Frederick Bingley to Mr Charles Bingley

Yorkshire, August 6

Well, my boy, you've done it now. It's 'Mr Darcy this' and 'Mr Darcy that'—your ma can talk of nothing else. She wants me to buy an estate so I can invite your friend to stay. 'Can't he stay here?' I asked, but she gave me a look, you know how she is. She expects me to go out tomorrow and buy an estate before breakfast. I won't deny I've been thinking of buying somewhere in the country, away from town, a nice plain house with a bit more space for all of us. Your brothers and sisters are growing up so fast I keep falling over 'em these days. Ned's as big as I am and little Amelia is shooting up like a dandelion. But nothing will do for your mother unless it's got corbels and columns. I've been scratching my head, trying to think what corbels might be, but I'm none the wiser, so if you know, let your old pa know, because your ma won't be happy without 'em. I remember the time when all it took to make her happy was a new bonnet. Those were the days! I do my best, but between you and me, my boy, there's no pleasing women. Just remember that and you won't go wrong.

Your proud Pa

Mr Charles Bingley to Mr Frederick Bingley

Pemberley, Derbyshire, August 8

My dear Pa,

I have no more idea of what a corbel is than you do, upon my honour. Why not ask Ma? If she is so set on them, she must know what they are.

As for pleasing women, I beg to differ when you say that there is no way of doing it. There are dozens of women here and they seem very easy to please to me. I only have to dance with them or smile at them and they look at me in the most admiring manner. Upon my word, I never knew so many pretty girls existed. Darcy's house is full of them. They come to dinner, they come to balls, they come to stay.

Caroline and Louisa were quite put out at first, but I believe they have rallied and they content themselves with saying that Miss Buchanan's nose is too long or Miss Pearson's neck is too short, when I believe that every nose and neck in the place is perfect.

Give my love to Ma and the little ones,
Charles

Miss Caroline Bingley to Mrs Bingley

Pemberley, Derbyshire, August 8

Greetings and felicitations, dearest Mama!

What a day we have had. The most elegant rooms, the most refined company, the conversation of intelligent people and the exhibition of the most superior accomplishments! But best of all, Mama, Mr Darcy. I am convinced he likes me. He smiled at me most particularly when I asked his sister to play for me, and he smiled again when I said how well she played.

It was no more than the truth, I am sure, and if that is all it takes to please him, then I will be happy to compliment her for the rest of my stay.

He never takes his eyes from her when she performs and so I suggested that we play a duet. I sat with my best profile towards him, you may be sure, and I was gratified to feel his eyes upon me. He was pleased with our performance and applauded us most assiduously when we had done!

There is a great deal of jealousy here, but that is only to be expected. One of the other young women tried to lower me in the eyes of the company by remarking that Papa owned a string of shops, but fortunately Mr Darcy had just stepped out of the room and the remaining gentlemen were all either old or married, so their opinions were of no importance.

I have much more to tell you but it is time to dress for dinner. Tell Papa I will be wearing my best jewels as well as the new brooch he gave me. I am going to dazzle Mr Darcy in my amber silk. I will send this letter at once to let you know how I get on and I will write again when I am able.

Your dutiful daughter,
Caroline

Colonel Fitzwilliam to Mr Darcy

Fitzwilliam House, London,
August 8

Darcy, I am sorry to inconvenience you, but I have been delayed in London and I will not be able to call on you at Pemberley as soon as I had hoped. Maud's new brother-in-law wants to go into the army and I have promised to give him what help I can. I am meeting him in town in a few days' time. He is travelling to town posthaste, as he is worried that all the fighting will be over before he has time to enlist. How I remember those days! I, too, used to fear that the war would be over before I had a chance to make my mark, but it is still dragging on, five years after Louis was executed, and despite a recent improvement in matters, I fear another five years will not see the end of it. Rumour has reached me of a naval victory at Aboukir Bay, and I hope it may be so, for it will give our navy command of the Mediterranean once more and ensure the safety of our trade in the Indies. But even if rumour speaks true, there are many battles to be won before we win the war. We need more men, and if Maud's brother-in-law seems promising, I will exert my influence to help him.

Maud is very happy, you will be pleased to know. She asks me to give you her love, and tells me to remember her to Georgiana.

Yours,
Henry

Mr Darcy to Colonel Fitzwilliam

Pemberley, Derbyshire, August 10

The delay in your visit is no inconvenience, and Georgiana and I are looking forward to seeing you. We have a large party here and I think you will enjoy yourself. Charles Bingley is here with his sisters. I was right to take the trouble to know him better; he is an affable addition to our party. Although his father made his money in trade, having a string of shops in the north, Bingley has escaped the evils of his situation. He is proud of his father's enterprise, but in a quiet way, and does not embarrass himself—or me—by seeking to ingratiate himself with the local gentry. He is just Charles, cheerful, honest and generous spirited, and it is a pleasure to have him here.

His sisters, Louisa and Caroline, are very different. I suggested they join us as they were staying with Charles and would have to pass close by on their journey home, but they are far more conscious of their position. However, they are company for Georgiana. They are well educated, accomplished and very kind to her. They sing with her and play duets with her and go out riding with her, and so I tolerate their attempts to win my attention—or rather, to win my hand and my house. They will try to win your hand and your house, too, or should I say your father's house? But you are used to such assaults and well able to defend yourself and so I will say no more.

Yours,
Darcy

Colonel Fitzwilliam to Mr Darcy

Fitzwilliam House, London,
August 12

My duty is done. I found Maud's brother-in-law to be a promising young man and I have helped him to a commission, and now I am free to join you. I am already looking forward to it. The army offers many things, but an excess of well-bred female company is not one of them. I have had little company in London whilst on leave, either. Town is empty in the summer and everyone is on their estates. I am sure I will enjoy talking to your houseguests, even Louisa and Caroline! They may set their caps at me if they please, but I will give them fair warning that an earl's son has expensive tastes and that, if he is not the heir, as is my own sad case, he must take an heiress to wife.

By the bye, I saw George Wickham in town yesterday. At first I was not sure it was he, but he saw me and recognised me. I would as soon have walked on but he hailed me and so we exchanged a few words—a very few, for he was roaring drunk, though it was the middle of the afternoon. He was with some very unsavoury people, a man—I can hardly call him a gentleman—Matthew Parker, and two women. One of the women was hanging around George's neck and the other was bestowing her ample attentions on Parker. I could not understand more than one word in three, for his speech was slurred and he kept forgetting what he was saying, but I think he was trying to ask me for money. I am very sorry for it. I remember him when we were boys. He was likeable enough then. Perhaps he used his charm too freely to get his own way, but nothing worse.

With all his advantages of person, and all the material advantages your father gave him, I thought he would do better for himself. I thought—or at least I hoped—he would take after his father, who was a good man. I liked Mr Wickham very much, as you did, but I fear that George will come to a bad end.

Yours,
Henry

Mr Darcy to Colonel Fitzwilliam

Pemberley, Derbyshire, August 14

Henry, it will do you no good to tell Caroline you are in need of an heiress as she has twenty thousand pounds. You must think of another excuse, unless you take a liking to her, in which case your problems are solved. I am sure she would like nothing better than to marry the son of an earl. Poor Charles is embarrassed at her antics, but she is young yet, and she has time to change. Once she is used to mixing in superior company, she will no doubt find it less exciting and behave herself accordingly. Let us hope so, for Charles's sake as well as our own.

I am sorry to hear about George Wickham, but not surprised. I watched him sink at university and although I tried to help him, it was impossible. He was always in the wrong company and spent much of his time drunk, and if not drunk, then not entirely sober. He spent more than his allowance and railed against fate for not providing him with more. Since leaving university he has sunk still further. I have seen him occasionally in town, drunk and in very low company.

To begin with, I gave him money, but despite his protestations that he would use it to furnish himself with a career, he abandoned everything he attempted.

I have done more for him than I was inclined to do, because of the love my father bore him, but to no avail. Once he runs through the money he has had from me, what then?

I would be obliged if you would not mention his shortcomings to Georgiana. She still remembers him fondly, as he was kind to her when he was a boy living on the estate. I do not want to spoil her memories of him, for she has precious few happy memories of that time. Her childhood was too often overshadowed by death.

You will be pleased to find her much grown, and very accomplished. She plays very well, and sings with a true sweetness of voice. Her painting is progressing and some of her work is now hanging in the parlour. She is working on a portrait of Ullswater at the moment and it is very promising. I have told her I will hang it in the library when it is finished, although I do not know when that will be: Ullswater has a dislike of sitting still, and is constantly hampering Georgiana's best efforts by bounding off after rabbits.

Mrs Reynolds has had your room ready for weeks and you may come as soon as you please. You know you are always welcome here at any time.

Your cousin,
Darcy

Miss Louisa Bingley to Mrs Bingley

Pemberley, Derbyshire, August 14

Dear Ma,

Pemberley is the most elegant house in all of England, and Mr Darcy and his sister are the most agreeable people, except for his pride and his aloofness and his air of looking down on everyone all the time. Caroline says that shows his quality. She is fast becoming as superior as he is. Not that it does her any good, for I can perceive no special regard when he looks at her, though Caroline is sure he is about to propose at any minute.

His sister is charming. She is a great deal younger than he, being about fourteen years old, but already very accomplished. She sings and plays extremely well, and Caroline practises assiduously every morning so that she shall not seem inferior.

We are to have another visitor soon. Mr Darcy's cousin Colonel Fitzwilliam will be here in the next few days. He was meant to be here sooner but he was delayed on business and this has given us an excuse to remain, for Caroline said how much she was looking forward to meeting him, and so Mr Darcy could hardly hurry us out of the house before he arrived. Of course, she has no interest in him, only in Mr Darcy. It is a pity, for I am sure a military man would suit Caroline. It would solve everything if she should take a fancy to him, and he to her; then I can marry Mr Darcy and live at Pemberley. I do not despair of it.

There is the dinner gong. I must go. Write and let me know if you have seen anything of Mr Hurst. Has he noticed my absence?

Your loving daughter,
Louisa

Miss Caroline Bingley to Mrs Bingley

Pemberley, Derbyshire,
August 16

Greetings and felicitations, dearest Mama.

What a week we are having! I hardly have time to tell you about any of it, but I had to let you know that Colonel Fitzwilliam has arrived. We have all been awaiting him with anticipation, and now at last he is here. He is tall and well built, and best of all he is the son of an earl, though a younger son and not very handsome. However, if his three elder brothers were to die, he would be Lord Fitzwilliam, and if I were to marry him, I would then be Lady Fitzwilliam. But as it is, a military man with no fortune and no title . . . perhaps he will do for Louisa. She says she prefers Mr Hurst, but if he has not come up to scratch yet, then perhaps he never will.

I hope we may meet some of Mr Darcy's other relatives whilst we are here. Georgiana speaks of them often and she thinks that her aunt Lady Catherine de Bourgh may join us.

There is a portrait of Lady Catherine hanging in the gallery—Ma, you must tell Pa we need a gallery when he buys an estate, and he must have someone paint my portrait—and she looks very commanding. She is the sister of Mr Darcy's mother. She has a daughter, Miss Anne de Bourgh, and I am sure that Anne and I would be great friends. I hope she comes to Pemberley, for then I might be invited to Rosings Park, which is said to be very fine. I have told Mr Darcy how agreeable Anne looks and I have dropped several hints about my desire to see Kent, which made Charles look uncomfortable. He took me to task, but I am sure Mr Darcy thought nothing

odd about it. He seemed pleased that I liked the look of his relations.

The other ladies here make me laugh with their blatant attempts
to win his favour, but I am persuaded he is not taken in by their flattery.

Your dutiful daughter,
Caroline

Miss Louisa Bingley to Mrs Bingley

Pemberley, Derbyshire,
August 17

Ma, you must tell Caroline not to be so superior, because she is
making herself ridiculous. She was admiring the portraits in the
hall yesterday, trying to pretend to be knowledgeable about art, and
then she went on to admire the miniatures by the fireplace, saying
that the dark boy was very handsome and pretending to be surprised when Mr Darcy said it was a picture of him. Then she said
that the fair boy next to him was handsome, too, thinking it to be
a relative, and no doubt thinking she might meet him and marry
him one day, only to find that it was a painting of Mr Darcy's late
steward's son, who has turned out very wild. I saw Colonel Fitzwilliam laughing at her, but when I told her about it later she said that
I had completely misunderstood the matter and that he had been
laughing *with* her because she had expressed her sorrow at George
Wickham's unsatisfactory nature and had said, 'How sharper than
a serpent's tooth it is to have an ungrateful child.' Now, don't worry,
Mama, it has nothing to do with serpents, there are no snakes here,
it is just something out of Shakespeare and Caroline wanted to

show the Colonel that she had been to a seminary. But I am still sure that he was laughing at her and not smiling admiringly as she said.

Let me know if you have any news of Mr Hurst.

Your loving daughter,
Louisa

Mr Wickham to Mr Darcy

The Black Bull, London,
August 23

My dear Darcy,

Can it really be three years since I last heard from you? It is, I am sure, and small wonder. You have been busy with the estate, and of course with your guardianship of Georgiana. How is she? Well, I hope, and as affectionate and pleasing as ever. I dare say she is becoming a beauty. I have many happy memories of the time we spent together, all three of us, inmates of the same estate, sharing the same amusements, growing up at Pemberley. They were happy days, and I know your father watched our friendship with pleasure and gratification. He was one of the best men that ever breathed, the truest friend I ever had, and his behaviour to me was beyond compare.

Your cousin Henry was often with us, too. I saw him in town recently; he was looking very well. The army has been working him hard but he has no complaints. He likes the life and says it has been good to him. I promised to send you his greetings, which is one of the reasons for this letter, the other being that it is too long since we have exchanged letters. My only excuse is that I have been busy.

When last I wrote, I was studying for the law, but it proved to be unprofitable. A man in my position, in such bad circumstances—for you know I have my way to make in the world, as I do not have an inheritance—must have something to live on. I looked about me for another career and the more I thought about it, the more I realised that I have a calling for the church, after all, so I plan to become ordained. I am sure you remember that your revered father, my dearest godfather, promised me the living of Kympton in his will. As I hear that the rector has recently died, and as you have no other person to provide for, I trust you will give it to me, as was your father's intention.

Your very great friend,
George

Mr Darcy to Mr Wickham

Pemberley, Derbyshire, August 25

I am deeply sorry that you have found the law unprofitable, but the church, or at least Kympton, is not for you. As you will no doubt remember, you relinquished all claim to it in return for a substantial sum of money. I cannot help thinking it was a narrow escape for the people of Kympton. They need someone who can save their souls and you, George, cannot even save your own. I respectfully, therefore, decline to present you with the living.

Darcy

Miss Louisa Bingley to Mrs Bingley

Pemberley, Derbyshire, August 25

Dear Ma,

The atmosphere has been somewhat strained today, on account of a letter Mr Darcy received this morning. I do not know what was in it, but it came from the late steward's son, Mr Wickham, and it angered Mr Darcy greatly. He read it at the breakfast table and his face darkened, then he screwed it into a ball, excused himself and walked out of the room.

Caroline is welcome to him if she wants him, for he is an awful sight when he is angry and I do not believe I would know what to do with such a man. But Caroline was nothing daunted. She followed him and tried to talk to him but he was brief with her and quickly left the house with Charles and some of the other gentlemen.

Caroline returned to the drawing room and we amused ourselves by playing the pianoforte and singing and then we invited Georgiana to join us at the pianoforte. She is a sweet girl with a pleasing manner and she is a great favourite with us. Then we all went out riding together. The countryside hereabouts is very beautiful, particularly on a clear day.

We met Charles when we arrived back at the house and we did not rest until we found out what was in the letter. Charles did not know everything but he said that George Wickham had behaved disgracefully, despite Mr Darcy's many kindnesses to him, and that Mr Darcy is well rid of him. There was something about an argument over a living which Mr Wickham thought himself entitled to, but was completely unsuited for.

Then Charles began to talk about our leaving Pemberley. Some of the other guests are talking of leaving, too. Colonel Fitzwilliam has been recalled to his regiment, something to do with a rumour that a General Bonaparte is leaving Egypt and returning to France. It has made the gentlemen uneasy, for if Bonaparte returns to France, there seems to be some feeling that it might be bad for us.

Caroline said that we had no need to fear a General Bonaparte when we had a Colonel Fitzwilliam on our side, but though Colonel Fitzwilliam bowed, it was clear he thought her a fool.

Lady Japhet smiled in a superior manner, like a cat who has got the cream, for she is setting her cap at Colonel Fitzwilliam and she knew Caroline had made a grievous mistake. She remarked that a colonel was not quite enough to rid us of a general, but that, as the daughter of a shopkeeper, Caroline could not be expected to understand the difference in the military ranks. Caroline tried to think of a cutting retort but could not do so, although she has thought of half a dozen since.

We have told Charles there is no need for us to leave but you must tell him so, too. Mr Darcy seems happy to have us here because we are company for his sister. Caroline wants to stay because she has not given up hope of winning his affections and I have little reason to return to Yorkshire.

Your loving daughter,
Louisa

Mr Wickham to Mr Parker

London, August 27

Matthew, it is all up with me. I asked Darcy for the living but he refused me. He said the people of Kympton need someone who can save their souls and I cannot even save my own. D——n him!

Kympton would have been perfect. The rectory is a large house and the income is generous. I could have left all the work to my curate and lived a life of ease. God knows what I will do now. You and I are both pockets to let. Did you have any luck with your family? Have they agreed to give you anything?

Wickham

Mr Parker to Mr Wickham

York, August 30

No luck here. You will have to write to Darcy again. It will not do to approach him at once. Wait long enough for it to seem reasonable that you have mended your ways, then write to him again. Thank him for his honesty and tell him that his words have made you look at yourself and realise what you have become. Tell him you have set your feet on the path of righteousness but tell him also how difficult it is for a man without connections to pick himself up. Play on his sympathy. Remind him of his father's love for you. Say anything and everything, but get him to give you some money.

Parker

❧ SEPTEMBER ❧

Mr Wickham to Mr Parker

London, September 5

I will do my best. I will wait until the New Year, a time of new
beginnings when he might, perhaps, believe I have mended my
ways. He will have filled the living of Kympton by then but he will
have other livings in his gift, almost as valuable, and why should I
not have one of them? A comfortable rectory, an annual stipend and
the position of a gentleman are things worth playing for. I will just
have to muddle through till then.

Wickham

Mrs Bingley to Miss Louisa Bingley

Yorkshire, September 6

My dear girl, come home at once. Mr Hurst is here! He got here this
morning and called at the house when I was out. Your pa entertained him but never mind, I'm sure Mr Hurst will overlook the
fact that your pa talked to him about his shops and then offered
him a glass of ale instead of something more genteel. Mr Hurst
asked about all the family and then asked about you particular like.
Mr Darcy is all very well, but 'a bird in the hand is worth two in the

bush.' You see, your old ma knows Shakespeare, too. Come home soon; we'll have you married before the year is out.

Your doting Ma

Miss Louisa Bingley to Mrs Bingley

Pemberley, Derbyshire,
September 8

Ma, I'm ready to come home straightaway but Caroline says there is no call for her to leave. Most of the other ladies have gone home and she is overjoyed that she has Mr Darcy all to herself. But it will look very odd if she stays, so tell her she must come with me. Charles has told her so already but she won't listen to him; she's too busy telling Mr Darcy that he does everything better than everyone else. She sings to him, she flatters him, she parades around in front of him, she does everything but ask him to marry her. Ma, tell her she's got to come, and get Pa to tell her, too. And whatever you do, don't tell Mr Hurst that 'a bird in the hand' is Shakespeare, dearest Ma, because it isn't, you know.

Your loving daughter,
Louisa

Mrs Bingley to Miss Caroline Bingley

Yorkshire, September 10

Now, Caroline, you've got to come home with your sister. Mr Darcy won't run away. If he hasn't asked you to marry him yet, then he's not going to do it, leastways not when you're there. Let him see how empty that big house of his is without you, and let him see how much his sister misses you—that's the way to do it. You'll have him eating out of your hand in no time. If not, your pa's going to buy an estate and then we can have this Mr Darcy to stay and we'll see what another few weeks will do. Your pa's writing to Charles and telling him to bring you both home, so let's have no more nonsense.

Your doting Ma

Miss Caroline Bingley to Miss Violet Cranmore

London, September 15

My dear, sweet, most amiable friend,

How good of you to write me such an estimable letter, setting my mind at ease about your family. I would have replied sooner, but Mr Darcy gave me no peace at Pemberley, wanting my opinion on this matter or that matter, until he quite wore me out. You will be relieved to know that your intelligence was altogether wrong, and that far from being an ill-favoured man he is very handsome, and as for his park being small, why, it is huge. We have but lately parted and he has invited Charles, Louisa and myself to spend Christmas with him.

Louisa thanks you for your kind defence of her and begs me to tell you that she is recently betrothed to Mr Hurst, a gentleman of fashion who adores her. As for myself, I will say nothing at this time, other than that I believe it is worth waiting for the right man, rather than jumping at the first man who offers. Pray do not go thinking I mean you and your sister, my dear Violet, for nothing could be further from my mind, but we both know that there are females for whom any husband is an object, no matter what he is like.

Your dear friend,
Caroline

❧ DECEMBER ❧

Mr Bingley to Mr Darcy

Yorkshire, December 1

My dear Darcy,

It is like your kindness to me to renew your Christmas invitation, and in other circumstances I would like nothing better than to spend Christmas at Pemberley. Caroline and Louisa feel the same as I do, but we have had a sad event here and so we must regretfully decline. My father died not six weeks ago and we are all cast down by his loss; upon my honour we find it very difficult to believe he has gone. He lived long enough to see Louisa married to Mr Hurst but no longer. My mama is downhearted but carries on. She grieves for him deeply but she has the little 'uns to look after and says she cannot afford to go into a decline. Besides, he was many years her senior and she knew it was likely that she would outlive him. As for the rest of us, we miss him deeply but we all must carry on. My brother Ned means to take over my father's trade and Caroline and Louisa will stay at home to help Mama for as long as they are needed. As for myself, once I have attended to all the matters arising from his death, I mean to carry out his plan of buying an estate sometime next year. Perhaps I can trespass on your kindness and ask for your help in the matter, since it is something I know nothing about. But for now I must remain in Yorkshire and tie up the rest of his affairs. I hope to be finished in time for Christmas, but it will be a sad affair without my father. We will celebrate in style for the sake of the little 'uns, but I think that otherwise we would all prefer a quieter affair.

Thank you again for your kind invitation.

Charles

Mr Darcy to Mr Bingley

Darcy House, London,
December 3

My dear Charles,

I know how difficult it is to lose a father. You have my sympathy. If there is any way in which I can help you, you have only to ask. Georgiana will be as sorry as I am that you are not to spend Christmas with us.

Of course I will give you my help with finding an estate, whenever you are ready to look for one. I think it an excellent idea. A man of your standing should have a family seat and I am sure your sisters would welcome it.

I will be going to my Fitzwilliam cousins for a few weeks in January and then to my cousin Philip's estate in Wiltshire in February but I hope to see you in town thereafter. You must spend the summer with us at Pemberley. Your sisters and your brother-in-law are welcome. Georgiana will be very glad to see you all again. She has been practising some new pieces on the pianoforte and I know she will be eager to play duets with Caroline and Louisa.

In the meantime, I hope that you and your family are able to make a tolerable Christmas.

Sincerely yours,
Darcy

Mrs Bennet to Mrs Gardiner

Longbourn, Hertfordshire,
December 4

Sister, you must come to us for Christmas as usual, we are all expecting it and the girls are looking forward to seeing their cousins.

We have need of you here, for the Lucases are getting above themselves now that Mr Lucas has been made a knight, though what he did to deserve it I cannot imagine, only made an address to the King, and I am sure that Mr Bennet could have done it just as well if only anyone had taken the trouble to ask him. And now we must call Mr Lucas 'Sir William' and see him give up his business and move out of town and call his new home Lucas Lodge, when it has been called Wayside Cottage ever since it was built. But there, they are putting a new veranda on, as if that made a difference, and think themselves very fine. Lydia laughed and said that we might as well call our house Bennet Palace, and I am sure she is right.

Ah! Lydia. She is a comfort to me, sister, and I do not know where I would be without her, for my other girls are a trial to me. You do not know what it is like to be a mother to five girls, and not one of them married, though Lydia is so spirited I swear she will marry before any of them. She is a little young to be going into company, to be sure, but she set up such a commotion when we left her behind the other day that we now take her with us wherever we go. She does not look out of place, for she is as tall as her sisters, and I believe she will soon overtop them all.

When you come to us, pray bring the latest fashion books. I will not have it said that my girls are behind the times.

There are rumours that the Sothertons are so heavily in debt they will have to leave Netherfield Park and then rent it out to strangers. I am sorry for them, I am sure, but if a family with five sons should happen to take the Park, it would be a very good thing for my girls.

Write soon and let us know if you will be joining us for Christmas.

Your fond sister,
Janet

Mrs Gardiner to Misses Elizabeth and Jane Bennet

Gracechurch Street, London,
December 6

My dear Lizzy and Jane,

Is it true, as your mama says, that the Sothertons might have to leave Netherfield Park? If so, I am sorry for it. Whatever your mama's hopes as to the possible tenants might be, old friends are never to be treated lightly, and any new people in the neighbourhood must be viewed with clear-sightedness—even if a family with five sons, all eligible, should take the house. Fortunately, you both have a great deal of sense, and I expect you to use it.

But perhaps things will not come to such a pass. There is yet a chance that Mr Sotherton will see the error of his ways and retrench before such a step becomes inevitable. I hope so, for it will be a blow to you both to lose Susan, and Mary will miss Lucy, just as Kitty and Lydia will miss Eleanor.

Speaking of your younger sisters, I do not like to think of Lydia being out so soon. She is not yet fifteen, and young for her age. She has always been giddy and prone to rashness, even if she is so very tall; in fact, I think her height is a danger, for it leads people to assume she is older than she is.

Your mother has been unwise to indulge her in this particular. I know that I can say as much to you, Jane and Lizzy, for you are sensible enough to have seen it for yourselves.

I hope to use what influence I might have to curtail your mother's indulgence of Lydia when I see you all in less than a fortnight. But in the meantime you must do what you can to lessen the evils of such folly, by reminding Lydia how she should behave and by dissuading your mama from including Lydia in the evening parties wherever possible.

It has been a long time since we have seen you. The children are already talking of nothing but coming to Longbourn and I am looking forward to seeing you all. You must tell me if there is anything you would like me to bring you from town. There will be some room in the carriage, although not very much, as the children are growing all the time. Your uncle complains that soon he will have to sit on the roof!

Give my love to your sisters,
Your fond Aunt Gardiner

Miss Elizabeth Bennet to Mrs Gardiner

Longbourn, Hertfordshire,
December 8

Dear Aunt Gardiner,

Nothing is certain with the Sothertons yet, but it seems likely that they will have to let Netherfield Park very soon as my mother says. Mr Morris—Mr Sotherton's man of business—is going to speak to him seriously in the New Year and try to persuade him of the necessity to economise, but Susan has little hope of him succeeding.

One thing is certain, however: they cannot remain at the Park unless there is a change in Mr Sotherton. And if every attempt to change him fails, then Mrs Sotherton is intending to go to Bath after Easter and look for some suitable property for them to rent.

It is hoped that the sober air of Bath might do something to cure Mr Sotherton of his propensities, and if not, at least the family will have the income from Netherfield Park to sustain them, for they hope it will be possible to live very cheaply in Bath.

I hope it does not come to that. I will miss Susan dreadfully if she goes, and Mary, I know, will find Lucy hard to replace. Jane will bear the loss of her friends as she bears everything, with goodness and grace, and I believe that Lydia will not mourn the loss of Ellie for very long. She has made a new friend since coming out, Miss Watson, and the two of them laugh and gossip whenever they get together, which is very often, since Miss Watson lives not far from my aunt Philips's house.

Papa has taken out a subscription to the library in Meryton and we are all now frequent visitors. Lydia goes there in the hope of meeting her friends, and with the desire of showing off her latest bonnet; Kitty is very much Lydia's shadow; Jane and I like to peruse the new books; and Mary is enthralled. She has borrowed a selection of improving books for young women and she reads to us over the breakfast table, then she copies her favourite extracts into a little book.

Did you know, aunt, that 'One of the chief beauties in a female character is that modest reserve, that retiring delicacy, which avoids the public eye'? Mary has taken this piece of advice so much to heart that yesterday she refused to take tea with my aunt Philips, since she would have to be seen by the public eye when she walked into Meryton, and would therefore lose one of her chief beauties.

Papa asked her whether the public eye were the left one or the right one, and he expressed his deep regret when she could not answer him. He recommended her to discover it, so that she could walk on either the right side or the left side of the road and therefore visit her aunt in safety.

'Or is it, perhaps, a Cyclopean eye, set in the middle of the forehead?' he asked. 'If so, it is something singularly lacking in all of our acquaintance and you might therefore go about as you please.'

It was very wrong of him to tease her, but we are all becoming tired of her moralising.

You ask if there is anything I would like from London. Apart from news of the latest fashions and yourselves, then no, there is nothing. I am eager to see you again.

Your affectionate niece,
Lizzy

1799

❧ JANUARY ❧

Mr Darcy to Mr Philip Darcy

Fitzwater Park, Cumbria,
January 15

Philip, the weather here is dreadful; I hope it is better with you. I have never liked being cooped up indoors for any length of time and I confess myself bored, though I would not say so to my aunt. She has made me very welcome here and she has been kindness itself to Georgiana since we arrived. Georgiana will return to school by and by, but I want her to have some fun with people of her own age before returning to her studies.

We had a full house at Pemberley over Christmas but there were only a few young people and none at all under fifteen, which meant Georgiana was deprived of many of the games she would otherwise have enjoyed. I played chess and backgammon with her, but here she plays at charades and indulges in other childish pursuits; for although she is turning into a young lady there are still days when she wants nothing better than to dress Ullswater in a stole and bonnet and push the gaily attired animal along the corridors in an old perambulator. Ullswater takes it all in good part and wags her tail in enjoyment, and I confess I like nothing better than to see my sister happy.

We were expecting to find Henry here in Cumbria but his leave was cancelled and we do not know when he will next see England. We thought, after Admiral Nelson destroyed the French fleet at the Battle of the Nile last year, that the tide was turning in our favour and that we would see more of him than hitherto. With the French navy decimated and the expeditionary force unable to return to their homeland, it seemed there was some chance of the French suing for peace, but it is becoming increasingly obvious the French are bent on conquering Europe and they will not rest until they have achieved their goal or been thoroughly crushed. Needless to say, we can never consent to the former and so it must be the latter, though it means another five years of war. However, it is good for Henry's chances of promotion and so we will not complain.

My aunt has arranged another ball for this evening. She has been tireless in her efforts to find me a wife but I am growing increasingly irritated with the whole affair. I have always hated talking to strangers and yet I must do it day after day and it puts me out of temper. It is even worse for the women. They have to try and win my favour and yet as soon as they try to catch my attention, I lose interest in them, for I cannot bear to be courted for my position or my wealth. And yet what alternative is there? Women must have husbands and men must have wives, and so I keep making myself attend all the balls and soirées to which I am invited; and of course I am invited to a great many of them. If not for the fact that I need an heir for Pemberley, I would be content to remain a bachelor. But I do need an heir and so I must do my duty and attempt to find a wife.

I have met any number of accomplished, beautiful and intelligent women from good families, with handsome dowries, but none of them tempt me. I am beginning to wonder if I am too hard to please. And yet I am convinced that the future Mrs Darcy must have something more: some indefinable quality which will make her not only a suitable mistress for Pemberley and a desirable sister for Georgiana, but a captivating and irresistible wife for me.

I remember my father's words very well. He told me that my wife will need to command the respect of the servants and the love of my family; she must reflect the greatness of the Darcys; she must be a gracious hostess and a model of feminine virtue; she must be a modest lady and she must be possessed of a refined taste and true decorum. And she must be a woman I can admire, respect and esteem, as well as love.

It is a great deal to ask. I fear he was spoilt by his own marriage, and I have been spoilt by it, too. I can still see the expression in my mother's eyes whenever she looked at him. There was a warm glow there, an unmistakable look of love and affection, and a certain lift to her mouth that I will never forget. If I must marry—and I must— I would like the same. But where am I to find it?

For advice on matters of this nature he referred me to you. We both bear the name of Darcy and we both have the responsibility of upholding the Darcy traditions and continuing the Darcy name. And so I ask you, Philip, have you ever met a woman who was necessary to you? A woman you would be glad to marry? Do you mean to marry when you are thirty, as you have always said, and if so, are you willing to marry without love? And how do you intend to choose your wife from the many caps that are set at you?

Yours,
Darcy

Mr Philip Darcy to Mr Darcy

Wiltshire, January 17

Of course you are hard to please, and so you should be: you are a Darcy. There are very few women who are good enough for you. My mother drew up a list of suitable wives for me before she died, and the same ladies are naturally suitable for you, but of the eleven names on the list, four are already married, one has lost her fortune and two are personally unappealing to me. Of the remaining four, one is your cousin, Anne de Bourgh, and she is sickly and not likely to provide a living heir. The three remaining ladies are all acceptable and I mean to propose to one of them in due course, though I have not yet decided which one. I am sending you a copy of the list in case it is of use to you, and I would be glad of the names of the women deemed suitable by your aunt, as they might perhaps be of use to me.

I am holding a house party next month and you are welcome. I will invite all the young women; it might help us to decide which ones we should favour with our hands if we see them all together.

I do not pretend to be looking for love, for although you say your parents found it—and I bow to your superior knowledge of them—I confess it seems to me that happiness in marriage consists of a large house, so that a husband and wife might speak to each other occasionally if they have a mind to do so, but otherwise go their own separate ways. As Pemberley is one of the largest houses in the country, I do not despair of you finding happiness, even if it is of my sort and not yours.

I am sorry Henry could not get any leave, though I know he would not feel sorry for himself. Ever since we were children he has longed to be a soldier, and now that he is a colonel his happiness is complete—or, perhaps no, he has still something to hope for, as I am sure he would like to become a general. If the war goes on much longer, he might have his wish. For myself, I would like to see an end to the war. I want to go over to Paris but at the moment it is impossible. God knows when it will end.

Have you heard anything of George Wickham lately? I met a friend of his, a Matthew Parker, in town last week. I know nothing of Parker, other than that he comes from a good family, but he says that Wickham is quite changed. He let slip it was a letter from you that brought about the change. I gather you wrote some harsh truths, which have done him more good than all the help he has been given and made him see the error of his ways. I hope it may be so. His father was a good man and I have not forgotten him.

Yours,
PD

Mr Wickham to Mr Darcy

London, January 20

My dear Darcy,

I cannot let the New Year go by without writing to wish you well for the future and without thanking you for everything you have done for me in the past. But above all, I want to thank you for the letter you sent me last summer. I was very angry with you when I received it, for I thought it the most unjust thing I had ever read. But I could not forget it and your words gradually pierced my haze of resentment until at last I was forced to acknowledge the truth of them. I had squandered my chances as well as my resources and I was unfit for the church, as I was unfit for everything else. Your letter made me look at myself and I did not like what I saw. I began to mend my ways and I mean to continue in the same way. I want to make you glad to call me your friend, as you were once before.

Do you remember the January when the lake froze at Pemberley and your father bought us both new skates so that we might take advantage of it? And do you remember how Georgiana followed us onto the lake and how I took off my skates and gave them to her so that she might take her first few tottering steps across the ice? And how we were certain she would fall, but how she surprised us both by skating unaided before half an hour was out? If this cold weather goes on much longer, the lake will freeze again. We should go skating there! It would be good for me to forget my present worries for a few days, for God knows I am sorely pressed. I have done everything I can to mend my fortunes, but it is very hard to be alone in the world, with no one to help me to some kind of preferment. I did think of going into the army, but I do not think it would suit my temperament. The church, now . . . When I rejected the idea before, I was a fool who did not understand the value of such an institution, but now my ideas have undergone a radical change. I have experienced sin and I know its temptations. I have seen, too, its darker side, and witnessed the effects on those who drink too deeply of forbidden fruits. I have drawn back from the edge, to find myself once more on solid ground and I hope to use my experiences to help my fellow man. Who better to understand the temptations of the sinner than a man who has himself been a sinner?

I know there was a time when you thought me unfit for the church, and you were right. I knew nothing then of the degradations awaiting me, but I know them now, as I know the healing power of redemption. I have seen the error of my ways, thanks to you, and I hope to use my life to help others see the error of such ways as well.

My godfather, and dear friend—your father—was always pleased to say that I had a good speaking voice and a good address, and that I could charm the birds from the trees if I so wished. He believed in me, and I know you believe in me, too. It was that thought which brought me back from the dark paths I walked in my folly and ignorance.

I know you will have given the living of Kympton elsewhere by now, but you still have other livings in your gift and I feel sure you would like to see me established in one of them. It will enable you to carry out your father's wish, and it will give you the satisfaction of seeing me, as I was meant to be, a good man guiding the souls of my parishioners as they walk the difficult path of righteousness through this world of sin.

Your friend, much humbled and chastened,
George Wickham

Mr Darcy to Mr Wickham

Cumbria, January 25

Wickham,

It will do you no good to importune me further—the living of Kympton is no longer vacant as you surmise and I have no other vacant livings in my gift. I am glad you have seen the error of your ways but you must help yourself now; I cannot help you any further. This letter ends the matter.

Darcy

Mr Wickham to Mr Darcy

London, January 27

By God, Darcy, how dare you write me such a letter? Do you think I am some beggar trying to scrape an acquaintance with you? Are you so puffed up in your own conceit that you forget we rode the same horses when we were children, swam in the same lake, climbed the same trees, worked together and played together as equals—nay, as brothers?

I thank God your father is not alive to see it. He would have been ashamed of you. He would have been disgusted and appalled that he had raised such a son, devoid of any kind of honour or loyalty or compassion. What gives you the right to say I cannot have the living, when your father expressly promised it to me? It is nothing to you, and nothing to the people of Kympton, either, who holds the living.

But think again. You surely do not mean to rob me of a livelihood. I have always known you to be proud and supercilious, but I never thought you would stoop to being a thief as well; in fact I am sure you will not sink so low. If I had half your riches, you know, and you were poor like me, I would not begrudge you a pittance of a living; quite the reverse, I would give you an allowance, and a handsome one at that, so that you could live as a gentleman. I cannot believe you mean to rob me of a livelihood without a second thought. How do you suggest I live? I must have something, and you have many livings in your gift.

In memory of all the times we played together as children and the love and affection your father showed me . . . but that is at the root of it, is it not? You are jealous because he loved me like a second son—in fact I believe he preferred me, and who can blame him? I, at least, took pains to entertain him, whereas you would never give yourself the trouble. By God, that is it. I have always suspected it and now I know, and this is how you mean to pay me out: by reducing me to nothing.

How could I help it if he preferred me? An old man will always like a handsome face and charming manners. Your face is handsome enough, I'll grant you, but your address is as stiff as a board. You have all the charm of a poker—is it any wonder that your father preferred me? He cannot be blamed for liking my cheerful manners or for being repulsed by your pride and your d——d self-righteous arrogance.

But you do blame him and now you are taking your revenge.

What do you want? Do you want me to crawl? Then be d——d to you. I will not crawl to you or any man. If you do not mean to help me, then you can go hang.

I wish you every ill that you have inflicted on me.

Wickham

Mr Wickham to Mr Parker

London, January 30

Well, Matthew, you will be surprised to get this letter after so long a silence, but I had no wish to write to bore you with my troubles, and debtors' prison is the most boring of all ills. But now I am out and living with a wealthy widow, though not for long: I would sooner be the master than the lapdog.

I have a mind to look about me for an heiress. Now that there is no chance of my getting the living of Kympton—I tried Darcy again, d——n him, but to no avail—I must look to some other way of supporting myself. Do you know any heiresses? Are there any in York? I am not known in that area, and I may pass there for a respectable man.

Let me know if you can help me. If I catch someone by your introduction, you may be sure you will always be welcome in my home.

Wickham

❧ FEBRUARY ❧

York, February 5

Good God, George, I could not believe it when I received your letter. I thought you were dead! Well, well, well, so that is where you
have been: debtors' prison. I should have guessed. It is very good to
know you are still alive and well, however, and looking for the love
of your life. George Wickham married! What a sight that will be. I
wish I knew any heiresses, but if I did, I would be making a play for
them myself. My pockets are empty, as always.

Let me know the name of your widow. If you are leaving, then
there will be a warm berth there for me, and it will suit me to leave
York just at this moment. You might be able to pass for a respectable man here, but alas! I cannot. I must leave the city, at least for a
while, and London would be as good a place as any for me to pass
the time.

Have you seen anything of Belle lately?

Parker

Mr Wickham to Mr Parker

London, February 13

The widow is Mrs Dawson. Meet me at The Black Bull and I will take you home and introduce you, and then I will be off in pursuit of a wife. A pity there are none in York, but never mind, I will try my luck with Anne de Bourgh. If I can catch her away from her dragon of a mother, then something might be done.

You ask about Belle but sadly I have not seen her for years. We had some times together, Belle and I! But neither of us had any money and although we managed to scrape along together for a while, in the end the creditors were pressing and so we had to part. The last I heard of her, she was thinking of turning respectable.

Wickham

Mr Parker to Mr Wickham

Leeds, February 16

Belle! Respectable? Good Lord! That is the best joke I have heard in a long time.

The de Bourgh girl sounds promising. Does she have any money? If so, you'll have to fight the mother for her. Not the first time a George has fought a dragon!

Parker

George Wickham to Matthew Parker

London, February 18

Of course she has money; why else would I want to marry her? Miss Anne de Bourgh is the heiress of Rosings. She not only has a fortune, but the property will pass to her on her marriage as well. I have only to marry her and I will be George Wickham of Rosings Park. It has a fine sound, do you not think?

Wickham

Mr Parker to Mr Wickham

Leeds, February 22

Better than George Wickham of Debtors' Prison at any rate. Hurry up and marry the girl. I am in low funds and need somewhere to stay. Let me know when you have tied the knot and I will join you at Rosings as soon as the deed is done. Summer in Kent would suit me well.

Parker

Mr Wickham to Mr Parker

Kent, February 27

It is going to be easier than I thought. I travelled down to Kent, where I took a room at the local inn and made discreet enquiries as to Anne's movements, hoping that once I knew them I could arrange to bump into her 'accidentally' whilst she was out taking the air. But the de Bourghs are no longer in Kent; they are in Bath as Anne is sickly and she has gone there to take the waters. It will be far easier for me to renew our acquaintance there, where there are a thousand and one ways of meeting her. I am on my way to Bath now and I will write to you when I get there.

Wish me luck!
Wickham

MARCH

Mr Parker to Mr Wickham

London, March 1

Bath, eh? You're in luck. You can bump into her easily in the Pump Rooms and it won't look suspicious. Tell her you've got a touch of gout!

It should be easier for you to get her alone there, too. Her mother will have a lot of acquaintances and be gossiping half the time, I don't doubt; either that or playing the grand lady and entertaining herself by patronising everyone else.

Parker

Mr Wickham to Mr Parker

Bath, March 2

Well, I have made a start. I found Anne at the Pump Room this morning and she was alone, apart from her companion. I took a glass of the waters and then sidled over to her, bumping into her and apologising, and then being concerned in case I had spilt the water on her dress. I affected surprise on recognising her and she blushed very prettily. She was flattered by my attentions, because of course I told her how well she looked—I am sure everyone else must tell her how sickly she looks—whilst the companion glowered at me and tried to hurry Anne away. So then I started talking about old Mr Darcy and mentioned that I was his godson and reminded Anne of all the happy times we had spent together at Pemberley. The companion was mollified and she was soon all smiles, for I bowed and kissed her hand, of course, and looked at her as though she were a beauty when in fact I am sure she must turn milk sour.

All was going well, very well, until Lady Catherine arrived. Anne shrank at once, and the companion looked nervous. I greeted Lady Catherine respectfully and told her that I had seen Darcy lately and that he was well. She raised her eyebrows but I saw that she remembered me and I thought everything was going to be all right, until she looked down her nose and said, 'Ah, yes, the steward's son,' and with that she turned her back on me.

I hid my disappointment, bowed and smirked, and accepted my

dismissal gracefully. But I have not given up. If I can only find Anne alone, I am certain I can win her. Let me have but half an hour with her and I will persuade her to leave her drab and dreary life behind and elope with me.

Wickham

Mr Parker to Mr Wickham

London, March 4

Use all your charm. I am sick of the Widow. I want my freedom, and the freedom of Rosings Park.

Parker

Mr Wickham to Mr Parker

Bath, March 5

I renewed my assault this morning, meeting Anne in the library. Her eyes lit up when she saw me and I bowed and kissed her hand. We were soon talking about her favourite books and all was going well until the companion hurried over from the other side of the room, saying that Lady Catherine had instructed them not to be more than ten minutes. I tried to talk to Anne again but it was no good. At the mention of her mother, Anne became anxious, and as the companion was evidently not going to leave her side, I had to withdraw with a good grace.

There is no use in my remaining: Anne and her mother are due to return to Rosings in a few days. But I have not given up. In a few years' time, Lady Catherine might have passed away and then I can try again.

In the meantime, I am returning to London. Meet me in The Black Bull on Saturday at midday and we will drown our sorrows together.

Wickham

Lady Catherine de Bourgh to Mr Darcy

Rosings Park, Kent, March 17

Dear nephew,

I called in at Darcy House on my way back from Bath and I spent the day with Georgiana. Her school has done well with her but it can do nothing more for her. She is old enough now to have an establishment of her own and you should form one for her in London. It is what your mother would have wished.

You will be pleased to hear that Anne's health is much improved by drinking the waters. I knew it must be so. Mr Feather was quite wrong when he said that Anne's condition was not the kind to benefit from a visit to Bath, and he has of course been forced to admit that I was right. I have been responsible for many cures by giving out good advice.

Your father's steward's son was in Bath. He did not seem to have any employment and I told him that he must apply himself if he wanted to get on in the world. It is amazing to me how many young men these days seem to squander their time and their energies. I told him that the Lymingtons were looking for a steward and I promised to mention his name. He told me he was very grateful for the attention.

Your friend Bingley was at Darcy House with his sisters when I arrived. They were visiting Georgiana and they had taken her riding in the park prior to my arrival. They were all impressed with Georgiana's equestrienne skills.

Mr Bingley's eldest sister is newly married to a Mr Hurst. He is a man who evidently suffers from fatigue and I told him that he would find the waters beneficial. Miss Bingley was much struck by the idea and assured me they would go to Bath forthwith.

'Let it be soon,' I said, 'for he will never recover without drinking the waters,' and she was forced to agree.

Mr Bingley is looking for an estate of his own. I advised him that he should look no further than Surrey. He said that he did not know if he would like the place but I told him he would like it very well: people in trade are always fond of Surrey.

Lady Catherine

Mr Darcy to Lady Adelaide Fitzwilliam

Pemberley, Derbyshire, March 20

I have had a letter from Lady Catherine and she raises a subject close to my thoughts at the moment, saying that she thinks I should set up a separate establishment for Georgiana in London. I have thought of it often recently but I have done nothing about it as I like to have my sister here at Pemberley when she is not at school. It is her home and she is very fond of it. I must also confess that I do not like to think of the place without her. But she is old enough now to leave school, and although it is one thing for her to spend the holidays at Pemberley, it is quite another for her to live here alone, for I cannot always be in Derbyshire.

If she had an establishment in London, she would have plenty of company all year round. There are always aunts, uncles and cousins in town on business or pleasure, and she would also have the parks, the picture galleries and the museums of London to educate and entertain her. I am more often in town than in Derbyshire and she would have my company then, as she would have it every summer when she would join me at Pemberley.

Let me have your thoughts on the matter; you know how much I value your opinion. I do my best for her, but it is at times like these that I realise how little I know about raising a child—or a young lady, I should say, for Georgiana is a child no longer—and I need advice.

Your affectionate nephew,
Fitzwilliam

Miss Anne de Bourgh to Miss Georgiana Darcy

Rosings Park, Kent, March 23

Dearest Georgiana,

How good it was to see you last week. How Ullswater made me laugh! And you are grown so talented. Your watercolour of the Thames was the prettiest thing you have done, and I am not surprised your brother wants to hang it in the drawing room. I wish I could learn to paint but Mama says that I am not well enough and that the lessons would fatigue me. I am sure they would not. However, I take my sketchbook out of doors whenever I can and I think the fresh air does me good, though Mama says it is injurious to my health.

We were sorry to miss your brother but your friends the Bingleys seem pleasant people. Mr Bingley is very handsome, is he not?

And so good-humoured. What a change it was to hear someone who was pleased with everyone and everything, saying that London was the finest place in creation, full of the most interesting gentlemen and the prettiest ladies. I liked his sisters less, but you know them better than I do and I must confess they were very elegant—even Mama said they were well dressed for people whose family are in trade.

Have you heard anything of Henry recently? We have not heard anything since Christmas, but as he is your guardian I thought you might have some more recent news.

Affectionately yours,
Anne

Miss Georgiana Darcy to Miss Anne de Bourgh

Darcy House, London, March 29

Dearest Anne,

Ullswater is very funny, is she not? She makes me laugh all the time, although sometimes I should not laugh, I know. She knocked my paint box flying yesterday and I had to scrub the carpet before my governess returned so that Ullswater would not be in trouble. My governess does not like dogs and looks for any excuse to criticise her. I am not allowed to take her with me when I go riding but she begs to come with me every time. I tell her she may not go, but I always relent. It is true she chases rabbits, but the sight of her lolloping along beside me makes up for any inconvenience.

My brother was sorry to miss you, too, and he was sorry not to be able to visit you for Easter, but he says we will see you in the summer. He is back in London now and he is staying with me at Darcy

House. He had a letter from Colonel Fitzwilliam yesterday and everything is well, or at least it was when the letter was posted, but it is difficult for letters to get through, you know. There was a lot in the letter about the war and the price of everything, also about military manoeuvres and some of the commanders, and there was a note in it for me. My guardian told me that the weather is good, much warmer than it is here, and the food bearable, and that he has some leave coming to him in the summer so that he will join us at Pemberley. The Bingleys will be coming, too. They are very agreeable people, are they not? Miss Bingley plays duets with me and she and her sister sing with me. They remained in Yorkshire over the winter on account of a sad bereavement but they returned to London recently and they are often here. I am glad of it. Mr Bingley dances with me after dinner sometimes whilst his sister plays the piano. I am preparing myself for the future, you see. I must know how to go on when I come out.

Miss Bingley is at present trying to persuade her brother to buy an estate. He is willing, but my brother does not think he will find it easy to settle because he enjoys travelling too much and meeting new people. He is at that time of life when friendships are growing and the circle of acquaintances is always expanding.

My brother says that Mr Bingley is so easily persuadable that if one of his friends only says to him, 'Bingley, I think you had better not buy an estate, you know,' Mr Bingley will probably not do it.

All the same, his sisters seem determined for him to have somewhere and I think they will prevail in the end.

Your affectionate cousin,
Georgiana

❧ APRIL ❧

Mr Bingley to Mr Darcy

London, April 3

Upon my honour, Darcy, it is good of you to invite us to dine with you. I am looking forward to seeing you again and to asking you for some advice about buying an estate. Caroline and Louisa can only see that it would give me somewhere to invite my friends, but there is a lot of work involved in running such a place and I do not know if I would be up to the task. Your aunt thought it a good idea and recommended Surrey, but Caroline did not take to the idea. Perhaps you would be so good as to give me your opinion when we meet next week.

Your friend,
Bingley

Lady Catherine de Bourgh to Mr Darcy

Rosings Park, Kent, April 8

Dear nephew,

I hear from Georgiana that your friend Bingley did not like Surrey and that he intends to buy an estate elsewhere. It is astonishing to me that gentlemen these days are so ignorant of what is to their own advantage. Your friend Bingley is not the only one to suffer from this complaint. The rector of Hunsford, Mr Green, is similarly afflicted, and saw fit to die last week, when it was clearly in his best interests to remain alive.

Like all inconsiderate people, he died at a most inconvenient time. If he had waited until next month, I would have had more leisure to replace him. I cannot think it would have mattered to him: having lived for ninety years it would surely not have troubled him greatly to have lived for another six weeks. However, it would have made a great difference to me as my guests would, by then, have departed. But that is the problem with people today: they have no thought for others. It is a universal complaint.

It is proving difficult for me to find a replacement. As the rectory is so near to Rosings Park, it is necessary for me to have a man of sound good worth and sobriety, with a respectful manner and a becoming gratitude for the favour bestowed. He must be a man of exceptional character as well as a man of great ability; a man who understands the difference of rank but who is at the same time a gentleman. In addition to this, he must have a proper humility. I will not have him subjecting Anne to the impertinent attentions her beauty is certain to inspire, for in point of true beauty, Anne is far above the rest of her sex. I cannot prevent him from worshipping her from afar, as, indeed, what man could resist? For such a refined and elegant young woman cannot help inspiring the tenderest feelings in the male breast. But her future lies elsewhere, as well you know.

I have so far seen four candidates but they have been impossible. Mr Frampton did not play cards so he would not do, for I must have some entertainment in the evenings; Mr Redding did not show the proper deference and I cannot abide a clergyman who is above himself; Mr Waring was so overcome by Anne's beauty that he could not remember her name and kept calling her Miss . . . Miss . . . and

Mr Ingers referred to me as Mrs de Bourgh. Another gentleman, a Mr Collins, has been recommended to me. I have no great hopes of him but I will see him nonetheless.

In my day, clergymen were all of them suitable. It is a sad sign of the times that not one of them today will take the trouble to be what I wish them to be.

Your aunt,
Lady Catherine

~ JUNE ~

Miss Elizabeth Bennet to Mrs Gardiner

Longbourn, Hertfordshire,
June 7

The Sothertons have left us at last and Netherfield Park is empty. We have all been cast down by their departure; all except Mary, who said that we must cherish in our bosoms the knowledge that vice, if allowed to flourish, will fell even the mightiest oak, and that we must take heed of the lesson so unwillingly taught to us by our unlucky neighbours. Papa asked her if vice would fell the mightiest elm, or if it was only the oak it could topple, which was very wrong of him, but Mary would try the patience of a saint.

We went over to my aunt Philips's house this evening, where Mary told Mr Shackleton that vice could fell any tree taller than a sapling, no matter what its species, and the rest of us spent most of our time bemoaning the loss of our friends. Charlotte felt it as much as Jane and I. She lifted our spirits, however, by saying that Mr Sotherton would have far fewer temptations in Bath and that the family could live there more cheaply, so that they would have a better chance of restoring their fortunes and then being able to return to Meryton.

My aunt Philips said that two people have already requested a viewing, for she saw Mr Morris, the Sothertons' man of business, in town this morning, and told us all about it. Mama made particular enquiries as to the nature of the prospective tenants but she was put out to discover that the first of them is a young man with a wife and two children and the second is a retired sea captain. She is hoping that neither of them take it, for she would like a family with five sons to come to the Park so that she can marry us all off at one fell swoop. The first son is to be the heir and he is to marry Jane. The second is to be a military man and he is to marry Lydia. The third is to be a clergyman with a handsome living and he is to marry Mary. The fourth is to be a sailor, the captain of a frigate, and he is to marry Kitty. And the youngest son is to marry me. I think my marriage was an afterthought, as I believe that Mama had forgotten about me!

Papa occasionally reminds her that no such family has taken the estate, but she is so happy in the imagining of it that for the most part he leaves her be.

She had some hopes that Jane might be about to marry last month. There was a gentleman from London who was staying with the Robinsons, but it all came to nothing. I am glad of it. Jane liked him, but when did Jane not like anyone? However, she was not downhearted when he went away, so it was nothing but a passing fancy. Mama was very upset, however, saying that Jane will soon be an old maid. Jane is one and twenty! Lydia of course believes everything Mama says, and declares that she will never be an old maid and that she will be married by the time she is sixteen. Since this puts Mama into a good humour, Papa says nothing to discourage it;

indeed he remarks that if she can find a man who is silly enough to marry her he will consider himself lucky and hand her over with his blessing. This leads Mary to reflect on the seriousness of matrimony, whilst Kitty fidgets and asks for a new bonnet. So you see we all go on as usual!

I will write again when I have any news.

Your affectionate niece,
Lizzy

Mr Charles Bingley to Mrs Bingley

Pemberley, Derbyshire, June 15

Dearest Ma,

I have been to see three estates these last few weeks and Caroline has disliked them all. She is such a fine lady that upon my honour I hardly dare speak to her anymore. She finds fault with everything, saying the drawing room is not as large as the Pemberley drawing room or the view from the dining room is not as splendid as the one at Pemberley. She will never find a house like Pemberley, and so I keep telling her, but she only smiles and says there are other ways to live in a house than buying it. If she thinks Darcy will marry her, she is mistaken. He will marry Miss de Bourgh if he marries to please his family, and he will certainly not marry Caroline if he marries to please himself, upon my honour he will not.

I am trying to persuade her to return to Yorkshire but she says I will need a hostess and she cannot leave me in my hour of need. I thought she might leave me last week, for there was some talk of Darcy sending Georgiana to the coast for a few weeks and Caroline said that she had a mind to visit the coast herself. But when she learnt that Darcy did not intend to go with his sister she changed her mind.

Are you sure you do not need her for a few weeks, Ma? I am certain the little ones would like to see her. We will be returning to London in a few days' time so send your reply to the London address.

Your loving son,
Charles

Mr Darcy to Lady Catherine de Bourgh

Darcy House, London, June 18

I sympathise with you over your difficulties in finding a new rector for Hunsford, aunt. I have had similar difficulties of my own. I had to dismiss my steward when I found he had been taking money from the estate and now I am looking about me for another one. I have had two since old Mr Wickham passed away but neither of them have been satisfactory. It has been a difficult position to fill, particularly as Mr Wickham's stewardship was exemplary. I am running the estate myself for the time being but the sooner I find a new steward the better. The grove at the far end of the lake needs coppicing and the home farm is in need of repair, to name but two pressing matters. Do you know of anyone who might suit?

I am also looking about me for a companion for Georgiana. Her governess has left her to marry and I think that a companion would be more suitable as Georgiana is now fifteen. She will still continue with her masters so you need not fear that her studies will be neglected, but she needs a woman who can show her, by example, how to behave in company. She is too young to come out but she is starting to attend small parties I hold at Pemberley, where she can learn adult manners amongst friends.

And speaking of friends, Henry writes to me that he will be home in a few weeks on leave and he will be coming to Pemberley, where I know he will be pleased to see the improvement in Georgiana. He has promised to bring her a collection of pressed flowers from Spain, species which flourish there but are not to be met with here, and she is planning to use them to decorate a screen. She has already made the design and although I have a brother's partiality, I think it very well done.

Henry has written to you, too, I know, but the mail being uncertain from the Continent he has asked me to say that he will call on you at Rosings in July. It is very hot in London and I am thinking of sending Georgiana to the coast following his visit, as I am persuaded it would do her good. Perhaps Anne would like to go with her? The two of them are good friends and they would be company for one another.

Your affectionate nephew,
Fitzwilliam Darcy

Lady Catherine de Bourgh to Mr Darcy

Rosings Park, Kent, June 20

You need not trouble yourself over the matter of Georgiana's companion. I have found you one, a very respectable woman by the name of Younge. She just happened to be mentioned to me the other day by Mrs Campbell, a very genteel woman whose husband is in the diplomatic corps. Mrs Younge is lately widowed and as her husband did not leave her very well provided for she is in need of a position. Mrs Campbell gave her friend the highest references and of course Mrs Younge will be only too delighted to find herself as companion to Miss Georgiana Darcy.

Your idea of sending Georgiana to the coast is a good one and with Mrs Younge to guide her she will be able to make the most of the opportunity to sketch and paint the coast. Anne, alas, will be unable to go with her. Mr Feather is quite wrong when he says the sea air would be beneficial to her health; it would certainly be ruinous to her.

You must send two menservants with Georgiana, as it would be highly improper for her to travel otherwise: Miss Darcy, the daughter of Mr Darcy, of Pemberley, cannot appear with propriety in a different manner. I am excessively attentive to all those things and you must be attentive to them as well.

I have arranged for Mrs Younge to call upon you on the twenty-second of June at ten o'clock, when you will confirm her appointment.

Your aunt,
Lady Catherine

Miss Anne de Bourgh to Miss Georgiana Darcy

Rosings Park, Kent, June 22

Dear Georgiana,

Mama says you are going to the coast. You must promise to write to me, for I do so like to hear from you. I get out very little and although we have people to dine they are always the same. We will have some variety soon, however, for Mama has just appointed Mr Collins as the new rector of Hunsford. He was ordained at Easter and seems very grateful for the preferment, which pleases Mama. He is also very agreeable and does whatever she asks him to do, as though it is his greatest pleasure on earth. He is an educated man, having been to university, but is not puffed up with conceit like so many young men nowadays, or so Mama says. He has a suitable humility, and a becoming gratitude towards her. She invited him to dinner yesterday, and he spoke at length on the duties of a clergyman and of the obligation he feels towards her for having given him such a splendid preferment so early in life.

Mama said, 'Mr Collins, I have chosen you for the living and I am a superb judge of character. I never judge wrong.' Mr Collins said that he had known as much from the moment he laid eyes on her, and Mama was impressed by his honesty and sense. He will be moving into the parsonage next month.

I hope you like Mrs Younge. Mama says she is a very agreeable woman and will make you an excellent companion. I believe your brother is seeing her today. I hope he likes her and that Colonel Fitzwilliam approves. Tell me, have you heard anything from Colonel Fitzwilliam recently? I must confess . . . but I had better not say any more.

Your loving coz,
Anne

Miss Georgiana Darcy to Miss Anne de Bourgh

Darcy House, London, June 30

Dearest Anne,

Mrs Younge has been appointed and I like her very much. Do you know, when Ullswater knocked over my screen this morning, instead of saying she was a horrible beast who ought not to be allowed in the house, Mrs Younge simply picked it up again, dusted off the footprints and said, 'No harm done.'

I am sorry you are not to come with me to the coast as it is now certain I am to go. It is so hot in London that I feel like a cut flower which someone has forgotten to put in water. I am to go to Margate or Ramsgate, just wherever Mr Hargreaves manages to find a suitable house. Poor Mr Hargreaves! He is having to do everything at the moment. My brother has not only instructed him to find me a suitable house by the sea, but also to supervise Pemberley until a new steward can be found. It is a pity that my brother has had a falling out with George Wickham, otherwise he could ask him to be the new steward. But when I ventured to mention it, Fitzwilliam became quite cold and said that it would be most unsuitable.

I hope to see Colonel Fitzwilliam when he comes home and I will tell you all about it. I am very fortunate to have him as my guardian. He always has some present for me, and I always make sure to give him something in return. I have painted a screen for him and I mean to present it to him when next we meet. I wish he did not have to go away to war, but someone must do it, I suppose, and all his life he wanted to be a soldier so I cannot complain.

Your affectionate cousin,
Georgiana

～ JULY ～

London, July 4

The biggest stroke of luck! I was walking in the park yesterday and who should I see but Belle. You remember Belle? Of course you do! We went to many parties with her and her friends when last we knew her, and you surely will not have forgotten them! If you remember, I told you that the last time I saw her she was thinking of turning respectable. Well, she has. I took her for an ice and she told me all about it.

It seems she happened to run across an old school friend who had seen nothing of her for years, and so of course she said nothing of the recent past. She drew a veil over her string of protectors and said only what she wanted her friend to hear: that she had married a good man, a Mr Younge, that he had tragically died and that she was left in difficult circumstances. This friend, a Mrs Campbell, gave her a glowing reference and helped her to a position as a companion to an heiress.

Ah! I thought that would make you sit up! But the best of it is, she is not just the companion to any heiress, she is the companion to Georgiana Darcy!

You can imagine how I felt when she told me. My heart leapt! An heiress, one I could approach and scrape an acquaintance with, and then reminisce about our happy childhoods with, for although I am some ten years older than her I was always kind to her when she was a little girl. Better yet, she is being sent to the coast by her brother for the summer, and what better place for me to approach her, where there will be no old servants watching, and no Darcy House to present a forbidding aspect? Only a promenade and many sheltered coves, with no friends or relatives nearby. A companion to guard her, of course—and that companion to be Belle!

I intend to run away with her to Scotland, where we can be married over the anvil, and then her thirty thousand pounds will be mine. Not only will I have a rich wife, but I will be revenged on Darcy for his contemptuous treatment of me.

Belle intends to work on Georgiana, encouraging her in romantic thoughts, so that she will be susceptible to my advances. I am to bump into them by chance when they are settled and then Belle will suggest I am invited to dinner. Before long, I will have Georgiana eating out of my hand.

I am going to buy a new suit of clothes but I will write to you again when I know where I will be spending the summer. Come and join me and we will celebrate: you, me and Belle together.

Wickham

Mr Parker to Mr Wickham

London, July 6

They say the devil looks after his own and it seems they speak truly. A rich wife and revenge into the bargain! By God, Wickham, you've fallen on your feet. Make the most of it!

Parker

Miss Georgiana Darcy to Mr Darcy

Ramsgate, July 8

Dearest Brother,

We arrived in Ramsgate yesterday evening and we are very happy
with the house. Mrs Younge says it is very convenient. It is small
compared to my London establishment, but it is very comfortable
and it has a pretty view of the sea. Mrs Younge and I are going down
to the beach this afternoon as I am eager to make a sketch of the
coast. I will send it to you when it is finished.

Your affectionate sister,
Georgiana

Mr Darcy to Colonel Fitzwilliam

Darcy House, London, July 10

It is good to know that you will soon be with us. I am in London at
present and I will be here until the end of July, certainly, and probably for August as well. I have sent Georgiana to Ramsgate for the
summer. Caroline Bingley was keen to go, too, until she learnt that
I would not be there. Her attentions to me grow ever worse. She
flatters and praises me, and drops hints as large as Derbyshire about
becoming the future Mrs Darcy. Poor Charles! He is mortified by
her attentions to me and he feels he has to apologise at least twice a
month. He is in town at the moment but he will be going north to
visit his family next week and then he intends to continue his search

for a country estate. His family want him to buy one, and he is not averse to the idea—indeed, he is of their opinion, although he asked sensible questions of me, about upkeep and other practical matters. But I have promised to look over any property he is thinking of buying and I have offered to help him appoint a steward. He thinks he will settle somewhere in the middle of the country. He has his family home in Yorkshire and he visits me often in Derbyshire, so he is thinking of somewhere in Hertfordshire or thereabouts. He has told his agent to look in that area.

I hope to see you next week. Until then, my dear Henry, I am

Your cousin,
Darcy

Mrs Belle Younge to Mr Wickham

Ramsgate, July 10

We are settled in Ramsgate, and a quieter spot you could not hope to find. Georgiana knows no one here and so there is no one to take an interest in any comings and goings. The servants are all local people. The only two who knew Georgiana were the footmen who accompanied us on our journey, but they have since returned to London. She receives letters from her cousin and from her brother and her guardian, but no one calls.

I have already encouraged her to take *Romeo and Juliet* out of the circulating library and she is reading it with interest. I spun her a yarn about my own love for my husband and said that I hoped she found a love of her own. I sighed and said how we had eloped and how it had been so romantic, without all the fuss of a society wedding, and she was enthralled.

Meet us on the promenade on Monday; we will be walking there between eleven and twelve.

Belle

Mr Parker to Mr Wickham

London, July 15

How are things going along? I have had to move out of The Black Bull and back in with the Widow. Hurry up and carry your prize off to Scotland.

Parker

Mr Wickham to Mr Parker

Ramsgate, July 17

I am off to a good start. I met Georgiana and Belle 'by accident' on the promenade. It was a fine day, exactly the sort of day I wanted, with a smiling sea, a gentle breeze, a blue sky and white clouds floating across it. The poets themselves could not have designed a better day for my purpose.

Georgiana was even more beautiful than I expected, the years since I have seen her having done remarkable things to her face and figure. I feigned a look of surprise as I drew close and said, 'Why, if it isn't Georgiana! Or Miss Darcy, I should say.'

Belle played her part magnificently, pretending to be very wary of me until she learnt that I was a friend, and the godson of old Mr

Darcy, and then she thawed and encouraged Georgiana to behave in a friendly fashion, saying that I must join them for dinner. Georgiana was hesitant, knowing that I had fallen out with Darcy but not why. However, Belle smoothed it over, saying that gentlemen often fell out and that it meant nothing.

A willing chambermaid helped me to pass the time agreeably until the evening and then I set out for Georgiana's house. I flattered her subtly, listened to her playing the pianoforte—why women must play the thing I cannot imagine, since no one can actually enjoy listening to the noise—and told her she was becoming very accomplished. I made friends with her dog and arranged to take her and Belle on a picnic.

Luck favoured me again. We took our picnic up on to the cliffs and Georgiana's bonnet blew off. We both ran to catch it, she went too near the edge of the cliff, and I caught her in my arms to prevent her falling—or so I said, though really she could have gone ten yards closer to the edge without any danger. But she did not object, far from it. I made the most of the opportunity, looked deep into her eyes and told her I was glad I had found her again. She blushed and said she was glad she had found me, too.

I bought her a new bonnet and presented her with it this morning. She is already half won. Another week to win her affections entirely, then a week to do away with her scruples over an elopement, and then we will run off before Darcy pays his planned visit at the start of next month.

Wickham

Miss Georgiana Darcy to Mr Darcy

Ramsgate, July 17

My dear brother,

It is another sunny day here in Ramsgate and I am very pleased to be here. Mrs Younge and I are in the habit of taking healthful walks by the sea every day, which I very much enjoy. Ullswater goes with us and you would laugh to see her running up to the waves and pouncing on them. You will be pleased to know that I am using the parasol you gave me, and it is much admired. The gloves and bonnet you sent me, too, are admired wherever we go.

We have met some old friends here and made some new. How good it is to see familiar faces when we are a long way from home! Mrs Younge encourages me to be sociable, saying it is good practise for me, so that I will know how to behave when I have my formal come-out. She is instructing me on how to behave, and giving me advice on how to deal with the ladies and gentlemen we meet, so that I know how far I may go in my friendship with them. I wish Mama were alive, so that I could learn from her, for I am not convinced that Mrs Younge always knows the right way to go on, but I must not repine. I have you, dear brother, to look after me, and my dear cousin Henry, and my other friends from Pemberley who will make sure that I do not go wrong.

It is a great thing to be young, is it not? To have one's life before one, and to know that love is never far away. How I long to see you, to share my joy with you, but perhaps I speak too soon. I am still very young, I know.

Mrs Younge is calling me. It is time for us to go for our afternoon walk. I wonder if we will meet our dear friend by the sea? I hope so! But for now, dear brother, adieu.

Your loving sister,
Georgiana

Miss Anne de Bourgh to Miss Georgiana Darcy

Rosings Park, Kent, July 17

I am thinking of you overlooking the sea as I sit here in my room overlooking the rose garden. It is very hot and I envy you a sea breeze.

Mr Collins dined with us last night. We learnt all about him, what little there is to know. He has a brother and also a family of cousins who live in Hertfordshire. Their property is entailed on him as they do not have a son, only five daughters. I am glad Rosings Park is not entailed away from the female line. I would not like to leave here even when I marry. I love the house and the grounds—even when it is very hot, as now.

We are looking forward to Henry's visit. Remember me to him if he should happen to visit you in Ramsgate.

Your cousin,
Anne

Miss Georgiana Darcy to Miss Anne de Bourgh

Ramsgate, July 19

I will have to leave Pemberley when I marry, but I do not think it will trouble me. I love it dearly, but I would gladly live in a crofter's cottage if I could be with the man I love.

I think you will see my guardian before I do. He is presently in London but I have had a letter from my brother this morning and he says that Colonel Fitzwilliam intends to go to Brighton before calling upon you in Kent, after which, I dare say, he might visit me in Ramsgate, perhaps arriving with my brother, who, I know, intends to visit me at the start of next month. How happy we will be, all friends together.

Your loving cousin,
Georgiana

George Wickham to Matthew Parker

Ramsgate, July 21

Why does anyone come to Ramsgate? The place is like death, all virtue and propriety. If not for my chambermaid, I would go mad with boredom. However, I will not be here for much longer. Darcy is due to visit at the start of August and so I must run off with Georgiana by the end of this month. She is nearly ready for my proposal. Belle has worked on her tirelessly, encouraging her romantic notions and saying that when two people are in love they do not need all the pomp and ceremony of a cathedral, but prefer a rustic wedding. The idea has borne fruit, for when Georgiana wrote to her cousin a few days ago she said that she would gladly live in a crofter's cottage with the man she loves. Not that an heiress with thirty thousand pounds will ever have to live in a crofter's cottage! I mean to treat her well when we are married and buy her all the frills and fripperies her heart desires. She will not regret having married me. And this will be my best revenge: for Darcy to see how happy she is with me and be unable to turn her against me. It cheers me every morning to think that he has no notion what is going on behind his back, for Belle reads all Georgiana's mail and prevents anything which mentions me by name from being sent. By the time Darcy learns that I have been in Ramsgate it will be too late. I cannot wait to see his face when he finds out what has happened and learns he will have to call me brother.

Wickham

Mr Parker to Mr Wickham

London, July 23

The end of the month, eh? Then you will need a week or two to get to Scotland and back, but by the middle of August, or the end of August at the latest, we will all be in clover.

Parker

Mr Wickham to Mr Parker

Ramsgate, July 28

Congratulate me, Matthew, for I have won the hand and the purse of Miss Darcy! Ah, life is good. I went to dinner there this evening and Belle left us alone on pretence of going to fetch her workbasket. Georgiana blushed very prettily and I satisfied every girlish dream, you can be sure. I told her how much I loved her and then I went down on one knee and proposed. Belle, who had been listening outside the door, came in at the right moment to hear our news and then congratulated Georgiana. 'Oh, this is wonderful news! You were made to be with each other! Just like my good, dear Stephen and me. Oh, the happy times we had together from the moment we met to all the magic of our wedding in Scotland, to all the happy years we had together until he died. I only hope you two young people can have the same,' she said.

At this I appeared much struck, and said, 'Why should we not go to Scotland?' I talked of the romance of it all and Georgiana, who has been encouraged to think of nothing else all month, was carried away with the idea. She hesitated only for a moment, thinking of her brother and worrying that he might not approve, but Belle rose to the occasion, saying that her family had thought it quite wonderful that she had eloped and had been full of admiration for her when she returned, praising her for following her dreams.

So take the best set of rooms at The White Hart, Matthew. No more Black Bull for us! No more living from hand to mouth or scraping along; there will be plenty for all.

Wickham

Mr Wickham to Mr Parker

Ramsgate, July 29

A note in haste. It is all up with me. Darcy is here. He arrived unexpectedly, d——n him, and foiled the elopement. What's more, he understood Belle's part in the scheme at once and dismissed her. He was in a towering rage, and only his sympathy for his sister and his desire to comfort her prevented him from pursuing me at once.

Belle and I are leaving Ramsgate together within the hour. Cancel the rooms at The White Hart, or play out the charade by pretending your wealthy friend will be arriving imminently, whichever you please, but do not expect to see us in London this month. We have nothing to live on but what we have on our persons, and we will have to find some cheap hole to hide in. God knows what we will live on when the money runs out.

Wickham

~ AUGUST ~

Mr Darcy to Colonel Fitzwilliam

Darcy House, London, August 2

Henry, are you still at Rosings? If so, find out all you can about Mrs Younge from my aunt. I must find her at once. She has proved to be a deceitful, scheming impostor—but you do not know all. And yet you must have it.

When Georgiana wrote to me about love and happiness and the future and old friends, I thought she meant nothing more than that she was enjoying her holiday, that she felt secure in my love, and that she had by chance met someone from Derbyshire. Little did I know she meant something quite different.

When I found myself with a free couple of days, on account of having finished some business more quickly than I expected, I went down to Ramsgate to pay her a visit before the appointed time. Thank God I did! For I found her about to elope *with George Wickham*.

Was there ever anything more villainous than his determined seduction of such an innocent girl? And the whole thing was cynically done, of course, with a view to persuading her to elope with him, whereupon he would become the master of her fortune.

He could not have done it without the help of Mrs Younge. I soon discovered that she and Wickham knew each other and that she was responsible for inviting Wickham to the house. It was child's play for her to encourage Georgiana's romantic notions and encourage my sister to see Wickham as a romantic hero.

Georgiana, poor girl, is heartbroken, and no wonder: the villain can make himself very agreeable when he chooses. He is handsome and charming and he knows how to make women admire him. He deliberately sought her out in Ramsgate and presented himself as a respectful and attentive cavalier who flattered her gently, bought her gifts, took her on outings, reminisced about their happy childhoods and expected nothing in return. What girl of fifteen could resist such a determined assault? He so worked upon her that she quite forgot it was wrong to run away, and thought instead it was romantic. It was not until she saw me that the glamour was broken, and she came to herself. She remembered the worry it would cause her family to find that she had gone, and remembered, too, that it would ruin her reputation.

That was Wickham's hope, of course: that once he had ruined her reputation, I would do anything to prevent the knowledge of her ruin becoming known; that I would recognise the marriage and disguise its beginnings; in short, that I would welcome him into the family for the sake of appearances. He would then have everything he wanted: a wealthy wife, an indissoluble connection with the Darcy family and his revenge upon me.

The latter, I am sure, was his chief motive. Revenge. He has never forgiven me for refusing to give him the living my father promised him. He conveniently forgot that he did not want it; that he asked me for money instead; that I gave it to him, knowing him to be unsuited to the church; and that he had willingly given up all claims upon it. Only when he had spent the money and found himself with nothing to live on did he remember the living, and try to claim it.

And now he has had his revenge.

Although, not quite. Thanks to Providence I was able to save Georgiana, and she is now upset and ashamed, but otherwise unhurt. In time, I hope, she will come to see it as a lucky escape, although at the moment her sense of relief is mingled with regret at what she has lost: a handsome suitor who engaged her affections and promised her a lifetime of bliss.

Once I find him, I mean to make him pay for what he has done and to this end I need your help. Find out everything you can about Mrs Younge, for where she is, Wickham will not be far behind.

Darcy

Colonel Fitzwilliam to Mr Darcy

Fitzwilliam House, London,
August 4

Darcy! I was appalled by your last. I discovered Mrs Younge's address in London and went there at once, intent on calling Wickham out, but the birds had flown. Let me know what you want to do. I am entirely at your disposal.

Henry

Mr Darcy to Colonel Fitzwilliam

Darcy House, London, August 5

I would call him out myself if I could find him. I have visited all his usual haunts but he has gone to ground. It is as well for him that he has. If he approaches Georgiana again, I will ruin him. She is devastated, poor child. She is pale and wan, and weeps at the slightest provocation. She has no appetite and she wanders the corridors of Darcy House, unable to settle to anything. Her painting lies untouched and she never sits down at the pianoforte without rising again a minute later with a heartfelt sigh.

I am doing my best to cheer her, taking her out and about to all her favourite places and doing everything I can think of for her pleasure, but she remains downcast. I hope you will help me to raise her spirits, before she goes into a decline.

Darcy

Miss Georgiana Darcy to Miss Anne de Bourgh

Darcy House, London,
August 15

Dearest Anne,

I must tell someone, though I have to swear you to secrecy, but I know I can trust you. I am so ashamed and so unhappy I do not know where to turn. My brother and guardian are both very kind, but I miss a woman to talk to. I had Mrs Younge, but now she has gone, and oh, Anne, I am so miserable. I have been very wrong and done something dreadful but even though it is all to be hushed up so that no one will ever know, I must have someone to tell. I have been in Ramsgate, as you know, but what you do not know is that I met George Wickham there. You know how charming he is and how handsome. He was kind to me when we were children and he was friendly to me in Ramsgate, and then more than friendly. Oh, always respectful! Never a hint of anything improper, unless it was to woo me without the consent of my brother. I did not know what he was doing to begin with, even now I can scarcely say when his friendship ended and his wooing began, but before I knew it I was falling in love with him. Mrs Younge smiled on the attachment, telling me of her own romantic past when she eloped with her husband and everyone said how much they admired her for following her heart. And all the while she was in league with Wickham and they were only after my fortune. My brother has dismissed her and is trying to find me a new companion, but it is a matter of indifference to me whether I have one or not. He is trying to cheer me by giving me his time and his company, but his kindness only makes me feel worse.

Oh, how could I have been so foolish! And, oh, Anne, how can I live without him; for without George the world is empty and dull. I wish, how I wish, his love had been real, for mine was heartfelt. You will think me very foolish I know, but I cannot help it. Even now I love him.

Tell no one, I beseech you.

Georgiana

Miss Anne de Bourgh to Miss Georgiana Darcy

Rosings Park, Kent, August 17

My darling Georgiana, how I feel for you! I do not think you foolish at all, for if Mama had not separated me from George in Bath, I think I would have fallen in love with him myself, had I not already been... And hearing your story, it is clear to me that he was hunting a rich wife even then. What a villain, to use you so! But you are lucky, Georgiana, though you cannot see it: you have escaped the clutches of a man who is not worthy of you. No scoundrel deserves your love, only a good and honest man, and there will be many, many men who will fall in love with you—you, who are so good and lovely—and who will care nothing for your fortune.

Your letter, I suppose, explains why Henry left us so suddenly. He received a letter from Darcy and then made some excuse about business and went at once. Your brother will find you a new companion, depend upon it, someone you can trust, and you know, dearest cousin, that you can always write to me.

I am sending you my love, my dearest Georgiana.

Your devoted cousin,
Anne

Miss Georgiana Darcy to Miss Anne de Bourgh

Darcy House, London, August 23

Dearest Anne,

Your letter heartened me and made me feel that I was not so alone. I am feeling a little better than the last time I wrote, and a little more able to see things clearly. The memory of George's charm is fading and what remains is not so pleasant to think of.

My brother has found me a new companion, as you knew he would. It was Cousin Henry who recommended her; she had been with a family he has known intimately for many years. My brother went to see her last week and looked into her background most carefully, speaking with all her employers and her family, too. He feels to blame for appointing Mrs Younge without examining her account of herself, and he has been determined not to make the same mistake again. I know, because I heard him and Cousin Henry talking about me. I have been a troublesome ward, I fear.

Mrs Annesley arrived a few days ago and she is very genteel and agreeable. I think I will like her. Fitzwilliam has suggested I invite a friend to stay as he has to go away for a while in order to help his friend Mr Bingley look for an estate to rent. I know that Mr Bingley has arranged to see three properties in the coming weeks. One is in Cheshire, one is in Staffordshire and one is in Hertfordshire. I hope he finds something to suit him; I know that Caroline and Louisa would like their brother to have an estate.

Your affectionate cousin,
Georgiana

~ SEPTEMBER ~

London, September 1

Greetings and felicitations, dearest Mama.

We have seen nothing of Mr Darcy these last few weeks, but Georgiana is in London once more and I intend to visit her tomorrow. She is such a dear girl, and such a favourite with her brother. I have told Charles that he must invite her to his estate just as soon as he has one.

We went to see one in Cheshire last week but it was quite hopeless. The drive was very short and the drawing room was small and dark. We could not have possibly invited the Darcys to such a place.

Charles has made arrangements to see two further properties. We are to go to Staffordshire next week and then to Hertfordshire. I only hope we might find something suitable before the autumn.

Your dutiful daughter,
Caroline

Mr Charles Bingley to Mrs Bingley

London, September 13

Dear Mama,

You will be pleased to know that I have at last found an estate. I did not take Caroline or Louisa with me, since they criticise everything and upon my word nothing seems to please them. Instead I persuaded Darcy to accompany me.

I was shown around by a Mr Morris, a very fine fellow who praised the house and the grounds; however, Darcy spotted some difficulties and made sure they were resolved before I settled. And now I am to have the run of Netherfield Park.

You must come and see it at once, and bring my brothers and sisters. You are all very welcome to come and live with me if you have a fancy to it. I am planning to move in by Michaelmas.

Your loving son,
Charles

Mrs Bingley to Miss Caroline Bingley

Yorkshire, September 14

Well, my girl, your brother has written to me and told me all about this estate of his, and I'm coming to see it just as soon as I can. Now don't you worry, your old ma won't go getting in the way. I've the little 'uns to look after apart from anything else, but Ned is driving me down to take a look at the place.

Make sure you invite Mr Darcy straightaway—these fashionable

gents get snapped up quick—and don't forget to let your old ma
know what's going on.

Your doting Ma

Miss Caroline Bingley to Mr Darcy

London, September 15

Dear Mr Darcy,

We can never thank you enough for helping Charles to choose a house
in the country. We are all beholden to you, and to show our gratitude
we hope you will visit us as soon as we move in to Netherfield Park.

Do not, I beg you, refuse on the suspicion that you will have to
mingle with the local burghers. Louisa and I will be there to provide you with the superior company to which you are accustomed.
I dare say you will never have to speak to the people of Meryton at
all, except to say, 'Good morning,' if you should be unlucky enough
to come across them whilst taking the air.

Hertfordshire is a pretty country, I hear. I am longing to see it!
And Netherfield, Charles says, is a very fine house. Not as fine as
Pemberley, I am sure, but then, what house is? For Pemberley, as I
frequently say to Charles, is the epitome of a gentleman's residence,
and I advise him constantly to model his own house upon it.

How happy we all were at Pemberley over the summer, before
you returned to London. I am longing to see Georgiana again, and
hear all about her trip to Ramsgate. I called upon her recently but
she was out.

Dear Georgiana! How I dote on her. Her manners are sweet and
engaging, exactly what a young lady's manners should be. How I
loved to see her dancing at Pemberley, at the private balls. They

were just the right sort of entertainment for her, introducing her to local society and allowing her to see how men and women of fashion behave. Most of all, allowing her to see some very superior dancing.

You yourself excel at the accomplishment, and I flatter myself that the partner with whom you opened the last ball was not deficient in her skills. It was very good of you to ask me to open the ball with you, though it gave rise to so much speculation that I was quite embarrassed by it all. I did not know where to look when your neighbour, Lord Sundy, said how well matched we were, and when his wife said there would be wedding bells at Pemberley before long, I am sure I must have blushed.

Georgiana, too, remarked that Pemberley needs a mistress. I am sure you would find it a help if you were able to leave the running of the household, and the care of your younger sister, to a wife, as long as the woman you chose was as fond of dear Georgiana as I am. I declare, I love her as much as I love Louisa, and you know my sister and I are very close. It is such a comfort for a woman to have another woman to talk to, and I think I may say, as your friend, that it would do Georgiana good to have some company from one of her equals. Mrs Younge is all very well, but a companion is only a companion, and can never be to a young girl what a sister can be.

But I must not lecture you. I am sure you will choose an estimable young woman to fill the role of Mrs Darcy when you are ready, and I can assure you that your friends would like nothing better than to see you happily settled. Who knows? Perhaps you will find your Mrs Darcy waiting for you when you visit us at Netherfield!

Do say you will stay with us. Charles would like nothing better, and Louisa and I quite depend upon it. It is our chance to repay you for all the hospitality you have shown us over the years. I am so glad that at last Charles has an estate of his own.

Sincerely yours,
Caroline Bingley

Miss Elizabeth Bennet to Mrs Gardiner

Longbourn, Hertfordshire,
September 14

My dear Aunt Gardiner,

Netherfield Park is empty no longer! I am sorry for Susan, as I know she hoped for a last-minute miracle, but I must also admit to being curious about our new neighbours. There has been talk of nothing else for days. According to Mama, who has been gossiping with Mrs Long, the house has been taken by a young man of large fortune from the north of England, a Mr Bingley. This is very pleasing to Mama, as you might imagine, for she has already married Jane off to him in her imagination, even though she does not know yet if he is single or married.

What is less pleasing to her is that Papa is refusing to visit Mr Bingley when he arrives. Mama teases him about it constantly, but he will not be moved. He says that Mr Bingley might call upon *him* if he pleases, but that he has no intention of being the first to pay the call. This has put Mama out of all countenance, for of course we cannot visit Mr Bingley until we have been introduced.

Jane and I have tried to console her by saying that one of our neighbours will perform the introduction at the Meryton assembly, but she refuses to be comforted, saying that Mrs Long is a hypocritical woman with two nieces and will therefore not introduce us. And even if these obstacles could be overcome—if Mrs Long were to suddenly become the kindest woman on earth and her two nieces were to become betrothed, or die, before the ball—it would still not answer, for Mrs Long will be away and will only return the day before the ball; therefore she will not have time to come to know him herself.

I dare say we will become acquainted with Mr Bingley sooner or later, whatever Mama thinks, since it is hardly possible we can be neighbours for any length of time without coming to know each other. Whether the acquaintance will be as welcome to her once it has been made I do not know, since it is almost impossible to find out anything for certain about Mr Bingley. This, however, does not stop the rumours. Almost everyone is sure they have heard something about him. Some say that he has three brothers, others that he has three sisters. He is, according to different informants, handsome, tolerably handsome and not at all handsome; temperamental, affable and condescending; a sportsman, an intellectual and a hermit. In height he is tall, medium and short; in figure he is portly, emaciated and spare.

However, we will have to wait until Michaelmas to find out for ourselves because he does not move into the Park before then.

Your loving niece,
Lizzy

Miss Susan Sotherton to Miss Elizabeth Bennet

Bath, September 25

Dearest Lizzy,

You will have heard by now that we have found a tenant for Netherfield Park, which has provoked different feelings in us all. Mama is relieved, because now, at least, some of the worst of our debts can be paid, whilst Papa is affronted at the idea of strangers living in our ancestral home, even though it is his own folly that has forced us to leave. My brothers and sisters are sad and angry in equal measure, and I must now become resigned to it. I must confess, I kept hoping against hope that Papa would see the error of his ways and stop drinking and gambling overnight, or that Mama would inherit a fortune from a hitherto unsuspected great-uncle, and that we could all return to Netherfield. But alas! It is not to be. Papa drinks as much as ever, though he gambles less, and unsuspected great-uncles are in short supply.

And so Netherfield has really gone and we will not be able to return there for at least a year, as that is the length of the lease. We know nothing about the man who has taken it yet, and I rely on you and Charlotte for the news. Papa takes very little interest in the affair and his man of business will talk to no one else.

We are settled in Bath for the autumn. It is cheaper to live here than anywhere else, at least with any pretence of gentility, and we will probably spend the winter here, too. After that, who can say?

Write to me soon, dearest Lizzy.

With fondest wishes,
Susan

✖ OCTOBER ✖

Miss Elizabeth Bennet to Miss Susan Sotherton

Longbourn, Hertfordshire,
October 1

Alas for unsuspected great-uncles: they are in short supply here, too. I am sure if we could find one, Mama would not be quite so eager to marry us to every man she meets. She has already decided that your new tenant will marry Jane. Poor Mr Bingley! He has hardly moved into the neighbourhood, and already he is considered as the rightful property of one or other of us.

But what is he like, you ask? I can answer that question. You will be pleased to know that he is a single gentleman and that he has a fortune of four or five thousand pounds a year. I hear that his money comes from trade, but we will not hold that against him.

Papa called on him as soon as he arrived, despite telling Mama that he would not go, and Mr Bingley returned Papa's call yesterday. We were not downstairs, but Lydia called to us as soon as she heard his horse and we managed to catch a glimpse of him from an upstairs window. There was much jostling for position as Lydia and Kitty pushed each other aside, first one gaining the prime spot and then the other, whilst Mary quoted a sermon on the beauties of sisterly self-sacrifice and the evils of the flesh.

Despite Lydia and Kitty's jostling, Jane and I managed to see him clearly and so I can also tell you that he is young and good-looking, that he rides a black horse and wears a blue coat. What more could you want? For if such a mode of dress and transportation does not declare an amiable disposition, I do not know what does.

However, if you press me for more, I will say that Mama asked him to dine with us and that he declined her invitation as he was obliged to be in town on business. Mama was afraid it meant that he would always be flying about, but as soon as it emerged that he was only going to town to gather a large party together for the assembly, she was content. For you know that an eagerness to attend the assembly means an eagerness to dance, and a fondness of dancing is a certain step towards falling in love.

Alas! for the young women of Meryton: Lady Lucas declared that he would be bringing twelve ladies as well as seven gentlemen to the assembly; however, Mrs Long says it is to be only six ladies, which means that instead of drowning us under a surfeit of ladies, the assembly will give us an overall addition of one gentleman.

The only thing that could make me look forward to the assembly more would be your presence, but I comfort myself with the thought that you have settled in Bath, that it is full of entertainments and so you will not be dull.

Write to me soon.

Lizzy

P.S. Mary is including a letter for your sister.

Miss Mary Bennet to Miss Lucy Sotherton

Longbourn, Hertfordshire,
October 1

Most noble Friend,

From all I have read, to lose a friend is one of the chief ills that can befall a young woman, but we must pour into each other's bosoms the balm of consolation and take courage from an exchange of scholarly letters. You and I, dear Lucy, were the only Learned Women in the neighbourhood and now that you are gone, I am the only one. I am determined not to let that prevent me from rational application and I have drawn up a plan of improvement for the coming autumn. I hope, dear friend, you have done the same.

However, it has met with little encouragement at home.

When I announced that I intended to spend four hours a day sewing blankets for the needy, Mama said that I had better sew blankets for our family, as we will soon be needy ourselves. 'If not for the entail, I should encourage you to help the poor,' she said, 'but once an entail is involved, there is no knowing what might happen.

As soon as your father dies we will all be turned out of our home and we will need those blankets because we will all be sleeping under the hedgerows.'

I explained to her again about the entail, but she was adamant that it was a deceitful invention, designed to cheat her out of what was rightfully hers.

This is not an easy house in which to be a Learned Woman, for there is no possibility of the exchange of rational or intellectual ideas.

At last I abandoned the attempt to explain the entail to her and continued to enumerate my plans, saying that I intended to devote four hours a day to learning a new instrument. Lydia said that I could not even play the pianoforte and that she would go mad if she had to listen to me learning to play the harp.

As you know, dear Lucy, Lydia is a Philistine. However, she only laughed when I said so, and danced around the room, saying, 'Phyllis Stein, Phyllis Stein, Lord! What a lark! Kitty, you must not call me Lydia from now on, my new name is Phyllis Stein.'

I did not let this daunt me, and merely remarked that I intend to spend four hours a day practising the pianoforte as well. I will, of course, ignore Mama when she comes into the room after ten minutes and says, 'What is all that noise? Really, Mary, have some compassion on my poor nerves,' and I will also ignore my younger sisters when they laugh at me and tell me to play a jig.

It is not easy to be a Learned Women in such a wilderness of ignorance. If not for Mr Shackleton, I do not know what I would do. He at least is capable of rational conversation and deep thinking on important subjects. He agreed with me when I said that preludes are of great intellectual beauty, whereas there is no intellectual value in a jig. I have promised him I will write a maxim on the subject.

It is also my intention to spend four hours a day in rational conversation, but this is impossible since Mr Shackleton is engaged in my uncle's office and no one at Longbourn House is capable of such a thing. Mama can talk of nothing except Mr Bingley and his five thousand a year whilst Kitty and Lydia can think of nothing but bonnets. Jane is a sweet girl but not even her best friend could accuse her of being a Woman of Brain, and Elizabeth confuses Levity with Wit.

Mr Shackleton agreed with me when I said as much at my aunt and uncle Philips's house this evening. Although he is only my uncle's clerk, he shows great signs of intelligence and I believe his friendship to be worth cultivating. Mr Shackleton also believes that our friendship is worth pursuing.

Shakespeare said: Friendship is constant.

Goldsmith said: Friendship is a disinterested commerce between equals.

I have copied these maxims into my book of extracts. I have also composed a maxim of my own: There is nothing so pure as friendship.

Mr Shackleton was much taken with it, and I told him he had my permission to copy it into his book of extracts.

And, lest I ruin my body in my pursuit of mental excellence, I announced that I intend to spend four hours a day in healthful exercise.

Elizabeth said that if I carried out all my resolutions they would amount to twenty hours of useful activity every day and when would I sleep? I replied that I was willing to sacrifice a few hours' sleep every night in order to preserve my position as the most accomplished young lady of the neighbourhood.

Write to me with your own plan of improvement, and we will sustain each other by showering each other's souls with the balm of true companionship.

Adieu!
Mary

Mr Darcy to Mr Philip Darcy

Netherfield Park, Hertfordshire,
October 2

Philip, I am staying with Bingley at present, but there is no need to address your correspondence to Netherfield as the Pemberley staff have instructions to send all my letters to me here until I return. Although I feel duty bound to remain with Bingley for a month or two, so that he can return my hospitality, the neighbourhood bores me. The countryside is featureless and the people have nothing interesting to say. They have been trooping into the house all week, examining us as though we were exhibits in a zoo, and I dare say to them we must seem as exotic, for there is not one person of fashion amongst them. There is, instead, the newly knighted Sir William Lucas, who has become suddenly fastidious and given up his previous occupations in favour of talking all day long about his presentation at St. James's. There is his daughter, Charlotte, the local spinster, who, at twenty-seven, is the despair of her younger brothers and sisters, and there is Mrs Long, the neighbourhood gossip.

When they invited us to the local assembly, I was just about to say that we could not attend when Bingley eagerly accepted. You know what Bingley is: he is as friendly and outgoing as a puppy and it was impossible to stop him. He did not care a bit that he might be mixing with the butcher, the baker and the candlestick maker; he thought only to make himself agreeable to his new neighbours. So now we must endure an evening of mortification and punishment as the local burghers ogle our clothes and whisper about our fortunes.

But I do not think we will be in Hertfordshire very long, for despite his willingness to attend the assembly, Bingley does not seem settled. He has already gone to London for the day. Not even a dinner invitation from one of his new neighbours could detain him, even though the Bennets have five reputedly pretty daughters, and you know how susceptible he is to a pretty face. I would not be surprised if he quits Netherfield before Christmas, once the novelty of having his own estate has worn off. That will suit me very well, for winter in such a place as this would be insupportable.

If you have a spare moment, call on Georgiana, will you? I know you are soon to be in town. She is always pleased to see you and you will be delighted with her. It is only a few months since you last saw her, but you will find her much grown.

Darcy

Mr Philip Darcy to Mr Darcy

London, October 4

I took Georgiana to the museum this afternoon as you requested and then entertained her to tea. You will be glad to know that she is well and happy and she sends you her love. She has been taking advantage of the fine weather to ride in the park, and Ullswater goes with her. I was pleased to see that Ullswater has reached a steady age and no longer runs off after every rabbit that pops out of a hole. Georgiana has done some very pretty sketches of the Thames and she has presented me with a monogrammed handkerchief, stitched with her own hand. I will call on her often, as I have decided to spend the winter in town. When you have had enough of humouring Bingley, I hope to see you here.

PD

Miss Anne de Bourgh to Miss Georgiana Darcy

Rosings Park, Kent, October 13

Dearest Georgiana,

We have had a visit from Philip and he tells us that he has seen you and that you are looking well. I am glad to hear it. I suggested to Mama that you should come and stay with us here, but she is entertaining herself with Mr Collins at present and has no need of any further diversion. He is the new rector of Hunsford, you know, and she is keeping herself busy by telling him how to manage his affairs. He is very grateful to her for her advice, and Mama has always liked gratitude so she invited him to dine a few days ago, that they might both continue to enjoy themselves. He remarked, not for the first time, that I seemed born to be a duchess, and I had to hide a smile behind my napkin. It is his idea of delicate flattery, I suppose, but I cannot altogether blame him, for Mama likes flattery as much as she likes gratitude.

We made up a pool of quadrille in the evening but it was not entirely satisfactory, so Mama hit upon the notion of providing us with some more company by telling Mr Collins that he should marry. He was dumbfounded, poor man, but it was useless for him to protest and five minutes later he was thanking Mama for her kind condescension. Indeed, he said he had often thought of marrying and that he meant to do so as soon as the parsonage was ready to receive a wife.

Mama was not one to accept this as a reason for delay and so she visited him yesterday in his parsonage and told him that, once he had put some shelves in the closets upstairs, the parsonage would be ready. I pity Mr Collins, for Mama means to have him married before the year is out.

He confided in me later that he was very willing to follow Mama's wishes, but that he did not know exactly where to find a wife. I could see that the matter troubled him and so I suggested he go to his cousins, for he has mentioned them on more than one occasion. They live in Hertfordshire and because they have no sons, only five daughters, they will be in some difficulties when their father dies, if they should not happen to marry, for the estate is entailed on Mr Collins.

He thought this a happy suggestion, for it would provide him with a wife and a means of doing good at the same time; and I think he is also not averse to the idea that his wife will likely be grateful to him. Indeed, I suspect that he likes gratitude as much as Mama does.

Whether his wife will be able to provide it for him as well as he provides it for his patroness remains to be seen.

But enough of my affairs. Tell me how you went on with your friend. Are you getting along with Mrs Annesley? And how is Mr Bingley liking his estate?

Your affectionate cousin,
Anne

Mr Darcy to Mr Philip Darcy

Netherfield Park, Hertfordshire,
October 13

Thank you for your kindness to Georgiana. I would like nothing better than to join you in town, as our time here grows ever more irritating. The assembly was even worse than I had expected. Bingley was happy, of course, particularly as he spent the evening dancing with Miss Bennet, the only pretty girl in the room, but there was no one I cared to stand up with, and as an assembly ball has no other purpose but dancing, the evening was tedious in the extreme. Bingley tried to tempt me to dance with one of Miss Bennet's sisters, saying that Miss Elizabeth, too, was a pretty girl. But although she was tolerable she was not handsome enough to tempt me, and besides, I was in no mood to give consequence to young ladies who were slighted by other men. I rather think she might have overheard me saying so to Bingley, which added to my ill humour, for of course I had not intended it. I danced with Caroline at last as a means of keeping boredom and irritation at bay; she, at least, dances well. She made her new neighbours the subject of her sharp wit and whilst Bingley said that he had never met with pleasanter people or prettier girls, and called Miss Bennet an angel, Caroline was more clear-sighted and laughed at the Bennets en masse. Mrs Bennet was excessively vulgar, the youngest two girls were common flirts and Miss Mary Bennet was almost worse, for despite being described as the most accomplished young lady in the neighbourhood she displayed neither talent, skill nor taste.

Caroline and Louisa allowed Miss Bennet to be a sweet girl, however, which did not surprise me, for they must have some company whilst they are here and there is no one else they could tolerate.

Remember me to your parents, and your brothers and sisters,

Darcy

Mr Philip Darcy to Mr Darcy

Wiltshire, October 14

What a time you have been having! But that is what comes of befriending a man whose fortune comes from trade. Lady Catherine feels the same. She is in town for a few days, having just returned from Cumbria, where she has been visiting her brother. Anne did not go with her, not being well enough. It says much about my aunt's new rector that she felt she could leave him alone in the neighbourhood with Anne, for she seems convinced of his probity and his respect. He is a very worthy young man, she tells me, 'though in need of a wife,' she remarked, 'for we are short of a fourth when we play cards.' It is not perhaps the best reason for marriage, but for my aunt it suffices. It seems to suffice for Mr Collins, too. I hope the woman he chooses is of a practical temperament, for her sake, and that she has a strong yet pliant character: living close to Lady Catherine will not be easy for a young woman, newly married, unless she has those qualities.

PD

Mr Collins to Mr Bennet

Hunsford, near Westerham, Kent,
October 15

Dear Sir,

The disagreement subsisting between yourself and my late honoured father always gave me much uneasiness, and since I have had the misfortune to lose him, I have frequently wished to heal the breach; but for some time I was kept back by my own doubts, fearing lest it might seem disrespectful to his memory for me to be on good terms with anyone with whom it had always pleased him to be at variance.

My mind, however, is now made up on the subject, for having received ordination at Easter, I have been so fortunate as to be distinguished by the patronage of the Right Honourable Lady Catherine de Bourgh, widow of Sir Lewis de Bourgh, whose bounty and beneficence has preferred me to the valuable rectory of this parish, where it shall be my earnest endeavour to demean myself with grateful respect towards her Ladyship, and be ever ready to perform those rites and ceremonies which are instituted by the Church of England. As a clergyman, moreover, I feel it my duty to promote and establish the blessing of peace in all families within the reach of my influence; and on these grounds I flatter myself that my present overtures of goodwill are highly commendable, and that the circumstance of my being next in the entail of Longbourn estate will be kindly overlooked on your side, and not lead you to reject the offered olive branch. I cannot be otherwise than concerned at being the means of injuring your amiable daughters, and beg leave to apologise for it, as well as to assure you of my readiness to make them every possible amends—but of this hereafter. If you should have no objection to receive me into your house, I propose myself the satisfaction of waiting on you and your family, Monday, November 18th, by four o'clock, and shall probably trespass on your hospitality till the Saturday sennight following, which I can do without any inconvenience, as Lady Catherine is far from objecting to my occasional absence on a Sunday, provided that some other clergyman is engaged to do the duty of the day.

I remain, dear sir, with respectful compliments to your lady and daughters, your well-wisher and friend,

William Collins

Mrs Gardiner to Miss Elizabeth Bennet

Gracechurch Street, London,
October 18

Dear Lizzy,

I have had such a strange and garbled letter from your mama that I thought I ought to write to you and find out the meaning of it. She says that Mr Bingley is on the point of marrying Jane. Is your sister really on the point of marriage, or is it one of your mama's speculations? And does your mama really like Mr Bingley? At first I thought so, for she called him the most agreeable young man of her acquaintance, and then, not two minutes later, she called him disagreeable. She also declared that he loved dancing and then went on to say that he did not dance at all. Perhaps you will be able to explain this paragraph to me:

> *We are all in raptures over Mr Bingley. He is the pleasantest young man imaginable, so affable and keen to please and be pleased, I am quite delighted with him! And dance! He danced all night long, and almost every dance with Jane. I am sure I am not surprised, for everyone knows my girls are the finest girls in the neighbourhood, and if he does not think so, then he has only himself to blame. Everyone is agreed that he is the proudest, most disagreeable man in the world and if he does not choose to dance, then, if I were her, I would choose not to dance with him next time.*

Pray tell me, Lizzy, what does it mean?

Your affectionate aunt,
Margaret

Miss Elizabeth Bennet to Mrs Gardiner

Longbourn, Hertfordshire,
October 20

My dear Aunt Gardiner,

It is really very simple: *two* young men have moved into the neighbourhood. The first, Mr Bingley, as you know, has rented Netherfield Park. The second, Mr Darcy, is his friend. Mr Bingley is affable and agreeable and although he has not had time to propose to Jane yet, he has at least made a good start by dancing with her twice at the Meryton assembly. Jane, in turn, likes him very well, and I do not object to it, for I am sure she has liked many a stupider young man. She declares him just what a young man ought to be: sensible, good-humoured and lively, with easy manners and perfect good breeding. She has only known him a week, but already I think she is falling in love with him. Mama is convinced he is on the brink of proposing, for when has she ever neglected to see a certainty of a marriage where anyone else would see nothing but a preference? And yet I will say this: it is generally evident whenever they meet that he admires her, and that Jane is yielding to her initial preference, so perhaps Mama is not so far from the truth this time, after all.

Mr Darcy, on the other hand, is the opposite of his friend. He is haughty, reserved and above his company. He is the kind of man who will always be well liked at first, for he is handsome, with a fine figure and ten thousand a year; but not all his estate in Derbyshire could save him from being discovered to be proud and disagreeable when he talked only to members of his own party, and declined being introduced to any other young lady in the room.

And here I must say that I have more reason than most to dislike him, because he slighted my attractions in a very public manner. He committed the grievous sin of refusing to dance with me, even though gentlemen were scarce and I was without a partner, and his friend Mr Bingley urged him to. But I dare say I will live, even though I am not handsome enough to tempt Mr Darcy. Yes, dear aunt, he did indeed say those very words, much to the consternation of poor Mr Bingley, who did not know what to reply; and much to the disgust of Mama. I am beginning to wish I had never told her about it, for although I told it as a joke against myself, she has used it as an excuse to be rude to him ever since.

You will be pleased to know that, despite this, we are all well. Mama complains constantly about her nerves—when she is not planning Jane's wedding or wishing Mr Darcy away from Meryton—but they are quickly forgotten when she has anything more agreeable to think of.

Papa continues to be amused by everything, including Mama. He had a letter from Kent the other morning which produced great mirth, but he has not yet told us what it contained. I hope he will let us in on the joke by and by.

Kitty and Lydia spend all their time visiting my aunt Philips and buying new bonnets whenever their allowance makes it possible.

Mary is as studious as ever. Her book of extracts is almost full and she has plans to embark on a second volume.

Give my love to my uncle and my cousins.

Your affectionate
Lizzy

Miss Charlotte Lucas to Miss Susan Sotherton

Lucas Lodge, Hertfordshire,
October 27

Dear Susan,

You have asked for more information about the new tenant of Netherfield Park, and you shall have it. Elizabeth has no doubt told you about the assembly ball, where Mr Bingley was the wonder of the evening, new neighbours being rare in this part of the world. I only wish his presence here were not at your expense, for you are sorely missed.

Mr Bingley is fond of company and prefers to spend time with his neighbours instead of with his horses and his dogs as so many men do. He drinks very little and shows no interest in games of chance, save as a means of being agreeable at parties. I must confess I find it refreshing. After living with so many brothers who can think of little but their hounds and their bottle, it is a relief to find someone who likes conversation and dancing. You will remember Alfred, my youngest brother, of course. He is only twelve but already he shows signs of following my other brothers in their favourite pursuits. His favourite occupation at the moment is bragging about how much wine he would drink and how many hounds he would keep if he were as rich as Mr Darcy. Unfortunately, he embarked on his usual bragging when we visited the Bennets and Mrs Bennet was not wise enough to let it pass. Instead she spent the visit arguing with him and so it went, back and forth, with her saying that she would take the bottle away from him if she saw him with it and he saying that she should not.

But there, I have said nothing of Mr Darcy yet. He is Mr Bingley's friend, though how two such dissimilar men came to be friends

I cannot imagine. Mr Darcy is sullen where his friend is lively; aloof where Mr Bingley is friendly; and superior where Mr Bingley is affable. He gave everyone a disgust of him at the assembly, and half of Meryton wishes he would go back to Derbyshire, where apparently he has a very fine estate. No doubt opinion of him would change if he showed any interest in one of the neighbourhood beauties, but he is far too superior for that. He talks only to Mr Bingley's sisters, who are handsome and fashionable women. The rest of us are beneath his notice.

Mr Bingley, though, seems ready to fall in love. He is very attentive to Jane Bennet. I am sure I hope it might come to something, for it would be a very good match for her. I am persuaded that she would be as happy as anyone ever is in marriage. I am not romantic, you know, and if a good man showed half as much interest in me as Mr Bingley is showing in Jane, I would have no difficulty in encouraging him. His wife will have a comfortable home, she will be respectable, and in addition she will have a husband who has no flaws for her to be ashamed of.

I have told Elizabeth that she should use her influence with Jane and advise her sister to show more interest in him, but Elizabeth is romantic and thinks that Jane needs more time to truly understand Mr Bingley's character. I cannot agree with her. Jane and Mr Bingley have spent four evenings together, and if she were married tomorrow, I should think Jane had as good a chance of happiness as if she were to be studying his character a twelvemonth. But it is no good. Elizabeth is content to let them go on as they are, and Jane has such a composed manner that Mr Bingley will never guess at her feelings unless she does or says something to make him understand.

It is a pity. It is clear that he likes her, and if she would only do something to help him on, I believe he would make her an offer. But otherwise I fear it will come to nothing. He is an unassuming young man, unaware of his own attractions, and he will not have the courage to ask for her hand unless she gives him some sign that it would be welcome.

My own prospects for marriage are no better than they were when you went away. Although I am happy enough at home, I would like my own establishment, rather than having to live my life with Mama and Papa; but unless another young man just happens to arrive in the neighbourhood, I fear my chances are slim.

But what of you? Has Bath cured your father of his unfortunate propensities? Has it brought you any new acquaintance worth having? Write and tell me all your news.

Your friend,
Charlotte

NOVEMBER

Miss Mary Bennet to Miss Lucy Sotherton

Longbourn, Hertfordshire,
November 5

Most noble Friend,

My plans for improvement have already reaped me rich rewards and I hope that your own endeavours have been as well received. As you know—for you, dear Lucy, are of a similar mind—I am not inclined to waste my time in the frivolity of social engagements, but I was compelled by my mother to attend a gathering at Sir William Lucas's house last night. She swept aside my arguments—for, not being a Learned Woman, she was unable to appreciate their potency—and said irritably, 'I thought you would want to show off, you have been practising that piece long enough.'

I was much struck, for though her sentiment was badly expressed, it echoed my own feelings that I should indeed be sharing my accomplishments with the world. I therefore condescended to attend the gathering. I was amply rewarded, for when I succeeded my sister Elizabeth at the pianoforte, Mr Darcy listened to my concerto with a look of astonishment. He had obviously not expected such a high degree of excellence from a young woman in such a small town.

Alas! My sisters then demanded a jig and I was forced to accede to their wishes, though as I remarked to Mr Shackleton afterwards, 'A jig might feed the body but a concerto feeds the soul.'

He was much struck and begged for permission to copy it into his book of extracts.

Lydia, Jane and Kitty danced for the rest of the evening, but I did not indulge in the activity. Elizabeth almost danced, for when Sir William saw that she was without a partner, he begged one for her, but it came to nothing. If Sir William had been a Learned Man, he would not have chosen Mr Darcy to be the object of his solicitations, for Mr Darcy had already said that he did not like to dance.

I believe that Mr Darcy and I have much in common. We share a love of music and, like Mr Darcy, I am not given to dancing. I think he had the right of it when he explained his aversion to the exercise by saying to Sir William, 'Every savage can dance.' I was much struck by the truth of it and I have copied it into my book of extracts.

Your friend,
Mary

Miss Elizabeth Bennet to Miss Susan Sotherton

Longbourn, Hertfordshire,
November 5

My dear Susan,

I should not triumph in it, I know, but I had a chance of turning the tables on Mr Darcy when we were at the Lucases' last night, thereby changing mortification to something far more satisfactory. Sir William, seeing me without a partner, entreated Mr Darcy to dance with me, and before Mr Darcy could refuse I replied coolly that I had no intention of dancing. Mr Darcy was confounded and my feelings were assuaged.

Jane's evening was even more satisfactory than mine, as Mr Bingley continued to pay her attention of the most particular kind.

I truly believe he is falling in love with her, and he is so agreeable that I think he might even be worthy of her.

Mama is effusive in her praise of him already, and if he offers for Jane, then her joy will know no bounds. Poor Mr Bingley! I fear he does not know what awaits him.

Your friend,
Lizzy

Mrs Louisa Hurst to Mrs Bingley

Netherfield Park, Hertfordshire,
November 12

Dear Mama,

We are now settled at Netherfield Park for the winter, it seems. Charles is very happy here, though Caroline and I are less so. The town is devoid of fashionable people and we have to make do with a strange assortment of neighbours. Mr Darcy is as bored as we are. He refused to dance at the first assembly and although he was nearly forced into it a few days ago, for the sake of politeness, it all came to nothing, for when Sir William Lucas tried to encourage him to dance with Miss Elizabeth Bennet, she refused him. I am not surprised. Sir William had all but begged a partner for her and no one with any spirit would have acquiesced. It did her no harm in Darcy's opinion—quite the opposite. He was caught by her refusal and remarked later that she had fine eyes. If only Caroline would take a lesson from this, she might have a better chance of catching him, but she can never bear to refuse him anything. She was annoyed when he praised Miss Elizabeth, and she vented her feelings by teasing him about his forthcoming marriage. Mr Darcy said he knew she would be jumping to conclusions and he bore it all with perfect indifference. It made Caroline so jealous that for a week she would not invite Jane Bennet to dine with us, but fortunately she has now relented, though it is more because we are to be alone this evening, the gentlemen dining from home, than any lessening in her jealousy. She is writing a note to Miss Bennet now.

Your daughter,
Louisa

Miss Caroline Bingley to Miss Jane Bennet

Netherfield Park, Hertfordshire,
November 12

My dear Friend,

If you are not so compassionate as to dine today with Louisa and me, we shall be in danger of hating each other for the rest of our lives, for a whole day's tête-à-tête between two women can never end without a quarrel. Come as soon as you can on the receipt of this. My brother and the gentlemen are to dine with the officers.

Yours ever,
Caroline Bingley

Miss Kitty Bennet to Miss Eleanor Sotherton

Longbourn, Hertfordshire,
November 12

Dear Ellie,

You will never guess! It is the most adorable thing! The town is full of officers! Yes, I know, is it not marvellous? They are all young and handsome and they wear bright red coats with brass buttons and they are so handsome you have never seen anything like it. Lydia and I go to my aunt's every day and we meet them there all the time. We see them on the way there, too, and on the way back again. I wish you were here, there are so many officers we have enough and to spare. I hate to think of you in Bath with all the old people with gout and corns. Tell your Papa to hurry up and win his fortune back again and then you can come back to Netherfield—although no, not too soon, because Jane is going to marry Mr Bingley or so Mama says, so Mr Bingley must remain at Netherfield until that is accomplished. But once he and Jane are married, then you must come back and meet all the officers. Lydia and I are wild to see them every day. Papa says we are the two silliest girls in the country, and to be sure that put a dampener on my excitement for a minute, but then Mama said that we are very clever and I believe she has the right of it.

The colonel of the regiment is Colonel Forster and Mama says that if a smart young colonel with five or six thousand a year should want one of her daughters she would not say him nay. He used to be always at Miss Watson's but they quarrelled and he does not go there so often now. Miss Watson does not mind, for she is besotted with Mr Robinson now. Lydia and I cannot understand it, and Lydia and Miss Watson have had a falling out about it. How can anyone like a man if he is not in a red coat? My aunt Philips says that now the colonel does not go to the Watsons' he is very often to be met with in Clarke's library. Lydia and I are wondering which of us he will pick, now that he is free again. Lydia thinks it will be her because she is the tallest, but I am the oldest. We are agreed that the other of us can have Captain Carter. We go to the library all the time and we are always changing our books but we never have time to read them. And now the officers are dining with Mr Bingley and we only found out because Jane has been invited to dine with Miss Bingley when the gentlemen are out. Mama thinks that that is unfortunate and I am sure I agree, for who would want to dine with Miss Bingley? But Jane has had to go. Mama sent her on horseback in the hope that it will rain and then Miss Bingley will have to ask her to stay overnight, so that Jane can see Mr Bingley in the morn-

Miss Elizabeth Bennet to Mrs Gardiner

Netherfield Park, Hertfordshire,
November 13

My dear Aunt Gardiner,

You will be surprised to see from the letter heading that I am writing to you from Netherfield Park, and I am very much afraid that the reason is not a happy one. Jane was invited to dine with Miss Bingley and it came on to rain as she rode over to Netherfield. She took cold and was invited to stay the night. Mama was delighted, for it meant that Jane would be thrown together with Mr Bingley, though why she wanted that to happen I cannot imagine, since a red nose and red eyes are hardly conducive to courtship.

Poor Jane was very poorly this morning and sent a note to Longbourn to inform us of her indisposition. I walked to Netherfield at once to keep her company. My appearance caused a great deal of surprise. Miss Bingley and Mrs Hurst found it incredible that I should have walked so far, though it is only three miles, and I am convinced they held me in contempt for it. Mr Darcy and Mr Hurst said nothing, but Mr Darcy looked down his nose at me, no doubt censuring me as much as the ladies. But Mr Bingley was all warmth. I like him better and better each day. He was concerned for Jane and he welcomed me openly, saying he was glad I had come and, I am persuaded, meaning it.

Jane was feverish and the apothecary was sent for. He promised her some draughts and advised her to return to bed, which she did, and she has remained there ever since. When it was time for me to go, Jane was so upset that Miss Bingley invited me to stay the night, and a servant has been dispatched to Longbourn to give them the news and to bring back a supply of clothes.

Jane was too ill to leave her room at dinnertime and I declared that I would not go downstairs, but she pressed me, saying that I must eat. I saw the sense of it but I would much rather have stayed with Jane, for I spent an uncomfortable evening. Miss Bingley and her sister made a few enquiries as to Jane's health but soon forgot her. Mr Hurst asked me a few questions about my favourite food and when he discovered that I preferred a plain dish to a ragout he had nothing more to say. Mr Darcy was engrossed by Miss Bingley, who evidently has designs on him, for she flattered his library, his house, his sister and indeed anything else she could think of that was connected with him. She echoed all his sentiments and enlarged them wonderfully. Where Mr Bingley can see nothing but good in everyone and everything, his sister and Mr Darcy can see nothing but what needs criticising: Mr Bingley is amazed that young ladies—all of them!—can be so accomplished, netting purses and painting tables and covering screens. Mr Darcy, on the other hand, knows only half a dozen accomplished young ladies, and his faithful assistant was quick to agree, saying that a lady must have a thorough knowledge of music, singing, drawing, dancing and the modern languages, as well as possessing something in her tone of voice, her way of walking and her expressions, to deserve the word. Mr Darcy was not even satisfied with this, but added that she must also improve her mind by extensive reading. When I remarked that I wondered he knew any accomplished young ladies, he regarded me with a look of contempt, and Miss Bingley did likewise. They make a delightful pair, both of them puffed up with their own importance and conceit. I am sure I hope they marry quickly, for two people who are better suited to each other would be hard to imagine. They can then indulge their love of criticising everyone else until the end of their days.

Mr Bingley was genuinely concerned about Jane and asked about her repeatedly. He did everything in his power to make the time pass pleasantly for me and I left the room in the end feeling that I would be very happy to have him as a brother-in-law.

Jane is sleeping now and I, too, will soon be going to bed, so for now, adieu.

Your affectionate niece,
Lizzy

Mr Darcy to Colonel Fitzwilliam

Netherfield Park, Hertfordshire,
November 13

Henry, I hear you are in London and so I will send you this in the hope it reaches you before you return to your regiment. I am staying with Bingley in Hertfordshire and I have met a friend of yours, a Colonel Forster, who is stationed nearby. He asks to be remembered to you. He is good company and seems resigned to spending his time with the militia in Meryton rather than fighting abroad, but perhaps this is because there seems to be a lady in the case, a Miss Watson who lives in Meryton. Whether it is a serious thing or not I cannot tell, but for the time being, at least, it makes him glad to be here.

If not for the military presence, our stay would be dull and boring. Like every other country neighbourhood, Meryton offers a confined and unvarying society. Bingleys' sisters occupy themselves as best they can with Miss Bennet, one of Bingley's neighbours, but they have little choice since she is the only tolerable young lady in the neighbourhood. At present she is indisposed, having taken cold when she rode over here to dine, and so they are deprived of even that small companionship; for although Miss Bennet is still at

Netherfield, being too ill to remove, she remains confined to her room.

Miss Bennet's sister is here, also, but Miss Elizabeth is not a favourite with Caroline and Louisa. They find her pert, and they amuse themselves at her expense by mocking her country habits. Miss Elizabeth, however, is not downcast; indeed, she seems to go out of her way to be different to the common herd. When she learnt of her sister's illness, she walked three miles to see her and arrived here with muddy petticoats. What is more, she did not seem to be the least bit ashamed of them. You may imagine what a torrent of ridicule this brought forth from Caroline as soon as Miss Elizabeth left the room, although I could not help noticing that, despite the state of her petticoat, Miss Elizabeth's eyes had been brightened by the exercise.

This, if nothing else, will convince you of the paucity of company to be found here, for not only did I notice Miss Elizabeth's eyes, I found myself attracted by them. In any other company, I am persuaded that I would not have given her a second glance. But she has a certain naturalness of demeanour and an independent spirit that make her something of a mystery to me. She seems to have no desire to attract my attention and is indifferent to my esteem. I must admit I find this intriguing, and if not for her vulgar family, I believe I would take some pains to know her better. But they are really beneath my notice. One uncle is a solicitor in the nearby town and the other lives in Cheapside. The mother is even worse than the uncles. She has taken against me because of an unfortunate remark which was never intended to be overheard, and she has not the wit to see that she makes herself ridiculous by her prejudice.

She paid us a visit today, to see her daughter and judge for herself the severity of Miss Bennet's fever, but finding her in no danger, she graced us with more of her presence than was necessary or desirable, and encouraged her younger daughters to beg Bingley for a ball. He is too good-natured to say no to anyone and so he has promised them that he will hold one just as soon as Miss Bennet is well again. Miss Lydia then remarked that, after Bingley's ball, she would persuade the officers to hold one. I have warned your friend Forster of it, but he just laughed and said that she is young and he has no objection to a ball now and again.

Bingley sees nothing wrong with Miss Bennet's low connections, but as his sisters so rightly point out, it makes it impossible for the Bennet sisters to marry men of consequence. Caroline fears his attachment to Miss Bennet, for he declares her to be an angel and the most beautiful girl he has ever seen. He has seen very few young ladies, however, and will, in time, find someone more suitable to marry. In fact, I believe he would make a suitable husband for Georgiana when she comes of age, and if they show a preference for each other, it is one I mean to encourage.

Luckily, Miss Bennet is improving daily and it will not be long before she returns home. I will be glad of it, for her sister will go with her and we will be left to ourselves again. Caroline and Louisa wish it, too. They like their friend well enough, but find it tiresome to have a sick person in the house.

Bingley is still enjoying the life of a country squire but as soon as he tires of it I mean to persuade him to return to town. The country is no place to be in November.

Your cousin,
Darcy

Mr Wickham to Mrs Younge

London, November 13

How are you faring, Belle? Have you found yourself a rich protector? I am pockets to let as usual. I met Denny yesterday. You remember him, perhaps? He went to school with me. He is now in the militia and he has suggested that I join. I cannot say I find the idea particularly attractive but I must do something; and, more importantly, it would give me a chance to establish myself in a new part of the country where my debts are not known. If I am one of the militia, I will find that credit is extended to me, at least for a while, and I will be able to dine and drink with my fellows for free. I am thinking of going to Hertfordshire to see him soon and decide if I can tolerate the discipline for the sake of the credit.

George

Colonel Fitzwilliam to Mr Darcy

Fitzwilliam House, London,
November 14

Dear cousin,

I had heard that Forster was with the militia but I did not know he was in Hertfordshire. You could not wish for better company. I have spent many an entertaining evening with him and I know he will collect the most interesting men around him. If he is stationed nearby, then you will not altogether lack for intelligent company, though you are living in a small neighbourhood in the middle of

Hertfordshire. I have not heard that he is to marry but I hope it may be so. He is at that time of life when a man must think of such things, and if Forster is not averse to giving a ball, it seems the rumour must be true: I cannot think why he would be so eager to do it otherwise, despite Miss Lydia's importunings.

The war continues to change course with every passing month. Everything was in our favour before Napoleon seized power: France was in disarray, and so was the army. But he is a natural leader and a man of considerable ability, and his recent victories against the Austrians have changed the balance of power again, so that I believe we will sign a treaty with him ere long. Even when it is signed, I doubt if the war will be truly over and I expect to see the outbreak of hostilities again before long. Napoleon is not a man to be content with peace, and the lull in hostilities will give him time to muster his forces and strike again, harder than before. If I had my way, we should crush him now whilst we can. But the politicians do not see it that way. The war is expensive and I think the government has no more stomach for it.

Your cousin,
Henry

Mr Darcy to Miss Georgiana Darcy

Netherfield Park, Hertfordshire,
November 14

Dearest Georgiana,

I was pleased to hear from Cousin Henry that you are well and happy and that you are making good progress with all your accomplishments. Ullswater is behaving herself, too, I hear, which will be a great relief to the rabbit population and no doubt the bird population as well! I remember you were going to paint her if she would only sit still long enough and I advise you to catch her when she is exhausted. I will look forward to seeing your portrait of her. I believe we will hang it in the gallery at Pemberley, at the far end between Cholmondley and Cerberus, a fitting filling between the sandwich of those other great Darcy dogs. And then you must paint your mare. Your last horse was so well done that it would be a pity not to take Milkfoot's likeness, and now that you are so accomplished, we will hang it with all the other horses.

Caroline asks me to tell you that she longs to see your paintings and that she is sure they will be worthy additions to the Pemberley gallery. She cannot wait to see them when they are done, and hopes they are finished in time for her next visit.

You asked in your last letter how we spend our time and so I will tell you. We are at present in the drawing room. Charles is playing piquet with Edmund, and Louisa is watching them. You and I must play again when I return to London. As I recall you beat me last time, and I must have my revenge.

Caroline is offering to mend my pen for me, but as you know, I always mend my own.

Miss Bennet is still indisposed and keeps to her room. Her sister, Miss Elizabeth, has spent most of the day with her but has now joined us in the drawing room, where she is at present busy with her needlework.

Caroline is complimenting me on my penmanship, which reminds me that I must compliment you on your own. Your hand was very fine and flowing in your last letter; it is a credit to you and your tutor.

Louisa has grown tired of watching the piquet and has begun to look through her music.

Caroline begs me to tell you that she is delighted to hear of your improvement on the harp.

Charles is now accusing me of searching for words of four sylla-bles and remarking that his own letters flow so fast that he has not time to express his ideas properly, but it is a boast, for he has always prized the idea of doing anything quickly. I hope you know that quickness is not a virtue and that considered thought is necessary in all things of importance.

Miss Elizabeth takes Charles's side in the argument and Caro-line takes mine. I fear it will not be over soon.

You must invite a friend to stay with you in London, for I find I will be in Hertfordshire for some time. You have your guardian in London at the moment, and Lady Catherine means to visit next week, but I am persuaded that you would like some company of your own age. I will be writing to Mrs Annesley about it, so pray invite whomever you wish. Perhaps Lady Catherine might be will-ing to let Anne remain with you for a few weeks. Though there are a good number of years between you, it makes me happy to see how well the two of you get on. Lady Catherine particularly commends you to practise your music, but I know you need no such reminders, as you are always diligent and your performance never fails to delight me.

And now I must go, for I am beginning to neglect Charles's guests. We will have some music, I think, and perhaps I might ask Miss Elizabeth to dance a reel.

Your loving brother,
Fitzwilliam

Mr Charles Bingley to Mrs Bingley

Netherfield Park, Hertfordshire,
November 16

Dear Ma,

When are you coming to visit me at Netherfield? It is all very well saying that you have already seen the house, but you have not seen it in the winter. You must come and stay with us for Christmas, and all my brothers and sisters, too.

I expect Caroline has told you already that we have houseguests, Miss Bennet and her sister. Miss Bennet is an angel, the most beautiful girl I have ever seen. We think alike on every subject, we dance together—upon my word I like her very much. She is not very well at the moment, a cold, but although I am sorry she is suffering, I cannot be sorry that she is here. Her sister walked over to be with her, which showed a very pleasing affection, though Caroline laughed at her for having a muddy skirt.

I believe Caroline does not like Miss Elizabeth very much, no doubt because Darcy is paying her some attention. I am not surprised. Miss Elizabeth does not hang on his every word as Caroline does. Indeed, when Darcy asked Miss Elizabeth if she would like to dance a reel, she refused, teasing him by saying that he only asked her so that he might despise her taste. A reel, you know, is not held to be a very genteel dance in society. Caroline was shocked that anyone should dare to speak to Darcy in such a fashion, but I could see that Miss Elizabeth did not disgust him, in fact quite the reverse—I am convinced he thought better of her for it. I am sure that Darcy does not like to be fawned over all the time, however much he expects it, and I think he liked to find someone who would stand up to him. I saw him watching Miss Elizabeth throughout the rest of the evening when he thought himself unobserved and there was a look of interest on his face. However, Caroline need have no fear, for it will not last. Darcy is not the man to lose his head over a woman. When he marries, it will be to someone whose pedigree is as long as his own. He can trace his family back to William the Conqueror, and there are very few families in England who can do the same. Upon my honour, I am glad I come from humbler stock. I am free to like whomever I will.

Write to me and let me know when I can expect you.

Your son,
Charles

Miss Elizabeth Bennet to Mrs Bennet

Netherfield Park, Hertfordshire,
November 16

Dear Mama,

You will be pleased to hear that Jane is now so much recovered that she is ready to come home, and I am writing to ask you if you will send the carriage for us this afternoon. We have already trespassed on Mr Bingley's hospitality far longer than we intended and I am sure he must be wishing us gone. His sister, I know, will not be sorry to see us leave. She is impatient for the day when she can have Mr Darcy all to herself again.

Your affectionate daughter,
Lizzy

Mrs Bennet to Miss Elizabeth Bennet

Longbourn, Hertfordshire,
November 16

Dear Lizzy,

You are quite wrong when you say that Mr Bingley is wishing you gone, for I never saw anything more promising than his attitude towards Jane when I called at Netherfield. Another few days will do the trick, you mark my words. I always intended Jane to stay at Netherfield for a week, and as the week will not be up until Tuesday, you may have the carriage then.

Your loving Mama

P.S. If Mr Bingley presses you to stay beyond Tuesday, then you must accept, for I can very well spare you for as long as he wishes.

Miss Elizabeth Bennet to Miss Susan Sotherton

Netherfield Park, Hertfordshire,
November 16

Dear Susan,

I owe you a letter. I would have written to you sooner but I have been busy looking after Jane, who was taken ill when she dined with the Bingleys at Netherfield some days ago. She was too ill to be moved—do not fear, it is only a cold, but she is very poorly with it—and so I came to look after her, for there is nothing so miserable as being among strangers when one is indisposed.

And that, you see, is why my letter comes to you from Nether-field Park. In fact, I am writing to you from your old room.

It seems very strange to be here without you. The company was much better when you were here, for, apart from Mr Bingley, there is not one person I wish to see again, and I am glad that we will be leaving this very day. Mr Bingley's sisters have been kind to Jane, to be sure—who could not be kind to someone so good?—but they have done everything in their power to make me feel unwelcome. They laughed at my taste and despised my occupations. But despite this, Miss Bingley fears me, I think. She sees me as a rival for Mr Darcy's attention.

Why she should have such an absurd notion I cannot imagine, for he never looks at me but to find fault. And yet she asked me to take a turn about the room with her one evening in order to try and catch his attention; then, once it had been caught, she did every-thing possible to keep his attention on herself.

He saw through her at once, however, and refused her when she invited him to walk with us. I suggested we tease him when she wanted to punish him for it, but Mr Darcy, arrogant, conceited man that he is, agreed with Miss Bingley that he was impossible to tease since he has no faults—except, perhaps, that his good opinion, once lost, was lost forever, but that is not a fault I could laugh at, and I said so.

He merely gave a superior smile, and Miss Bingley, tired of his attentions to me, suggested we have some music.

She need not have worried. As if realising that he had been too agreeable—agreeable by his own standards, though not by anyone else's—Mr Darcy relapsed into a hostile silence, which he has pre-served ever since.

We are now waiting only for Mr Bingley's carriage to be brought round to take us home, and I hear it below. I will write some more when we are back at Longbourn.

Lizzy

Miss Susan Sotherton to Miss Elizabeth Bennet

Bath, November 17

Dearest Elizabeth,

I have been hearing so much about Netherfield from you and Charlotte that I feel almost as though I had never left. I am very glad that Mr Bingley is such an agreeable gentleman—and already halfway in love with Jane, Charlotte says. I think Charlotte is right, Lizzy: if Jane likes him, she should encourage him. Jane has always been of a calm and equable temper and, not knowing her as we do, he might mistake her gentleness for indifference. It would be a good match for her and I would be happy to see her so well settled in life.

What a pity that all young men cannot be as pleasant as Mr Bingley, for I hear nothing but bad reports about Mr Darcy. However, I know you will tolerate him, for Jane's sake. Perhaps he will return to town, leaving Mr Bingley behind. That would be better for everyone.

We have our own share of conceited company here. There are two titled people in Bath, and they expect the rest of us to give way to them in all things. Luckily, we do not see them very often, for it is tiresome to be always having to bow and scrape to those who have nothing to recommend them but their illustrious name.

There are some interesting people here, too, however, and we meet them regularly at the assemblies and concerts. Mama and Papa do not particularly enjoy going out, but Mama makes sure we attend all the entertainments because she is hoping that my sisters and I will find wealthy husbands and so relieve her of our keep. It is for this reason that she thinks the expense of all our outings worth it.

I am sure I would like to find a wealthy husband as well as the next person, as long as he should happen to be young, handsome and agreeable as well. Alas, the young men in Bath are poor and the wealthy men are disagreeable, so much so that the thought of dwindling into an old maid seems positively welcome next to the thought of marrying any of them. But we are expecting an influx of new visitors next week and must hope that some of them are more inspiring.

Do not forget what I have said: tell Jane to encourage Mr Bingley. If anything could reconcile me to the loss of Netherfield Park, it would be knowing that my dear friend was living there.

Your friend,
Susan

Miss Mary Bennet to Miss Lucy Sotherton

Longbourn, Hertfordshire,
November 18

Most noble Friend,

Our family circle has been much improved by the arrival of Mr Collins, one of Papa's cousins and the heir to the Longbourn estate. He has made clear his intention of marrying one of us, in order not to deprive us of our home when Papa dies. Jane must be his first choice, she being the eldest, though she is perhaps as good as betrothed to Mr Bingley. Elizabeth must be his next choice, but she is unsuited in every way to being a clergyman's wife. Were it not for the fact that I have foresworn the nuptial veil, I might be prevailed upon to marry him. He is a man of taste, refinement and solid worth, as evidenced by his company and his letter to Papa. His ideas were well expressed, if all of them were not new, and I have used them, as well

168 · AMANDA GRANGE

as my brief knowledge of him, to make a thorough analysis of his character.

He is a clergyman with a pleasing gallantry not unbecoming to a man of his profession; indeed, his comment that he did not doubt of seeing us all well disposed of in marriage in due time was delicately expressed, for he could not be expected to know that I have foresworn the state of matrimony.

He is a man of some ability, for he has won the patronage of a very great lady, Lady Catherine de Bourgh. She is a woman of sound understanding and intelligence, as Mr Collins himself has said. She is thought proud by many who know her, but Mr Collins has found her to be all affability—no doubt because she appreciates his superior powers.

He is a man of foresight, for he prepares elegant compliments with which to compliment Lady Catherine and her daughter, Anne, when the chance arises.

He is also a man of great perspicacity, for he looked with disapproval on Kitty's novel and chose to read from Fordyce's Sermons instead.

As befits his calling as a clergyman, he is full of the milk of human kindness and Christian charity, for when Papa apologised to him for Lydia's inattention, he remarked that he bore her no ill will.

If I were ever to abandon the ways of Intellect and embrace the Fleshpots of Matrimony, I believe it would be with a man such as Mr Collins.

Your sister in the pursuit of learning,
Mary

Miss Lucy Sotherton to Miss Mary Bennet

Bath, November 19

Hail!

The clarion call of alarm sounded in my bosom when I received your last epistle. Although it was written in no less erudite a style than that which I have come to expect from you, it showed a disturbing wavering in your devoutly held principles, never to forsake the path of Learning and succumb to the Lure of the World. Take succour from me, dear friend, and let the strength of womanly sisterhood flow into your veins from a fellow ardent supporter of Athena. The owl sees all but flies alone. Pray reassure me that Mr Collins has not ensnared you with his masculine charms.

Your ardent friend,
Lucy

Miss Mary Bennet to Miss Lucy Sotherton

Longbourn, Hertfordshire,
November 19

Most noble Friend,

Your letter made me think, for I must own that I was considering whether or not it might be my Duty to forsake the path of spinsterhood in order to spread my gifts amongst the parishioners of Rosings. But your remark about the owl gave me pause, for it was very well expressed; indeed, I have copied it into my book of extracts.

With your help, dear friend, I have seen that I can best spread my wisdom by helping Mr Collins to write his next sermon. I have given him the benefit of my thoughts on the Iniquity of Frivolity and the Wickedness of Vanity. My sister Lydia could gain much by such a sermon. It would prevent her from running after the officers, a habit which has grown worse since the arrival of Mr Wickham, a handsome young man from London. But as I said to Lydia, a handsome face does not always auger a handsome heart. She only laughed and continued to trim her new bonnet, but Mr Shackleton said the thought was well expressed.

If not for the fact that he is a man, I would invite him to join our exclusive group of Learned Women.

Your dearest friend,
Mary

Mr Darcy to Colonel Fitzwilliam

Netherfield Park, Hertfordshire,
November 19

Dear Henry,

Wickham is here! In Hertfordshire—indeed, in Meryton! I saw him not an hour ago. It was an unpleasant shock, and I cannot help wondering what mischief he is planning. He has never forgiven me for denying him the living, though he knows he should never have had it, and he has hated me even more since I frustrated his attempts to elope with Georgiana. After that, I was sure I would never see him again, and yet here he is, in my very neighbourhood. I cannot think it is an accident, it must be by design, yet he seemed as shocked as I was at our meeting. What can it mean?

It happened like this. Bingley and I were riding over to Long-bourn to see how Miss Bennet did, when we saw the Miss Bennets walking to their aunt's house with a small party. They were all talking together with perfect ease until we came upon them, when they stopped to talk to us. Bingley enquired after Miss Bennet's health and I was in the act of turning away from her sister when I saw Wickham. He saw me at the same moment and went red, and then touched his hat with the coolest impudence I have ever seen. Does he mean to torment me with his presence? Is that his idea in coming here? Is it his revenge, to force himself into my company, knowing that if he is with the officers there is nothing I can do about it?

I cannot say. And yet I wish I knew.

Our meeting lasted only moments but it has left me feeling unsettled and I find myself worrying about Georgiana. Perhaps Wickham is hoping she will join me here, and perhaps he thought to make himself agreeable to her again, and relied on being able to escape my notice. Or perhaps he wanted to assure himself that I was really settled in the country, so that he could arrange a meeting with her in London whilst I was away.

I am perhaps being overly cautious, but I am writing to Philip, as he is presently in London, and I have asked him to visit Georgiana. He does not know what happened at Ramsgate and I have no intention of telling him; it is not at all necessary, as he will think my concern is nothing more than brotherly interest. If anything is amiss, I am sure he will tell me.

I will write to you again tomorrow. We are dining with the officers tonight and I hope to learn more from them. I only hope that Wickham is not with them.

I dare say this all seems very trivial to you, caught up as you are in the war. Tell me everything you can, without compromising your troops; I rely on you for news. The papers are full of such conflicting reports it is impossible to know what is really going on. Half of them are motivated by patriotic fervour and promise us that victory is imminent, and the other half are motivated by a desire to ridicule the government and its handling of the war and write daily of the certainty of our being invaded before the year is out.

Your cousin,
Darcy

Mr Darcy to Mr Philip Darcy

Netherfield Park, Hertfordshire,
November 19

Mr dear Philip,

I know you are in town and I would be much obliged if you would call on Georgiana and let me know how she goes on. I had to dismiss her last companion, as you know, because the woman did not know what company was suitable for Miss Darcy, and although I have every confidence in Mrs Annesley, I think it does no harm to keep a brotherly eye on things.

Your cousin,
Darcy

Mr Wickham to Mrs Younge

Meryton, Hertfordshire,
November 20

Belle! I miss you! The women of Hertfordshire are nothing to you. I have met them all, and not one of them can hold a candle to you. I wish I was in town with you, but London is too hot to hold me, and many other towns as well. I had an uncomfortable feeling yesterday that Meryton was going to be too hot for me as well, not because I have run up a mountain of debts already, but because Darcy is here! Can you believe it? Was there ever a man plagued by such d——d bad luck as I am? I saw him whilst out walking with one of the officers here. We had just fallen into conversation with a family of young ladies—not a patch on you, Belle, none of them—when who should ride up but Darcy. He was with his friend Bingley, and the two of them were evidently acquainted with the ladies, for they stopped to talk to them. I thought Darcy was going to have an apoplexy! I was none too comfortable myself. I knew he could make things very difficult for me if he chose, and though in order to destroy me he will have to destroy his sister, I am not certain he will not do it. He hates me enough, I am sure. He went white when he saw me and his hands clutched the reins of his horse so tightly I thought he would tear them in two. I went red. How could I help it? But I quickly recovered myself and touched my hat. He was incensed. He did not want to acknowledge me. But rather than make a scene, he saluted me in return. Our greeting would have passed unnoticed, but for the glance of Miss Elizabeth Bennet, which happened to notice all. I saw her surprise, and on learning that her sister is shortly to become betrothed to Darcy's friend—for her aunt told me so—I was afraid that Miss Elizabeth might have the whole story out of her future brother-in-law. I could do nothing about it at the time, but being invited to a party at her aunt's house, I sought her out and sat next to her, hoping to discover what she knew. And then at last I had a stroke of good luck, for a change, as I quickly discovered that she did not like Darcy. Moreover, half the town did not like him, for his superior airs had given them a disgust of him. Thank God for Darcy's d——d snobbishness. It has served me well. I was able to give Miss Elizabeth an account of my dealings with Darcy which, you may be sure, were favourable to me: how his revered father left me a living, which Darcy chose not to give me; how he was jealous of me, because of his father's love for me; how I was not meant for a military life, but meant to make the best of it. I tempered it with remarks on his liberality to his tenants and his affection for his sister, but I took care to portray Georgiana as proud, so that if word ever reaches Miss Elizabeth about that unfortunate affair, she will put it down to malicious gossip.

I had an uncomfortable moment when she said that he deserved to be publicly disgraced, for if my lies came out, then Darcy would not hesitate to refute them, but I recovered quickly and said that I should never breathe a word of it, out of respect for his father.

Although quick-witted enough in other respects, Miss Elizabeth believed me, without it ever occurring to her that I *had* just breathed a word of it, indeed many words of it, to her. I wonder what he has done to her, to give her such an immoveable dislike of him? Insulted her, no doubt. Not deliberately, but in that superior way he has of making everyone else feel that they are beneath his notice.

So now I am firmly established in her good opinion, and in the good opinion of the rest of the town. A handsome face and a charming manner will always win friends for the man who puts himself out to win them. A bit of flattery thrown into the mix and it is soon done. Whether or not I will stay here I do not know. Much depends on Darcy. I do not know at present how long he intends to stay here.

If it is only for a few weeks, then it will be worth my while to stay, but if he intends to stay here for months, then things might become uncomfortable. I am still undecided. But I must live somewhere, and until anything better offers, in Meryton I must stay.

George

Mrs Younge to Mr Wickham

London, November 21

Ah, Georgy, you don't fool me, it's your Belle you're talking to. You've been charming the young ladies of Meryton and you've singled out Miss Elizabeth as your flirt. She must be pretty, then, and lively, and witty, for you wouldn't waste your time on her otherwise. You'll leave a mountain of debts and a string of broken hearts behind you when you leave the neighbourhood, I dare say.

Fancy you seeing Darcy there, of all places. That was a piece of bad luck, but I don't suppose he will be there for long; he will be wanting to see his sister again soon and he will be riding back to town.

Hurry up and find an heiress. We've had a lot of good times, you and me, and will have some more before we're done, but we need money to do it with.

Belle

Mr Darcy to Colonel Fitzwilliam

Netherfield Park, Hertfordshire,
November 22

My dear Henry,

You will be relieved to hear that Philip has been to see Georgiana and that he has found nothing to alarm him. I mentioned that Georgiana's last companion allowed her to mix with unsuitable people and, being a brother himself, he understood my concern and made minute enquiries. He found out what letters were received and sent from the house and they were all unexceptionable. He spoke at length with Mrs Annesley and found her to be as reliable and trustworthy as I had found her, and he spoke to Georgiana and found her happy and intent on painting Ullswater. He then spoke to the groom and discovered that Georgiana never spoke to anyone in the park who could be considered undesirable and that she was attended at all times.

So my worst fears were ungrounded.

Indeed, it seems now certain that Wickham's presence in the neighbourhood is pure chance. I dined with the officers again and discovered that Wickham came here at the invitation of Mr Denny. The two were already acquainted and Denny persuaded Wickham that a life in the militia would suit him. Wickham, as always, has pockets to let, and so he is to purchase a lieutenant's commission. Where he will find the money I do not know, nor do I care, as long as he does not ask me for it, and after our unfriendly greeting I have no fear of it.

If not for the fact that I will have to accustom myself to seeing him from time to time, I would not think of him again. Unfortunately, Bingley has invited him to a ball at Netherfield—not him especially, but as one of the officers. I could not very well ask Bingley to make an exception of Wickham, at least not without arousing curiosity, and so I said nothing. Caroline, though, suspects something, but I believe she has put my aversion down to pride, and thinks that I do not wish to mix with the son of my father's steward. It is better than her discovering my real reason for hating him—and hate him I still do. My good opinion, once lost, is lost forever.

Your cousin,
Darcy

Miss Charlotte Lucas to Miss Susan Sotherton

Lucas Lodge, Hertfordshire,
November 22

Dearest Susan,

We have two new additions to Meryton society. The Bennets have a cousin staying with them, a Mr Collins, and there is a new officer—or soon-to-be officer—Mr Wickham. My brothers and sisters are all hoping that one or other of the gentlemen will make me an offer, but I think it unlikely. It is a pity, for I would certainly accept. My feelings on this matter have brought home to me what a very great difference there is between twenty-seven and one and twenty. Jane is the object of Mr Bingley's attentions, but she does nothing to encourage him. Such reticence is very sweet at her age, but if she does not have a care, she might find herself having to encourage someone far less agreeable in another five years' time.

Elizabeth is meanwhile the object of her cousin's attentions. I think she has only just begun to suspect it and is mortified. To be sure, he is not a sensible man, and has nothing in the way of personal virtues to recommend him, but he has a good living, a comfortable establishment and the patronage of Lady Catherine de Bourgh. His wife will be respectable and respected, and I must confess that if such a man were to appear interested in me, I would encourage him in every way available to me. But Elizabeth is yet young enough and romantic enough to think that true love still awaits her. As for myself, I have never been romantic. I have no belief in love, true or otherwise, but I would be glad of my own home and my own life, away from my family, no matter how much I love them.

I am invited to a ball at Netherfield and there I will no doubt dance with all the officers, make myself agreeable, and hope that one of them will be as unromantic as I am and decide that he needs a sensible wife.

But what of you? Are you still liking Bath? Is your father any better? Is your mother any happier? Have you any prospects?

Write to me soon,
Charlotte

Mr Wickham to Mrs Younge

Meryton, Hertfordshire,
November 22

Ah, Belle, how strange a thing is life, one minute up, one minute down, and then up again! After my recent holiday in debtors' prison it was balm to my spirit to find myself invited to a ball at Netherfield Park. That is an arena in which I can shine. I am not asked there for my own sake, but that is not important; I have an invitation and that is all that counts. As Mr Bingley did not make an exception of me when he invited all the officers, he evidently does not know what happened in Ramsgate last summer. Darcy must have been too proud to tell him, for which I am grateful. Bingley will be useful to me as long as he stays in ignorance. He can give me an entrée into the best society here and, better yet, he has a wealthy sister. The gossip is that Caroline Bingley has her sights set on Darcy, but I know him too well to think that he will ever marry her, for she has no pedigree and her money comes from trade. Sooner or later she will realise that she is wasting her time and then she will be vulnerable to a handsome charmer and there might be a chance for me.

In the meantime, I am keeping my wits about me. There are bound to be some wealthy young women in the neighbourhood and they are bound to be at the Netherfield ball. I am looking forward to seeing the look on Darcy's face when I walk in! No matter what his true feelings, he will have to be polite to me, as a guest of his friend. I am looking forward to it.

George

Mrs Younge to Mr Wickham

London, November 23

I think you would do better to avoid the ball; it might provoke Darcy into revealing something you would rather have concealed. The people of Meryton believe you to be a good, honest citizen at the moment. They give you ready credit and you have friends who will be useful to you, but all that will change if Darcy lets slip something about your habit of running up debts, let alone your habit of trying to run off with rich young girls.

Your own,
Belle

Mr Wickham to Mrs Younge

Meryton, Hertfordshire,
November 25

Perhaps you are right. I will say that I have business in town. It is as good an excuse as any. Expect me tomorrow at midday.

George

Miss Lydia Bennet to Miss Eleanor Sotherton

Longbourn, Hertfordshire,
November 26

You will never guess what we have been doing all week: getting ready for the Netherfield ball. Lizzy has been telling Mama that my dress is too low and Mama has been busy telling her that it is not! Mama says that Mr Bingley's giving a ball is a compliment to Jane but I think it is a compliment to me since I am the one who asked him for it, and you may be sure I intend to tease everyone else in the neighbourhood into giving a ball as well, just as soon as this one is over.

Kitty and me have been wanting to walk into Meryton a dozen times since Miss Bingley brought us the invitation but it has been raining so hard we have not been able to go once. It is wet enough for a river in the lane. Mary says that it is a punishment on us for being so frivolous and she has been writing about it in her book. La! You never saw such nonsense.

If we all take a soaking on our way to the ball, I wonder if we will all have to stay at Netherfield until we are well again? Lord!

What fun it would be, especially if Mr Wickham had to stay there, too. Me and Kitty are going to dance with him half the night apiece, and the other half we are going to dance with the rest of the officers. We both intend to marry a man in a red coat.

I cannot wait for this evening, the time is going so slow. Mr Collins is prosing on and Lizzy is telling me I must behave and Mama is talking of nothing but Mr Bingley. Only another hour to go and then I can get dressed. I am wearing my blue sarsenet and Kitty is going in yellow.

Your affectionate friend,
Lydia

Miss Elizabeth Bennet to Miss Susan Sotherton

Longbourn, Hertfordshire,
November 27

Dear Susan,

You will be pleased to hear that the ballroom at Netherfield has been put to good use, for last night Mr Bingley hosted a ball. I had high hopes for the evening and I dressed with unusual care, as I was looking forward to dancing with Mr Wickham and conquering what was left of his heart, but he did not attend. But I forget, you do not know about Mr Wickham. He is new to the neighbourhood and the most amiable young man in existence. He is charming, sincere, intelligent and handsome: in short, he is my model of what a young man should be. And I believe I may say without undue vanity that he is equally pleased with me. He singled me out at my aunt's house and we spent most of the evening talking together. I looked out for him in the ballroom as soon as we arrived at Netherfield but

I was disappointed in my expectations for he did not attend. He had some urgent business in town, or so Mr Denny said, but Denny knew as well as I did that Mr Wickham was driven away by Mr Darcy.

It seems that Mr Darcy's father left Mr Wickham a valuable living in his will, but Mr Darcy was jealous of the affection his father bestowed upon Mr Wickham and so he gave the living elsewhere.

I am not surprised that Mr Wickham decided to avoid the ball. I would have avoided it myself if I had known how it was going to turn out. No Mr Wickham, and instead I had to dance with Mr Darcy. I would have refused him, but he asked me so unexpectedly that I could not think of any excuse and so I was doomed to dance with the one man in the room who, above all others, I had no desire to partner. I cannot imagine why he asked me, as he seemed to take no pleasure in my company and I certainly took no pleasure in his. I could not resist the urge to question him about Mr Wickham and I was not surprised that he quickly changed the subject, but not before he had said that Mr Wickham found it easy to make friends but less easy to keep them.

I have no desire to think about Mr Darcy and yet I must admit that he puzzles me. He is a thoroughly disagreeable man, monstrous in his dealings with Mr Wickham, and yet Mr Bingley likes him; and Mr Bingley, you know, is the most pleasant of men. How can this be?

Jane is certain that there has been some misunderstanding, that Mr Darcy and Mr Wickham are both amiable men who have been set against each other by some third party, but this is impossible—and besides, Jane's opinion is not to be trusted, for when did Jane ever think ill of anyone?

It is a mystery. For my part, it can remain so. I have no interest in Mr Darcy, and if he is going to make life difficult for Mr Wickham, then I hope he will soon leave Netherfield so that we might all be comfortable again.

My dance with Mr Darcy was not the limit of my vexations. Indeed, it seemed as if almost my whole family was conspiring to disgrace themselves. Mr Collins insisted on dancing with me, and a more mortifying partner it would be impossible to imagine. He went left when he should go right, forward when he should go back, and he stood on my toes at least three times. I am beginning to fear, too, that his interest in me does not end in dancing and that he has it in mind to marry me. But I will not think of that until I am certain.

He further made himself ridiculous by attempting to ingratiate himself with Mr Darcy, as he knows Mr Darcy's aunt, Lady Catherine de Bourgh, and Mama spoke in the loudest voice about Jane and Bingley's forthcoming marriage, though nothing has been agreed upon. She would not lower her voice no matter how much I asked it of her.

As if that were not enough, Mary sang. Oh, Susan, how good it is to write to you, because you know exactly what I mean when I say that Mary sang! Why she will persist in doing it when she has no voice I do not know. Ordinarily it does no harm, but in front of Mr Bingley's sisters and Mr Darcy, who are ever looking for something to ridicule or despise, it was humiliating. I caught my father's eye, but instead of managing the situation with tact he almost pulled Mary from the piano, saying that she had delighted everyone long enough.

Caroline Bingley added her share to my vexations by trying to ridicule my friendship with Mr Wickham, saying that he was the son of the late Mr Darcy's steward, to which I replied that he had told me so himself. When she could not discomfit me that way, she said that Mr Darcy had always been excessively kind to Mr Wickham but that Mr Wickham had never deserved his kindness and had returned it with infamous behaviour. When I questioned her she could give me no particulars, which did not surprise me, as her motives were transparent. She sought to lower Mr Wickham in my estimation because he is the son of a steward, and the son of a steward must always come beneath a man with ten thousand a year in her eyes.

I was very glad when the evening came to an end. Mama would not leave, however, but managed by some ruse to keep us there for a quarter of an hour after everyone else had gone, so that I saw how heartily we were wished away by most of the party. Not Mr Bingley, however, for I believe he would never send Jane away of his own accord.

It was the one good thing to come out of the evening, for he sought Jane out at the start of the ball and devoted himself to her for the entire evening. I am sure he will propose to her before long, and how fortunate an outcome that will be. Jane happily settled, and married to a good and cheerful man—it is almost worth the mortifications of this evening to see that come to pass!

And now I must go to bed. I am cross and out of sorts, but I hope that things will look better in the morning.

Write to me soon,
Lizzy

Miss Mary Bennet to Miss Lucy Sotherton

Longbourn, Hertfordshire,
November 27

Most noble Friend,

I have endured many serious trials this week on account of the Netherfield ball, but you will no doubt be pleased to hear that the rigours of my intellectual pursuits have allowed me to bear the follies of my family with stoicism. Indeed, I used the occasion to impart some knowledge to my sisters. When Kitty and Lydia filled the house with their idle chatter about officers, remarking on the importance of a red coat, I told them that Hannibal had managed to cross the Alps without a red coat, and so, too, had his elephant. But my attempts to awaken them to the joys of sisterly scholarship fell short of my hopes, as Lydia took no notice of me but instead embarked on a long and not very interesting story about when Mr Denny pretended to be an elephant and chased her all around the room.

Jane has spent the week sighing over Mr Bingley, encouraged by Mama, and Elizabeth talks of no one but Mr Wickham, who, it seems, is a paragon of virtue. I likened him to a young Apollo, hoping to awaken in her bosom an interest in the ancient Greeks, but her brain, alas, is not suited to such erudition. Nor is my sister Lydia's, for she ran around the room shouting, '*à pollo, à pollo.*' She persisted in thinking that Apollo meant 'like a chicken,' flapping her arms and squawking in a noisy manner, even when I protested that Mr Wickham was nothing like the aforementioned bird.

The only sensible conversation has come from my cousin, Mr Collins. We were both of us in agreement over the necessity of attending the ball, despite my family's expectations that we would find such an entertainment unworthy of our superior powers, but as I remarked to them at the time, I think it no sacrifice to join occasionally in evening engagements. Society has claims on us all. I was much taken with this phrase and I have written it into my book of extracts. As a maxim it is both elegant and true, for I profess myself one of those who consider intervals of recreation and amusement as desirable for everybody.

Mr Collins agreed with me. He was able to set Elizabeth's mind at rest when she feared that he might suffer a rebuke from the Archbishop or from Lady Catherine if he should venture to dance. In proof of his confidence, he asked her for the first two dances. It was very noble of him, for he could expect nothing by the way of a sensible conversation. My sister Elizabeth means well, but alas, dear Lucy, she is not a Learned Woman.

This was brought home to me when I was solicited to sing after supper. She looked at me in consternation, realising that if she had applied herself to her music as I had done, she could have been the centre of attention; and determining, no doubt, to apply herself to the pianoforte as soon as she returned home.

My performance was much enjoyed and I was gratified to think that I had brought some culture to the gathering, for Mr Bingley and his London friends expect it. Indeed, I saw Miss Bingley and her sister exchanging looks of frenzied delight, whilst Mr Darcy listened in stunned silence, amazed to have found such sophistication in the country. His frozen features showed his determination to catch every note of my performance, despite Miss Bingley's attempts to distract him.

I was preparing to embark on a third song when Elizabeth caught my father's eye and he drew me from the pianoforte, saying that I had delighted the company long enough. I was startled, for the assembled company was evidently enjoying the music, but his following words showed his real thoughts: 'Let the other young ladies have time to exhibit.' And it is true that, whilst I sang, the other young ladies were squirming with embarrassment, knowing that they would have to follow my superior performance with one of their own. It would have been mortifying for them if I had continued any longer and shown their own efforts to be the effusions of mere amateurs.

Mr Collins was applied to, and made the most sensible speech of the evening, saying that he considered music an innocent diversion and perfectly compatible with the profession of a clergyman, as long as he did not devote too much time to it and neglect his other duties, such as the writing of sermons. My mother nodded her approval and remarked to Lady Lucas that he was a very clever man.

It is the first sensible remark I have ever heard my mother make. Perhaps there is hope for her yet.

Mr Shackleton surprised me by saying that he did not see anything so very clever about Mr Collins, only the sort of cleverness which comes with being in the pocket of a Lady Catherine de Bourgh. Mr Shackleton is of the opinion that true cleverness comes in enhancing the lives of one's neighbours in a quieter way, by carrying out such necessary duties as those of a clerk. It is an interesting opinion, and one that is worthy of further consideration.

I hope your own studies are improving and that you are growing daily in virtue and understanding.

Your sister in all but family relations,
Mary

Miss Kitty Bennet to Miss Eleanor Sotherton

Longbourn, Hertfordshire,
November 27

Dearest Ellie,

We have been to a ball and danced all night. I danced the first two with Mr Denny and the third with Colonel Forster, then the two fourth with Mr Collins—urrgh!—and the two fifth with Captain Carter. I went into supper with Mr Saltrum and then danced with Mr Shackleton and then Mr Dacres. Lydia danced the first two with Captain Carter and the third with Mr Collins—she was lucky and only had one dance with him, and she says it was the most tedious affair and he would keep stepping on her hem and turning all the wrong ways—then the two fourth with Mr Dacres and the two fifth with Mr King. She went into supper with Mr Denny and afterwards danced with Colonel Forster, when he was not dancing with Miss Graves, and then Mr Pratt. I do wish you were here—what fun we would have had! I hope there are lots of officers in Bath. Lydia is fagged. She says I must send you her love and tell you that she had new shoe roses, and says that she will write a note in the morning.

I do wish your papa would mend his fortunes and you would come back to Netherfield, but not before Mr Bingley has married Jane.

Love and kisses,
Kitty

Miss Charlotte Lucas to Miss Susan Sotherton

Lucas Lodge, Hertfordshire,
November 27

Dear Susan,

You are no doubt longing to hear all about the ball, and so here I am at my writing desk before breakfast. It was an interesting affair, and made a change in our daily routine. I was lucky and danced several dances, though Elizabeth was the focus of attention throughout the evening. I am not surprised. She was in looks, and attracted the admiration not only of her cousin but also of Mr Darcy. She did not see it, thinking that he asked her to dance only to mock her in some way, but that would have been out of character for him and I am surprised she did not realise it, she who is a great studier of character. He is proud and arrogant, yes, and I could well imagine him avoiding anyone he felt to be beneath him, but he does not have a propensity to mockery. I advised her to make herself agreeable to him, and cautioned her not to let her fancy for Mr Wickham make her appear unpleasant to Mr Darcy, who is a man of ten times Wickham's consequence. But Elizabeth has no interest in a man's consequence, and I believe she would rather marry a man she liked with a thousand a year than a man she did not particularly like with ten thousand a year. I cannot understand it. Happiness in marriage is very much a matter of chance, and those who start it in love very often fall out of love, whereas those who start it without love frequently end up the happier for it.

Jane was still the object of Mr Bingley's affections, a fact my mama privately resented, not because she wishes Jane ill—though she would be happier if Mr Bingley had fallen in love with me—but because Mrs Bennet would talk of nothing else. She drove Mama almost to tears by enumerating the virtues of the match, crowing about Mr Bingley's face, fortune, manner and address, and hoping that Mama might soon be equally fortunate in having a daughter wed.

She thought there was no chance of it, but I believe she might be mistaken, for Mr Collins has come to Meryton with the express wish of finding a wife. His first object was Jane, until he found she was likely to be soon engaged, and then Elizabeth became the object of his attentions. But Elizabeth has given him no encouragement—quite the reverse, in fact. She makes no secret of her irritation with him and last night she was grateful to me for drawing his attention to myself. She saw in it nothing but an act of kindness to herself. Such is the difference between twenty and twenty-seven!

Am I wrong, do you think, Susan, to try and win his—I will not say affections, for I doubt if he has any, unless they be for his patroness, Lady Catherine de Bourgh—but his addresses, and his hand? I thought so at first, but if neither Jane nor Eliza will have him, then I see no reason why I should not be his third choice. He seems to have a comfortable home, Lady Catherine seems to be a sensible, if dictatorial, woman, and he has no vices. He has no virtues either, it is true, but his parsonage has two sitting rooms, so he tells me, and it seems to me that a wife might have one whilst her husband has the other. He is also fond of gardening. A man who is fond of such a pursuit will be out of doors a great deal in the summer and a sensible wife might see him very little, after all.

It might all come to nothing. He might offer for Mary if Elizabeth refuses him. But I believe he is my best hope. The next few days should prove interesting.

Yours affectionately,
Charlotte

Mr Collins to Lady Catherine de Bourgh

Longbourn, Hertfordshire,
November 27

Lady Catherine, I give thanks that I am in a position to inform you that your most estimable nephew, Mr Darcy, is in full and vigorous health, as I had the honour of meeting him last night at a private ball given by some gracious neighbours of my most revered cousins. It was an elegant entertainment, marked by the hospitality and politeness of the beneficent hosts, and one at which your nephew, if I might be permitted to say so, shone brightly. I was much struck when I learnt of his relationship to you and made so bold as to introduce myself, whereupon I was able to tell him that your ladyship and Miss Anne were exceedingly well a sennight ago. He was grateful for the knowledge and much pleased with the attention.

Of the other matter I cannot yet speak, but I am certain that before very long I will be able to introduce you to Mrs Collins, if you should be gracious enough to allow the familiarity.

Your humble servant,
William Collins

Mr Darcy to Colonel Fitzwilliam

Netherfield Park, Hertfordshire,
November 27

Dear Henry,

I spoke at length with Colonel Forster at Bingley's ball last night, and he shares your opinion of the war. It is a pity, because if a lasting peace could be secured it would be of benefit to the country as a whole, but if the French are determined to fight on then we have no choice but to defend ourselves and our interests overseas.

Bingley was less interested in the war and more interested in his first ball, or at least, the first he has hosted. He need not have worried, for it was generally well received. He danced every dance and charmed everyone, playing the perfect host, and Caroline was an excellent hostess. She arranged the whole thing very well and was gratified when I said so.

I saw nothing of Wickham, who cried off at the last minute, but his influence was felt still, for, when I asked Miss Elizabeth Bennet to dance, it became clear that he had been blackening my character and that she believed everything he had said. I could not correct her without disgracing my sister and the dance ended in silence.

The rest of the evening was no better. The company, though well enough for a small country neighbourhood, irritated me considerably.

I will be glad to leave the country. The weather has been abominable, and as Bingley has to return to town on business for a few days, I believe I will go with him. I have found myself attracted to . . . well, enough of that. Suffice it to say, I would do well to remove myself from certain temptations. Bingley, too . . . it will be better for both of us once we are in London again.

I will write to you again from there and send you news of Georgiana. I am thinking of having a miniature painted of her. It would please me to hang it next to the miniature of myself as a boy which my father so loved, in the drawing room at Pemberley.

Darcy

Miss Lydia Bennet to Miss Eleanor Sotherton

Longbourn, Hertfordshire,
November 27

Lord! What a time we are having, not only the ball last night—I danced every dance—but now Mr Collins has proposed to Lizzy! He said he wanted a private audience with her this morning and Kitty and I were agog, as you might imagine. Mama said of course, and Lizzy said he could have nothing to say to her that anyone might not hear, and Mama insisted on her staying and talking to Mr Collins, and then Mama took Kitty out of the room and left Lizzy alone with Mr Collins, and he rambled about Lady Catherine—for you know I just happened to be passing the door and just happened to hear every word he said—and he told Lizzy he had to marry because he is a clergyman and needs to set a good example, and that Lady Catherine told him to!

I wished he had asked me. Lord! What a lark it would have been, to have a proposal before any of my sisters.

But that is not the best of it. The best of it is that Lizzy would not have him! And he would not believe her, and said it was only delicacy on her part that kept her from accepting, and she kept telling him she would not have him over and over again, and he kept saying he wasn't discouraged but he was certain of leading her to the altar when she'd refused him a few more times. It is even better than the ball!

And then of course Mr Collins told Mama that Lizzy refused him because she was a delicate female and Mama said she would never speak to Lizzy again if she did not marry Mr Collins, and then Papa said that *he* would never speak to Lizzy again if she *did* marry Mr Collins, and the whole house was in an uproar!

If it was me, I would much rather never speak to Papa again, for he is always saying how silly we are, but Mama understands what it is like to be young and thinks we are very clever.

Oh, Lord! Here is Charlotte coming down the drive. I hope you are having half as much fun in Bath as we are having here.

Lydia

Miss Charlotte Lucas to Miss Susan Sotherton

Lucas Lodge, Hertfordshire,
November 28

My dear Susan,

You will be surprised, perhaps, to have another letter so soon, but I am sure you will like to know that Mr Collins proposed to Elizabeth and that she refused him. Mrs Bennet was very doleful when I arrived at the house, and wanting sympathy for having such an unnatural daughter. Elizabeth bore her mother's reproaches well but she escaped from the room as soon as she could, and I do not blame her.

Mr Collins was equally affronted. He told me at least seven times that he did not resent Elizabeth's behaviour and as many more times that he had meant well throughout the whole business and that if his manner had been at fault he must beg leave to apologise, but I listened to it all patiently.

At length I managed to lead him away from the topic by asking him some trifling questions about Rosings Park, Lady Catherine and his parsonage. He reluctantly let go of his complaints and overcame much of his stiffness as he talked about the cost of the chimney piece, the condescension of his esteemed patroness and the improvements he had made to his humble dwelling.

He was gratified at finding a ready listener and I hoped he might offer for me before I left Longbourn. Alas, he did not, but I think I am not deceiving myself when I say that I believe an offer will be forthcoming. There is no better salve for a rejection than an acceptance. You may be sure I will write to you as soon as I have any news.

Your good friend,
Charlotte

Miss Caroline Bingley to Miss Jane Bennet

Netherfield Park, Hertfordshire,
November 28

My dear Friend,

When my brother left us yesterday, he imagined that the business which took him to London might be concluded in three or four days; but as we are certain it cannot be so, and at the same time convinced that when Charles gets to town he will be in no hurry to leave it again, we have determined on following him thither, that he may not be obliged to spend his vacant hours in a comfortless hotel. Many of my acquaintances are already there for the winter; I wish that I could hear that you, my dearest friend, had any intention of making one in the crowd, but of that I despair. I sincerely hope your Christmas in Hertfordshire may abound in the gaieties which that season generally brings, and that your beaux will be so numerous as to prevent your feeling the loss of the three of whom we shall deprive you. We mean to leave at once and we intend to dine in Grosvenor Street, where Mr Hurst has a house.

I do not pretend to regret anything I shall leave in Hertfordshire, except your society, my dearest friend; but we will hope, at some future period, to enjoy many returns of the delightful intercourse we have known, and in the meanwhile may lessen the pain of separation by very frequent and most unreserved correspondence. I depend on you for that.

Mr Darcy is impatient to see his sister; and, to confess the truth, *we* are scarcely less eager to meet her again. I really do not think Georgiana Darcy has her equal for beauty, elegance, and accomplishments; and the affection she inspires in Louisa and myself is heightened into something still more interesting, from the hope we dare to entertain of her being hereafter our sister. I do not know whether I ever before mentioned to you my feelings on this subject, but I will not leave the country without confiding them, and I trust you will not esteem them unreasonable. My brother admires her greatly already; he will have frequent opportunity now of seeing her on the most intimate footing; her relations all wish the connection as much as his own; and a sister's partiality is not misleading me, I think, when I call Charles most capable of engaging any woman's heart. With all these circumstances to favour an attachment, and nothing to prevent it, am I wrong, my dearest Jane, in indulging the hope of an event which will secure the happiness of so many?

Yours ever,
Caroline Bingley

Mrs Bennet to Mrs Gardiner

Longbourn, Hertfordshire,
November 28

Ah! Sister, was there ever anyone so cruelly used? Nobody is on my side, nobody takes part with me, nobody feels for my poor nerves. We have had such a few days I wonder I have survived. First Lizzy turned down Mr Collins, and now Mr Bingley has gone to London when he was to have married Jane. Everybody said so. Sir William Lucas himself said it was as plain as a pikestaff that Mr Bingley was head over ears in love with her, and now he has gone to town and we do not know when he will return. And if Lizzy takes it into her head to go refusing every offer of marriage she receives, she will never get a husband at all. I do not know who is to maintain her when her father is dead. *I* shall not be able to keep her. Nobody can tell what I suffer. But it is always so. Those who do not complain are never pitied.

Your affectionate sister,
Janet

Miss Jane Bennet to Miss Caroline Bingley

Longbourn, Hertfordshire,
November 29

My dear Caroline,

Thank you for your letter; it was good of you to let me know that you are leaving Hertfordshire. You will be sorely missed but I console myself with the thought that we can continue our friendship through correspondence as you suggest, and I hope that you will one day return to Netherfield so that we might continue our friendship in person.

Truly yours,
Jane

Miss Charlotte Lucas to Miss Susan Sotherton

Lucas Lodge, Hertfordshire,
November 29

Susan, you are to congratulate me. I am to marry Mr Collins. I was sure a proposal was coming, having listened to him all day yesterday, but knowing that he was to leave Hertfordshire very soon, I feared that he might not have time to speak before he left. However, I need not have worried. I happened to see him from an upstairs window as he approached the house and so I went out to accidentally meet him in the lane. No sooner did he see me than he proposed, assuring me of his wholehearted devotedness, and the approval of his noble patroness, Lady Catherine de Bourgh. By the time we returned to the house I was engaged.

He speedily applied to my mother and father for their consent, which, as you might guess, was readily forthcoming, and my father set his seal on the match by saying that we should make our appearance at St. James's. My brothers and sisters were overjoyed, my sisters knowing they will be able to come out more speedily now that I am to be married, and my brothers freed of the fear of me dying an old maid.

I am content. To be sure, Mr Collins is neither sensible nor agreeable, but still he will be my husband. I am convinced that my chance of happiness with him is as fair as most people can boast on entering the marriage state.

I have not yet told Elizabeth. I fear she will be disappointed in me, but if so, I must bear it. I thought the news would come better from me and so I charged Mr Collins not to speak of it when he returned to Longbourn. I am not sure how far I can trust him, however.

Wish me courage!
Charlotte

Miss Susan Sotherton to Miss Charlotte Lucas

Bath, November 30

My dear Charlotte,

I wish you happy with all my heart. It is a good match for you. Mr Collins is a respectable man with a good living and a useful patroness, by all accounts. I am happy for you, indeed I am. I know you are not romantic, and that you have never been romantic, and I think that you are lucky to have found a man who is also not romantic. Think how awful it would have been if he were in love with you and you could not return his affections. He wants a wife; you want a husband; and although I know it is not Lizzy's way of going on, we are each of us different. I long to hear all about Kent, and how lucky you are to be going somewhere so agreeable.

Now I have some news for you. I, too, have met a gentleman. I will not say more at the moment, only that he is very handsome and agreeable, and that I like him more than any other man I have ever met. His name is Mr Wainwright. Would it not be strange if we were all to marry within a few months of each other?

Write to me soon. Tell me all about your wedding. Are you to be married in Meryton? Are you to go to London to buy your wedding clothes? Are you to leave for Kent straight afterwards, or are you to have a wedding tour first? You see, I am insatiable!

Your dear friend,
Susan

Miss Elizabeth Bennet to Mrs Gardiner

Longbourn, Hertfordshire,
November 30

My dear Aunt Gardiner,

I have been remiss in my letter writing, particularly since much has been happening. Just over ten days ago a visitor arrived, one of Papa's cousins, Mr Collins, who is to inherit the estate. This upset Mama, as you might imagine, until he made it clear that he had come to make amends for his inheritance by marrying one of us, after which Mama was all smiles. His first choice was Jane, made in less than twenty-four hours of his arrival. On learning that she was likely to be soon engaged, he quickly transferred his favours to me, and three days ago, having known me for no more than ten days, he proposed. Naturally I did not accept, for even leaving aside his dubious motives for marriage, he is one of the most ridiculous men I have ever met. You do not know him, and so perhaps you doubt me, but I am not alone in my opinion of him: Papa thinks him one of the most absurd of men and even Jane can scarcely find anything good to say about him.

In refusing him, I incurred Mama's disapproval and I fear she has still not forgiven me. She makes constant allusions to it, and her ill will was matched by Mr Collins's resentment until, three days after being rejected by me and less than a fortnight after arriving in Hertfordshire, he proposed to Charlotte! The love which he offered me is now hers, as is the parsonage at Hunsford and the patronage of Lady Catherine de Bourgh. Poor Charlotte. I do not know which I mind most: the thought that she has accepted him, for it has sunk her in my estimation, or the knowledge that she will not be happy.

This is a letter of wonders, is it not?

Mr Collins has now left us, although he intends to return very shortly, much to Papa's despair, for Mr Collins is very fond of company and follows my father even into his library. Mama, too, is not eager for his return, thinking, not unnaturally, that he would be better staying at Lucas Lodge.

She has still not accepted the situation and consoles herself by variously saying that she disbelieves the whole story, or by thinking that Mr Collins has been taken in by Charlotte's artfulness, or by trusting they will never be happy together, or by hoping that the match will be broken off.

Papa amuses himself by saying that he is relieved to know that Charlotte is just as silly as his wife and more foolish than his daughter. Jane is surprised but endeavours to see good qualities in Mr Collins and to believe that they will be happy. Kitty is entertained, being eager to spread the news as quickly as possible. Lydia is astonished, asking Sir William—who brought the news—how he could tell such a story, for Mr Collins wants to marry me!

Mama scolds me every time she sees me. I have some sympathy for her, as Lady Lucas cannot help speaking of having the comfort of a daughter well married whenever she visits, which is rather oftener than usual.

My other news is neither ridiculous nor happy. Mr Bingley has left Netherfield, and there is some doubt as to when, and if, he will return. Jane bears it bravely but she is deeply upset. I am sure his sisters are behind the separation, for I never saw a man so violently in love as Mr Bingley.

Your loving niece,
Lizzy

↞ DECEMBER ↠

Mrs Gardiner to Miss Elizabeth Bennet

Gracechurch Street, London,
December 1

Dear Lizzy,

Thank you for your letter, which as you will imagine I found impossible to put down. I did not know that Mr Collins planned to visit, and I am surprised your Mama did not mention it, which leads me to assume that you did not have much warning of his visit yourself. He certainly seems to be an extraordinary young man.

I am relieved that you refused him, though not surprised, for you have always had good sense. He must be very foolish, for who but a foolish man would propose to one woman he did not know, let alone propose to two? What can he have been thinking of? And after his rejection by you, to propose to another woman whilst staying under your roof? There is not only foolishness but a lack of delicacy in the matter.

Your mama has also written to me and feels herself very cruelly used, although at the time I did not understand what she was complaining of, as I had never heard of Mr Collins and her letter did not make it clear who he was, much less what he had been doing. Her talk of you rejecting an offer of marriage also made no sense as she gave me no details, so I am grateful that your letter has enlightened me.

Never fear, her anger will soon fade—far sooner than your problems would have faded had you indeed accepted Mr Collins.

You say that you are disappointed in Charlotte. I understand your feelings towards your friend, but remember that Charlotte is twenty-seven, and that her situation, as well as her temperament, is very different to your own. She has no congenial companion at Lucas Lodge, no sister with whom she shares everything, as you share everything with Jane, and this will necessarily give her less of an attachment to her home. Then, too, she knows that if she does not accept Mr Collins, she will very likely end up an old maid. Yes, my dear Lizzy, I know that you would far rather be unmarried than marry a man you did not love, but for Charlotte it is different. She has a practical nature, and, for her, being the mistress of her own home is preferable to remaining under her father's roof. I would rather she had been able to love her husband, but I think, knowing Charlotte, that she will not repine over her lot. She will rejoice that she has so much, rather than mourn that it is not enough.

Your uncle and I will be with you on the twenty-third for our visit, and if your mama has not given over her ill humour by then, I will do what I can to restore her to civility. And if your sister has not recovered her spirits, perhaps she will like to come back to London with us for a holiday and a change of scene. I believe that some time away from your mama might be beneficial to her.

Your loving aunt,
Margaret

Mr Collins to Mr Bennet

Hunsford, near Westerham, Kent,
December 2

Dear Sir,

The delightful and felicitous stay I have just enjoyed in your munificent home, where I was overwhelmed by the gracious hospitality and genteel congeniality of your entire family, not excepting yourself, dear sir, of whose condescension in receiving me I am fully and nobly aware—also, I beg to assure you, most suitably and humbly obliged—has prompted me to write this letter of grateful and sincere thankfulness.

It has fallen to my happy lot in life to secure the affections of your most noble and amiable neighbour, Miss Lucas, whose modesty and economy have already won her the favour of my most estimable and gracious patroness, Lady Catherine de Bourgh. My esteemed patroness has humbled me by the excessive kindness of her reception of my news, and the assurance that the future Mrs Collins will be welcome to partake of a hand of quadrille at Rosings Park whenever Lady Catherine should need to make up a table.

It was merely to enjoy the society of my amiable Charlotte that I closed so rapidly with your wife's kind invitation to visit Longbourn again when I last departed, whither I hope to be able to return on Monday fortnight, for Lady Catherine so heartily approves the marriage that she wishes it to take place as soon as possible. This will, of course, be an unanswerable argument with my amiable Charlotte for her to name an early day for making me the happiest of men.

William Collins

Mrs Bennet to Mrs Gardiner

Longbourn, Hertfordshire,
December 4

Ah, sister, how good it is I have you to turn to, for nobody here is on my side, no one listens to me and no one cares about my nerves. And now on top of everything I am to receive Mr Collins, who belongs to Lizzy, for you know he proposed to her, but who has turned, like a snake in the grass, and proposed to Charlotte Lucas instead. Lady Lucas crows about it all the time, saying how good it is to have a daughter well married, and talking of his parsonage and his Lady Catherine, till I have to bite my tongue in order not to tell her that she is welcome to him, for never a more disagreeable man have I ever met; and I am sure that the parsonage is nothing to brag about, for I am convinced it will be small and dark and, I dare say, full of pigs.

I do not see why he does not go to Lucas Lodge instead of plaguing us here at Longbourn. I hate having visitors in the house while my health is so indifferent, and lovers are of all people the most disagreeable, especially lovers who do nothing but talk all day long and never let one get away. Though if Mr Bingley were here it would be quite different, and do not go thinking I am meaning him. But ah! sister, there again I have been cruelly used, for Mr Bingley has been away a week and we have not heard a line from him. There is a report abroad that he does not mean to return to Meryton, but I never fail to contradict it as a scandalous falsehood.

Jane bears it like a saint, but if he does not come back she will think herself very ill used and most likely go into a decline and die. And then Mr Bingley will be sorry, I am sure, but of what use will it be to us then?

But here is Charlotte Lucas at the door, come to cast her eye over Longbourn, I make no doubt, and to anticipate the hour of possession. That I should live to see Charlotte Lucas take my place as the mistress of Longbourn! I have told Mr Bennet he must outlive Mr Collins and he has promised to do his best, but oh! sister, when he dies, what will become of us? We will be turned out of the house before Mr Bennet is cold in his grave, and if my brother does not take us in, I do not know what we will do!

I cannot bear to think of the Collinses having this estate. If not for the entail, I should not mind it, but no one takes pity on me. How can anyone have the conscience to entail an estate away from their own daughters? I cannot understand, and all for the sake of Mr Collins, too. Why should *he* have it more than anybody else? He has done nothing to earn it, except be Mr Bennet's cousin, and I am sure anyone would be Mr Bennet's cousin if they knew there were such rich rewards to be had.

Do say you will come to us at Christmas, sister, and my brother must come too, we need you here. Your own children can manage without you if there is not room in the carriage for all of them. I have still not given up hope of Mr Bingley returning to Netherfield for Christmas, and I am sure he would be very welcome here, even if it meant we had to tolerate Mr Darcy.

Your poor sister,
Janet

Mr Darcy to Mr Philip Darcy

Darcy House, London,
December 6

Philip, I am once more in London and likely to be here for some time, so pray send all letters to Darcy House. Bingley is here as well and has at present no intention of returning to Netherfield. His sisters and brother-in-law are with him, and I have invited them to spend Christmas with Georgiana and myself. I have some thought of Bingley marrying Georgiana when she is old enough. He is just the sort of man I would like to see her with. He is honest, reliable, trustworthy, friendly, good-natured and good-humoured. I think he would be a good match for her. There is some disparity in fortune, it is true, but fortune is not everything and I want to see her happy. I believe such a match would suit him, too. He has always liked Georgiana, and he was much struck by the change in her when he dined here last night. She has grown considerably these last few months and is becoming a very lovely young woman. But such thoughts are for the future. It is enough that he will be spending some time with her over the next few weeks and renewing his friendship with her.

Tell me, Philip, as we are talking of matches, are you any nearer to finding a woman to take to wife? I have never heard you talk of anyone in particular, but perhaps you have never found anyone you were particularly attracted to. Unless . . . have you ever found yourself attracted to someone unsuitable? A woman whose standing was so far beneath your own that it would be a degradation to marry her because her family were, let us say, country gentry, with uncles engaged in the professions or in trade? Whose mother talked of nothing but marrying her daughters off, and whose father failed to correct the behaviour of either his wife or his children, allowing them to grow up wild and unrestrained? Did you ever find that, despite all these disadvantages, such a woman attracted you, against your will, and that a pair of fine eyes caught your attention and would give you no peace? Or that an impertinent manner, instead of revolting you, attracted you? Or that her lack of respect for your standing served to make you more interested, and not less?

Did you ever think it necessary to remove yourself from the company of such a woman, lest your interest should become ungovernable and your behaviour should give rise to expectations? And did a part of you feel that, if such expectations should arise, it would be no bad thing? That your feelings would actually like it if you were obliged to offer for her, though your character revolted against the idea? Did you find it difficult to be rational where she was concerned? Did you, in short, feel in the grip of something out of your control? Let me know if anything similar has ever happened to you.

Darcy

Mr Philip Darcy to Mr Darcy

Wiltshire, December 8

Darcy, I was surprised by your last letter and took up my pen to reply to you straightaway. I never thought you would be the man to succumb to the charms of someone unsuitable. You are the last person I would ever expect to lose your sense of your own importance and become beguiled by someone as low as your object of desire seems to be. She is wholly unworthy of your hand, however, as you know yourself, and as she is from the gentry you cannot even assuage your desires by offering her carte blanche; therefore, I advise you to put her out of your mind. Occupy yourself with business, take plenty of exercise, ride hard, make time for fencing every day, go to your club when you do not have company at home, never leave yourself with a moment to think of her. If you do all this, then by and by the attraction will fade. There is a great deal to be said for 'out of sight, out of mind' and you were wise to take yourself out of her way. And after Christmas, come to Wiltshire. I am having a large party of friends here in the New Year. You will be amongst your own kind and they will soon drive this woman from your mind.

But before you banish her from your thoughts entirely, answer me this: who is she? I am curious to know just what woman has won your reluctant admiration, for I have never heard you speak so of a woman before. She must be something out of the common way to make such an impression on you.

PD

Mr Darcy to Mr Philip Darcy

Darcy House, London,
December 10

Philip, you misunderstand me. It is not I who was bewitched by someone beneath my station, it was my friend Bingley. He became enamoured of a local girl when we were staying in Hertfordshire. Her father was a gentleman but her mother was a silly, vulgar woman who was always trying to make a match, and her younger sisters spent their lives running after officers. However, we rescued him from the situation and all is well, for when he came to town on business, his sisters and I followed him and persuaded him to remain.

I have just been to Howards and Gibbs to have my mother's pearls restrung for Georgiana; I mean to give them to her for Christmas. I am debating whether or not to have some further items of family jewellery remodelled for her. She is still a little young for them, but as I am having the pearls restrung, I think it would be easier to have it all done together. She will look very well in them, for she has my mother's colouring.

I thank you for your invitation to Wiltshire but I am engaged to go to Cumbria in the New Year to see my aunt and uncle there. Maud has just had a child and I am to be the godfather.

Darcy

Mrs Bingley to Miss Caroline Bingley

Yorkshire, December 12

Now, Caroline, what's all this I hear from your brother about this angel of his? Tell me all about it. I've had some of it from Charles, he sent me a letter, but such a letter! I thought, 'What's wrong with Charles?' It wasn't in his usual cheerful style; it was full of misery and gloom. He met her at that fancy house, he said, and never a prettier nor more agreeable girl lived, but somehow or other she didn't take to him? I'd like to see the girl silly enough not to take to my Charles. Any girl would be lucky to get him, and that's not just a mother talking. Now, what's the tale, Caroline? Has this Mr Darcy persuaded him the girl doesn't like him? Shall I come down to London and sort things out? Or shall I go to Hertfordshire and see this girl for myself? I will in a trice if you think it will help, only Ned's not well and the little 'un has colic. I can't bear to think of your brother unhappy. A nice, pretty girl is just what he needs.

Your Ma

Miss Caroline Bingley to Mrs Bingley

London, December 16

Greetings and felicitations, my dearest Mama.

There is no need for you to come to London or Hertfordshire; indeed, I beg you will not leave my brothers and sisters if they have need of you, for you must not neglect them on any account. It is true that Charles became enamoured of a sweet girl in Hertfordshire, but it was nothing more than a passing fancy on her part. I am persuaded that it was nothing really but a passing fancy on his part, either, and now that he has settled in London he will soon forget all about her, particularly as he has Miss Darcy to entertain him. She is just the sort of nice, pretty girl you would like for Charles. She is unaffected and sweet, and I am persuaded that her family would like the match as well as his. There is no need for you to meet her just yet, Mama, she is still young and nothing is fixed, but do not worry about Charles, he has already recovered from his infatuation with Miss Bennet.

Your dutiful daughter,
Caroline

Miss Caroline Bingley to Miss Jane Bennet

London, December 16

My dear Friend,

As I suspected, Charles is now settled in London for the winter, and we expect to remain here with him, to keep him company whilst he is in town. We will be celebrating the season with Mr Darcy and his sister. Georgiana Darcy grows more beautiful every day, and the bond of friendship between her and Charles is deepening into something more before our eyes. We are all very happy for it. They are well suited, and I am sure you will join with me in wishing them every happiness when the accomplishment of all our wishes should come to pass.

Mr Darcy and Charles are seldom apart. It is good for Charles to have an older, steadier friend who can advise him in the ways of the world, but I believe the friendship is not all in Charles's favour: Mr Darcy asked his opinion only the other day on some new furniture he is buying, and Charles was able to give his approval of Mr Darcy's choice.

Charles is very sorry that he did not have time to pay his respects to his friends in Hertfordshire before he left, but he has asked me to repair the omission and I do it gladly, telling you how much he enjoyed his stay in Hertfordshire and the delightful, friendly company he found there.

Write to me soon, my dearest friend, and tell me how you go on in Hertfordshire.

Yours ever,
Caroline

Mr Wickham to Mrs Younge

Meryton, Hertfordshire,
December 18

Dear Belle,

Luck has favoured me. Darcy has left the neighbourhood! His friend became attached to one of the local girls and so Darcy whisked him back to London.

It has been a relief to me, for it means that I can now stay here for as long as I want. Moreover, I can say of Darcy whatever I want, without fear of contradiction. His pride, his arrogance and his over-bearing attitude have already given the people of Meryton a dislike of him, and it is child's play for me to fan that dislike into disgust. Whilst speaking always in sorrow and not in anger I have let it be known that he ruined my chances in life. I was forced to whisper this before, but I now proclaim it in the open. The result is that Darcy is universally despised, and everyone feels how clever they were to dislike him, even before the full weight of his iniquities was known. In this way I have protected myself, for if he should happen to return to the neighbourhood, my friends will be so numerous and his so few that nothing he says will be believed. Indeed, the people of Meryton are happy to condemn him as the worst of men.

I have taken the opportunity to paint Miss Darcy as proud and disagreeable, too, so that if any rumour of my conduct there is abroad, it will look as though I am an innocent victim of a slander.

My standing as an officer allows me to live on credit but I cannot live on credit forever and so I must look about me for an heiress. I like Miss Elizabeth Bennet very much, in fact if she had a fortune I would be happy to marry her, but discreet enquiries have led me to understand that she has nothing but a thousand pounds, and that would be gone in a month. I am presently keeping my eyes and ears open, and hope to hear something of an heiress soon. Let me know if you hear of anything.

In the meantime, I hope all goes well with you. I wish you a wealthy husband and I wish myself a wealthy wife, and let neither of us end up in the position of Charlotte Lucas, being forced to marry a Mr Collins!

Love and what you will,
George

Miss Charlotte Lucas to Miss Susan Sotherton

Lucas Lodge, Hertfordshire,
December 20

Dear Susan,

I am just returned from London, where Mama and I have been shopping for my wedding finery. We have bought white silk for the dress, which is to be trimmed with lace, and a short veil. Mama has promised to help me make the gown so that it will be ready in time. We do not yet have a date, but Mr Collins wishes to be married sooner rather than later and I believe the ceremony will be early in the New Year. I am particularly pleased with my shoes, which are of a silk so similar to the fabric I have bought for the dress as to be almost identical.

We are now busy cutting and stitching. As well as my wedding gown, I am having three new gowns to take away with me: two evening gowns, such as I might wear at Rosings Park, and one for everyday wear. My sisters are all helping, and I think we will have them finished in time.

You ask about a wedding tour. We are not to have one, but are to go straightaway to Kent; indeed, we will be leaving from the church door. Mr Collins has already been away from his duties for weeks, and cannot expect Lady Catherine to allow him more time away. I am looking forward to meeting her. Although she seems to like her own way, as many great people do, she sounds to have a great deal of common sense, and I think we could have a far worse neighbour.

Warm wishes,
Charlotte

Miss Jane Bennet to Miss Susan Sotherton

Longbourn, Hertfordshire,
December 23, four o'clock

Dear Susan,

I have not written to you for some time and I should have done. I have no excuse to make except low spirits. They are recovering, however, greatly helped by my aunt Gardiner, who arrived today bearing presents, and bringing us news of all the latest London fashions.

She spent much of the day listening to my mother, which was a great relief to me, since Mama talks of Mr Bingley constantly and bemoans the fact that he has left us and has no plans to return. I wish she did not talk of it so relentlessly; she can have no idea how much she wounds me when she talks of it, but I will not repine. It cannot last long. He will soon be forgot; indeed, he must be, for it is clear that he means to return to Netherfield no more. His sister, you must know, put me on my guard, telling me that he is destined for Miss Darcy. Elizabeth would have me believe that it is his sister's wish only, but I must believe that it is his wish also, or else why would he not return?

With his sister Caroline I am still in communication, and I am glad of it. I would be sorry to lose her friendship. Lizzy is not of the same opinion—she thinks that Caroline simply uses me—but I am sure that Caroline is incapable of using or deceiving anyone.

Mr Bingley may live in my mind as the most amiable man of my acquaintance, but that is all. I have nothing either to hope or fear, and nothing to reproach him with. Thank God! I have not *that* pain. A little time is all I need to recover, and my aunt's company is of great help in that direction. It is of great help to Elizabeth, too: Mama has still not forgiven Lizzy for refusing Mr Collins and will not let the matter rest. She bemoans the fact to my aunt, saying that Lady Lucas will have a daughter married before her, and that the estate is as much entailed as it ever was.

I must go. Mama has invited some of the officers to dinner and I hear their horses outside. Mr Wickham is one of them, and if all goes well, I believe he will soon propose to Elizabeth. He is certainly very warm in his regard and I know she likes him immensely. I will write more after dinner.

Eleven o'clock

My dear aunt has invited me to stay with her in London. Nothing would give me greater pleasure, or more relief, for a sojourn away from home is just what I need. I hope that, as Caroline does not live in the same house as her brother, I might occasionally spend a morning with her, without the risk of seeing him.

I must go.

Truly yours,
Jane

Miss Susan Sotherton to Miss Jane Bennet

Bath, December 24

My dear Jane,

I envy you your visit to London, and your chance to visit the parks and the museums, and of course the shops! I am more sorry than I can say about Mr Bingley, but he must be very stupid to leave so good and lovely a woman as you, Jane, and I will console myself with the fact that you do not deserve a stupid husband.

I have some good news of my own to report. I think I am not precipitate in saying that, although our removal to Bath has had little effect on my father, it appears to have had a beneficial effect on my brother. He used to be courted wherever he went, and so he had no incentive to curb his taste for spending unwisely and drinking to excess. Now, however, instead of pursuing him, the mamas look at him coldly and draw their daughters out of his path. It has shaken him. He is beginning to realise that he is no longer Frederick Sotherton of Netherfield Park—a prime catch—but Frederick Sotherton of nowhere in particular, with nothing to inherit but a mountain of debt.

At first he sneered at those who treated him differently; then he laughed at them; but lately he has started to drink less, take more care over choosing those with whom he associates and conduct himself in a more agreeable manner.

If Bath has not been the saving of my father, I believe it might be the saving of my brother.

Your dear friend,
Susan

Miss Lucy Sotherton to Miss Mary Bennet

Bath, December 27

Hail!

Do not start back in horror, I beg you, when you see the enclosed, for I have not left the path of Athena, indeed I have opened my mind to her wisdom, for on reading the dedication of this book, which at first I took to be a novel, I see that it is in fact a true story, and that the events described, though seemingly impossible, actually took place. They are of great historical and geographical value, as they occurred in Italy in the sixteenth century. Lest you should be reluctant to open it, let me state the full title here: *The Mysteries of Udolpho: A Romance, Founded on Facts; Comprising the Adventures & Misfortunes of Emily St. Aubert.*

Emily is a young woman of noble virtue, superior sense and understanding. In short, dear friend, she is a Learned Woman. She would make a very useful addition to our select circle, were it not for the fact that she has been dead these two hundred years. Her conduct is exemplary, despite the many trials she passes through; similar, dear Mary, to the trials we daily pass through, though for her there were more dungeons and fewer bonnets.

With this in mind I read it thoroughly, learning much about the Italian landscape, and the cruel and barbarous banditti who inhabit the hills, as well as the villainous nature of many of the men across the ocean. I enjoin you to read it, and to share with me your thoughts on the nature of the citizens of Europe, who, it would seem from this informative book, are prone to locking up innocent women and sacrificing them upon the altar of matrimony to wealthy, ignoble men. If you and I, dear Mary, were in such a position, forced into marriage by our coldhearted relations, I am sure that you and I, too, would escape by flying through the forests of England and taking refuge on holy ground.

Your sister in study,
Lucy

Miss Mary Bennet to Miss Lucy Sotherton

Longbourn, Hertfordshire,
December 29

Most noble Friend,

Your gift has enlarged my knowledge of the Continent and its strange practises, for which I thank you. I perused it assiduously this afternoon, and could scarcely put it aside when we had to leave for Lucas Lodge, so enlightening did I find it. I believe you are right in your conjecture that, should we ever be forced into marriage with wealthy counts who have murdered their previous wives, we would take refuge in holy places. It is therefore convenient that I am acquainted with Mr Collins, who would, I am sure, accommodate me at the rectory in the event of such a misfortune, and who, I am persuaded, would also find room for you.

Mr Collins was the chief topic of conversation at the Lucases' tonight. Sir William happened to mention that Charlotte had been blessed with her husband, who was in every way an estimable son-in-law, and who combined the virtues of an excellent living with the blessings of a noble patroness in the form of Lady Catherine de Bourgh. Mama was so annoyed that she said, 'If Elizabeth had not been such an obstinate girl, she could have had Mr Collins, and not Charlotte.'

I believe it was this very obstinacy which caused Mr Collins to withdraw his offer and seek consolation elsewhere. Mama was of the opinion that if Charlotte Lucas had not been so artful, Mr Collins would have proposed to me. If he had done so, I might have felt it my Duty to accept him, for although I have otherwise foresworn marriage, I think that Mr Collins has some intelligence and with a settled course of reading, such as that on which you and I are now embarked, he might have one day become, if not a Learned Woman, a Learned Gentleman. And might it not be our Duty, if such is the case, to put aside our own feelings and embrace the marital path?

However, as he was ensnared by the feminine wiles of Charlotte Lucas, such questions need not trouble us, dear Lucy.

Your sister in learning,
Mary

Miss Jane Bennet to Miss Caroline Bingley

Longbourn, Hertfordshire,
December 31

My dear Caroline,

Thank you for your letter. I was pleased to hear all your news and I am glad that you and Louisa are keeping well. I was sorry to hear you were not to return to Netherfield, but I hope we will be able to see each other soon, for I am happy to say that I will be travelling to London tomorrow, as I am to stay for some time with my aunt and uncle. I am enclosing my uncle's address so that we might arrange a meeting. I will be very glad to see you again.

Truly yours,
Jane

1800

∼ JANUARY ∼

Longbourn, Hertfordshire,
January 1

My dear Susan,

My aunt and uncle have gone, taking Jane with them. I am glad she is to have a change of scene and, although I did not say so to her, I think there is some chance she might renew her acquaintance with Mr Bingley. My aunt told me it must not be thought of, as they live in such a different part of town that a meeting is unlikely, but if Mr Bingley learns that Jane is in London, I think it not unlikely that his former affection will be restored.

As for his sister Caroline, I wish that Jane could see her in her true colours, for she is a cold, supercilious young woman who will drop Jane just as soon as it suits her.

I hope your affair with Mr Wainwright is prospering, since our affairs all seem doomed at the moment. I am still very fond of Mr Wickham, who grows more agreeable every day, but my aunt has cautioned me against him—not because of his character but because of his lack of fortune. I have promised her to do my best not to fall in love with him. But it makes me think, Susan, where fortune is concerned, where does good sense end and avarice begin? If it is wrong to marry a man for his fortune, why is it then equally wrong to marry a man without a fortune? I will only hope that Mr Wickham will discover one of the wealthy great-uncles who have been so singularly lacking in our own lives, and that the said uncle will leave him a moderate fortune: not substantial enough to make me a fortune hunter, but large enough for us to live on with a degree of comfort.

Charlotte's—I cannot say *love*, I had better say *affairs*—are, however, prospering. Mr Collins has returned to Meryton, but thankfully this time he is staying at Lucas Lodge and not at Longbourn. Tomorrow is to be the wedding day.

Charlotte has asked me to write to her often and I have promised to do so. I have also promised to visit her in Kent in March, when her father and her sister go there. I promised only reluctantly at first, as there can never be the closeness between us that there once was, but I find that I am looking forward to it. It will make a welcome change from home, I must confess, for Mama has still not stopped complaining that she has been cruelly used by Mr Collins, by Mr Bingley and by everyone else of her acquaintance. Besides, I am curious to see the parsonage and to meet Lady Catherine de Bourgh.

Your dear friend,
Lizzy

Miss Jane Bennet to Miss Elizabeth Bennet

Gracechurch Street, London,
January 2

My dear Lizzy,

A short note to let you know that we have arrived safely and it is already doing me good to be here. I have nothing further to say, but when I write to you again, I hope to be able to give you news of the Bingleys. Now that Caroline knows I am in town, I am sure she will call here soon.

Your loving sister,
Jane

Mrs Charlotte Collins to Miss Elizabeth Bennet

Hunsford, near Westerham, Kent,
January 5

Dear Eliza,

You will be wanting to hear all about my new life and I am only too ready to tell you. Everything here is much as I expected, and it is all to my satisfaction. The parsonage is a good house, better even than I had hoped. It is well proportioned and although it is rather small it is well built and convenient. It is set back from the road amidst a large and well laid out garden which slopes down to the road at the front, so that we can see everyone who passes and, beyond the road, we can see Rosings Park. To the back, we have fine views over fields, and I know you will enjoy walking in them.

We have dined already at Rosings. I believe that Lady Catherine wanted to take a look at me, her curiosity being natural, and I was not sorry to become acquainted with her. She is a respectable, sensible woman and a most attentive neighbour.

There is not much in the way of society, as the parsonage is some way from the nearest town, but I knew to begin with that it would take time for me to settle into my new neighbourhood and so I do not complain. I have my home and my housekeeping, my parish and my poultry to keep me busy, and I am getting to know my way about the place. I am pleased with everything and have no fault to find.

Write to me soon,
Charlotte

Miss Jane Bennet to Miss Elizabeth Bennet

Gracechurch Street, London,
January 6

My dearest Lizzy will forgive me for not writing sooner, but I have had very little to report. I have been a week in town without either seeing or hearing from Caroline. I am surprised, and I can only account for it by thinking that my last letter to her must have gone astray. My aunt is going tomorrow into that part of the town, and I shall take the opportunity of calling in Grosvenor Street. I will write more then, when I hope I will have more to say.

January 7

I have paid my call. I did not think Caroline in spirits, but she was very glad to see me, and reproached me for giving her no notice of my coming to London. I was right, therefore; my last letter had never reached her. I enquired after their brother, of course. He was well, but so much engaged with Mr Darcy that they scarcely ever saw him. I found that Miss Darcy was expected to dinner. I wish I could see her. My visit was not long, as Caroline and Mrs Hurst were going out. I dare say I shall see them soon here.

Your loving sister,
Jane

Miss Elizabeth Bennet to Mrs Charlotte Collins

Longbourn, Hertfordshire, January 8

I am glad you find everything to your liking in Kent. The parsonage and garden sound everything you want, and if anyone could bring out the best in them, dear Charlotte, it is you.

Life in Hertfordshire is much as it was before you left. My sister, Jane, as you know, has gone to London, and finds the amusements lively, but she has not had a chance to see Mr Bingley. It is obvious that his sisters do not mean to let her have him. Poor Jane! Always so good. She cannot see through Caroline's lies, for Caroline did not visit her in London and then, when Jane called, pretended that news of Jane's stay in London had not arrived. I do not know whether to wish that Jane would see through her false friend, or whether to wish that she should preserve her goodness despite the fact that Caroline does not deserve her confidence.

We have our share of amusements here. The weather is fine and I walk a great deal, sometimes accompanied by the officers. I must confess that I like Mr Wickham more and more each day, despite my efforts to resist his charms. If only he had a fortune! Or at least the rectory he was promised, and the living he should have had, if Mr Darcy had not deprived him of it. That odious man! To ruin forever the prospects of such an admirable young man as Mr Wickham. I am glad that Mr Darcy is not to return to the neighbourhood, for I would almost certainly tell him what I thought of him and his cruel behaviour.

I have heard from Susan. Her affair with Mr Wainwright proceeds apace. I think it is serious on both their sides and would not be surprised to hear news of an engagement soon.

Kitty and Lydia send their love.

Lizzy

Mr Wickham to Mr Parker

Meryton, Hertfordshire,
January 10

A stroke of luck. One of the Meryton ladies, Miss King, has been left a fortune of ten thousand pounds. I heard of it by chance and managed to pay her some compliments before it was generally known, so that she did not suspect me of being a fortune hunter. She was flattered and giggled encouragingly: she is a plain girl, and I believe it was the first time anyone had ever taken any notice of her. Ten thousand is not a great fortune, it is true, but in my present circumstances it is better than nothing.

I have had to gradually withdraw my attentions from Miss Elizabeth, which is a pity, as I like her very well; in fact, if things were different I might be tempted by her. But as they are, I cannot marry a woman with so little and I must look elsewhere. She has noticed my defection, of course, but there was a look of understanding and resignation in her eye and I think she does not despise me for it. She knows how the world works as well as I do. A man must have something to live on, and that is the way of things. And so I pursue Miss King and if I am lucky, I will soon be the master of her ten thousand pounds. Then you must come and stay with us. It will relieve you of the expense of living and give me some company, for Lord knows I need someone lively here. The other officers are well enough in their way, but their interests are not mine and I feel I am always playing a part in front of them. With you I can be myself, for you are as bad as I am.

Wickham

Miss Mary Bennet to Miss Lucy Sotherton

Longbourn, Hertfordshire,
January 12

Most noble Friend,

I am sending you my thoughts on our latest history, misleadingly entitled *A Sicilian Romance*, when *A Young Lady's Exploration of the Geology of Her Native Country* would have been a more suitable title. It was a very illuminating document and I was enthralled by the account of the labyrinthine catacombs to be found beneath the marquis's castle. The rock on which it was built must have been of some soft variety, and the caves were no doubt made by the act of water upon the stone.

I was also entranced by the musical content of this most worthy tome, and interested to know that Julia's singing had alerted her dead mother's friend to her presence in the wilderness. This aspect of the human voice is often overlooked in histories, but its power for reuniting lost loved ones is nevertheless an important one. And how deeply philosophical were the reflections of Hippolitus. I am glad that you found such a useful book in the circulating library, and I am gratified that it was written by a woman. I have written to Mrs Radcliffe and invited her to join our select circle of Learned Women.

I have recommended the work to Mr Shackleton. It is good to know that there is one person in Meryton who has a brain, even if, when I told him I was thinking of becoming a bluestocking, he said that he was sure I would be the most intelligent girl in Meryton, whatever the colour of my stockings. I had to inform him that a bluestocking was a Learned Woman who spent her time in rational activities, and who discussed literature and other intellectual things, instead of wasting her time on balls and bonnets. He listened attentively and then apologised earnestly for his mistake. I told him graciously that it was no matter, and we continued to have a lively discussion about music and literature.

To be sure, I thought I had misjudged him when I felt his hand on my knee. But when I reproved him, saying that we were in Meryton and not in Sodom and Gomorrah, he was heartily offended and said that he had merely been brushing a moth from my gown.

It was then my turn to apologise.

Your sister in all but relatedness,
Mary

Miss Lydia Bennet to Miss Eleanor Sotherton

Longbourn, Hertfordshire,
January 18

Dear Ellie,

Such larks! We were at my aunt Philips's house last night and Captain Carter was there and he pretended to be Colonel Forster. He cut off a lock of my hair and used it to make a moustache. We laughed and laughed.

Talking of Colonel Forster, the rumours are true, he is to be married.

Miss Watson pretends to care nothing of it, but Kitty says that Miss Watson suspected something last November and told him that if he could not tell her it was a lie he had better not come to her house again. So that is why he stopped going there.

It seems he has known Miss Harriet Brown for years. She lives in his hometown and there was an understanding between them, but then she was cool to him the last time he was home on leave and so that is why he took up with Miss Watson. But now Miss Harriet is smiling on him again.

He is to be married next month, or soon after, and he is to bring Miss Harriet to Meryton. She is not much older than I am, and Mama said if he had not been spoken for already she was sure Colonel Forster would have proposed to me. I wonder what his wife will be like. I hope she will be fond of dancing and give lots of balls.

Lizzy has not been so lucky. Mr Wickham has deserted her for Mary King—nasty freckled thing—just because Miss King inherited ten thousand pounds. I am sure I cannot blame Miss King for wanting him, he is ever so handsome, but I wish Lizzy could inherit ten thousand pounds and then she could have him. Or even better I could inherit it and then I could be Mrs Wickham! I will be sixteen in June and I hope to be married soon after. What fun it would be to be married before my sisters, and to be married to someone as handsome as Mr Wickham!

Kitty sends her love but is too busy to write as she is trimming her bonnet.

Your good friend,
Lydia

Miss Eleanor Sotherton to Miss Lydia Bennet

Bath, January 20

I wish we had some officers here, everyone is ancient, at least a hundred, and they talk of nothing but their gout, all except my sister Susan, who is newly engaged to Mr Wainwright. He is very handsome and very rich and I wish he had a brother for me to marry but he has only three sisters.

Frederick is surprisingly sober. Lucy is as prosy as ever. She is busy reading a novel which she insists is a history book. She is making extracts from it and then making notes on the extracts, just as if it were a learned work. She thinks it is a treatise on the iniquities of the Catholic Church and the causes of the French Revolution, when it is nothing but a story about a girl whose wicked father has locked her mother in the catacombs so that he can marry someone else. But at least it is better than her sermonizing and telling us to study all the time.

Hurry up and marry someone and then invite me to stay. If I have to live in Bath much longer I will die of boredom.

What is Kitty doing to her bonnet?

Your devoted friend,
Ellie

Miss Jane Bennet to Miss Elizabeth Bennet

Gracechurch Street, London,
January 22

My dearest Lizzy will, I am sure, be incapable of triumphing in her better judgment, at my expense, when I confess myself to have been entirely deceived in Miss Bingley's regard for me. But, my dear sister, though the event has proved you right, do not think me obstinate if I still assert that, considering what her behaviour was, my confidence was as natural as your suspicion. I do not at all comprehend her reason for wishing to be intimate with me; but if the same circumstances were to happen again, I am sure I should be deceived again.

Caroline did not return my visit till yesterday; and not a note, not a line, did I receive in the meantime. When she did come, it was very evident that she had no pleasure in it; she made a slight, formal apology for not calling before, said not a word of wishing to see me again, and was in every respect so altered a creature, that when she went away, I was perfectly resolved to continue the acquaintance no longer. I pity her, though I cannot help blaming her. She was very wrong in singling me out as she did; I can safely say that every advance to intimacy began on her side. But I pity her, because she must feel that she has been acting wrong, and because I am very sure that anxiety for her brother is the cause of it. I need not explain myself further; and though *we* know this anxiety to be quite needless, yet if she feels it, it will easily account for her behaviour to me; and so deservedly dear as he is to his sister, whatever anxiety she may feel on his behalf is natural and amiable.

I cannot but wonder, however, at her having any such fears now, because if he had at all cared about me, we must have met long, long ago. He knows of my being in town, I am certain, from something she said herself; and yet it would seem, by her manner of talking, as if she wanted to persuade herself that he is really partial to Miss Darcy. I cannot understand it. If I were not afraid of judging harshly, I should be almost tempted to say that there is a strong appearance of duplicity in all this. But I will endeavour to banish every painful thought, and think only of what will make me happy— your affection, and the invariable kindness of my dear uncle and aunt. Let me hear from you very soon.

Miss Bingley said something of his never returning to Netherfield again, of giving up the house, but not with any certainty. We had better not mention it. I am extremely glad that you have such pleasant accounts from our friends at Hunsford. Pray remember me to them, and do go to see them, with Sir William and Maria. I am sure you will be very comfortable there.

Yours truly,
Jane

Miss Elizabeth Bennet to Mrs Charlotte Collins

Longbourn, Hertfordshire,
January 22

My dear Charlotte,

I am commanded to send you my sister Jane's best wishes, and I do so gladly, knowing that you will be happy to receive them. Mr Bingley, alas, is not so willing to receive them, or rather, I suspect, his sister is determined that he should not have them. Jane has been three weeks now in London and has finally seen through Miss Bingley's protestations of friendship, having been treated coldly and with incivility. Miss Bingley wishes her brother to marry Miss Darcy, and she is determined that Jane shall not come between them. From everything Mr Wickham has said of Miss Darcy, she will make him abundantly regret what he has thrown away in Jane, being an imperious girl, every bit as proud and disagreeable as her brother.

It seems that everyone is playing us false this New Year, when at the end of last year everything seemed so promising: Jane unhappy, and my own situation not much better, though I believe I have a temperament which can better bear the loss. Mr Wickham has become less and less attentive, and although my head applauds this turn of events, my affections cannot be so triumphant. I still think him one of the most charming young men of my acquaintance, but his poverty has caused him to transfer his attentions to Miss King, who has recently inherited ten thousand pounds. It is an inducement, is it not? Though I believe that I would have been his choice had his fortune permitted it.

I am looking forward to visiting you in March.

Your friend,
Lizzy

Mrs Gardiner to Miss Elizabeth Bennet

Gracechurch Street, London,
January 22

My dear Lizzy,

I know you have heard from Jane, and so you are aware that Miss Bingley has been a false friend to your sister, and that Jane does not intend to see Caroline again. I cannot say that I am sorry. It would have been very difficult for the two young women to be friends when the spectre of the brother's previous affection lay between them. And even if this were not the case, I would not like Miss Bingley as a friend for Jane; she is a very cold and supercilious woman. Your sister has now accepted that her intimacy with the Bingleys is at an end.

But what of you? When last we met you promised me you would not encourage your feelings for Mr Wickham. Have you been successful in your endeavour, or is he still a favourite with you? Let me know how you go on.

Your affectionate aunt,
Margaret

Miss Elizabeth Bennet to Mrs Gardiner

Longbourn, Hertfordshire,
January 24

My dear aunt,

I have that to tell you about Mr Wickham which will please you more than it pleases me: his attentions are at an end. I am now convinced, my dear aunt, that I have never been much in love; for had I really experienced that pure and elevating passion, I should at present detest his very name, and wish him all manner of evil. But my feelings are not only cordial towards him, they are even impartial towards Miss King, to whom he has transferred his affections.

I cannot find out that I hate her at all, or that I am in the least unwilling to think her a very good sort of girl. There can be no love in all this. My watchfulness has been effectual; and though I should certainly be a more interesting object to all my acquaintance were I distractedly in love with him, I cannot say that I regret my comparative insignificance. Importance may sometimes be purchased too dearly.

Kitty and Lydia take his defection much more to heart than I do. They are young in the ways of the world, and not yet open to the mortifying conviction that handsome young men must have something to live on as well as the plain.

Your loving niece,
Lizzy

~ FEBRUARY ~

Mr Charles Bingley to Mrs Bingley

Bath, February 10

Dearest Ma,

Caroline said that I looked seedy, she thought London was not doing me good and she persuaded me to take a house in Bath, so here we are. Upon my honour it is lively enough but somehow the concerts and amusements do not entertain me as much as I thought they would. I am glad you are coming to stay with us; I am looking forward to seeing you again and you must stay until Easter.

I thought of going back to Netherfield Park next month but as I would have to see Miss Bennet again, and as Darcy and Caroline assure me that Miss Bennet had no affection for me, I have decided against it. I think it would be hard to be with her and know that she did not care for me. I am not complaining. She is an angel and can do far better I am sure, for I am a very ordinary sort of fellow. Come soon, Ma, you will like it here. If Ned cannot tear himself away from business, then come without him.

Your loving son,
Charles

Mrs Bingley to Mr Charles Bingley

Yorkshire, February 12

If that girl doesn't think she's the luckiest girl alive to have won your affections, Charles, then she's not worth a candle. There are plenty of other girls who know a good thing when they see it. You'll have them falling all over you before long, you mark my words. Never you fret, your old ma will be there next week and we'll have a high old time of it. Is that friend of yours, Mr Darcy, there? How is Caroline getting along with him?

Your doting Ma

Mr Charles Bingley to Mrs Bingley

Bath, February 14

Dear Ma,

Caroline thinks she is getting along very well with Mr Darcy but she is no further forward than before. He is not in Bath; he has gone to stay with his cousins in Cumbria. Caroline wanted me to take a house there also but I told her I will not chase Darcy round the country like a puppy and so she has had to make do with Bath.

Your loving son,
Charles

Mr Darcy to Mr Bingley

Fitzwater Park, Cumbria,
February 19

Dear Charles,

I have just had a letter from Georgiana and she asked after you particularly. I know how much she enjoyed your company over Christmas and I hope you will come to stay with us at Pemberley after Easter.

I find myself in the middle of unusually clement weather up here in the Lake District, thank God, for you know how much I detest bad weather in the country. But the days are fine and we spend them out of doors, sailing on the lake, riding, fishing, and taking outings to entertain the ladies. They are all of them very accomplished and they paint and sketch; they are as pleased as we men that the weather is fine.

Maud is well and my godson is thriving. He was christened yesterday. He has a fine set of lungs and he displayed them to us throughout the ceremony. Maud made several comments about wanting to repay me by standing godmother to my children and exhorted me to provide her with them without delay. My aunt was of the same mind and introduced me to a very pretty young woman by the name of Miss Barton; however, I made it clear to her that I have no plans to marry this year.

The rector, Mr Grayson, accompanied us back to the Park and I was glad of it for I wanted to ask if he could recommend a deserving young man to fill the living of Kympton. It is only eighteen months since I had to appoint a new incumbent when Mr Rogers died, but now his successor has met with an unlucky accident and I am having to fill the living again. Luckily Mr Grayson was able to recommend a young man who is newly ordained but who is known to Mr Grayson personally and sounds very promising. I mean to speak with him tomorrow and see if he would be suitable.

The only complaint I have to make of my present circumstances is that my aunt is fond of charades and I am obliged to play, though I avoid it whenever I can.

I hope you are well entertained in Bath. Pray write to Georgiana and let her know how you get on—she has never been to Bath and she is longing to hear all about it. I know that Caroline and Louisa have promised to write but I believe Georgiana would value a letter from all of you. I have encouraged her to reply to everything she receives, as it will give her some practise in the art of letter writing, which will be very useful to her.

Darcy

Mr Bingley to Mr Darcy

Bath, February 25

My dear Darcy,

Of course I will write to Georgiana. You should bring her here, there are concerts and balls and all manner of entertainments. She is a little young for some of them, to be sure, but Caroline is convinced she would like the libraries and the firework displays and begs me to ask you to join us here as soon as you return from Cumbria. One of my younger sisters is here, who is not yet sixteen, and two of my younger brothers, and they are all very taken with the place. My mother is enjoying herself, too.

Have you heard anything from Colonel Forster? You will remember we met him in Meryton. I have written to him several times to ascertain his thoughts on the war. It seems a long way away, but my brother Ned is interested in the future of the hostilities because it affects the future of trade. Upon my soul, Ned has done very well for himself and we are all very proud of him, though Caroline says he needs to buy himself a new coat.

You will like to hear something of our neighbours at Netherfield. Colonel Forster happened to mention something about them in his letters and it seems that Charlotte Lucas has married Mr Collins. Did you know? If you remember, Mr Collins was the cousin of the Bennets, and also, I believe, your aunt's rector. If you go to Rosings at Easter as usual, it seems likely you will see her there.

Bingley

~ MARCH ~

Mr Darcy to Mr Bingley

Fitzwater Park, Cumbria,
March 7

My dear Bingley,

I knew of Mr Collins's marriage, as you surmised. Hurst heard something of it as we left Netherfield and he happened to mention it to me. It seems that Mr Collins proposed to Miss Elizabeth Bennet at first but was refused and then found more favour with her friend. He is fortunate in his wife, I think—I remember Miss Lucas as being a sensible young woman.

I have given the living of Kympton to Grayson's protégé, Mark Haydock. I heard him preach as part of his duties as the curate of Highwater, and my aunt invited him to Fitzwater Park so that I could see something more of him. He is young, intelligent, sensible and committed to the church, whilst understanding the foibles of human nature and being prepared to encounter them in all their forms. He is popular with the people hereabouts as he does not preach, unless it is from the pulpit, and yet he sets a good example in his daily life. He attracts a great deal of attention from the ladies, as he has a handsome face but he does not trade on it. I think he will do very well.

Darcy

Mr Mark Haydock to Mrs Haydock

Cumbria, March 7

Mama, I have had a piece of astonishing good fortune. The Fitzwilliams have guests and one of them is a cousin of theirs, a Mr Darcy of Pemberley in Derbyshire. He happened to need a rector for one of his livings and I was recommended to him. In short, he has given me the living! It is a great thing for me, a very great thing indeed, the kind of preferment I could only dream of. The living is a handsome one and, from all I hear, the rectory is a fine house in large gardens. Mr Darcy himself is an imposing gentleman. I was nervous of him at first, although he is not many years older than I am, for he has an air of pride about him, but once I began to know him, I found him to be intelligent and—I will not say agreeable, for he remained aloof throughout our meetings—but at least not disagreeable. I think I have been very lucky and I have given thanks for it, you may be sure.

I am to travel to Derbyshire at the end of March and take up my duties shortly thereafter. I will write to you when I have any more news.

Your loving son,
Matthew

Mrs Charlotte Collins to Miss Elizabeth Bennet

Hunsford, near Westerham, Kent,
March 10

Dear Eliza,

The daffodils are out and the banks outside the parsonage are covered in them. Mr Collins has spent the morning digging up some of the bulbs and moving them around the garden, a healthy recreation which I have encouraged, though I believe they looked prettier where they were.

He is a little out of sorts at the moment. When we went to Rosings Park for dinner last night, Lady Catherine happened to mention that her nephew, Mr Darcy, had been looking for a new vicar to fill the living of Kympton and I could tell that Mr Collins hoped he might be given it, for it would have meant an extra two hundred pounds a year. He began to say that he had been most impressed with Mr Darcy when he met him at Netherfield, and that it would be an honour to serve such a bountiful man, but hardly were the words out of his mouth than Lady Catherine finished by saying that Mr Darcy had already appointed a Mr Haydock. Mr Collins was disappointed, I could see, but he immediately remarked that he was sure a nephew of Lady Catherine's could never appoint

244 · AMANDA GRANGE

anyone unworthy to such an important position, and to console himself with the fact that Mr Darcy may have other livings to give.

I hope you have not forgotten your promise to visit me. I miss you, Eliza, and I look forward to seeing you and to showing you my new home. My father and sister are to set out on the twenty-third and you promised to be one of the party, you know. Indeed, I quite rely upon it. We are unlikely to leave Kent for some time, Mr Collins being unable to leave his duties, and I would like to remind myself of my Hertfordshire life and Hertfordshire friends.

Your friend,
Charlotte

Miss Elizabeth Bennet to Mrs Charlotte Collins

Longbourn, Hertfordshire,
March 15

My dear Charlotte,

How can I refuse you? Besides, I am looking forward to seeing you again. The arrangements have all been made, and even improved, for now we are all to stay with my aunt and uncle for a night on our way down to Kent. We will be leaving Longbourn on the twenty-third and as it is only twenty-four miles, there will be plenty of time for us to spend the morning shopping and the evening at the theatre before we leave again. We will be with you by the twenty-fourth.

I am longing to see Jane again. She writes to me often but although she takes great pains to make sure her letters are cheerful, and although I know she loves being with our aunt and uncle and our troop of little cousins, I know she still misses Mr Bingley. That odious Caroline! She has deliberately separated them, I am sure of it, and that odious Mr Darcy! He is as bad as Caroline, if not worse. Who are they to decide how Jane and Bingley shall be happy? What business is it of theirs? And now Jane is pining for him. I hear it in her letters, for try as she might she cannot make them as light-hearted as they once were. But I console myself that I will be with her again soon and then I will be able to better judge how far she is from recovery.

I must confess that, quite apart from the joy of seeing you and Jane again, I will not be sorry to get away from home. Mary practises the pianoforte, very loudly, for hours every day and my only escape is to go for a walk; which, as the weather is cold and wet, brings me no pleasure. Kitty and Lydia are worse than ever. Colonel Forster's new wife is very young and just as silly as my sisters, and she is always having parties where they dress up and make a lot of noise, laughing with the officers. Officers are all very well, but I confess since the loss of the attentions of one, the others hold very little interest for me.

He is still friendly, still attentive, but in a different way. He makes it clear by small words and looks and gestures that he is not free to marry as he will, and I understand him perfectly. We are still very much of one mind on most things, however, and, whether married or single, he must always be my model of the amiable and pleasing. It is perhaps a good thing, then, that I am to go away, for it cannot be long before he marries Miss King and I would rather not be here when the wedding takes place.

Your friend,
Lizzy

Miss Mary Bennet to Miss Lucy Sotherton

Longbourn, Hertfordshire,
March 23

Most noble Friend,

My sister Jane is in London still and my sister Elizabeth has left for Kent, which means that I can practise on the pianoforte for hours together without any interruption. To be sure, Mama says my playing gives her a headache and Papa asks if I would not rather be outdoors, and Kitty cries whenever I approach the instrument, but these are no more than the ordinary obstacles which fall into the path of the Learned Woman.

Mr Shackleton agrees with me. I discussed the matter with him this evening, when we both dined with my aunt Philips, and he said that the lives of the great were always fraught with difficulty.

I was prevailed upon to play the pianoforte after dinner. I was just embarking on my second sonnata when I was alarmed to find Mr Shackleton's arm around me. He was shocked when I reproved him and said that I had mistaken his motives entirely, explaining that he had merely been reaching round me to turn over the pages of my music.

Harmony was restored, as I remarked to him as I embarked on a third sonnata, and he laughed at my witticism and said that I should make a note of it in my book of extracts. I have duly done so. My only regret is that no one ever reads the book. I am sure my sisters would benefit from it, for it would be sure to impart learning and wisdom to anyone who opened its pages. I have tried to encourage Lydia and Kitty to read it, and to be sure Lydia started to do so, but she only laughed when she read that Mr Shackleton had had his hand on my knee, and Kitty was no better, saying that there should only be one *n* in sonnata.

Your sister under the skin,
Mary

Miss Elizabeth Bennet to Miss Susan Sotherton

Hunsford, near Westerham, Kent,
March 24

You will be anxious to know all about my visit to London and my arrival in Kent, and so I sit down now to write you a letter.

Jane was very happy to see me and I to see her, as you can imagine. We have been apart for a long time and we had much to talk about. But on questioning my aunt later, I found that my dear sister has periods of dejection, and who can blame her? She has lost the attentions of a most amiable young man, through no fault of her own, and does not see how she will ever meet a man she likes half as well. I sympathise with her deeply, for I am no luckier in my attachment to Mr Wickham, but I believe my spirits are of a sort to better bear the disappointment. Besides, I was not separated from him by others, but by his own choice, and that I think makes it easier to bear.

Through all this, though, I cannot help blaming Mr Bingley, for if he was as much in love with Jane as he appeared he should have resisted his friends' efforts to influence him and followed his heart; which leads me to think that it is possible for a young man to be *too* amiable. But even as I write this I remember Mr Darcy saying that Mr Bingley was easily swayed by his friends; how much more blame-worthy, then, must those friends be for influencing someone they knew would not be able to resist. But blame will not help Jane, and I believe that she is in the best place, where there is congenial company and plenty to do.

The company here at Hunsford is not so congenial. Charlotte is the same, but I cannot place such confidence in her as formerly, for I cannot forgive her for marrying such a stupid man. She has a home, it is true, and a life of her own, but the price she paid is a heavy one and although she does not resent it, I resent it for her. Oh, why can there not be as many amiable and sensible young men in the world as there are women who deserve them! She welcomed me affectionately, however, and I was very pleased I had come. Despite everything, I miss her. Meryton is unfortunately not supplied with so many sensible young women that I can easily bear the loss of another one.

Mr Collins was in all his glory, displaying the good proportions of the rooms, their aspects and their furniture—everything from the sideboard to the fender—and showing us around the garden, pointing out the numbers of fields beyond. Sir William and Maria were as admiring as he could have wished for, pleased with everything they saw and exclaiming over the sight of Rosings Park in the distance.

Luckily I did not have the right shoes for walking over the fields, nor did Maria nor Charlotte, and whilst Mr Collins conducted Sir William thither, we three returned to the house. With Mr Collins forgotten there was an air of comfort throughout, and I believe he is very often forgotten. And when he cannot be forgotten, and says something particularly foolish, then Charlotte is wise enough not to hear.

We are to have the honour of seeing Lady Catherine at church on Sunday, and I am assured by Mr Collins that she is all affability and condescension; although I was warned by Mr Wickham that she is authoritative and self-important, and I suspect his judgement is the true one. Apparently, she is likely to include Maria, Sir William and myself in every invitation issued to the Collinses for the length of our stay—courtesy indeed!

And so our time is to be spent sharing Charlotte's daily activities, which will be enjoyable enough. It will only be made vexatious when we are interrupted by Mr Collins or patronised by Lady Catherine.

Then, my dear Susan, I will have more pleasures to look forward to, for my aunt and uncle have invited me to go on a tour of the Lake District with them in the summer. I am already looking forward to it.

Write soon and tell me all your news.

Lizzy

Miss Susan Sotherton to Miss Elizabeth Bennet

Bath, March 25

Dearest Lizzy,

Your letter makes me ashamed—I have not written to you in an age, for my Mr Wainwright is keeping me busy. I have been to visit his family and found them all charming, and a wedding date has been set. We are to be married in August. My mama is very happy, for it is a better match than she hoped for me, and I am overjoyed, as I truly love my Mr Wainwright. Papa is happy, as Mr Wainwright's mother has insisted on arranging the wedding, so it will not cost Papa a penny, and he went out to celebrate by getting drunk. Frederick, however, said he wished me happy and gave me a small present, a brooch, bought with money he had saved himself from his inheritance from our late aunt. Although it is not a large fortune, it is not inconsiderable and he has begun to husband it, spending less than its income so that he is gradually restoring the capital. News of this has spread and he is no longer shunned so resolutely by the Bath mamas. Eleanor is now more hopeful of finding a husband for herself, and Lucy hopes that Frederick will restore the library at Netherfield so that she might continue her studies there when we return home. If we return home. But as Jane no longer needs Netherfield to be let to Mr Bingley, I hope we will return home sooner rather than later. Alas, until Papa mends his ways it is not likely.

I am glad that Charlotte is happy. I wish her many fine days and a husband who is busy elsewhere. And to you, Lizzy, I wish fine weather for country walks and a handsome stranger.

Your dear friend,
Susan

Miss Elizabeth Bennet to Miss Jane Bennet

Hunsford, near Westerham, Kent,
March 26

My dearest Jane,

I have had my first sight of Lady Catherine de Bourgh. We dined at Rosings last night and saw her in all her glory. She is a tall, large woman with strongly marked features and a sense of self-importance which rendered Sir William speechless and reduced Maria to perching, in fright, on the edge of her chair.

Miss de Bourgh was as unlike her mother as it was possible to be, for she was thin and small, with insignificant features; there was neither in face nor figure any likeness between the ladies.

The dinner was exceedingly handsome, and Mr Collins could not have been happier as he took his place at the bottom of the table, by her ladyship's desire. Lucky Mr Collins, to be so easily pleased! He commended every dish, his flattery echoed by Sir William, so that I wonder Lady Catherine could bear it; however, she seemed very pleased. We ate almost in silence, although when we retired to the drawing room after dinner, there was a great deal of talking, all on Lady Catherine's side. She held forth at length, enquiring into Charlotte's domestic concerns and giving her a great deal of unnecessary advice, and then turned her attention to me. Oh, Jane! I could scarcely keep from expressing my astonishment at her impertinence when she asked about my sisters, demanding to know if any of them were handsome or likely to be married soon, where they had been educated and what kind of carriage my father kept! She then demanded to know about our governesses, and on learning that we had none, remarked that our mother must have been a slave to our education! I did not know where to look, nor how to keep from smiling! She then deigned to tell me that my sisters should not all be out at once, and was surprised when I answered her back, saying that I saw no reason why the younger girls should not have their share of society and amusement as well as the older. I do not believe anyone has ever answered her back before.

The gentlemen soon joined us and we played at casino, but there was no conversation that did not pertain to the game. When Lady Catherine and Miss de Bourgh had played as long as they wished, the tables were broken up and the carriage was ordered, and I was asked for my opinion of Lady Catherine on our way home. I gave what praise I could, but Mr Collins was not satisfied and took matters into his own hands, praising Lady Catherine as he felt she deserved. He had not done by the time we reached the parsonage, and he followed me upstairs so that he could continue singing her praises. It was only when I bid him a firm 'Good night' that he gave over, but I heard him saying, 'affable ... condescending ...' to Charlotte as they went downstairs.

How I am to manage here over the next few weeks I do not

know. I am sure I will find it more and more difficult to remain silent whilst Lady Catherine gives her decided opinion on everyone and everything; however, I am determined to be on my best behaviour for Charlotte's sake.

Sir William will be here only for a week and will then return to Meryton, but Maria will stay here for six weeks with me. I wish you could be here, too, Jane, but I am persuaded you will be much happier where you are.

Your loving sister,
Lizzy

Miss Jane Bennet to Miss Elizabeth Bennet

Gracechurch Street, London,
March 30

Dearest Lizzy,

Your letter made me smile. I am sure I am glad it is you and not I who have to face Lady Catherine; she sounds to be as formidable as I had expected. I am very glad to be here with my aunt and uncle instead. We have had fine weather since you left and I walk in the park with the children every day. We have been to the theatre again and this evening we go to a concert. My aunt has invited a number of young men to dine. She says nothing but I know she is hoping to help me over my disappointment by reminding me that other young men exist. And indeed, I know that they do, only none I like as well as . . . But there, I will not mention his name, it is better not. He is destined for another and there is no use repining.

I have had a letter from Mama, telling me not to hurry home, for she is sure there are many more eligible young men in London than in Meryton. Lydia included a note, asking me to send her a sketch of the latest fashions, for she is going to one of Colonel Forster's balls, and Kitty asked me for some sarsenet. My aunt and I are going to Grafton House tomorrow to buy it. Mary has asked for some music, as she is planning to play a sonata. I cannot help thinking that there will be little call for a sonata at a ball.

Your loving sister,
Jane

⸙ APRIL ⸙

Mrs Charlotte Collins to Miss Susan Sotherton

Hunsford, near Westerham, Kent,
April 14

Dear Susan,

As you know, Elizabeth is our guest at the parsonage, together with my sister, but what I think you do not yet know is that Mr Darcy is here also, staying with his aunt Lady Catherine. He has only been here a few days and yet I suspect as much as I did last autumn that he is attracted to Elizabeth, though she persists in thinking he does not like her. It is possible that he looks at her only to find fault with her, as she thinks, but I do not believe it. When Mr Collins went to pay his respects to Mr Darcy and his cousin Colonel Fitzwilliam, who is also a guest at Rosings, the gentlemen returned to the parsonage with him. I am sure that Mr Darcy would not have waited on us so soon if Elizabeth had not been here. He had little to say for himself, but his eyes were drawn to her and at last remembering his manners, he enquired after the Bennets. Eliza could not resist saying that Jane had been in town for three months and asking if he had seen her, to which Mr Darcy replied that he had not. Elizabeth pursued the subject no further and I think Mr Darcy was happy to let it drop. However, he continued to look at her until he and his cousin returned to Rosings.

We dined with Lady Catherine, and Mr Darcy was once again very attentive to Elizabeth, as was his cousin, and I am not surprised for Elizabeth was at her liveliest. Even Lady Catherine demanded to have her share of their conversation. When coffee was over, Colonel Fitzwilliam invited Eliza to play the piano and Lady Catherine engaged Mr Darcy in conversation, but the latter abandoned her soon enough and walked over to the piano to listen to Eliza. He positioned himself so as to be able to see her face and Elizabeth teased him, saying that he had come to frighten her. He looked surprised, but not displeased. I am sure he has never met anyone like Elizabeth before. She continued to tease him, saying to Colonel Fitzwilliam that Mr Darcy had danced only four dances at his first Meryton assembly. I thought he would be angry, but instead a smile played about his lips. He is ready to fall in love with her, if he is not in love with her already. I wish she would show him some encouragement, for I am sure he would offer for her if she did. It would be a brilliant match for her. Mr Darcy is a man of consequence and wealth, and moreover he is very well-thought-of hereabouts. His cousin joined in with the teasing, saying that Mr Darcy would not give himself the trouble to talk to strangers, and instead of being angry, Mr Darcy took it all in good part.

But that is not all. This morning, Maria and I walked into the village and when we returned we found Mr Darcy in the parsonage, and learnt that he had been talking to Elizabeth for half an hour. I was sure he must be in love with her, or he would never have called on us in such a familiar way, but when I said as much to Elizabeth, she said that he had been silent for most of the visit. It is very odd, but I cannot shake the feeling that he is deeply attracted to her. I do not want to press the idea with her, however, because I do not want to raise expectations which might only end in disappointment. But if she were sure of his affections, I think her dislike of him would evaporate, and why should it not? He is tall, handsome, intelligent, well-bred, wealthy . . . the sort of man that any woman would be proud to call husband.

I cannot help thinking that it would be a good thing if Lizzy were to marry him, for he has several wealthy livings at his disposal and it would be no bad thing if Mr Collins were to be appointed to one of them. But only time will tell.

Charlotte

Mr Bennet to Miss Elizabeth Bennet

Longbourn, Hertfordshire,
April 16

Lizzy,

You will no doubt be surprised to receive a letter from me, though I half promised one, but I find I cannot manage without you here at Longbourn. Your sisters grow sillier every day and your mother is no better. Without you and Jane, all sense has gone and I am longing for your return. I am sure that you will find it difficult to tear yourself away from Mr Collins, and I know that my company cannot possibly compensate you for the loss of his sensible and erudite conversation, but I miss you, Lizzy, and I am writing to hurry you home. Come as soon as you like; it cannot be too soon for me.

Your affectionate
Father

Miss Elizabeth Bennet to Mr Bennet

Hunsford, near Westerham, Kent,
April 18

Dear Papa,

I will come as soon as I can, but it will not be for a few weeks, I fear. Charlotte depends upon me to remain with her until the start of May and my aunt Gardiner expects me to stay for a few days with her before returning home. Though I doubt if my sisters will ever be sensible, yet something might be done to curb the worst of their excesses and in the process you might make them better companions for yourself. Lydia would benefit from some attention and Kitty, too. At present they have nothing to think of but red coats. Could you not give another turn to their minds? I doubt if they will ever become scholars but there are some books in the library they might like; if you will take the trouble I am sure you will find them willing to give over at least a small portion of their day to rational enterprise.

There is very little that is rational here, save Charlotte, of course. She tends her household and her parish with great success. Mr Collins continues to flatter Lady Catherine, who accepts every word graciously as though it is her due. Maria is in awe of everyone and everything. Mr Darcy stares us all out of countenance—yes, he is here. It is not so very surprising, I suppose, as his aunt is Lady Catherine. What pleasure he gains from his visit I cannot guess, since his aunt's behaviour is such as to make any sensible person blush. But perhaps he likes it. I suppose he must, for he is his own master, and he could just as easily spend Easter in Derbyshire or London if he had a mind to do so. Instead he plagues us here at Rosings.

Your loving daughter,
Lizzy

Mr Darcy to Mr Philip Darcy

Rosings Park, Kent, April 20

Philip, this letter might surprise you, or then again, not. I think you guessed that I was speaking of myself when I wrote to you about an inferior woman at Christmas, and not Bingley as I protested; or, at least, not entirely about Bingley, for it is true that he was attracted to a woman of inferior birth and that I saved him from an imprudent attachment. But it is my own case that now concerns me, for I was also enamoured of a woman who was unsuitable in every way.

I first met her at a local assembly and paid no attention to her, thinking her, quite rightly, beneath my notice. But the more I came to know her, the more I came to be intrigued by her, for her quick wits and lively intelligence stimulated me and made me want to know more of her. I began to seek her out, enticed by her conversation, which gleamed like a vein of gold amidst the dull talk and endless flattery of everyone else around me.

I found myself looking forward to seeing her and I started each day by wondering when and where we would encounter each other. My pulses quickened and the blood ran more swiftly in my veins whenever she entered a room. I was alert, where usually I am bored. I was further attracted by the fact that she was not in awe of my wealth or my position and that she treated me as she would anyone else. She was constantly challenging me, making no allowances for my name or fortune, in fact she seemed to delight in teasing me and tormenting me. She had a way of looking at me, as if daring me to cross swords with her, which fascinated me; it called forth all my instincts, base and otherwise, and made me so far in danger of forgetting myself that on more than one occasion I was tempted to kiss her. I did not do it, of course, but the urge grew stronger and stronger, and the energy I needed to resist was becoming more and more powerful, until I felt that I was in some danger from her.

I knew the remedy: to avoid her. But by some unlucky chance her sister became ill whilst visiting Bingley, and when Elizabeth called to see her sister, Bingley invited her to stay. I was thrown more and more into company with her and it was not long before I had to admit to myself that I was at risk of being overwhelmed by my feelings entirely. Where I had once thought she had not one good feature in her face, I found myself thinking her uncommonly pretty, with a pair of fine eyes which, when she teased me, sparkled. And tease me she did. What is more, I looked forward to it.

But I was still not lost, at that time. I recognised my weakness and I attempted to control it by putting her in her place, to remind her—as well as myself—that she was beneath me. But every attempt I made failed. When I asked her if she wanted to dance a reel, she saw at once what I was about, and knew that I wanted her to admit to liking the unrefined dance. So instead she outwitted me, replying that if she said yes I would despise her taste, so she would refuse—then challenged me to despise her if I dared. And indeed I did not dare! Or, rather, I did not want to, for she had outmanoeuvred me and I felt nothing but admiration for her.

I was still enough the master of my feelings to resist her charms, however, and to force myself to avoid her whenever I felt it necessary. But the pull towards her was so strong that when Bingley left Netherfield Park for a few days to attend to business in town, I followed him. I gave as my reason my concern for his attachment to an unsuitable woman; but I was just as concerned, if not more so, about my own unsuitable attachment. I encouraged him to remain in town, away from the object of his affections—and away from mine. I was sure that, with no reason to return to the neighbourhood, I would soon forget her. And for a time it seemed that I was right. Back in my own world, I saw the folly of becoming entangled with someone from such a low level in life. I knew that she would never be able to fit in with my kind; that, in short, it would never lead to anything but disaster.

And so I occupied myself with business and friends and family, taking myself off to Cumbria and surrounding myself with people I knew. But thoughts of her would intrude at the most inopportune moments and I found myself comparing every other young woman I met to her—unfavourably, I might add. None of them had her playful disposition or her lack of deference or her complete uncon- cern for my position, my wealth, or indeed anything else that young women usually court.

How things would have turned out if I had not visited Rosings I do not know, but the fact of the matter is that I did visit Rosings— indeed, I am still here—and by some unlucky chance she was here also.

I never thought to meet her in Kent, but her friend had lately married the rector of Hunsford and Elizabeth is visiting her friend. There! I have said her name. It is a name which haunts me and plagues me and delights me and gives me no peace.

Elizabeth.

Elizabeth, Elizabeth, Elizabeth.

It seems folly to me now, but when I first found out she was here, I thought it would be a useful test of my resolve. I flattered myself that I was no longer in any danger from her, but the more I see of her, the more I find it impossible to resist her. I find myself drawn to her as if to a magnet whenever she dines with us; and when she does not cross my path by accident, I walk in the park, following her favourite routes in the hope of seeing her. If she is not to be met with in the park, my feet turn of their own accord towards the parsonage, where I know I will find her. The other day I went in, even though I knew her friend to be away from home, and almost found myself proposing to her.

It is madness! The inferiority of her family, who are small country gentry; the wild behaviour of her younger sisters, who spend their time flirting with the officers stationed nearby their home; the vulgarity of her mother; the irresponsible nature of her father; the family's lack of connections or fortune; all of these things make it impossible. It would degrade me to marry her. I would be laughed at by all my friends, jeered at by my enemies and pitied by all. I could never possibly marry her. And yet—and yet I cannot keep away from her. The lightness of her spirits, her humour, her arch smile, her teasing, her eyes—oh! Philip, her eyes! which sparkle when she teases me and show she knows her power over me—all these things drive me to distraction.

I can tell no one but you. You know my character, you know how proud and disdainful I am, but against my better judgement I have been enraptured by her. It is out of the question for me to marry her; out of the question to make her my mistress.

I would leave if I could, but if I go now it will look particular and that is something I very much want to avoid. I do not know what to do.

Your beleaguered cousin,
Darcy

Mr Philip Darcy to Mr Darcy

London, April 21

Darcy, leave at once. Make some excuse and go today, this minute, never mind if it looks particular, it will soon be forgotten. Do not linger another moment. This kind of fever is virulent and the only thing that can control it is a prolonged absence from its source. Have your valet pack your things and meet me in London straightaway. If you stay, you will regret it.

PD

Mr Darcy to Mr Philip Darcy

Rosings Park, Kent, April 22

Philip, your letter arrived too late. I have proposed. I never meant to. I was in a ferment of passion, I did not know what I was doing. I was looking forward to seeing her, for she was engaged to drink tea with my aunt, and I was surprised and humiliated at the bitterness of my disappointment when she did not attend. She had a headache, her friend said. I wondered what could have occasioned it; I wondered how bad it was; I wondered if she needed a physician. I could not ask without it causing interest and so I said nothing, but excusing myself on account of a letter which I said needed an urgent reply, I bent my steps to the parsonage and before I knew what I was doing I was inside.

I do not know what possessed me, but possessed I was. I enquired after her health in a hurried manner and she replied coldly, not pleased to see me. Her manner only inflamed me more. I sat down in an effort to collect myself but my passions rose within me like a volcano and I believe it would have killed me to keep them in. They erupted from me as I told her that in vain had I struggled, but that I ardently loved and admired her.

Once started, I could not stop. I poured out my feelings: my horror at the behaviour of her family, the inferiority of her station in life, and the degradation it would be for me to marry her; but that, despite all this, I could not root out my feelings, that they were impossible to conquer, and I expressed my hope that she would accept my hand in marriage.

I did not doubt she would accept me and I was resentful even as I waited for her answer—resentful because she had brought me to this pass, resentful that she had taken control of my thoughts and feelings and reduced me to a state of helplessness—but that was nothing compared with the feelings I had when she rejected me. Can you credit it? I confess that I cannot. It is incredible to me. I am still smarting with the humiliation of it. To be rejected by anyone—I, Fitzwilliam Darcy of Pemberley—is inconceivable. And yet to be rejected by Elizabeth Bennet, who is no one from nowhere, and who should have been honoured I even noticed her, let alone proposed to her? The thing is incredible. And all because I listed the scruples that had long kept me from forming any previous proposal. Had I flattered her into the belief of my being impelled by unqualified, unalloyed inclination, by reason, by reflection, by everything, then I am convinced she would have accepted me, whatever she might say. But disguise is my abhorrence and I made no scruple of my struggles. And how did she repay this honesty? With contempt, telling me that she had never sought my good opinion, never wanted it and had no difficulty, in short, of throwing my proposal back in my face.

It has done one thing for me, however. It has cured me of my feelings for her. I am only now ashamed of what those feelings have been. I pray you will never mention this to anyone, not even to me.

I have only to answer the remarks she threw at me in her refusal, and then I have done with her. An encounter would not be wise for either of us, but a letter—yes, a letter will show her how wrong she has been.

I am looking forward to seeing you again. Tell me you will be in London for the Season. I myself will be there. I cannot leave Rosings soon enough. I am now ashamed of myself for ever having thought well of her, for being attracted to her and—above all—for proposing to her. This unfortunate affair is over. Once I have placed the letter into her hands, I hope I never see Elizabeth Bennet again.

Darcy

Miss Elizabeth Bennet to Miss Susan Sotherton

Hunsford, near Westerham, Kent,
April 22

I scarcely know where to begin . . . I cannot believe . . . and yet, did not Charlotte always say . . . But how was I to know, how to think she was right? Of all men, Mr Darcy! And yet there is no doubting it now. Oh! *That man!* How right my mother was to call him so! To come here and . . . but I must tell you all.

You know that Mr Darcy is here. He has visited us constantly and I never knew why. I laughed at Charlotte when she said he came for me, for his attentions were certainly not loverlike; indeed, when he called here one day and found me alone, he scarcely opened his mouth. But now . . .

I was unwell, a headache—caused by Mr Darcy, for I had discovered he played a role in separating Bingley from Jane; Colonel Fitzwilliam told me so—and so I stayed at the parsonage when

Charlotte, Maria and Mr Collins went to Rosings for tea. I read Jane's letters again, mourning her lack of cheerfulness and the knowledge that Mr Darcy was the cause, when the doorbell rang. Thinking it might be Colonel Fitzwilliam come to ask after me, I put the letters aside, but what was my astonishment when Mr Darcy walked in!

You will readily imagine my feelings: he was the last man in the world I wanted to see. I could not understand what he was about. He asked after my health, but seemed to be labouring under some heavy burden, and then he burst out, saying that he admired me and loved me! I have never been so astonished in all my life. I thought he had run mad, or else had taken too much wine. But it soon became apparent that he was perfectly sane and sober, for he strode around the room and told me that I was beneath him, that my family were in every way reprehensible, that it would be an insult to his own relations, but that he was determined to marry me!

My moment of feeling flattered—for who could be insensible to the compliment of a proposal from such a man?—swiftly passed, to be replaced by anger, mortification and contempt, and I roundly rejected him. He started; he had not expected it. He thought I would fall at his feet and thank him for his condescension, which shows how little he knows me! And then he asked why he was rejected with so little civility! When he had spent ten minutes roundly abusing my parents, my sisters, my station in life and his own wayward feelings!

You may be sure I answered him in kind, asking him why he had couched his proposal in such insulting terms. But I could not wait for his answer, for my feelings against him were such that they had to be given voice. I told him that I could never marry a man who had ruined my sister's happiness, and he changed colour, which removed every last shred of doubt in my mind that he was indeed the person responsible. He did not apologise, as might have been expected, but said only that he had been kinder to Bingley than to himself. This civil reflection did not do anything to lessen my anger, as you may imagine, and I set about him for his cruel and inhuman treatment of George Wickham. And what was his reaction? Shame for his misdeeds? Not a bit of it! He waved them aside and declared that I had only rejected him because he had not flattered me enough!

Why do men find it so hard to understand that we will not fall at their feet if they ask us to marry them? I am beginning to think that they are all either too stupid or too arrogant to see that we are not all eager to spend the rest of our lives with cruelty or pride; that we might draw back from trusting our future happiness to a man who has shown no interest in our feelings, but only in his own needs and desires.

I dare tell no one else of this proposal. I would tell Jane—how I miss her!—but I would then have to reveal that Mr Darcy interfered in her affairs, and I do not want to reopen that wound. I cannot tell any other member of my family. Can you imagine what Mama would say if she knew? And what she would say if she knew that I had refused him? She would not speak to me when I refused Mr Collins, and what is Mr Collins to Mr Darcy? She would no doubt banish me from the country if she knew I had denied her the right of visiting Pemberley and the opportunity to talk of it constantly to Lady Lucas!

Neither can I tell Charlotte, for she would certainly counsel me to marry him. She has been advising me to encourage him since almost the first moment I laid eyes on him, and I do not want to hear any arguments in his favour. I am still boiling with anger.

I am not even certain enough of my aunt to confide in her, for she would ask me if I refused Mr Darcy on account of Mr Wickham, and I would not know how to reply; for although I would have refused Mr Darcy even if I had never met Mr Wickham, I cannot deny that it gave added anger to my rejection of him.

Thank goodness I have you, Susan.

You must promise to tell no one of this. I hereby swear you to secrecy.

How I am longing to see you again. Is there any chance of you coming to Meryton, even for a few days? For I am afraid there is no chance at all of me coming to Bath.

And now I must go and bathe my face, for I was so angry that, once Mr Darcy left, I sat down and cried for half an hour. I can scarcely believe it even now, that he should have proposed to me; that he should have been in love with me for months without my knowing it; that he should wish to marry me, despite all his objections to the match. In another man it would have been gratifying indeed. But his pride! His abominable pride, his shameless avowal of the part he played in Jane's unhappiness and the unfeeling manner in which he mentioned Mr Wickham, his cruelty towards whom he did not even attempt to deny! No, I do not regret my decision, quite the reverse.

But already I hear the sound of the carriage. I am not equal to facing Charlotte. She is sure to tell that something is wrong and I cannot face her like this, with my face streaked and my eyes no doubt swollen.

Write to me soon. Tell me how you go on in Bath, where life is normal and no impossible men seek to disturb you.

For now, adieu,
Lizzy

Miss Susan Sotherton to Miss Elizabeth Bennet

Bath, April 23

How cruel, Lizzy, to confide in me and then swear me to secrecy, for with such a secret I could amaze the whole of Bath! Mr Darcy in love with my Lizzy! Though it does not surprise me, for you know I love you and so how can I be amazed when you are loved by someone else? It shows that, if nothing else, Mr Darcy has some sense, even if he has no manners and is evidently in need of some lessons in humility.

How I longed to say something when your letter arrived, for several ladies arrived a few moments later as they paid a morning call. Miss Violet Cranmore launched into her favourite topic at once—well, almost her favourite topic, for her favourite topic is herself—but her second favourite topic, then, of Caroline Bingley, and Caroline's attempts to win Mr Darcy. They were at the seminary together and hate each other, it is plain to see.

'Caroline's efforts are pitiful,' said Violet. 'She keeps writing to me and telling me how important she is to him, but everyone knows Mr Darcy will never marry beneath him. He is as good as betrothed to Miss Anne de Bourgh.'

I wanted to smile sweetly and say that, actually, Mr Darcy had no intention of marrying Miss de Bourgh; that he was in love with my friend and that he had just proposed marriage to her.

Oh, how I wish you had accepted! Not really, of course, I could not bear to see you marry a man you do not love. But if you could have loved him, what fun it would have been to see her face, and the face of her superior mama, for they both of them look down on me. They are annoyed that I have caught Mr Wainwright, who has a handsome fortune, far larger than that of Violet's intended.

Have you told Charlotte yet? Do you think you ever will? And what about Jane? She will want to know, even if it hurts her to begin with, I am sure of it. And anyway, there is no need to tell her that Mr Darcy interfered in her own life, only that he proposed to you. When will you be seeing her again? It is so exciting. And that is always the way of things; either there is nothing to tell, but one has perfect liberty to tell it, or something so momentous it would rock everyone, but one is unable to breathe a word!

Write to me soon, dearest, you know you can tell me anything, and I promise faithfully to keep your confidence, whatever it costs me!

Your loving friend,
Susan

Miss Elizabeth Bennet to Miss Susan Sotherton

Hunsford, near Westerham, Kent,
April 23

My dearest Susan,

I must unburden myself again, and again I must swear you to secrecy, for I have had such a letter . . . When I think of it, I . . . But let me collect myself. Charlotte is busy about her household affairs and Maria is helping her, Mr Collins is out in the garden and I am alone in the house. Only now am I able to drag myself out of my thoughts, and needing someone to turn to, someone to tell . . .

By now you will have had my previous letter, about Mr Darcy's proposal. I was angry with him, disgusted with his behaviour, but now . . .

I do not know what to think. He has written me a letter, and such a letter . . . I expected nothing from him, I thought he would avoid me, since I knew that he intended to return to London very soon, but instead, this morning as I walked, I found him waiting for me. I tried to avoid him but he detained me by stepping forward and calling my name. He held out a letter, which I instinctively took, and said haughtily that he had been walking in the grove for some time in the hope of meeting me, and then asked me to have the goodness to read the letter.

With no expectation of pleasure, but with the strongest curiosity, I opened it, and to my increasing sense of wonder I saw an envelope containing two sheets of paper, written quite through in a very close hand. The envelope itself was likewise full. I did not know what he could have to say to me, let alone what he could have to say which would take so much saying, but I could not contain my curiosity.

I cannot begin to tell you my feelings as I read everything contained therein; indeed, it is only now, several hours later, that I can begin to sort them out. Everything was presented to me with such a different slant that I find myself, against my will, beginning to see things differently; or, at least, to acknowledge that there might be a different interpretation to be put upon things.

The letter started arrogantly enough, all pride and insolence, saying that I had accused him of two offences in my rejection of him. He claimed that, although he knew his friend was becoming increasingly attached to Jane, he convinced himself by watching her that her feelings were not similarly touched. I was at first outraged by this, until I remembered Charlotte saying that Jane ought to show what she felt if she wanted to attach Mr Bingley. Susan, reluctant though I am to do it, I find I have to admit that Jane's feelings, though fervent, were little displayed, and that there was a constant complacency in her manner not often associated with great sensibility.

His comments on my family, though mortifying, I could not help admitting had some justice. You left Meryton before the militia arrived and so you do not know how my sisters have been throwing themselves at the officers' heads, whilst Mama and Papa did nothing to stop them.

But it is in his details of his dealings with Mr Wickham that he chiefly sought to exonerate himself. At first I did not believe it, for his account of events differed so strongly from Mr Wickham's account, but he referred me to his cousin if I doubted him, and this helped convince me that he was not misleading me. Then, too, when I was forced to think about Mr Wickham's behaviour, I had, in the end, to think it was not as spotless as it first appeared.

I cannot tell you all, but I can say this: that Mr Darcy claims his father left the living to Mr Wickham provisionally only, and that, as Mr Wickham did not want it, Mr Darcy gave him the sum of three thousand pounds instead.

At first I doubted, but as I thought back over my acquaintance with Mr Wickham it struck me as odd that he had confided so much at our first meeting, which was surely wrong of him, and that he had not noised his grievances in public until Mr Darcy had left the neighbourhood and was therefore no longer in a position to defend himself.

And now I am left feeling perplexed and wounded, scarcely knowing what to think, who to believe. To begin with, I believed resolutely in Mr Wickham, but Mr Darcy's story had the ring of truth and, together with the fact that he referred me to his cousin—who is an honest and upright man—I find myself believing Mr Darcy.

He was sent to plague me, I am sure of it, first of all with his haughtiness, then with his unwanted attentions, and now with his unsettling news about my favourite. He has brought me nothing but torment. And yet I cannot help thinking that he is a better man than I had supposed and, although undoubtedly proud, much maligned.

How much easier would it have been if Mr Darcy had continued to be a villain, and Mr Wickham a saint. But as Mr Wickham transferred his affections from me as soon as Miss King inherited a sizeable dowry, I am faced with the fact that he was never quite the saint I believed him.

My one consolation is that Mr Darcy is leaving the neighbourhood tomorrow, and that I will not be here much longer, either.

How I long to see Jane and the familiar walls of home; how I long to talk with Papa and have everything back to normal.

Your dear friend,
Lizzy

Miss Susan Sotherton to Miss Elizabeth Bennet

Bath, April 24

Lizzy, you are trying me hard! First I must mention nothing of your proposal, and now I can mention nothing about Mr Wickham's relations with Mr Darcy. I wish I were coming to Meryton again, but there is no chance of it, and after all I am glad, for I do not think I could keep so many secrets if I were to find myself at home again.

You say I know nothing of your sisters' goings-on, but do not forget that Ellie writes to Lydia and Kitty—indeed a letter from Kitty arrived this morning—and I have seen enough of their correspondence to know how silly they are, but this does not excuse Mr Darcy for saying so. It is up to him, as your lover, to make light of your family's failings, not to make much of them. Your father and mother are not the most sensible parents, it is true, but at least your father has not gambled away your inheritance and forced you to leave your home. I am not surprised you miss him. My own papa, alas, is no better: every time we think he is improving he relapses, and goes from bad to worse.

I eagerly await your next letter. I fully expect to find that the Archbishop of Canterbury has proposed to you when next you write!

Your loving friend,
Susan

Miss Lydia Bennet to Miss Eleanor Sotherton

Longbourn, Hertfordshire,
April 24

La! Ellie, what do you think? The officers are leaving Meryton, they are to be gone in a month, and what shall we do without them? They are going to be encamped near Brighton. How I wish I could go with them, for it will be deadly dull here without them. I have said so time and time again, and Mama agrees with me and says we should all go to Brighton. It would be a delicious scheme, and I dare say would hardly cost anything at all. Mama would like to go too of all things, but Papa says he will not stir from Longbourn, and we may not go without him. He says Kitty and I are the silliest girls in the country, but I do not think we are as silly as Mary, who has made so many books of extracts her bedroom is full and now she wants a shelf in the library for them. Papa says she may not have one and Mama tells her to wear her hair differently and Mary preaches in return, so that I am sick of the sound of her. If only we could go to Brighton! Papa says he cannot wait for Jane and Lizzy to return, so that he can have some sensible conversation, but what can they have to talk of? Jane has been in London and Lizzy has been in Kent and there are not any officers in either place.

Your greatest friend in all the world,
Lydia

Miss Elizabeth Bennet to Miss Susan Sotherton

Hunsford, near Westerham, Kent,
April 25

Dear Susan,

I know I try you hard, but I shall endeavour not to do so in future. The Archbishop has not proposed and so that is one less secret for you to keep! The gentlemen—Mr Darcy and his cousin—have now left Rosings, and I have only Lady Catherine to contend with.

We dined with her yesterday evening and I could not help thinking that, if I had answered Mr Darcy differently, I might by this time have been presented to her as her future niece. What would she have said? How would she have behaved? I amused myself with these questions as an antidote to an otherwise dull evening.

Lady Catherine mourned the absence of the gentlemen, and Mr Collins alleviated her suffering with some clumsy compliments.

Then she turned her attention to me and thinking, quite wrongly, that I was quiet because I did not like to leave, she said that I must write to my mother to beg that I may stay a little longer. Nothing could be further from my wishes, for I long to be at home. She would not accept it, however, but went on saying that my mother could certainly spare me for a fortnight or so. She dismissed the idea that my father was missing me and added, in her goodness, that she could take either Maria or myself as far as London in early June, though what the other one was supposed to do, I do not know—run behind, I suspect! Though she did say, condescendingly, that as we were neither of us large, if the weather should happen to be cool, she did not mind taking us both.

Surprisingly enough, I said we must abide by the original plan.

How tired I am of Rosings: Lady Catherine with her officious interference; Mr Collins with his obsequiousness and stupidity; even Charlotte, who has chosen this lot in life. How I long to be away.

Your dear friend,
Lizzy

➤ MAY ➤

Miss Lydia Bennet to Miss Eleanor Sotherton

Longbourn, Hertfordshire, May 7

Lord, Ellie, I never knew I could be so fagged. We have been to balls and parties every night this week, we are setting up a store of them to remember when the regiment has left Meryton, though I have still not despaired of going to Brighton. Say nothing to Kitty, but Harriet has said she will ask her husband, Colonel Forster, if I might go with her as her especial friend. Just think! I might be spending the summer in Brighton, surrounded by officers!

Tomorrow Kitty and I are going to meet Jane and Lizzy on their way back from Aunt Gardiner's. We are going with the carriage to meet them at the inn and we plan to get there early so that we might look in the milliner's, then we intend to treat them to a meal at the inn before we return.

I dare say Lizzy will be wild to know about Wickham. He is not to marry Mary King after all—she is gone down to stay with her uncle at Liverpool. She is a great fool to have gone away, he will not follow her, you know. He will probably pay court to Lizzy again, though Harriet says she is sure he has an eye for me. Would that not be fun! I am sure I should not mind if he wanted to pay court to me.

As for Lizzy and Jane, I hope they come back with husbands, for they will very soon be on the shelf. Jane is almost three and twenty. I am sure I should be ashamed to be single at that age, she will be quite an old maid soon.

My aunt Philips wants them both to get husbands. She says Lizzy had better have taken Mr Collins but I do not think there would have been any fun in that. Lord! How I should like to be married before any of them, and then I would chaperone them around to all the balls! Dear me! We had such a piece of fun last night, what do you think we did? We dressed Chamberlayne in women's clothes, on purpose to pass for a lady—only think what fun! Not a soul knew of it but Colonel Forster and Harriet and my aunt, for we were forced to borrow one of her gowns, and you cannot imagine how well he looked! When Denny and Wickham and Pratt and a few of the others came in, they did not know him in the least. Lord! How I laughed! And so did Harriet Forster! I thought I should have died. And that made the men suspect something, and then they soon found out what was the matter!

Mama is hoping that Mr Bingley will come back to Netherfield, or that your papa will let it again to someone else, some nice family with five sons for our five daughters!

Write and tell me all about your beaux in Bath. Are you having as much fun as we are?

Lydia

Miss Mary Bennet to Miss Lucy Sotherton

Longbourn, Hertfordshire, May 9

Most noble Friend,

My sisters have returned from their sojourn and are once more enwrapped in the bosom of their family. Lydia and Kitty went to meet them and returned in high spirits. I remonstrated with them gently, saying far be it from me to depreciate such pleasures, which would doubtless be congenial with the generality of female minds, but that they would have no charms for me. I said that I should infinitely prefer a book, and Lydia asked whether I would prefer *The Necromancer* or *Horrid Mysteries*. Like the generality of people, she is under the mistaken impression that these are salacious works, and does not realise that they are erudite works of art which give us an understanding of our ancestors, the topography of their landscapes and their historical importance. However, I am heartened by her desire to visit Brighton. Travel broadens the mind, and a few weeks on the south coast will no doubt make her aware of the rich flora and fauna to be found within these isles; that is, if our father relents and lets her go.

Your sister in wisdom,
Mary

Miss Jane Bennet to Mrs Gardiner

Longbourn, Hertfordshire,
May 10

Mr dear aunt,

I am writing to thank you for your kind hospitality over these last few months; it has given me new heart and the courage to face home again. I am glad to be with Lizzy, and Papa says he has missed me. My sisters, too, have welcomed me warmly.

The garden at Longbourn is very pretty with its new foliage and its blossoms. The weather is mild, and we are to walk to my aunt Philips's house this evening.

Give my love to my cousins.

Your loving niece,
Jane

Mrs Bennet to Mrs Gardiner

Longbourn, Hertfordshire,
May 10

Well, sister, Lizzy says the Collinses live very comfortable. I suppose they often talk of having Longbourn when Mr Bennet is dead. They look upon it quite as their own, I dare say, whenever that happens. Well, if they can be easy with an estate that is not lawfully their own, so much the better. *I* should be ashamed of having one that was only entailed on me.

Lydia is wild to go to Brighton, for the regiment are to leave us, and I am sure I cried for two days together when Colonel Millar's regiment went away when I was a girl, twenty-five years ago, though it does not seem a day. I thought I should have broke my heart. If only Mr Bennet would consent to the idea, we could all of us go to Brighton. A few weeks on the coast would set me up wonderfully, but Mr Bennet will not hear of it. Ah! Sister, you do not know what I have to bear.

You must ask Lydia and Kitty to stay with you soon. I am sure I do not see why they should not have their share of the pleasure and enjoy themselves in London if they cannot go to Brighton.

I do not know what you think of this sad business of Jane's, for I made sure before she went away that she would be married by the time she returned. Four whole months she has been in London, and not even an engagement.

For my part, I am determined never to speak of Mr Bingley again to anybody. He is a very undeserving young man, and I do not suppose there is the least chance of her getting him now. There is no talk of him coming to Netherfield again in the summer; and I have enquired of everybody, too, who is likely to know. Oh, well, it is just as he chooses; nobody wants him to come. Though I shall always say that he used my daughter extremely ill; and if I were her, I would not have put up with it. My comfort is that Jane will die of a broken heart, and then he will be sorry for what he has done.

Your affectionate sister,
Janet

Miss Caroline Bingley to Mr Charles Bingley

Yorkshire, May 12

Dear Charles,

I had forgotten how boring it is in the country, for there is nothing to do all day. You were right to leave Netherfield; it had outlived its charm. I do not say that an estate is a bad thing, but one closer to London would be better suited to our needs. I cannot think why you keep Netherfield when you have no intention of returning. You should give up the lease and look for something closer to town. Louisa and I will help you, for there is nothing to keep us here. We have taken the waters at Harrogate and exhausted the York shops. Ned is busy all the time and never takes us anywhere. Besides, his friends are of a low sort, manufacturers and the like. He is talking of buying a mill. Mama says if that is what he wants then that is what he must have, but you must write and talk him out of it; it would be too humiliating to have a brother with a mill.

Your dearest sister,
Caroline

Mr Charles Bingley to Miss Caroline Bingley

London, May 16

Dear Caroline,

I agree with Ma—if Ned wants a mill, he must have one. He does not tell me how to be happy and upon my honour I will not tell him.

You talk of me quitting Netherfield but the lease has still some months to run and I might go there again before it has expired. It is in a very pretty part of the country and I still think fondly of it, though it is a very long time since we were last there. I left on the twenty-seventh of November, the day after the Netherfield ball. I believe I have never enjoyed myself more than I did that night; all our friends were there and I remember it often.

You will be pleased to know that Darcy has invited us to a picnic he is giving with Georgiana next month. He wants her to gain more experience of entertaining, nothing much at first, just small parties for friends, so that she learns how to go on. She is sixteen now and going more into the world. Upon my soul she is a very pretty girl, a credit to Darcy and much loved by everyone in London.

Give my love to Ma and my brothers and sisters.

Charles

Mr Philip Darcy to Mr Darcy

Wiltshire, May 18

My dear Darcy,

It is almost a month now since you left Rosings and I hope your infatuation has run its course. Do you ever think of the woman you spoke of, or has she faded into memory? Whatever the case, it would be better not to try yourself too far. You should continue to avoid her until the end of the year at least, and distract yourself with thoughts of other women. There are plenty here for you to choose from. Join me in Wiltshire, and bring Georgiana, too—I have not seen her for months and she will have changed a lot in that time. It will give her an opportunity to meet some new people, always good for a girl of her age. Besides, I would like your opinion on a young woman I am intending to marry. She offers everything a man of my standing has a right to look for in a wife. She is beautiful, well-bred and accomplished. I mean to offer for her next month.

PD

Mr Darcy to Mr Philip Darcy

Darcy House, London, May 20

My dear Philip,

Ashamed as I am to admit it, I have not been able to forget Elizabeth, though God knows I have tried. I have thrown myself into the Season and I have never been at home. By day I attend to business—and I have started several new works in order to fully occupy myself, including commissioning a new orangery at Pemberley—and when I am not dealing with business affairs I am riding or boxing or fencing; either that or escorting Georgiana on pleasure trips. By night I go to soirées, balls—indeed, any entertainment rather than remain at home and give myself time to think. But try as I might, the thought of her haunts me. I see her everywhere I go. I catch sight of the back of a woman's head and think: Elizabeth! Then the woman turns and I see it is not she, and I am disappointed, even though I should not be; even though our time together was categorized by verbal sparring and not by pleasantries, and should be easy to forget. But the memory of her lingers. The day I proposed in particular will not leave me. I said some things to her that were, perhaps, better left unsaid. Even worse, I cannot forget her face as she told me I was the last man in the world she could ever be prevailed upon to marry.

It used to make me angry when I thought of it, but now I find myself doubting, and wondering whether I deserved her anger. I have been too used to having my own way, perhaps. It was not well done of me to throw the inferiority of her connections in her face, nor their behaviour. She has no control over either and so of what use was it to mention it, save to show my own magnanimity in overlooking them? And that was not only condescending but arrogant of me. I am beginning to understand why she refused me, and to think that if I had managed things better . . . but no, I said so at the time and she returned that I could not have offered her my hand in any way that would have induced her to accept it.

I feel myself growing angry again as I think of it . . . but also to admire her. How many women would have refused me, even if they did not love me nor even like me? I cannot think of one. But she refused me, even knowing she was turning down Pemberley, my fortune, my position, everything that goes with being my wife. There are few enough people with principles in the world, and even fewer who stick to them when temptation to abandon them offers, but she is that rare person, a woman of honour and integrity. And I have lost her. By my own arrogance, conceit and pride, I have disgusted her.

But I was not intending to think of her, let alone write of her. Your invitation comes at a good time, you see. A change of scene will perhaps encourage a change of thoughts. I will be glad to come to Wiltshire and I will bring Georgiana with me. You will be very pleased with her; she is quite lovely.

I have to be back in London in a few weeks—I have already sent out invitations to a picnic, or rather, Georgiana has—but you may expect us on Saturday.

Darcy

Miss Lydia Bennet to Miss Eleanor Sotherton

Hertfordshire, May 21

I am going to Brighton! I am going to Brighton! Lord! What a lark! Harriet is a darling! I knew she would invite me. Mama is delighted. Kitty is jealous and says she should have been invited because she is older than me, but Harriet is my *particular* friend. La! The streets will be paved with officers and I will be able to flirt to my heart's content. There will be Denny and Pratt and Wickham and all the rest. They dined with us last night and Kitty was wild when we all talked about Brighton. Wickham spent a great deal of time talking to Lizzy about her stay in Kent as well, but he did not seem to like what he heard. I dare say he did not like to hear that Mr Darcy had been there. Who would like to hear about Mr Darcy? He does not even have a red coat.

You must write to me every day in Brighton, though I am sure I will be too busy to write to you. But I will write when I can. Tell your mama she must take you to Brighton—I am sure you can live there as cheaply as Bath—then we will have fun together. I am writing this in haste from Colonel Forster's house because we leave here early tomorrow.

Love,
Lydia

Miss Elizabeth Bennet to Miss Susan Sotherton

Longbourn, Hertfordshire,
May 22

Dearest Susan,

The house is much quieter without Lydia, and Meryton seems deserted without the officers. Mama gave a last dinner for them and I had a chance to speak to Mr Wickham. The more I saw of him, the more I was convinced that Mr Darcy spoke the truth, for there was something alarmed in Mr Wickham's eye when he saw that I had heard about the conditions attached to the living he was left, and he coloured when I said that I understood Mr Darcy better than I had done. I could not repress a smile when he said that Mr Darcy must have been on his best behaviour in front of Miss de Bourgh, as he wishes to marry her! But all in all I am not sorry that Mr Wickham has left us—a state of affairs I could not have guessed at a few short weeks ago.

As for Mr Darcy, I find that I view him with more compassion and respect than formerly, but I cannot forgive him for wounding my sister, and I am glad that he shows no signs of returning.

Although I am glad to see the regiment go, I must confess that our lives are much duller now. Our parties are less varied and we go out less often. I find myself looking forward more and more to my trip to the Lakes with my aunt and uncle.

Your friend,
Lizzy

Miss Lydia Bennet to Mrs Bennet

Brighton, May 27

Mama, you will never guess what we did yesterday: we went first of all to the library, where Denny and Wickham attended us, and where I saw such beautiful ornaments as made me wild. I have ordered a new gown and bought a new parasol, it is the darlingest thing, only I can say no more, Harriet is calling me, we are going out again!

Give my love to my sisters,
Lydia

Miss Lydia Bennet to Miss Kitty Bennet

Brighton, May 30

Kitty, you would die if you could see what we have all been up to here, we have been sea bathing, Harriet and I went in our underwear, DO NOT LET MAMA OR ANYONE ELSE KNOW. Things are different in Brighton, not so stuffy as they are at home. Lord! What fun we have. The men are all wild for me, I have a dozen different flirts. There are parties every night and I went to one last night dressed as a man. I borrowed Denny's coat and breeches and wore a piece of wool as a moustache, I thought I would die laughing. Wickham was in on the joke, he laughed as much as anyone. There are a lot of new officers here, Jakes and Little and Madison, and a whole host of others, all laughing and joking and teasing and dancing and flirting; well most of them anyway. Some of them are ancient, friends of Colonel Forster's who are here on leave, and all they talk about is the war. I am glad I am not married to Colonel Forster, he is far too old and stuffy, poor Harriet! She should have married Denny. Lord! Was there ever such a place as Brighton? Tomorrow we are going to have a bathing party by moonlight, I have bought a new bathing dress, it is quite scandalous. DO NOT TELL ANYONE.

Lydia

ᨑ JUNE ᨑ

Colonel Fitzwilliam to Mr Darcy

Brighton, June 2

Darcy, I am home on leave and am visiting friends in Brighton before heading north. Colonel Forster is here and asks me to remember him to you. His wife is here, too, and a prettier creature it would be hard to imagine. She is young and gay and it is a pleasure to see her enjoying herself. She has a friend with her, a Miss Lydia Bennet. I cannot help wondering if she is any relation to your Miss Elizabeth Bennet—though perhaps I should not call her *your* Miss Elizabeth, as I am sure you will have overcome your feelings for her now. I have not yet seen Miss Lydia so I do not know if there is any resemblance, but I mean to ask her if there is a relationship when we meet.

Another acquaintance is here, and one less welcome: George Wickham. He bowed when he saw me but looked uncomfortable, as well he might. I was tempted to call him out but did not want to cause a scandal: any action I take against him would lead to speculation and that is something I am determined to avoid. If not for this, I would gladly run him through.

How is my ward? Growing more beautiful every day, I am sure. I hear you are in Wiltshire at the moment: Mama knows everything! She and Maud are hoping for news of Philip's intended, so you must write to them and let them know your opinion of her. Philip will have chosen some paragon, I am sure, but what is she really like? We rely on you to tell us.

My sister Maud will soon be presenting you with another god-child, so you must look about you for a christening present.

I do not believe I will have time to call in at Wiltshire on my way north to see my family, but I hope to see you in London, either on my way up to Cumbria or on my way back down again. When will you be leaving Wiltshire? I must be back with my regiment in a few weeks' time. I would be there now if not for this confounded injury. With the French advancing towards Turin my place is on the Continent, not here, but I am little use as I am. I cannot sit a horse nor walk for any length of time and my right arm will not do my bidding. I only hope the Austrians throw Napoleon out of Italy and save me the trouble.

Your cousin,
Henry

Mr Darcy to Colonel Fitzwilliam

Wiltshire, June 4

Henry, it is good to hear from you, though frustrating for you to be home at such a time. The war shows no sign of ending and if not for the troops stationed at Brighton and other likely landing spots, we would be in some danger of Napoleon invading these shores. But the Channel protects us, as it has done before.

I did not know you had been injured. Would you like my physician to attend you? I can send him down to Brighton if you think he would be of use.

I will be returning to London in a few days' time. Georgiana is hosting a picnic on the seventh and we must be there for that. You are welcome to join us. If you will not be returning to London so soon, then call in at Darcy House whenever you arrive; you know you are always welcome.

You ask about Philip's intended bride. She is everything you imagine: beautiful, accomplished, elegant, well-bred, and yet—Henry, it is not enough. It is enough for Philip, he is pleased with his choice and she with him, but it is not enough for me. There are two similar females here, they possess everything a man could require of a wife, and yet I have no wish to marry either of them. I am happy to escort them in to dinner, to dance with them and converse with them, but to spend the rest of my life with them? No. I already know everything about them. There is nothing to discover, nothing to intrigue or stimulate. They never change. Their thoughts and feelings are what they were a year ago, and will be the same when another year has gone by. Marriage to either one of them would be like bathing in tepid water: nothing to complain of, but nothing to desire either.

You will tell from this that I have not forgotten Elizabeth. I have tried, but the more I see of other women, the more I know that Elizabeth is the only one I have ever wished to marry. She is not perfect—far from it—but it is her flaws and imperfections that entrance me—those, and her eyes. I want to see them looking back at me across the breakfast table; I want to see them sparkling with mischief as she teases me; I want to see them widen as I show her all the delights of Pemberley and offer them to her, not with arrogance but with humility.

But it is pointless to think of such things.

I am beginning to wish I had not encouraged Bingley to leave the neighbourhood. But of what use would it be for me to return there? Elizabeth made her feelings for me clear; though perhaps it would lessen her ill opinion of me if she could see that some of her reproofs have been attended to.

But this is idle speculation. I will torment myself with it no more.

Come to us as soon as you can in London; Georgiana is longing to see you.

Your cousin,
Darcy

Colonel Fitzwilliam to Mr Darcy

Brighton, June 5

I will not be in town in time for your picnic, alas. I am here with Wilkins and I am at his disposal. He arranges the business just as he pleases: the privilege of wealth! I do not think we will remain here very much longer, however, and I hope to join you in London soon. I will be glad to see you again but I will be sorry to leave Brighton. The sea breeze is refreshing and the fishermen's nets set out to dry on the Steine give the place charm.

You must bring Georgiana here for the summer, Darcy; the sea air will do her good and the south coast will not have the unpleasant memories for her that the east coast must have. The pleasure gardens, the promenades and the libraries will amuse her. They are all flourishing, thanks to the patronage of the Prince of Wales, who spends more and more of his time here. They say he means to leave London altogether and live in Brighton permanently. It is certainly possible; he is enlarging his marine pavilion and making it fit for a prince. It is a very handsome dwelling, but even so I think he is in error for spending so much on his amusements when the country is at war. He ought to be retrenching so that he can better equip the troops. I said so only last night to Colonel Forster when we dined together.

By the bye, Forster's wife's friend, Miss Lydia Bennet, is indeed a relation of your Miss Elizabeth, a sister. I have seen her only once, briefly, as she was going out with Colonel Forster's wife, but I had a chance to speak to her and ascertained that her family were well before she set off for the shops with Harriet. It amazes me that women can spend so much time shopping, but Lydia and Harriet look very well on it.

Look for me on the sixteenth.

Henry

Miss Elizabeth Bennet to Miss Susan Sotherton

Longbourn, Hertfordshire,
June 20

Dear Susan,

It is very quiet here at Longbourn. Kitty has at last given over lamenting her absence from the Brighton scheme and consoles herself with reading and re-reading her letters from Lydia. She keeps them close and runs out of the room with them if anyone draws near her. I dread to think what they contain; stories of flirtations, most likely, and the names of a dozen officers. The letters are all so heavily underlined it is a wonder there is any paper left to write them on! I laugh, but all the same, I wish my father had been more sensible of the dangers to Lydia of such a trip. She is heedless and headstrong and loves to be the centre of attention, and I fear this trip will be the death warrant of all possibility of common sense for her. To put such a girl, at the tender age of fifteen, in the way of dozens of young men who are all bored and away from home, is to put temptation in her way, and Lydia has never known how to resist temptation. Her behaviour in Meryton was abominable; how much worse must it be in Brighton, with no one there to curb her worst excesses? I can only hope that the young men are better able to control themselves than Lydia is, and that my father is right when he says that Colonel Forster will see that no harm comes to her.

Mary continues to try Mama's nerves with her constant practise on the pianoforte, and if not for Jane I would not know what to do. But with Jane's companionship I can bear anything. How she came to be so different from my other sisters I do not know, but she is everything Kitty is not. She bears her disappointment without complaint and busies herself about the house, treating Mama with her usual calm patience and providing me with a confidante when I feel I must talk of Mr Darcy or burst. How can I have been so wrong about him? How can I not have seen him for the man he is, and instead seen him for a man he is not? I thought myself so clever when I teased him, and yet I could not have been more mistaken. But I am well rewarded for it, am I not? For I never think of him now without mortification and shame, and I cannot help thinking of what might have been . . . that is, until I remember that he parted Jane and Bingley, and then I regret neither him nor Pemberley nor his ten thousand a year! You see, I can laugh at myself still, and a good thing, too, or I fear I should go into a decline!

Mama, I am sure, would be very pleased if I did—it would add to her consequence to have a daughter who was brought low by love. As it is, she continues to lament the absence of Mr Bingley, saying that she will never mention him again and then talking of him in the very next breath. I spare Jane from these outbursts as often as I can by listening to them myself and by turning Mama's thoughts into a happier direction, though unfortunately that direction is always towards Lydia and how many flirts she has in Brighton. I am not surprised that Papa has retreated to his library and emerges only at mealtimes.

And so now I am looking forward to my trip with my aunt and uncle. We cannot go to the Lakes as we planned, for my uncle cannot spend so long away from his business, and my aunt has suggested that we go to Derbyshire instead. I was taken aback by the suggestion, but I did not hesitate for long before writing and agreeing to the change, for I might venture into Derbyshire, I think, without meeting Mr Darcy. It is a large enough place. And a good thing, too, for what would I say to him if I were to meet him again? It would be humiliating. And yet I cannot help wishing that I had had a chance to speak to him after receiving his letter.

And that, my dear Susan, is all my news.

Your loving friend,
Lizzy

Mr Philip Darcy to Mr Darcy

Wiltshire, June 24

Darcy,

We have set a date for the wedding: December 4. You will be receiving an invitation any day now. It will be a grand affair held in the cathedral and we look forward to seeing you there.

PD

Mr Darcy to Mr Philip Darcy

Darcy House, London, June 26

My dear Philip,

I am glad your affairs are prospering and I look forward to seeing you married. It is good to know that at least one of us will be continuing the Darcy name. I only wish my own affairs were going half so well. I have tried to forget Elizabeth Bennet but there is always something to remind me of her. Only yesterday Henry dined with me—he is in town once again after a spell in Brighton—and I learnt something disastrous to my peace of mind. When I revealed that I regretted my interference in Bingley's affairs, Henry said that I agreed with Miss Elizabeth Bennet, then. When I looked surprised, he said that he had mentioned the matter to Elizabeth when they walked together at Rosings. Oh, not by name, nor in any great detail: he said only that I had saved a friend from the inconveniences of an imprudent marriage, and that there were strong objections to the lady. He meant to show me in a good light, never suspecting that Elizabeth was a relative of the lady involved, but she must have guessed that the friend in question was Bingley and that the lady was her sister. Small wonder then that she was angry, both when speaking to Henry—she told him that I had had no right to interfere—and when rejecting me. I admire her for her anger, and for her partiality, though at first it exasperated me, for what kind of woman would she be if she could stand by and hear a beloved sister abused in such a way? It cannot have been pleasant for her to hear of the matter spoken of in such a casual way, nor can it have been pleasant for her to think that anyone could object to her sister. I confess that as to Miss Bennet herself, there cannot be any rational objection. She is a very pretty girl, sweet natured and good-hearted, and singularly untainted by the vulgarity of the majority of her family. Moreover, she has an optimistic temperament that suits Bingley's own. If he seems no happier in another month then I mean to give him a hint that a return to Netherfield would not be a bad thing. I once thought he would make a good husband for Georgiana but I no longer think they will suit.

Darcy

Mr Philip Darcy to Mr Darcy

Wiltshire, June 28

I am sorry to hear that you have still not recovered from your infatuation, but I could not agree with you more when you say that Bingley and Georgiana will not suit. He is a pleasant enough young man but his family are in trade and I once had the misfortune of meeting his mother. He is not nearly good enough for Georgiana; she can look far higher for a husband. I have one or two young men in mind for her, and I will introduce you to them the next time you are in Wiltshire. Better yet, I will introduce you to them at the wedding, and Georgiana, too. It will be just the right atmosphere for the introduction. They are both the kind of men she should be marrying.

PD

JULY

Darcy House, London, July 9

Dearest, dearest coz,

It seems an age since I have seen you. You will come and stay with us at Pemberley, won't you, when we go there for the summer? It will not be long before we go; indeed, Fitzwilliam is already there, overseeing plans for the house party next month and making sure that work is progressing on the orangery. He will be returning to London shortly and then he will be escorting me back to Derbyshire. Oh, I am so looking forward to it. I am tired of London, though I dare say I am ungrateful, for Fitzwilliam arranged a host of picnics and parties for me, and took me to all the museums and galleries. But I am longing to be in the country once again. Ullswater is looking forward to it, too. She will much prefer to be there, where she can run around to her heart's content and sniff and nose about in the shrubberies without anyone bothering her or telling her it is time to go home.

Caroline Bingley will be joining us, and her brother and sister, but although she is very accomplished and I like singing and playing duets with her, I cannot talk to her as I can to you. I believe she wants me to marry her brother—she is always telling me what a good, kind man he is—but I have no wish to marry him. Charles is a kind friend, but I dream of love and I do not love him.

I have guessed your secret. I believe you are in love with my guardian. I do not know why I did not see it before. I was too young, I suppose, but happening to take out your letters the other day in order to renew the ribbon tying them about, I read them again. How long have you been in love with him? Is he to visit you at Rosings? Or will you be able to persuade your mama to take you to Cumbria to visit his family?

I believe that Fitzwilliam, too, is in love. He has been distracted recently and he has spoken to me of love and marriage more often than formerly. He keeps telling me that I will be able to marry whomsoever I choose and that he will not stand in my way if I truly love a good and honourable man who deserves me, whatever his background might be. It might be idle fancy on my part, but I think not.

I wondered if Caroline Bingley was his choice. That would seem to explain his remarks about a lover's background, but I am certain she is not good enough for Fitzwilliam, and besides, he would tell me if it were Caroline. But I can think of no one else in our intimate circle who might have won him. Can you? Whoever the lady is, she must be very special to have captured Fitzwilliam's heart and I am sure an announcement cannot be long in coming. I speak with a sister's partiality, but I truly believe that no better man lives, and that any woman would be lucky to marry him.

Write to me soon.

Your loving cousin,
Georgiana

Miss Anne de Bourgh to Miss Georgiana Darcy

Rosings Park, Kent, July 11

What a relief it is to be able to speak of it at last! You have guessed correctly, dear coz, I am in love with your guardian and always have been, ever since we were children. He has always been so good to me and has always paid such kind attention to me that it has kindled in me a long-lasting affection which eventually deepened into love. But alas! he does not see me, or if he does, he sees me not as a woman, but as a sickly creature he has known all his life.

Oh, this confounded illness! If only I were healthy, I could go for long country walks and put some colour into my cheeks. I could eat more and fill out my figure so that I would look more womanly, and buy some lower-cut dresses instead of the high-necked gowns that Mama always forces me to wear. I have no desire to flaunt myself indecently, but it is very hard to be starched up to the ears when everyone else is looking devastatingly beautiful in scoop-necked gowns. If I could only be well enough to go to London and look around the shops, I would encase myself in colourful silk from head to foot instead of the grey brocade Mama thinks so suitable. Then he would look at me in the way he looked at Miss Elizabeth Bennet.

I am not surprised he was drawn to her, both men were, Henry and your brother. She was so lively and *healthy* looking, with her bright eyes and her pink cheeks and her air of youth and vigour; whereas my air is one of tiredness. And her clothes! Nothing vulgar, but at the same time they could not help but display her figure, which believe me was noticeable, though she seemed unaware of it herself.

I go out in my phaeton whenever I can to improve my looks, and I am sure I could walk if Mama would only let me, but she says it would tire me too much. I sometimes think it is sitting indoors all day long that tires me, and that brisk exercise would instead put new life into me. But alas! When I said as much to Mama, I was unfortunately seized with a coughing fit, which led her to raise her eyebrows and declare that I was delicate and must not think of going out of doors on foot.

But hold. I wonder if Elizabeth Bennet is the woman who has entranced Darcy? He was certainly very attentive to her when she was here. He walked over to the parsonage almost every day and he has never done that before. The only differences between this year and last were the presence of the new Mrs Collins and Miss Elizabeth. Since I cannot imagine Darcy putting himself out for Mrs Collins, who is very pleasant but unremarkable, I can only think he went there to see Miss Elizabeth.

If he is in love with her, I hope he marries her. In fact, I hope he marries anyone, as long as the woman is not me. Mama has always wanted a match between us but I could not marry him, even if I were not in love with Henry. You are right, dear coz, Darcy is one of the noblest men alive, but he frightens me. He is so very determined. He needs a stronger woman than I to be his wife. Miss Elizabeth, though, was not in awe of him; she teased him in a way that astonished me. She would make him an excellent wife. Her liveliness would counteract his stateliness and she would be a merry sister for you, and a merry cousin for me. But no, it cannot be. If she were the woman, then Darcy would have proposed by now and she would have accepted him, and we would all know of it. Unless they are waiting for her father's permission? It is interesting to speculate. But it is probably someone else who has caught his eye, or no one at all. I do hope there is a woman and that she is Elizabeth. Would it not be fun?

You must tell me if you hear anything more about a wife for Darcy, and send me any news you may have about Henry. I treasure everything I hear about him and I rely on you, since no one else knows my secret. I sometimes think I should make my feelings clear to him but alas! I am a woman and we are not allowed to do such things, otherwise I would gladly shout my love from the rooftops. Imagine Mama's face if I did! And imagine Mr Collins's face as he tried to decide whether to applaud me for my honesty or revile me for my forwardness, wondering all the time what Mama's reaction might be! I have half a mind to do it, just to see.

Write soon, dearest.

Your loving coz,
Anne

Mrs Charlotte Collins to Miss Elizabeth Bennet

Hunsford, near Westerham, Kent,
July 12

Dear Eliza,

I have some news which I hope will please you as much as it pleases me. I am going to have a child! I have just written to Mama but I wanted to write to you by the same post so that you will hear it first from me. I fear my mama will be a little too vocal in her delight. I fear, too, that your mama will be similarly vocal in her lack of delight. But I hope you will be pleased for me. I know you thought my marriage ill-advised but last year at this time I was nothing but Charlotte Lucas, spinster, with no life to call my own. Now I have my own home to care for, my parish affairs to interest me and a child on the way. I am happy with my lot.

Your friend,
Charlotte

Miss Elizabeth Bennet to Mrs Charlotte Collins

Longbourn, Hertfordshire,
July 18

Charlotte, of course I am delighted for you. Mama is less pleased and is even more vocal than you might imagine. Papa has retreated to his library and Jane and I now take regular refuge out of doors. Thank goodness for fine weather! Mary amuses herself by spouting words of wisdom, remarking on the blessing of an olive branch, and Kitty has written of it to Lydia. We were not allowed to see Lydia's reply. Kitty read it with many smothered giggles and furtive glances towards us, as though we were likely to steal it away from her, and when Papa asked her what it contained she said only that she would not betray a sister's confidence nor spoil Lydia's happiness. With this cryptic reply we had to be content, although I doubt that Lydia's letter contained much about your happy event, and suspect it contained a great deal about officers, red coats, private balls, assemblies and flirting.

Poor Kitty! It is very hard for her to read all about the exciting times Lydia is having when she is having so little excitement herself, apart from my aunt's card parties. I must confess, they are not so lively now that the officers have gone, but I am not sorry on the whole that they have left us.

My dear Jane is still quietly melancholy but does not complain. I am full of admiration for her fortitude. Luckily, she will have the little Gardiners to play with soon, for my young cousins are to stay here at Longbourn whilst I travel to Derbyshire with my uncle and aunt. The children's high spirits will lift Jane's own low mood, and Jane's steady sense and sweetness of temper will be exactly what they need as she teaches them, plays with them and loves them.

I have started a cap for the baby and hope to have finished a dozen by the time it arrives.

Lizzy

Mr Darcy to Colonel Fitzwilliam

Darcy House, London, July 20

Henry, it is done. I have encouraged Bingley to think of Jane Bennet once more. I told him something of my meeting with Miss Elizabeth at Rosings: that she had been staying with the Collinses and that I had spoken to her about her family. He asked hesitantly after her sisters and I told him that Miss Bennet had been out of spirits. I saw the workings of his mind flit across his face: that Jane was out of spirits because she missed him, and I saw hope rising within him. When he said he thought that he might return to Netherfield Park after his visit to Pemberley, I gave him my blessing.

It is enough that I have ruined my own chances of happiness; I will not ruin his as well.

I never before knew what a burden it was to be so admired. I have become so used to looking after everyone and everything since my father died—my sister, the tenants, the estate, the Pemberley staff, my friend—that I had forgotten that some of them were capable of taking care of themselves. And I have come to realise something else as well: that I do not always know what is best for everyone else. I wish I could say that I had come to this knowledge on my own, but it is Elizabeth who has shown it to me. I resented her for it at first, but now I thank her for it.

I will be taking Georgiana to Pemberley in August. If you have not returned to your regiment by then, I hope you will join us. We will be quite a party, and you will be well entertained. You will meet

Caroline, Louisa and Charles there, and I have invited the rector of Kympton, Mr Haydock, too. I like him. He is intelligent and sensible and yet he is also lively and a favourite with his parishioners. I think he will like Georgiana and she him. Not that I am thinking of her marrying him, but it will do her good to have some more young men to mix with; she knows so very few of them at the moment and I want her to become accustomed to their ways before she has her formal come-out.

Darcy

Miss Elizabeth Bennet to Miss Jane Bennet

Derbyshire, July 30

My dearest Jane,

Our Derbyshire adventure is filled with as much novelty and amusement as I had hoped; indeed, if not for your absence, it would be perfect. We have passed through Oxford, stopping to see the university and then going on to visit the palace at Blenheim. As we travelled farther north, passing through Birmingham and then on into Derbyshire, the landscape began to change into something altogether wilder than anything I have so far seen. I never thought such hills existed in our country. The roads climbed constantly, so that we often left the carriage and walked in order to spare the horses until they reached the summit of the moors, which are truly splendid. I have never seen such grandeur of landscape. Standing on top of the moors it is possible to see for miles, and to believe oneself at the end of the world, for apart from a few sheep there is nothing to be seen in the remoter areas, save swathes of harsh grasses, large boulders and picturesque stone walls. We are too early to see the heather, but my aunt tells me it covers the moors with a purple cloak in the late summer and I hope to come back again one day and see it.

We have been blessed with fine weather and we walk each day, sometimes by the side of boulder-strewn rivers and sometimes through woodland, as well as visiting any houses of note along the way. My aunt is eager to see Chatsworth, and I am just as eager to visit it.

One place I am not so eager to visit is Lambton. Although I have some curiosity to see my aunt's old neighbourhood, it is so close to Pemberley that I am apprehensive about it, for Pemberley is exactly the kind of great house my aunt likes to visit. I have thought of taking her into my confidence, but it would lead to so many questions that I cannot bring myself to do it. If she insists on seeing Pemberley, therefore, I intend to make enquiries as to whether or not the family is at home, and if they are, I think I will plead a headache and remain at the inn.

How are my cousins going on? Are they plaguing you? Not too much, I hope. I dare not ask if Kitty and Mary are plaguing you, let alone our mother, as I fear I know the answer to that already.

I must go. My aunt is ready to go out. We will be at Lambton by the time a reply is able to reach us, so write to me at the inn there; we plan to reach it by August fourth.

Your loving sister,
Lizzy

✤ AUGUST ✤

Brighton, August 1

Lord! Kitty! What a lark. You will never guess and you must not tell, not until it is done and I can sign my name Lydia Wickham! Is it not a good joke? My dear Wickham and I are eloping. The next time I write to you I will be Mrs Wickham! You must come and stay with us, we will be returning to Brighton or perhaps London, just as soon as we get back from Gretna Green. Is it not romantic? We will be married in Scotland, over the anvil. I will be married at sixteen! And my sisters not yet married, and all of them older than me. I will get a husband for you as soon as I return, never fear. There are officers aplenty in Brighton and we must go back there eventually, for Wickham's regiment is there. You might marry Denny or Pratt or Colonel Fitzwilliam, though he is not very handsome, but they cannot all be as handsome as my Wickham. Lord! What a lark! I thought I would die laughing when Wickham said we could run away together! How surprised Harriet will be. They will all be astonished. It will be the talk of Brighton and I dare say I will be the toast of the officers. Only tell no one of it. You know how Lizzy and Jane tried to stop me going to Brighton in the first place, they will only try to spoil my fun if they know. Mama would not do anything to spoil it, but she would tell everyone and I want to tell them myself, you know.

Your soon-to-be-married sister,
Lydia

Mr Wickham to Mrs Younge

Brighton, August 2

Belle, I am in a fix. I thought I would have longer credit here but the shopkeepers in Brighton are used to being swindled and they have started demanding payment. I found a line of creditors at my door this evening and had to climb out of the window. Lydia Bennet saw me but thought it was all a lark. When I said I would have to leave Brighton, she said we should elope. You know me, Belle, I cannot say no to a woman, and the upshot is that I am on the point of escaping to London. I will need somewhere to stay until things blow over. Do you still have your boarding house? I hope so, for I have nowhere else to go. I will be there sometime tomorrow.

Hoping this letter reaches you before I do,
George

Miss Lydia Bennet to Mrs Harriet Forster

Brighton, August 2

My dear Harriet,

You will laugh when you know where I am gone, and I cannot help laughing myself at your surprise tomorrow morning, as soon as I am missed. I am going to Gretna Green, and if you cannot guess with who, I shall think you a simpleton, for there is but one man in the world I love, and he is an angel. I should never be happy without him, so think it no harm to be off. You need not send them word at Longbourn of my going, if you do not like it, for it will make the surprise the greater, when I write to them, and sign my name Lydia Wickham. What a good joke it will be! I can hardly write for laughing. Pray make my excuses to Pratt for not keeping my engagement, and dancing with him tonight. Tell him I hope he will excuse me when he knows all, and tell him I will dance with him at the next ball we meet, with great pleasure. I shall send for my clothes when I get to Longbourn; but I wish you would tell Sally to mend a great slit in my worked muslin gown before they are packed up. Good-bye. Give my love to Colonel Forster. I hope you will drink to our good journey.

Your affectionate friend,
Lydia Bennet

Miss Jane Bennet to Miss Elizabeth Bennet

Longbourn, Hertfordshire,
August 3

Dearest Lizzy,

I knew you would enjoy yourself with my aunt and uncle and I am glad you are now having your share of the amusements. I would have liked to have you with me in London earlier in the year, but it would have been too cruel to deprive our father of both of us at once. He misses you sorely, and I believe he might even write to you in a few days' time. In the meantime, you will want to know what we have been doing in Hertfordshire. We had a card party at my aunt Philips's house the night before last and then yesterday we went to dinner with the Lucases. Lady Lucas could talk of nothing but Charlotte's impending happy event and Mama could not help being disagreeable. I have started a bonnet for Charlotte's baby. I could not decide whether to make it blue or pink and so I have settled on yellow.

My cousins keep me busy. In the morning I help them with their reading and in the afternoons we spend most of our time out of doors. Mary, too, helps with their education, although I do not think that Fordyce's Sermons are of much use to the little ones, since they cannot understand one word in ten. Kitty plays with them sometimes but more often she is shut up in her room, writing to Lydia or reading letters from her. I must say that Lydia has surprised me. I did not think she would be such a regular correspondent. She still sends no more than a few short notes to Mama and Papa, but her letters to Kitty arrive with increasing frequency and Kitty laughs and giggles as she reads them. I am glad she is happy again.

I can write no more at present, my cousins need me, but I will finish my letter tomorrow. For now, adieu.

August 4

Since writing the above, dearest Lizzy, something has occurred of a most unexpected and serious nature; but I am afraid of alarming you—be assured that we are all well. What I have to say relates to poor Lydia. An express came at twelve last night, just as we were all gone to bed, from Colonel Forster, to inform us that she was gone off to Scotland with one of his officers; to own the truth, with Wickham! Imagine our surprise. To Kitty, however, it does not seem so wholly unexpected. I am very, very sorry. So imprudent a match on both sides! But I am willing to hope the best, and that his character has been misunderstood. Thoughtless and indiscreet I can easily believe him, but this step (and let us rejoice over it) marks nothing bad at heart. His choice is disinterested at least, for he must know my father can give her nothing. Our poor mother is sadly grieved. My father bears it better. How thankful am I that we never let them know what has been said against him! We must forget it ourselves. They were off Saturday night about twelve, as is conjectured, but were not missed till yesterday morning at eight. The express was sent off directly. My dear Lizzy, they must have passed within ten miles of us. Colonel Forster gives us reason to expect him here soon. Lydia left a few lines for his wife, informing her of their intention. I must conclude, for I cannot be long from my poor mother. I am afraid you will not be able to make it out, but I hardly know what I have written.

Jane

Miss Mary Bennet to Miss Lucy Sotherton

Longbourn, Hertfordshire,
August 4

Most noble Friend,

My sister Lydia is ruined. I am not surprised. If ever a girl was born to be ruined, it is Lydia. She has run away with an officer. Mama has spent the day bewailing her poor baby's fate, though as I remarked to Mama, Lydia is not in point of fact a baby, but a young lady of sixteen summers. Mama ignored me, saying that if she had only had her way we would all have gone to Brighton. When I said that if she had carried the day, she might now have four daughters who had run away with officers instead of only one (since I would never have done anything so foolish), she told me that she wished I would run away and then I would not be able to plague her with my moralising. Poor Mama! She would never be accepted into the bluestockings, for she has far too many nerves.

My sister Jane has spent the morning writing to Elizabeth,

whilst I have spent my time more profitably by searching for suitable extracts to sustain my family in their hour of need.

Your sister in moral rectitude,
Mary

Miss Jane Bennet to Miss Elizabeth Bennet

Longbourn, Hertfordshire,
August 5

By this time, my dearest sister, you have received my hurried letter; I wish this may be more intelligible, but though not confined for time, my head is so bewildered that I cannot answer for being coherent. Dearest Lizzy, I hardly know what I would write, but I have bad news for you, and it cannot be delayed. Imprudent as a marriage between Mr Wickham and our poor Lydia would be, we are now anxious to be assured it has taken place, for there is but too much reason to fear they are not gone to Scotland. Colonel Forster came yesterday, having left Brighton the day before, not many hours after the express. Though Lydia's short letter to Mrs Forster gave them to understand that they were going to Gretna Green, something was dropped by Denny expressing his belief that Wickham never intended to go there, or to marry Lydia at all, which was repeated to Colonel Forster, who, instantly taking the alarm, set off from Brighton, intending to trace their route. He did trace them easily to Clapham, but no farther; for on entering that place they removed into a hackney coach, and dismissed the chaise that brought them from Epsom. All that is known after this is that they were seen to continue the London road. I know not what to think. After making every possible enquiry on that side of London, Colonel Forster came on into Hertfordshire, anxiously renewing them at all the turnpikes, and at the inns in Barnet and Hatfield, but without any success—no such people had been seen to pass through. With the kindest concern he came on to Longbourn, and broke his apprehensions to us in a manner most creditable to his heart. I am sincerely grieved for him and Mrs Forster, but no one can throw any blame on them. Our distress, my dear Lizzy, is very great. My father and mother believe the worst, but I cannot think so ill of him. Many circumstances might make it more eligible for them to be married privately in town than to pursue their first plan; and even if *he* could form such a design against a young woman of Lydia's connections, which is not likely, can I suppose her so lost to everything? Impossible! I grieve to find, however, that Colonel Forster is not disposed to depend upon their marriage; he shook his head when I expressed my hopes, and said he feared Wickham was not a man to be trusted. My poor mother is really ill, and keeps her room. Could she exert herself, it would be better; but this is not to be expected. And as to my father, I never in my life saw him so affected. Poor Kitty has incurred their anger for having concealed the attachment; but as it was a matter of confidence, one cannot wonder.

I am truly glad, dearest Lizzy, that you have been spared something of these distressing scenes; but now, as the first shock is over, shall I own that I long for your return? I am not so selfish, however, as to press for it, if inconvenient. Adieu!

I take up my pen again to do what I have just told you I would not; but circumstances are such that I cannot help earnestly begging you all to come here as soon as possible. I know my dear uncle and aunt so well that I am not afraid of requesting it, though I have still something more to ask of the former. My father is going to London with Colonel Forster instantly, to try to discover her. What he means to do I am sure I know not; but his excessive distress will not allow him to pursue any measure in the best and safest way, and Colonel Forster is obliged to be at Brighton again tomorrow evening. In such an exigence my uncle's advice and assistance would be everything in the world; he will immediately comprehend what I must feel, and I rely upon his goodness.

Jane

Mr Darcy to Colonel Fitzwilliam

Carriage, on the way to London,
August 8

Something terrible has happened. Wickham! How I curse his name! Oh, do not fear, it is not Georgiana he has run away with this time, but another young woman. If you have not yet returned to your regiment, meet me in London at my club. If you cannot meet me, pray let me know Mrs Younge's address as soon as possible; I know you discovered it last year and I have urgent need of it.

But I must explain. I must go back, in fact, to make you understand my interest in the matter, nay my determination to put everything right.

I returned to Pemberley a few days ago and having occasion to ride on ahead of the rest of the party in order to attend to some business with my steward, I turned the corner of the stables to find myself looking into the eyes of Elizabeth Bennet! Never had they looked more beautiful, and never had I been more tempted to take her in my arms and kiss her, but I could do nothing except stand and stare. I thought for a moment it must be a dream, a hallucination, for the day was very hot, but when she blushed I knew it was not a dream. Recovering myself, I advanced and spoke to her, if not composedly, at least civilly. As I spoke I could not stop my eyes from roving over her, taking in every small detail of her face and hair. From the depth and beauty of her eyes to the remaining blush on her cheek, I was drinking her in.

She turned away, embarrassed, but she turned towards me again when I spoke to her. I know not what I said; something about the weather, her journey, my surprise at seeing her, the date on which she left Longbourn, her stay in Derbyshire and the health of her family; in short, nothing, but simply words to hold her so that I would have more time to look at her and love her and wonder how I ever thought I would be able to conquer my feelings for her. And all the while she was as uncomfortable as I was, and yet she did not turn away; not after the first time, which, I am convinced, was only because of embarrassment.

And when I could think of nothing further to say, I still remained rooted to the spot, unable to leave, unwilling to relinquish one second of her company, glad to be with her, wanting to be near her; wanting to look at her, and to hear the sound of her breathing and to feel my fingers shiver with the desire to reach out and touch her.

I still want her. I cannot disguise it from myself. No one else will ever do. Only Elizabeth.

I knew it as I stood there, unable to leave, whilst the gardener looked at me curiously and her aunt and uncle watched me from a distance and I knew I must depart, but could not.

At last I tore myself away and went indoors, making sure that the house was ready to receive my guests, as had been my original plan. But I could not remain long indoors. I wanted to be near her, and to show her that her reprovals had been attended to; that I was no longer insufferable or disdainful of the feelings of others; that I had changed.

And so I left the house. I found her at last as she walked by the river. She was at that part of the grounds where the path is open and I saw her long before I reached her. I could tell she saw me, too. The walk seemed endless. A turning in the path hid her from view and then I was suddenly in front of her. Mindful of her previous words about my incivility, I set out to please and to charm her. She seemed to sense it and to want to imitate my politeness. She remarked on the beauty of the place, then blushed and fell silent, as if remembering that, had she accepted my proposal, it could have been hers. Any other woman would have made it hers, even if she despised me. But not Elizabeth. Only love will do for her. And I have known, deep down, for many years, that only love will do for me.

Our conversation faltered and I asked if she would do me the honour of introducing me to her friends. Something of her mischievousness returned, for she smiled with a gleam in her eye as she introduced them as her aunt and uncle. I was surprised; I knew they lived in Cheapside and had therefore not expected them to be so fashionable. To please her, and to show her I was not the rude, arrogant and unfeeling man she thought me, I walked with them, all the time wondering how I could make sure I saw her again. Her party were on a travelling holiday and I did not want them to leave Derbyshire, and so I hit upon the happy notion of inviting her uncle to fish at Pemberley.

And so we continued, the two ladies in front and the two gentlemen behind. I was just wondering how I could alter things when luck played into my hands. Her aunt became tired and leant on her husband's arm, leaving me free to walk with Elizabeth. There was a silence, but I was not anxious. I was content to catch her scent and to watch the play of colour on her cheek. But she was not easy and soon made it clear that she had been told the family were away from home, and that she would not have taken the liberty of visiting Pemberley otherwise.

I blessed my good fortune. A day later and I would have been in residence, in which case she would not have come; a day earlier and I would have been in London and missed her. I acknowledged that I had arrived earlier than expected and told her that Bingley and his sisters would be joining me.

It was not a happy thought. She became withdrawn and I could tell that her thoughts had returned to her sister and my interference in the matter of Bingley's attentions. I sought to divert her and found a happy topic in my own sister, asking if I might introduce Georgiana to her during her stay at Lambton. She was surprised, but agreed, and I was content. I would very much like the two of them to come to know each other.

We walked on in silence, each deep in thought. My mind was wondering how I could have stayed away from her so long and wondering how soon I could offer her my hand again. Her mind I did not know, but I hoped it was not entirely set against me.

We reached the carriage and I invited her to walk into the house as her relations were some quarter of a mile behind. She declined, saying she was not tired, and we talked of nothing in particular but each one of us, I am sure, was thinking a great deal. At last her aunt and uncle joined us and the three of them departed.

My thoughts were turbulent, as you might imagine, but the following morning I took Georgiana to meet her and the two of them liked each other. Bingley was with us, and talked of the Netherfield ball. It showed me once and for all that he has not forgotten Miss Bennet, and I am now resolved to do everything in my power to encourage him to see her again.

The meeting was not without its embarrassments, but they were less than formerly and I courted the good opinion of not only Elizabeth but her relations. She saw it, and from time to time a gleam of astonishment lit her eye. I had not realised until then how rude my behaviour had been at Netherfield, for my present civility surprised her.

We stayed only half an hour. I wanted to stay longer. I would have been happy to remain there for the rest of my life. But courtesy compelled me to take my leave—not, however, until I had secured her promise to dine with us the following day.

The evening passed slowly but not unpleasantly, and when my guests had gone to bed I walked the halls of Pemberley, imagining Elizabeth's step on the stairs, her laughter in the garden, her singing in the drawing room, her brightness and vivacity filling the house and bringing it back to life; for ever since my parents died, a part of Pemberley has been dead.

Her visit to take tea with Georgiana the following day only intensified my feelings and all was going well until this morning, when I paid a visit to the inn at Lambton and found Elizabeth in a state of great distress. I was immediately alarmed and thought she must be ill, but she broke down and revealed that she had just received a letter from home, and that her sister Lydia had run away with George Wickham!

I longed to comfort her, to go to her and put my arms around her, to let her cry against my shoulder, but I could do nothing without outraging propriety and occasioning gossip, so I did what little I could, sending for her aunt and uncle. But I am determined not to rest until I have rescued her sister and relieved her from the agony of this despicable affair.

And so now you see why it is imperative I find Wickham.

I hope you can decipher this letter. I am writing it in the carriage and the potholes are playing havoc with my penmanship. I never thought it would be so long but my feelings have run away with me. A glance out of the window shows me that we are approaching London and I must finish my letter quickly. I must right this wrong, for my own sake as well as Lydia Bennet's. If I had explained his character, given some hint of it when I was at Netherfield last autumn, this could not have happened. The girl would have been on her guard against him; or, at least, if she was too foolish to heed the warning, then Forster would have been alerted to the danger and kept a better eye on her.

I pray you are still in London and that I will find you there, but if not, I will leave this letter for you at Fitzwilliam House. Come to me at once, and of course say nothing of this to anyone. All may yet be well and the girl's reputation saved. Though she is not a blameless innocent, as Georgiana was, still she does not deserve this, and neither does Elizabeth.

Darcy

Miss Susan Sotherton to Mrs Charlotte Collins

Bath, August 9

How very glad I was to hear your exciting news. If it is a girl, I hope she grows up to be just like you, if a boy, I hope he grows up like . . . well, I cannot think of any suitable man for him to emulate. It would certainly be better if he did not grow up like any of the men in my family. I hope he grows up to be someone very good and brave and intelligent. In fact, if he is a boy, I think it would be simpler if he should just grow up to be like you as well! Pray let me be a godmother.

My news is less exciting, but glorious nonetheless. I have chosen my wedding dress. Madame Chloe is to make it for me, after one of the fashions in *La Belle Assemblée*. It is in the latest Grecian style, with a high waist, a round neck, short sleeves and a sash. I am enclosing a sketch so that you can see how delicious it is. Mama and I are going to London tomorrow to buy the silk at Grafton House. We intend to stay there for a few days so that we can buy everything else I will need as well; all except my shoes, which I am having made here in Bath. They will be made of white silk to match the dress.

I never thought my wedding outfit would be half so fine. Indeed, there were times in the last few years when I thought I would have to dress in rags, but now that I am to marry a rich husband I can buy whatever I please. I am very vain, I dare say, but I am enjoying every minute of it.

We are going to have the ceremony in Bath. I did hope, when Elizabeth said Mr Bingley had left Netherfield, that he would give notice, then we could return there for a few months and I could be married from home. But although Mr Bingley stays away, it seems he does not want to relinquish his tenancy. I am disappointed for my own sake but I am pleased for Jane. I have quiet hopes that he keeps Netherfield Park because he wants to see her again, and wishes to continue his pursuit of her. Let us hope so, for never a dearer creature lived than Jane Bennet.

By the bye, do you have Elizabeth's address? I know she is in Derbyshire with her aunt and uncle, and her last letter told me where she expected to be for the next week, but I have somehow misplaced it. Or, to tell the truth, my father burnt it with a pile of other papers in a fit of rage. I believe he thought it was a bill. You will tell from this that he is no better and that we all despair of him ever retrenching and conserving what little is left of his fortune. Luckily, I will soon be married and I will not have to worry about his temper any longer, nor his drinking nor his gambling nor anything else. I am very glad my dear Mr Wainwright has none of these vices; he is the most amiable man that ever lived and I am very much looking forward to being his wife.

If you have Elizabeth's address, pray let me have it, for I want to send her a sketch of my wedding dress. I hope she is enjoying herself in Derbyshire. Indeed she must be, for her aunt and uncle are sensible, intelligent people and Derbyshire itself is very fine. After all the vicissitudes of her life over the last few months I am sure that no one deserves a little happiness more than Elizabeth, and I wish her a handsome husband, just like my Mr Wainwright.

Write to me soon,
Susan

Lady Lucas to Mrs Charlotte Collins

Lucas Lodge, Hertfordshire,
August 10

Charlotte, such news! Far be it from me to take pleasure in the misfortune of our neighbours, but the Bennets are disgraced! Lydia has done what I always said she would, and run away with one of the officers. You probably remember him, he was here before you married: a handsome fellow by the name of George Wickham. He was very charming to be sure, but there was something about him that was not quite right. I thought so at the time. 'Depend upon it,' I said to your father, 'that man will come to a bad end.' And now I am proved right, for not only has he run off with Lydia, he has left a mountain of debts behind. Mrs Bennet keeps to her room and will have no one but Hill to look after her, for fear the other servants will gossip, but it is impossible to keep such a thing quiet. I had it from the butcher's boy, who had it from the Bennets' maid. Mrs Bennet is in hysterics and even Mr Bennet is shaken out of his customary complacency.

I am sorry for them, of course, but they are sadly to blame. If they had looked after Lydia better, and not indulged her so much, it would have been a different tale. But Mrs Bennet *would* bring Lydia out when she was only fifteen, instead of waiting until she was sixteen as is customary, and then encouraged her in her wild ways. I am sure I would have been mortified if one of my daughters had flirted with all the officers in such a way, laughing and joking and getting up to who knows what kind of mischief. And then to let her go to Brighton, unguarded, with no one but Colonel and Mrs Forster to take care of her...it is no wonder she came by such an unhappy fate. If the Bennets had looked after her properly, as Sir William and I looked after you, she could have one day married a good and decent man like Mr Collins.

Ah, Mr Collins! You have done well, Charlotte, very well, with your marriage. Such a fine parsonage! And such a patroness! And the chimney piece at Rosings costing eight hundred pounds!

I am to visit Mrs Bennet again this afternoon, and I mean to take her some jam. I am sure there is nothing like it for making the world seem a brighter place and she will need it, poor woman, to comfort her in her family's disgrace.

Your affectionate
Mother

Mrs Charlotte Collins to Miss Susan Sotherton

Hunsford, near Westerham, Kent,
August 11

Susan, have you not heard? There is great trouble in the Bennet household. Mama has written to me about it three times already. Elizabeth is once more at Longbourn, and Lydia has run away with George Wickham. It is the talk of the neighbourhood.

Mrs Bennet went off into hysterics and of course it was then impossible to keep it from the servants and it was all round Meryton in the hour. Mama went round to the Bennets' at once, to condole with Mrs Bennet and to offer her services. She wrote to me of it as soon as she returned to Lucas Lodge. Poor Elizabeth and Jane! They have to bear the burden of it, for Kitty is no help and Mary is more interested in sermonizing than making herself useful. This will be a sore trial for our friends. It seems that Mr Wickham is not the man everyone thought him, for he has not paid his debts and it transpires that this is not his first attempt at seduction.

He was very attentive to Mary King when she inherited a fortune and he was also very attentive to Elizabeth at one time. Thank God she resisted him!

The latest news is that Mr Bennet has gone to London to try and find Lydia. I hope for everyone's sake that she is soon discovered. But I must go, I hear Mr Collins's step in the corridor. Alas! he was in the room when I read the first letter from Mama, and as I could not help exclaiming when I read of Lydia's elopement, it was impossible for me to keep it from him. I fear he means to write to the Bennets, despite my best efforts to discourage him.

Your dear friend,
Charlotte

Miss Mary Bennet to Miss Lucy Sotherton

Longbourn, Hertfordshire,
August 11

Most noble Friend,

Let us rejoice that we have followed the path of womanly virtue and that we have not strayed into the wilderness of infamy that is the present abode of my sister Lydia, for she has run away with George Wickham. Let us give thanks that our studies have prepared us for the wickedness of men, so that we are warned against them, and that their blandishments have not succeeded in luring us from the tranquillity of our families to a certain doom.

My sister Elizabeth has returned home, summoned by Jane, and she is much chastened, for she sees now the sense of my studies, which she was inclined to deride. She sits with my mother and attempts to console her, but Mama is beyond consolation.

My father has gone to London to look for Lydia, and to make Wickham marry her, but I fear his efforts will be in vain. Mama expects Lydia to be found and talks often of Lydia's marriage, but Lydia is not the sort of young lady that men marry. She is the sort of young lady that men run off with and then abandon to a life of poverty and vice.

I have memorised some of my extracts and I comforted my sisters by telling them that although it was a most unfortunate affair, and one which would be much talked of, we must stem the tide of malice and pour into the wounded bosoms of each other the balm of sisterly consolation.

Elizabeth was humbled into silence by my wise words, and, seeing how affected she was, I added that, unhappy as the event must be for Lydia, we could draw from it a useful lesson: that loss of virtue in a female is irretrievable; that one false step involves her in endless ruin; that her reputation is no less brittle than it is beautiful; and that she cannot be too much guarded in her behaviour towards the undeserving of the other sex.

Elizabeth was speechless with admiration.

Mr Shackleton, too, who had learnt of the matter from my aunt, thought the sentiments very well expressed.

I have given him leave to copy them into his book of extracts.

Your sister in virtue,
Mary

Mr Gardiner to Mrs Gardiner

Gracechurch Street, London,
August 11

My dear wife,

You will be anxious to hear what little news I have, though I wish it could be more, and more to the point. However, I have found Mr Bennet and persuaded him to come to Gracechurch Street, so that we are both here now at home. He has already been to Epsom and Clapham to try and discover something from the hackney carriage drivers, though without gaining any satisfactory information, and he is now determined to enquire at all the principal hotels in town in case the young couple spent the night at one of them before procuring lodgings. I do not expect any success from this measure, but as he is eager to be doing something, I mean to assist him in pursuing it. I have tried to persuade him to leave London when it is done, but he will not hear of it. I wish he would return to Longbourn. There is nothing he can do here that I cannot do, and his agitation makes him ill suited to doing what little can be done. However, if he will not leave then he will not leave and I must hope for better things tomorrow. I will write again very soon and let you know how we go on.

Your loving husband,
EG

 P.S. I have written to Colonel Forster to desire him to find out, if possible, from some of the young man's intimates in the regiment, whether Wickham has any relations or connections who would be likely to know in what part of the town he has now concealed himself. If there were anyone that one could apply to, with a probability of gaining such a clue as that, it might be of essential consequence. At present we have nothing to guide us. Colonel Forster will, I dare say, do everything in his power to satisfy us on this head. But, on second thought, perhaps Lizzy could tell us what relations he has now living, better than any other person.

Mr Collins to Mr Bennet

Hunsford, near Westerham, Kent,
August 12

My dear Sir,

I feel myself called upon, by our relationship, and my situation in life, to condole with you on the grievous affliction you are now suffering under, of which we were yesterday informed by a letter from Hertfordshire. Be assured, my dear sir, that Mrs Collins and myself sincerely sympathise with you, and all your respectable family, in your present distress, which must be of the bitterest kind, because proceeding from a cause which no time can remove. No arguments shall be wanting on my part that can alleviate so severe a misfortune—or that may comfort you, under a circumstance that must be of all others most afflicting to a parent's mind. The death of your daughter would have been a blessing in comparison of this. And it is the more to be lamented, because there is reason to suppose, as my dear Charlotte informs me, that this licentiousness of behaviour in your daughter has proceeded from a faulty degree of indulgence; though, at the same time, for the consolation of yourself and Mrs Bennet, I am inclined to think that her own disposition must be naturally bad, or she could not be guilty of such an enormity, at so early an age. Howsoever that may be, you are grievously to be pitied; in which opinion I am not only joined by Mrs Collins, but likewise by Lady Catherine and her daughter, to whom I have related the affair. They agree with me in apprehending that this false step in one daughter will be injurious to the fortunes of all the others, for who, as Lady Catherine herself condescendingly says, will connect themselves with such a family? And this consideration leads me moreover to reflect with augmented satisfaction on a certain event of last November, for had it been otherwise, I must have been involved in all your sorrow and disgrace. Let me advise you then, my dear sir, to console yourself as much as possible, to throw off your unworthy child from your affection forever, and leave her to reap the fruits of her own heinous offence.

I am, dear sir, your faithful servant,
William Collins

Miss Lucy Sotherton to Miss Mary Bennet

Bath, August 12

Hail!

I am saddened, nay grieved, to learn of the fate of your sister, but—may I say it?—not surprised. Many are the times I tried to tempt her back to the path of Athena by my sagacious reasoning and learned erudition, but she only laughed at me and said that she preferred men in pantaloons to women in pulpits. And now we see the end of the path of perdition, where your sister lies prostrate with grief, weeping over her lost virtue; or, worse yet, laughing in the face of virtue and drinking cheap spirits from the bottom of life's grimiest bottle.

If news reaches you of Lydia's ultimate fate, you will find a sympathetic listener in me, no matter how shocking that news might be; for too well do I know that you do not share in her immorality and that you have renounced the fleshpots for the pure world of wisdom where you and I, dearest friend, will reside for eternity.

Your faithful friend,
Lucy

Miss Mary Bennet to Miss Lucy Sotherton

Longbourn, Hertfordshire,
August 13

Most noble Friend,

Thank you for the noble sentiments expressed in your reply to my last and for your belief in my own unsullied virtue. I am continuing to write in my book of extracts, and my family now see the wisdom of it, indeed they are dumbstruck every time I open my book. If only they had paid more attention to their own education, they, too, could have had a ready store of solace close to hand.

The only one of my family to have emerged from this disaster in a favourable light is Mr Collins. He has written to my father and, Jane being instructed to open and read any letter that arrived in my father's absence, I have had the pleasure of discovering its contents. It was a very sensible letter in which he has advised my father to throw off his unworthy child from his affection forever, and leave her to reap the fruits of her own heinous offence. His sentiments were so ably expressed that I have borrowed his letter and I have copied it into my book of extracts.

Your fellow sister along the path of wisdom and virtue,
Mary

Miss Lucy Sotherton to Miss Mary Bennet

Bath, August 14

Hail!

I am glad that you are continuing with your studies at this grievous time, but I must warn you that I detected in your letter a lingering admiration for your enticing cousin, Mr Collins. Let your sister's fate serve as a warning. Mr Collins is not for you. He has given his hand elsewhere, and no matter how learned his discourse or how just his sentiments as he expresses his proper opprobrium of your sister's fall, you must not sink into the pit of depravity by coveting your neighbour's ox nor ass; not even when that ass is as alluring as Mr Collins.

With any other correspondent I would have to explain myself, dearest friend, but you will understand at once that I am alluding to the scriptures and that I am not likening your revered cousin to a farmyard animal; for his voice is the honeyed voice of reason and not the braying of a donkey. But no matter how soft his voice or how perspicacious his reasoning, he belongs to Mrs Collins, your erstwhile, if not wholly deserving, neighbour.

Take comfort, dear friend, in the history I am sending you, of an orphan lost in the forest. Arm yourself with her fortitude, and give thanks that your tragedies are not those of one whom the fates have abandoned, for you still have your parents, woeful though they may be, and a dear friend who will call your feet back to the straight and narrow whenever they are tempted to stray.

Your sister beneath the skin,
Lucy

Mr Gardiner to Mrs Gardiner

Gracechurch Street, London,
August 15

My dear wife,

I am sorry for the long gap between this letter and my last but I did not want to write again till I had received an answer from Colonel Forster; I only wish I had something of a more pleasant nature to send. Colonel Forster has made extensive enquiries but as far as he can discover, Wickham does not have a single relation with whom he kept up any connection, and it was certain that he has no near one living. His former acquaintances have been numerous; but since he has been in the militia, it does not appear that he was on terms of particular friendship with any of them. There was no one, therefore, who could be pointed out as likely to give any news of him. And in the wretched state of his own finances, there was a very powerful motive for secrecy, in addition to his fear of discovery by Lydia's relations, for it has just transpired that he had left gaming debts behind him to a very considerable amount. Colonel Forster believes that more than a thousand pounds would be necessary to clear his expenses at Brighton. He owes a good deal in the town, but his debts of honour are still more formidable.

The only good news that I have to send is that I have persuaded Mr Bennet to return to Longbourn. He has been rendered spiritless by the ill-success of his endeavours and he has at last yielded to my entreaties, for which I am very grateful. He will be more use to his family in Meryton than he is here. I will continue the search and do everything in my power to discover the young couple.

I hope you will then feel free to return to Gracechurch Street. I believe that Jane and Elizabeth are over the worst of the shock, and once their father is home, they will have someone to support them through this time of trial.

Your loving husband,
EG

Mr Darcy to Colonel Fitzwilliam

Darcy House, London, August 17

My dear Henry,

Thank God you knew Mrs Younge's address, for it is only that which allowed me to discover Wickham. I tried to persuade Miss Lydia to leave him, promising to escort her back to her family, but she refused my help and expressed her intention of staying with him. It was evident that she believed him when he said he would marry her, and she thought an elopement to Gretna Green was imminent, just as soon as he had raised the money for the carriage fare. Nothing I could say would change her mind and at last I could do nothing more for her than make him agree to marry her; although, I say 'for her' when in fact I did it all for Elizabeth. It was Elizabeth I thought of as I engaged with Wickham, and the thought of her suffering which forced me to continue long after I would have left him otherwise.

He was insolent and impertinent, as you can imagine, and he soon returned to his favourite subject, the living of Kympton. He had the audacity to tell me that if I honoured my late father's wishes, he would be happy to become a clergyman, and as a clergyman he would take Miss Lydia to wife.

I replied in short order that the living had been given to Mark Haydock, an excellent man of intelligence and sound common sense, who was in robust health and likely to hold the position until he was ninety, and that therefore the living was no longer available.

He hung out for as long as he could, but when he saw that I was immovable on the subject, he started to bargain more rationally. I had little inclination to bargain with him, God knows! but I promised to pay his debts and, furthermore, give him something to live on. He at last agreed, for he knew that his only choice was to face his creditors: I left him in no doubt that if he did not marry Miss Lydia, then I would give them his address. With no money to fly, he was caught.

My next step was to visit Elizabeth's uncle and tell him what had been arranged. He was surprised, and at first refused to let me help in any way. But a thoughtful look gradually crept over his face and I could see that he guessed I had done it for Elizabeth's sake.

From that moment on, he had no more objection to make. He agreed to say nothing of my involvement to anyone, and he further agreed to ask Mr Bennet to make a small contribution to the affair, in order to convince Mr Bennet that matters were not so bad and to make him feel that he is, himself, setting matters to rights.

I, of course, will bear the burden of Wickham's debts.

As for Wickham, he will quit the militia, where he is no longer welcome and where Lydia's disgrace is known, and he will go into the regulars. I have undertaken to help him acquire an ensigncy in the north. Lydia will now stay with her uncle until the wedding takes place. It cannot be until September because the banns must be read, but once it is done, Lydia and Wickham will go north and, I very much hope, out of my life for good.

It is a bad business, but I am thankful it is no worse.

I have sworn Mr Gardiner to secrecy. I do not want Elizabeth to know what I have done. She would be grateful and I do not want her gratitude, I want her love. I have done little enough to earn it but I must win it, for nothing else will make me happy.

Darcy

Mrs Bennet to Mrs Gardiner

Longbourn, Hertfordshire,
August 19, ten o'clock

Sister! What a fortunate day this is! I knew that Lydia would be married if only she could go to Brighton, and see, she is! Only sixteen! Lucky, lucky Lydia, to be marrying such a handsome man! And to be married before all her sisters! Tell her she must have the finest muslins from Grafton House and to send the bills to her father. And she must have a new carriage. I believe there are some very good carriage makers in town. There are one or two houses within a few miles of Longbourn which I think might suit her. Haye-Park might do, if the Gouldings would quit it, or the great house at Stoke, if the drawing room were larger; but Ashworth is too far off! I could not bear to have her ten miles from me; and as for Purvis Lodge, the attics are dreadful. But we will find somewhere for her before very long.

I will include a note for my own dear girl; pray give it to her for me.

Your affectionate sister,
Janet

Mrs Bennet to Miss Lydia Bennet

Longbourn, Hertfordshire,
August 19, eleven o'clock

My dear Lydia!

Happy was the day you went to Brighton! If I had had my way, we would have all gone, and I dare say all of your sisters would have found husbands by now, but I was overruled. Is it any wonder I am a martyr to my nerves? But at least one of my daughters has found herself a husband, and at only sixteen! Clever, clever Lydia! What fun you will have, showing your ring off to everyone in Meryton. I was wild to come down to London to be with you but your father has forbidden me to leave the house. He says your aunt and uncle will do everything that is necessary, but what is an aunt to a mother? I wanted to help you buy your wedding clothes but your father is being most disagreeable and he has told me he will not give you a shilling. It is fortunate, then, that your mother has some small income of her own, and here it is, dear Lydia, everything I have. You must go and buy yourself some new clothes. To be sure, there is not enough time to buy everything I would wish for you, but something can be done. You must have a new dress and a new bonnet, and do not forget to buy a new pair of gloves and a fan.

Oh, how I am looking forward to seeing you again and calling you Mrs Wickham! How green everyone hereabouts will be. You can have no notion of how spiteful they have been. Lady Lucas has been exceedingly unpleasant, though I put that all down to jealousy because Mr Collins is not as handsome as dear Wickham, and Mr Collins does not have a blue coat.

I am going out now to spread the news of your engagement. It is perhaps a good thing I am to remain in Meryton, to be sure, for I am certain that no one can do that as well as your own dear mother.

Mama

Miss Lydia Bennet to Mrs Bennet

Gracechurch Street, London,
August 20

My dear Mama,

Lord! How I laughed when I got your letter. I wish you could come to London, how happy we would be. My aunt and uncle are being horrid unpleasant and they will not allow me to set foot out of the door, let alone buy any new wedding clothes. My aunt preaches and sermonizes all the time, indeed, she is almost as bad as Mary; however, I do not listen to one word in ten, for as you might imagine I am busy thinking of my dear Wickham. I would marry him tomorrow but the banns have to be read and the ceremony cannot therefore be held until the first of September. We are to be married at the church of St. Clement's. I am quite wild for it as you can imagine. How I am to pass the time until then I do not know, since my aunt and uncle never let me have any fun. The Little Theatre is open and I am wild to go; do write to my aunt, Mama, and tell her to take me.

Tell my sisters to write to me, too. They must take the opportunity of addressing me as Miss Lydia Bennet for the last time: before very long I will be signing myself

Lydia Wickham!

Miss Mary Bennet to Miss Lucy Sotherton

Longbourn, Hertfordshire,
August 22

Most noble Friend,

I know you will give thanks with me when you learn that the worst disaster has been averted and that my sister Lydia will now wed her vile seducer, George Wickham. I had thought that such enforced marriages happened only on the Continent. Though I know from my reading—our reading, dear Lucy—that young women are frequently seduced in Italy, and then chained up in dungeons beneath sinister castles, I never expected to encounter it here in England (though without the chains), and we must hope (since Gracechurch Street is a respectable establishment) without the dungeon.

It only shows what dangers are all around us. We must be on our guard, you and I, and make sure that no seducers charm us with their sweet words, robbing us of our virtue—our most treasured possession. Mr Shackleton agrees with me. He says that seducers are more common than is usually supposed and that he has his doubts about Alfred Courtney. I was surprised, as Mr Courtney has always been a pleasant young man—indeed, he was good enough to compliment me on my playing the other evening—but Mr Shackleton assures me there are Rumours. He has warned me to preserve a stoical silence in the presence of the man. I think, after my sister's unfortunate experiences, I will follow his advice.

It is lucky that I already have some experience of stoical silence, or else nothing would have enabled me to remain quiet when my mother heard the news that Lydia was to be married. She was in transports of delight, saying that she longed to see Lydia again, that

Lydia and Wickham must come to stay as soon as they are married, and what fun it would be to introduce her to all the neighbourhood as Mrs Wickham.

Papa took a more rational view of the matter and said that he would never let Kitty or me out of his sight, that he would not reward Lydia's impudence by recognising the marriage and that she should never again set foot in the house. An argument ensued and Papa vowed that he would not be moved on the subject. But Mama prevailed and Lydia and Wickham are to visit us.

Your true sister—for you are more surely my sister than the fallen woman who is Lydia,
Mary

Miss Elizabeth Bennet to Miss Susan Sotherton

Longbourn, Hertfordshire,
August 23

Dear Susan,

I am sure you will have heard by now of our troubles, for Mr Collins could have learnt of them from no one but Charlotte, and as she knows of them she has certainly told you. He wrote Papa a very stupid letter; however, he is a very stupid man and I expected no better.

Forgive me, I am out of sorts this morning. I meant to write and send you all my love, for this is the last time I will be able to write to you as Miss Sotherton; by this time next week you will be Mrs Wainwright. And not long afterwards, Lydia will be Mrs Wickham.

I cannot bear it. The more I think about it, the worse it seems, not only for Lydia but for me.

Oh, Susan! My confusion about Mr Darcy is growing daily. If only I could go back to thinking him rude and above himself, how happy I would be. If only I could tease him and laugh at him and pay him back for slighting my charms! If only he had never proposed to me, or written me that letter: for it was the letter which forced me to see him as a very different man. If only I had not met him again in Derbyshire . . . but you do not know about my visit to Lambton, and how everything there changed things.

You know that I was going to Derbyshire with my aunt and uncle. Once there, my aunt had a wish to see Pemberley, for as you know she grew up in the neighbourhood, and once I had discovered that Mr Darcy was not at home, I decided I could visit his estate without ill effect. It would have looked very odd if I had refused to go, and indeed, I will admit that I was curious to see a place about which I had heard so much.

Susan, it is the most beautiful estate you ever saw. Nothing vulgar or ostentatious, but everything has been done to make it the loveliest place in England. The park contains a variety of grounds and as we drove in at the lodge, we found ourselves travelling first through a wood, the prettiest wood you have ever seen, then ascending for half a mile before finding ourselves at the top of an eminence. The trees gave way to open ground and my eye was immediately caught by Pemberley House, which was situated on the opposite side of the valley, beyond a meandering stream. It was basking in the sunlight and I found myself thinking, Of all this I might have been mistress!

But then I reminded myself of Mr Darcy's feelings towards my family and I knew my aunt and uncle would not have been welcome, and so I ceased to regret it as a home, but yet to admire it as a splendid residence.

We drove on, crossing a bridge and then rolling to a halt by the front door. We were greeted by the housekeeper, who is used to showing people around the house, and I discovered that, inside as well as out, it is the most charming place. There are sweeping views from every window and the most elegant wallpapers and furnishings decorate the rooms.

When we had seen all of the house that was open to general view, we were passed over to the gardener, who led us towards the river. I stopped to look back at the house, and my aunt and uncle looked back also, wondering as to the date of the building, when suddenly Mr Darcy appeared round the corner of the house! I could not believe it. I thought at first he must be an apparition but I quickly realised that he was real. He was coming from the direction of the stables and it was apparent that he had come home unexpectedly.

I wished the ground would open and swallow me up. I felt a wave of humiliation and I could not keep a blush from spreading over my face. I could not bear him to think that I had sought him out deliberately. I wanted to tell him that I was there by accident, at the wish of my aunt and uncle, and that we believed he was from home. But I was too embarrassed to speak, let alone cross the twenty yards that stretched out between us, and so I turned away with my feelings in a whirl.

You may imagine my horror when I heard his footsteps approaching, and my embarrassment when I received his compliments. I scarcely dared lift my eyes to his face, and I know not what answer I made to his enquiries after my family.

I was dumbfounded by the change in his manner. Gone was his pride, his haughtiness and his arrogance. To my astonishment he was speaking to me in the most affable manner; indeed, it seemed as though he were putting himself out to please me, and to set me at my ease.

Presently he fell silent and then, after standing a few moments without saying a word, he took his leave. My aunt and uncle joined me, but I was so overcome by my own feelings that I did not hear a word they said. I was overcome with shame and vexation, certain that he would think I had deliberately thrown myself in his way again.

And yet he had not met me with derision or disgust. He had met me with great civility. I could not make him out.

We walked on round the lake, but yet my thoughts were all fixed on the one spot of Pemberley House where Mr Darcy might be. I longed to know what was passing in his mind, and whether, in defiance of everything, he still held me dear.

It seemed that he must, for he soon joined us again and spoke to my aunt and uncle in the most affable manner. He even invited my uncle to go fishing with him! And, what is more, he asked if he might be allowed to introduce his sister to me.

My aunt and uncle were curious at the sight of so much attention, but I did not feel I could enlighten them. I scarcely knew what his attentions meant myself.

The next day, he brought his sister to see me at the inn where we were staying, and she is the sweetest, most charming girl imaginable—not at all the proud young woman Mr Wickham described.

He brought someone else, too: Mr Bingley. And oh, Susan! Say nothing of this to anyone, in case I am mistaken, but I believe he still has feelings for Jane. In fact, if Mr Darcy gives his approval, I believe Mr Bingley will return to Netherfield and seek Jane out again.

But will Mr Darcy give his approval? I thought so, because he was very changed, and spoke well of her and did not discourage Mr Bingley from speaking of her.

Things were going very well . . . he was attentive, charming, generous, kind . . . and then Lydia ran away with Wickham! Even worse, I told him! I could not help it. The letter arrived just before Mr Darcy entered the room and I was so horrified that I could not conceal my distress. For Lydia's elopement to happen at such a moment, when I had just acknowledged to myself that Mr Darcy was the one man in the world I could be prevailed upon to marry, was cruel indeed.

I had thought it was all over; that I had no chance with him; that, having offered me his hand once he would not do so again. But then the meeting at Pemberley and his evident efforts to please aroused hope in my breast and made me hope that things had changed . . .

But now those hopes are broken before they were ever fully formed. To marry me? When Lydia has disgraced herself and the rest of the family, thereby justifying everything he said to me about my family: my sisters' behaviour and my father's lack of any kind of control? No, it is impossible. And even more impossible, because if he married me, he would be related to Wickham, his worst enemy. It is unthinkable.

And yet I do think of it, Susan, all the time. I remember every word spoken between us. I remember his looks, his expression, his voice, the touch of his hand.

I cannot forget.

But I must.

I must.

But I have been writing only of myself. What of you? Tell me of more pleasant things. Give me all your news. Distract my thoughts. Make me forget about Mr Darcy, and make me cease to regret everything I have lost, for it is a comfort to me, at least, that you, dear Susan, are happy.

Lizzy

Miss Susan Sotherton to Miss Elizabeth Bennet

Bath, August 24

My poor Lizzy,

How I feel for you. I wish that everyone could be as happy as I. Only a few more days and I marry my dear Wainwright, and I wish with all my heart that you could marry your Mr Darcy. I have never heard you talk about a man in this way before, and you are too sensible to think such things about a man unless they are true. I believe you are in love with him and I will hope for some miracle which might yet unite you.

You are right when you say that I had already heard about Lydia's escapade from Charlotte, but do not judge her too harshly. She did not tell Mr Collins deliberately, rather she was reading a letter from her mama when Mr Collins was in the room and could not help exclaiming over the news, and then she could not keep it from him. I am sure she would have kept your confidence otherwise.

And now I must go, there is time for no more; Mama is calling me and I must see to the final preparations for my wedding. I will write to you again as soon as I can, but I must now sign myself for the last time,

Susan Sotherton

⌒ SEPTEMBER ⌒

Colonel Fitzwilliam to Mr Darcy

Fitzwilliam House, London,
September 2

Darcy, you must be relieved that Wickham is safely married and the whole business is over with. What are your intentions now? Are you planning to visit Hertfordshire? You mentioned something about revealing the truth to Bingley; that you suspect Miss Bennet has feelings for him, but what of your own feelings? Are you going to speak to Miss Elizabeth?

I think she would make a worthy mistress of Pemberley.

Henry

Miss Caroline Bingley to Mrs Bingley

Pemberley, Derbyshire,
September 3

Greetings and felicitations, dearest Mama!

It is raining today and I am full of ennui. Mr Darcy left us a few days ago to attend to business in London. I cannot think what he finds to do in London at this time of year. However, he insisted he must go and that no one could conduct the business for him.

Louisa and I are entertaining Georgiana, but it is not the same without Mr Darcy here. He graces everything with his presence, and notices every time I give his sister a kind word. He should, however, return to Pemberley later today.

I hope his business prospered, for he was not in the best of tempers when he left. I do not believe he was looking forward to it, whatever it was. No doubt it is something to do with the war; it unsettles everything, but Mr Darcy's fortune is large enough to withstand even these turbulent times.

I had hoped to see Colonel Fitzwilliam here, but he has returned to his regiment. There are plenty of other gentlemen, however, even if none of them are as handsome as Mr Darcy, but I have not despaired of fixing him, though Miss Bennet's eyes are so fine.

She was here several weeks ago and had the impertinence to visit Pemberley. The housekeeper had no choice but to show her round, and poor Mr Darcy was quite taken in by her, believing her story of being in the neighbourhood with her aunt and uncle, who wanted to see the house. A likely tale! But luckily Mr Darcy had to leave on business shortly after her arrival, whereupon she and her relatives hastily decamped, their supposed tour of Derbyshire entirely forgotten. What simpletons she must think us!

But I hear the carriage! Mr Darcy has returned. I must go!

Your dutiful daughter,
Caroline

Miss Mary Bennet to Miss Lucy Sotherton

Longbourn, Hertfordshire,
September 5

Most noble Friend,

My sister has had the benefit of clergy and is now Mrs Wickham. She arrived here at Longbourn in high spirits, not at all abashed as she should have been by her disgrace. I am very disappointed in Papa. When Lydia arrived, he had an opportunity to tell her how grievously she had sinned, and to extol her to be a better woman in the future, instead of which he laughed at her iniquities and those of her husband.

It emerged that Mr Darcy had been at her wedding, indeed, he seems to have arranged it. That was very wrong of him. He should have roundly condemned Lydia, as Mr Collins did. I think that Mr Collins would have made me a better husband, after all. Mr Shackleton agrees with me. He said that wealthy gentlemen never make good husbands and that the best husbands are often clerks. I was surprised at this, but he assured me that he had read it somewhere and he has promised to find the passage so that I might make an extract of it.

Your devoted sister in morality,
Mary

Miss Elizabeth Bennet to Mrs Gardiner

Longbourn, Hertfordshire,
September 5

My dear aunt,

I cannot contain myself, I must beg your indulgence and hope you will put me out of my misery. Lydia let slip that Mr Darcy had been at her wedding and that she had been sworn to silence on the subject.

You may readily comprehend what my curiosity must be to know how a person so unconnected with any of us, and (comparatively speaking) a stranger to our family, should have been amongst you at such a time. Pray write instantly, and let me understand it—unless it is, for very cogent reasons, to remain in the secrecy which Lydia seems to think necessary; and then I must endeavour to be satisfied with ignorance.

Your loving niece,
Lizzy

Mrs Gardiner to Miss Elizabeth Bennet

Gracechurch Street, London,
September 6

My dear Niece,

I have just received your letter, and shall devote this whole morning to answering it, as I foresee that a *little* writing will not comprise what I have to tell you. I must confess myself surprised by your application; I did not expect it from *you*. Don't think me angry, however, for I only mean to let you know that I had not imagined such enquiries to be necessary on *your* side. If you do not choose to understand me, forgive my impertinence. Your uncle is as much surprised as I am—and nothing but the belief of your being a party concerned would have allowed him to act as he has done. But if you are really innocent and ignorant, I must be more explicit.

On the very day of my coming home from Longbourn, your uncle had a most unexpected visitor. Mr Darcy called, and was shut up with him several hours. It was all over before I arrived; so my curiosity was not so dreadfully racked as *yours* seems to have been. He came to tell Mr Gardiner that he had found out where your sister and Mr Wickham were, and that he had seen and talked with them both—Wickham repeatedly, Lydia once. From what I can collect, he left Derbyshire only one day after ourselves, and came to town with the resolution of hunting for them. The motive professed was his conviction of its being owing to himself that Wickham's worthlessness had not been so well known as to make it impossible for any young woman of character to love or confide in him. He generously imputed the whole to his mistaken pride, and confessed that he had before thought it beneath him to lay his private actions open to the world. His character was to speak for itself.

He called it, therefore, his duty to step forward and endeavour to remedy an evil which had been brought on by himself. If he *had another* motive, I am sure it would never disgrace him.

He had been some days in town before he was able to discover them; but he had something to direct his search, which was more than *we* had; and the consciousness of this was another reason for his resolving to follow us. There is a lady, it seems, a Mrs Younge, who was some time ago governess to Miss Darcy, and was dismissed from her charge on some cause of disapprobation, though he did not say what. She then took a large house in Edward Street, and has since maintained herself by letting lodgings. This Mrs Younge was, he knew, intimately acquainted with Wickham; and he went to her for intelligence of him, as soon as he got to town. But it was two or three days before he could get from her what he wanted. She would not betray her trust, I suppose, without bribery and corruption, for she really did know where her friend was to be found. Wickham, indeed, had gone to her on their first arrival in London, and had she been able to receive them into her house, they would have taken up their abode with her. At length, however, our kind friend procured the wished-for direction.

He saw Wickham, and afterwards insisted on seeing Lydia. His first object with her, he acknowledged, had been to persuade her to quit her present disgraceful situation, and return to her friends as soon as they could be prevailed on to receive her, offering his assistance as far as it would go. But he found Lydia absolutely resolved on remaining where she was. She cared for none of her friends; she wanted no help of his; she would not hear of leaving Wickham. She was sure they should be married sometime or other, and it did not much signify when. Since such were her feelings, it only remained, he thought, to secure and expedite a marriage, which, in his very first conversation with Wickham, he easily learnt had never been *his* design. He confessed himself obliged to leave the regiment on account of some debts of honour, which were very pressing; and scrupled not to lay all the ill-consequences of Lydia's flight on her own folly alone. He meant to resign his commission immediately; and as to his future situation, he could conjecture very little about it. He must go somewhere, but he did not know where, and he knew he should have nothing to live on.

Mr Darcy asked him why he had not married your sister at once. Though Mr Bennet was not imagined to be very rich, he would have been able to do something for him, and his situation must have been benefited by marriage. But he found, in reply to this question, that Wickham still cherished the hope of more effectually making his fortune by marriage in some other country. Under such circumstances, however, he was not likely to be proof against the temptation of immediate relief.

They met several times, for there was much to be discussed. Wickham, of course, wanted more than he could get, but at length was reduced to be reasonable.

Everything being settled between *them*, Mr Darcy's next step was to make your uncle acquainted with it, and he first called in Gracechurch Street the evening before I came home. But Mr Gardiner could not be seen, and Mr Darcy found, on further enquiry, that your father was still with him, but would quit town the next morning. He did not judge your father to be a person whom he could so properly consult as your uncle, and therefore readily postponed seeing him till after the departure of the former. He did not leave his name, and till the next day it was only known that a gentleman had called on business.

On Saturday he came again. Your father was gone, your uncle at home, and, as I said before, they had a great deal of talk together.

They met again on Sunday, and then *I* saw him too. It was not all settled before Monday: as soon as it was, the express was sent off to Longbourn. But our visitor was very obstinate. I fancy, Lizzy, that obstinacy is the real defect of his character after all. He has been accused of many faults at different times, but *this* is the true one.

Nothing was to be done that he did not do himself; though I am sure (and I do not speak it to be thanked, therefore say nothing about it) your uncle would most readily have settled the whole.

They battled it together for a long time, which was more than either the gentleman or lady concerned in it deserved. But at last your uncle was forced to yield, and instead of being allowed to be of use to his niece, was forced to put up with only having the probable credit of it, which went sorely against the grain; and I really believe your letter this morning gave him great pleasure, because it required an explanation that would rob him of his borrowed feathers, and give the praise where it was due. But, Lizzy, this must go no further than yourself, or Jane at most.

You know pretty well, I suppose, what has been done for the young people. His debts are to be paid, amounting, I believe, to considerably more than a thousand pounds, another thousand in addition to her own settled upon *her*, and his commission purchased. The reason why all this was to be done by him alone was such as I have given above. It was owing to him, to his reserve and want of proper consideration, that Wickham's character had been so misunderstood, and, consequently, that he had been received and noticed as he was. Perhaps there was some truth in *this*; though I doubt whether *his* reserve, or *anybody's* reserve, can be answerable for the event. But in spite of all this fine talking, my dear Lizzy, you may rest perfectly assured that your uncle would never have yielded, if we had not given him credit for *another interest* in the affair.

When all this was resolved on, he returned again to his friends, who were still staying at Pemberley; but it was agreed that he should be in London once more when the wedding took place, and all money matters were then to receive the last finish.

I believe I have now told you everything. It is a relation which you tell me is to give you great surprise; I hope at least it will not afford you any displeasure. Lydia came to us; and Wickham had constant admission to the house. *He* was exactly what he had been when I knew him in Hertfordshire; but I would not tell you how little I was satisfied with *her* behaviour while she stayed with us, if I had not perceived, by Jane's letter last Wednesday, that her conduct on coming home was exactly of a piece with it, and therefore what I now tell you can give you no fresh pain. I talked to her repeatedly in the most serious manner, representing to her all the wickedness of what she had done and all the unhappiness she had brought on her family. If she heard me, it was by good luck, for I am sure she did not listen. I was sometimes quite provoked, but then I recollected my dear Elizabeth and Jane, and for their sakes had patience with her.

Mr Darcy was punctual in his return and, as Lydia informed you, attended the wedding. He dined with us the next day, and was to leave town again on Wednesday or Thursday. Will you be very angry with me, my dear Lizzy, if I take this opportunity of saying (what I was never bold enough to say before) how much I like him? His behaviour to us has, in every respect, been as pleasing as when we were in Derbyshire. His understanding and opinions all please me; he wants nothing but a little more liveliness, and *that*, if he marry *prudently*, his wife may teach him. I thought him very sly—he hardly ever mentioned your name. But slyness seems the fashion.

Pray forgive me if I have been very presuming; or at least do not punish me so far as to exclude me from P. I shall never be quite happy till I have been all round the park. A low phaeton, with a nice little pair of ponies, would be the very thing.

But I must write no more. The children have been wanting me this half hour.

Yours, very sincerely,
M. Gardiner

Miss Lucy Sotherton to Miss Mary Bennet

Bath, September 14

Hail!

I am not surprised at your father's behaviour, nor your mother's, for I see such things all about me in Bath. There are but a handful of Learned Women in the whole of England, dear Mary, and you and I are two of them. Nor does it surprise me that there are vile seducers everywhere. Men are slaves to their evil lusts and we must be ever on our guard, for they will assail our virtue if we give them any encouragement.

One such gentleman is returning to Netherfield Park, no doubt with the intention of seducing your sister Jane. Yes, Mr Bingley is to once again take up residence. I know this because Papa, hearing of Mr Bingley's absence, hoped we might be able to let the property to another tenant, whilst at the same time keeping Mr Bingley's payment. Such are the low standards I live amongst! But Mr Bingley replied that he will be taking up residence once again on the seventeenth of this month. Your sister must take care. Let her walk nowhere unchaperoned. Having had an opportunity to propose to her in the usual manner last autumn, he did not do it, no doubt because he has designs on her virtue. We are not so very far from Italy after all.

My sister Susan has succumbed to worldly lures and is now married to Mr Wainwright. She has not written to us yet, and I must hope it is because the post is slow and not because she and her husband have been slain in the mountains and eaten by wolves or banditti (eaten by the wolves and slain by the banditti, I mean; even the worst of the banditti do not, to my knowledge, eat their victims, although nothing would surprise me about the inhabitants of the Pyrenees).

Your dear friend,
Lucy

Miss Mary Bennet to Miss Lucy Sotherton

Longbourn, Hertfordshire,
September 21

Most noble Friend,

Mr Bingley has indeed returned to the neighbourhood. He called on us yesterday with his friend Mr Darcy, though, as Mama says, she does not know why Mr Darcy called, for no one wants him here. He said very little, only asked after my aunt and uncle Gardiner, though he made no enquiries after our cousin Mr Collins and his wife, Charlotte Collins. I did think at one time that Charlotte might have become a Learned Woman, since she showed no sign of frivolity and occasionally opened a book, but she was lost to us when she succumbed to the lure of Mr Collins's masculine charms and walked along the bridal path with him as her chosen mate.

Mama believes that Mr Bingley means to make Jane an offer, and in an endeavour to hasten the courtship she remarked that when Mr Bingley has killed all his own birds he must come and kill Papa's. But I believe it will take more than an invitation to deal out death to our wingèd friends to ensnare Mr Bingley, who is a slippery customer: as I said to Mr Shackleton, we have been down this path before. I only hope that Jane is not too disappointed when Mr Bingley disappears again.

Mary King has also returned to the neighbourhood. She was taken away by her relatives when Mr Wickham began to court her, having been alerted to his infamy by their cousin, Mark Haydock, who, as the rector of Kympton, knew something of Mr Wickham's past. But now that Mr Wickham is married to my poor sister Lydia, Mary King is safe and so she has taken up residence here again.

Perhaps she might be persuaded to join our select circle.

Your vestal sister in humility,
Mary

Miss Elizabeth Bennet to Mrs Susan Wainwright

Longbourn, Hertfordshire,
September 22

Dear Susan,

By now you will have returned from your bridal tour. I hope it was everything you wished for, but I am glad, selfishly so, that you are back at home—that is to say, your new home—because I need someone to turn to, and only you will do.

Everything is in turmoil here. Mr Bingley has returned to the neighbourhood and I believe he is as much in love with Jane as ever. He called on us the day before yesterday, bringing Mr Darcy with him, and I think he is waiting only for his friend's approval before proposing.

Jane, of course, says that he is just being friendly and that she expects nothing from him. She declares that, now the first meeting is over, she will never be embarrassed by his coming here again, and says that she is glad he is to dine here tomorrow, so that everyone can see that they meet only as common and indifferent acquaintances.

So common and indifferent that I believe he will propose to her before very long, even if he does not have Mr Darcy's approval!

I hope he does, for I cannot bear to see Jane unhappy and I wish Mr Bingley would put her out of her misery sooner rather than later, for there is no denying that his company is very uncomfortable for her whilst the situation is unresolved between them. It would not be apparent to anyone who does not know her well, but I can see that she is anxious and uneasy, whatever she might say. And small wonder, when everything she longs for in life is so near and yet so far away.

Mama increased her misery by fawning over Mr Bingley in the most embarrassing manner, and increased mine by treating Mr Darcy with the scantest civility. If she only knew what she owed him, for it was he who forced Wickham to marry Lydia, and without his influence I dread to think what would have happened to Lydia. But all Mama does is to revile him, saying she hates the very sight of him; whereas I find myself longing to speak to him, so that I can thank him for his kindness.

Susan, I do not know what to think. When Mr Darcy came to Longbourn, I found myself hoping against hope that his affection was unshaken and that, despite everything, he still loved me. But he did not speak to me, not even about commonplace things; in fact he scarcely opened his mouth. I was so embarrassed I buried myself in my needlework, but I could not resist glancing at him from time to time; however, his eyes were fixed on Jane more often than on me. On seeing this, I was overwhelmed with disappointment, and then was angry with myself for feeling that way, for how could I expect him to love a woman who had rejected him, and in so vehement a fashion?

And so I determined to treat him like any other guest. I summoned the courage to ask about his sister, but once he had told me that she was well, he lapsed into silence again, and at length both he and Mr Bingley went away.

Why, if he wished to see me, did he not speak to me? And why, if he did not wish to speak to me, did he come?

Did you ever have such moments with Mr Wainwright? Did you ever feel so painfully embarrassed that you wished never to see him again, whilst hoping with all your heart that you would?

Tell me, Susan, what do you think he is about? For I cannot live with this uncertainty.

Your dear friend,
Lizzy

Mr Darcy to Colonel Fitzwilliam

Darcy House, London,
September 25

Henry, I am sorry it has taken me so long to reply to your last but I have been in Hertfordshire, making amends for the wrong I did Charles in deceiving him about Miss Bennet. As soon as I told him that I suspected she had feelings for him, and that she had been in London earlier in the year without his knowledge, he returned to Netherfield Park at once. He paid a call at Longbourn straightaway, where he was warmly welcomed by Mrs Bennet. She is as vulgar as ever, but I believe he would tolerate ten such Mrs Bennets for the chance of marrying his beloved Jane; as I would gladly tolerate a hundred Mrs Bennets if I thought that Elizabeth might marry me.

I had hoped, when I went to Longbourn, that I would find Elizabeth welcoming; that the warmth of our meetings in Derbyshire would be continued in Hertfordshire; but instead I found her ill at ease in my company.

Henry, I do not know what to think. I was sure we were coming to know each other in Derbyshire, and that she was starting to forgive me for my former rudeness. I could see that she was surprised by my courtesy to her aunt and uncle, but nevertheless pleased by it, and I felt sure that she looked more kindly on me, realising I had changed. If not for her wretched sister eloping with Wickham, I am certain we would have come to an understanding. But the mood was broken when she was forced to return home—forced to it by the elopement of her sister, whom I could have protected if I had only made Wickham's character known.

And now I do not know if I have any hope of ever winning her affections, or if I have disgusted her too much for her to forgive me.

I fear the latter. If she had given me any encouragement, any hope when I visited her in Hertfordshire . . . but there was none. She scarcely looked at me, let alone spoke to me, and I can see no reason to return.

I fear my chance of winning her has gone forever.

Darcy

Lady Lucas to Mrs Charlotte Collins

Lucas Lodge, Hertfordshire,
September 29

Dearest Charlotte,

We all hope you are taking care of yourself and not working too hard; also, make sure you eat well. You must look after yourself. Your father talks of nothing but the happy event and is looking forward to introducing his grandchild at St. James's.

Meryton is full of news, though none so good as your own. The Bennets are insufferable because Jane Bennet is engaged to Mr Bingley. Mrs Bennet can talk of nothing else, and grows very tiresome, for you know what a gossip she is. It is 'Jane and Mr Bingley this,' 'My future son-in-law, Mr Bingley, that' and 'My daughter, who will be Mrs Bingley.'

She was less pleased to play hostess to Mr Darcy, who accompanied his friend, although no one knows why he went. It is not as though he can have anything to take him to Longbourn. Poor Elizabeth! She had to entertain him whilst her sister sat with Mr Bingley, though he has now gone back to town on business, but everyone says he plans to return and Mrs Bennet is quite put out. 'What does he come here for?' she asks. 'I quite detest him.' But as the friend of Mr Bingley she has to tolerate him.

You have been lucky in your choice of husband, Charlotte, but I do hope he is not plaguing you too much. Remember to encourage his hobbies. I have always encouraged your father to take up outside employment of one kind or another. I cannot be doing with him under my feet all day long. Press upon Mr Collins the advantages of gardening. A man can never be too much in the garden.

Your loving
Mother

Mrs Charlotte Collins to Mrs Susan Wainwright

Hunsford, near Westerham, Kent,
September 30

Susan, how glad I was to hear of your wedding and your bridal tour, and it seems that one wedding has brought on another, for you will have heard by now that Jane Bennet is betrothed. Things happen in threes, so they say, and I think there will be another betrothal in Meryton before long. Mr Darcy has been often at Longbourn, so my mother says, and if I do not miss my guess, he will propose to

Elizabeth very soon. I thought, as long ago as last year, when we were all together in Meryton, that he was attracted to her, and I counselled her to make herself agreeable to him. She would not do it, but her impertinence did her no harm with him; indeed, I think it attracted him more. To be sure, things did not look so promising when he went away, but now that he is back, and visiting Longbourn for no reason, I think it certain that he intends to marry her. I am glad of it. I like him. His manners are not prepossessing to begin with, but they improve on acquaintance. I have seen him many times, both in Hertfordshire and Kent, and I believe he would make Elizabeth an excellent husband, as well as being an excellent catch.

Your dear friend,
Charlotte

⤙ OCTOBER ⤚

Miss Anne de Bourgh to Miss Georgiana Darcy

Rosings Park, Kent, October 1

Dear coz,

Mama had a letter from Colonel Fitzwilliam this morning and he mentioned that you were unwell and so I write to cheer you. He sent us news of his deployment and I was glad that his injuries have healed so that he will soon be where he wants to be, back on the Continent and fighting Napoleon. I fear for him each time he goes into battle but I am glad for him nonetheless: he came to Rosings when he was injured and he was frustrated and bored, unlike his usual self. I only hope we may see him again soon.

We have more excitement here than usual. Mrs Collins is expecting a child in the spring and Mr Collins is very proud of the fact, though I fear he is more delighted because the news has pleased Mama than for his own sake. Mama has already told Mrs Collins what she must eat and what exercise to take, as well as how to raise the child and how to educate it. She has also suggested the child follows Mr Collins into the clergy and said that by the time it is grown, Mr Collins will no doubt have inherited Longbourn and so the child may have the living he now holds. Mr Collins was very grateful, as you can imagine, and bowed most profusely, though whether he will be so humble when he inherits his own property I do not know.

Having been in favour for a few weeks or so, even since the Collinses gave Mama the news, Mr Collins is now very markedly out of favour, however. He happened to say that Mr Bingley is to marry Miss Bennet, a circumstance which held no particular interest for Mama, and which Charlotte learnt in a letter from her mother, for it is the talk of Hertfordshire. He then went on to say, most unluckily, that Mr Darcy had accompanied his friend to Longbourn on several occasions and that he was on the point of proposing to Miss Elizabeth Bennet. I felt my heart soar at the news, for although I like Darcy very well as a cousin, you know my heart is elsewhere. But Mama sat as one stunned. She quickly recovered and said it was unthinkable that Darcy, descended from kings and related to earls, should offer for a woman with neither family nor fortune to recommend her. Seeing that he had displeased Mama, Mr Collins quickly remarked that the news was unreliable, mere gossip, and as Lady Catherine was so gracious as to remark, it was unthinkable, preposterous, ludicrous, and a dozen other such words.

Mama was for the moment mollified, but she kept returning to the subject and she has now announced that she means to go to Hertfordshire and make sure that Miss Elizabeth has no intention of marrying Darcy, and to tell her that she forbids the match. I think Mama is mistaken in thinking it will have any effect, for Miss Elizabeth has a decided personality and I believe she will not be browbeaten.

Mama means to take me with her, and I must confess I am looking forward to seeing the battle, although I am less happy at the thought of the rest of Mama's plan; for after she has visited the Bennets, Mama intends to make sure that Darcy offers for me. She has never been in a hurry for the engagement before, since she likes to have me with her—or, perhaps it is better to say, she likes to have *someone* with her—but now I believe she is beginning to think that if the engagement is not formalised, Darcy might look elsewhere.

I am sending you a sketch of the park, which I have just completed, and I console myself with the thought that, if Mama is determined to visit Darcy, then at least I will have the consolation of seeing you.

Your dear coz,
Anne

Miss Georgiana Darcy to Miss Anne de Bourgh

Darcy House, London, October 2

Dearest Anne,

I think your sketch is beautiful, I have sent it to be framed and I intend to hang it by the fireplace in my bedroom. I do hope you call here, for I would so love to see you again.

How I wish the rumours might be true, and that my brother will marry Miss Bennet! I liked her very much when I met her and I know that she is special to him. He told me a great deal about her before I even met her, and all of it good. That is not like Fitzwilliam, for you know he is easily bored and has very little time for the women who cluster around him. But I know he was taken with Elizabeth. There, I am calling her Elizabeth, quite as if she were my sister already!

I am sure Fitzwilliam would like to marry her. I can think of no other reason for him introducing me to her, and being so pleased when we got on well together. He introduces me to very few people, thinking that I am too young to come out, which in general is true, and in the past he has only introduced me to young women who are related to his friends, like Miss Bingley.

Oh dear, poor Caroline: I know she would like to be Mrs Darcy, but it will never happen, even if my brother does not marry Elizabeth. He does not like her very much. He admires her accomplishments and he thinks her a suitable companion for me, and of course he likes Mr Bingley a great deal, but Caroline is not always wise and does not see when her amusing remarks become spiteful. Fitzwilliam sees it and hears it, though. He is ill-humoured himself sometimes—you see, I know my brother, and much as I love him I know that he is not perfect—but there is a generosity and kindness at the heart of him that I think Caroline lacks.

Elizabeth does not lack it. When I met her in Derbyshire she put me at my ease and went out of her way to protect me from some comments that Caroline made about George Wickham.

It seems odd to me now that I was ever betrothed, however secretly, to George. He ran off with Miss Bennet's sister Lydia, you know. It was all hushed up but I could not help seeing that my brother was very agitated, and I could not help overhearing the directions he gave to his coachman, nor seeing what was in one of my guardian's letters, for my brother was so distracted that when he gave it to me to read, he forgot to remove the sheet which had been intended for him alone. By the time I realised what I was reading, I had already learnt the truth: that George had preyed upon another young woman and that, having ruined her, he was refusing to marry her.

I do not think that he would have refused to marry me; indeed, I think that was his intention, but only because of my fortune. And if I had not been an heiress but had been foolish enough to believe him—which I am ashamed to say that I would have been—then my fate would have been the same.

Fitzwilliam had to pay George in the end to marry Lydia—and it is that, I think, which has persuaded me that my brother is really in love with Elizabeth, for he would not have sought out George Wickham for anyone else.

I do hope he is about to propose to her, and I do hope she says *Yes*. I would love such a sister. But whether it will ever come to pass . . . we must just wait and see.

I am sending you one of my own sketches and I hope you find it pretty.

Your loving coz,
Georgiana

Mr Collins to Mr Bennet

Hunsford, near Westerham, Kent,
October 2

Dear Sir,

I must congratulate you on the approaching nuptials of your eldest daughter, whose beauty is matched only by her modesty and elegance. As a clergyman it is my duty to encourage the institution of matrimony and I am sure that the marriage of your uniformly charming daughter to so estimable a man as Mr Bingley will bring joy to all who know them.

Having thus offered you the sincere congratulations of Mrs Collins and myself on this happy event, let me now add a short hint on the subject of another; of which we have been advertised by the same authority. Your daughter Elizabeth, it is presumed, will not long bear the name of Bennet after her elder sister has resigned it, and the chosen partner of her fate may be reasonably looked up to as one of the most illustrious personages in this land. This young gentleman is blessed, in a peculiar way, with everything the heart of mortal can most desire—splendid property, noble kindred, and extensive patronage. Yet in spite of all these temptations, let me warn my cousin Elizabeth, and yourself, of what evils you may incur by a precipitate closure with this gentleman's proposals, which, of course, you will be inclined to take immediate advantage of. My motive for cautioning you is as follows: we have reason to imagine that his aunt, Lady Catherine de Bourgh, does not look on the match with a friendly eye.

After mentioning the likelihood of this marriage to her ladyship last night, she immediately, with her usual condescension, expressed what she felt on the occasion; when it became apparent that, on the score of some family objections on the part of my cousin, she would never give her consent to what she termed so disgraceful a match, I thought it my duty to give the speediest intelligence of this to my cousin, that she and her noble admirer may be aware of what they are about, and not run hastily into a marriage which has not been properly sanctioned.

I am truly rejoiced that my cousin Lydia's sad business has been so well hushed up, and am only concerned that their living together before the marriage took place should be so generally known. I must not, however, neglect the duties of my station, or refrain from declaring my amazement, at hearing that you received the young couple into your house as soon as they were married. It was an encouragement of vice; and had I been the rector of Longbourn, I should very strenuously have opposed it. You ought certainly to forgive them, as a Christian, but never to admit them in your sight, or allow their names to be mentioned in your hearing.

And now, dear sir, I must give you some news of my own which I am sure will delight you. My dear Charlotte is in an interesting condition and she will soon grace us with a young olive branch, which, if we are blessed with good fortune, will be a boy, a son and heir to come after me and to come, if I may so put it, good sir, after you; a child who will inherit Longbourn and continue the noble tradition of elegance and hospitality so charmingly begun by your own grandfather and so estimably continued by your father and yourself.

I remain, sir, your humble servant,
William Collins

Mr Darcy to Colonel Fitzwilliam

Netherfield Park, Hertfordshire,
October 5

Henry, direct your letters to Netherfield Park, as I am once again with Bingley. I have hope, hope at last! My aunt sought to interfere in my affairs and in so doing has done me an unexpectedly good turn.

Having heard a rumour that I was about to propose to Elizabeth—it seems that Mrs Collins's mother suspected my feelings and guessed my reasons for going to Longbourn—Lady Catherine visited Longbourn herself to tell Elizabeth that she must not marry me. When Elizabeth refused to give her any undertaking that she would never marry me, my aunt bore down on me like a Fury and demanded that I give her an undertaking never to offer my hand to Elizabeth. I did not give it. I would not have given it anyway, as she has no right to interfere in my affairs, but I was in no mood to even contemplate it when I learnt that Elizabeth had refused to put paid to the rumours.

My spirits lifted, for I knew that Elizabeth would have been only too happy to declare her intention of never marrying me if she had decided definitely against me, and so I set out at once for Hertfordshire. And now here I am, with hope in my heart, and tomorrow I must put that hope to the test.

I mean to ask her to marry me again. One way or another, tomorrow my fate will be sealed.

Pray for me, Henry.

Your cousin,
Darcy

Miss Kitty Bennet to Miss Eleanor Sotherton

Longbourn, Hertfordshire,
October 6

Dear Ellie,

Everything here is horrible. Lydia is having all the fun in the north and if I had only been allowed to go to Brighton, I could have married an officer and I could be having fun flirting up in the north, too, instead of stuck here in the middle of nowhere. There are not even any new bonnets in the milliners'. Jane is the only one enjoying herself. She is having fun with Mr Bingley, though it is no fun for the rest of us as she sits and talks to him all the time and the rest of us might as well be dying of the plague for all she cares about us.

That Mr Darcy is here all the time, too. I do not know why he keeps coming, he never says anything to anyone, and as Mama says, he is the most disagreeable man in existence.

Mama keeps making me and Lizzy entertain him so that Jane can have Mr Bingley all to herself. We had to go for a walk with him today so that Jane and Mr Bingley would not have the bother of talking to him, but I managed to run off to the Lucases'. Lizzy said she did not have anything particular to say to Maria Lucas and so she walked on with Mr Darcy, which I must say was very noble of her; there could have been no pleasure in it for her.

Poor Lizzy! I would not be her for a kingdom, having to walk about with Mr Darcy. They are still out walking, though Jane and Mr Bingley returned an hour ago. Mama thinks they must have got lost. How horrid for Lizzy, to be lost with that man, and to have to wander through the country lanes with him all afternoon!

I would rather be here, writing to you, though it would be better to go somewhere like Bath or Brighton and get a husband. But Papa says he will never let me go anywhere, and if he does not relent, I will turn into an old maid.

Kitty

Miss Elizabeth Bennet to Mrs Charlotte Collins

Longbourn, Hertfordshire,
October 7

My dear Charlotte,

You were right! Mr Darcy is in love with me, he proposed to me yesterday and I have said yes! I am so happy that I cannot even be angry with you for being right where I was wrong, and for seeing what I could not. To think, you knew it all along, before I knew it myself, before even my dear Mr Darcy knew it; though he tells me now that he was struck with the beautiful expression in my eyes almost the first day he met me, as soon as he had roundly condemned my looks to everyone else! It seems that when Sir William Lucas begged a partner for me at Lucas Lodge last November, Mr Darcy was ready to oblige, although he liked me better for my spirit in refusing.

I am sure I cannot claim any virtue for it, as I was motivated by a wish to confound his expectations and remove any reason he might have for disdaining me rather than by any nobler instincts. He had slighted my charms and so I was determined never to like him, and I was certain that he would never like me. Such is the blindness that prejudice brings with it.

But I was wrong! Charlotte, we have been talking all day, and you may imagine how much we have to say. We have a year's worth of conversation.

When I stayed with Jane at Netherfield to nurse her through her cold, he found himself so much in danger from me by the end of the visit that he withdrew into silence lest he should raise any expectations in my breast. And I thought he was simply being arrogant and disdainful; particularly after Mama's visit, which I knew had disgusted him. And when he left the neighbourhood with Mr Bingley, my loss caused him a great deal of unhappiness; more unhappiness than his loss caused me, for by then I had heard Mr Wickham's tale of woe and I was foolish enough to believe it.

When I think how Mr Wickham duped me, and how easy I was to dupe, I am ashamed. And when I think of how I treated my dear Mr Darcy at Easter, when I was still in the grip of all my blind prejudices, I blush with mortification.

But let me not dwell on such things. As soon as Mr Wickham's villainy was revealed I began to think differently about everything, though I thought it too late, because by then I had lost my dearest Mr Darcy.

And now I must tell you of something which happened at Easter, when I was staying with you and Mr Collins, and which I did not tell you about at the time because of my confusion and my uncertainty as to my own feelings. It is this, Charlotte: that when I was staying at the parsonage, Mr Darcy proposed to me.

And now you are shocked, I suppose—or perhaps not, as you always suspected he had a partiality for me. It was on the night of Tuesday, the twenty-second of April that he offered me his hand. The date is ingrained in my memory. You and Mr Collins and Maria had gone to dine at Rosings Park, but I had stayed behind pleading a headache. And indeed I did have a headache, for I had just discovered that Mr Darcy had separated Mr Bingley and Jane. You may guess at my feelings towards Mr Darcy then, and my unwillingness to meet him at dinner.

But what should happen, when I was sitting alone in the parsonage, but that Mr Darcy should walk in! Oh, Charlotte, the things I said to him! And the things he said to me! He criticised my family, my person, my station in life, and then had the temerity to propose to me. You may imagine my reply. I not only condemned him for separating Mr Bingley and Jane, but for ruining Mr Wickham's hopes as well.

In reply, he wrote me a letter. He told me the truth about Mr Wickham: that Mr Wickham was a wastrel and other, less savoury, things; and I realised how wrong I had been about everything. But it was too late to put matters right.

And there matters would have ended, had I not met Mr Darcy again in Derbyshire. How changed he was, how polite and attentive to my aunt and uncle, how unfailingly courteous to me. And then came Lydia's elopement and I thought all hope had gone forever. But I was wrong!

Oh, Charlotte, I cannot tell you how happy I am! What does it matter what happened in the past, when everything in the present is so right? My dearest Mr Darcy smiling at me, my darling Jane happily betrothed, Susan blissfully married, and you, dear Charlotte, with your olive branch on the way.

I have time for no more. I must go. Give my love to Mr Collins, though I fear he will be horrified at my news! And perhaps it would be better to stay away from Lady Catherine for the next few days. My dear Mr Darcy intends to write to her and apprise her of our betrothal, and you know her feelings towards me. She liked me well enough as a friend of her rector's wife, but not as the mistress of Pemberley. I fear the shades will be polluted after all.

Your friend,
Lizzy

Mr Darcy to Mr Philip Darcy

Netherfield Park, Hertfordshire,
October 7

Philip, you must forgive me, but I have offered my hand to Elizabeth Bennet and she has accepted. I know you wanted me to make a great match, one which would enhance the standing of Pemberley and the Darcy name, but believe me, I have made the right choice. Elizabeth is the only woman I could ever take to Pemberley and the only woman I could ever make my wife. I am persuaded my father would be pleased. How well I remember his letter, telling me what I must look for in a wife, and I have found it and more besides. I have found something my parents had, something better than rank or wealth; I have found love. You must come to the wedding. When you meet her, you will understand.

Darcy

Mr Bennet to Mr Collins

Longbourn, Hertfordshire,
October 8

Dear Sir,

I must trouble you once more for congratulations. Elizabeth will soon be the wife of Mr Darcy. Console Lady Catherine as well as you can. But, if I were you, I would stand by the nephew. He has more to give.

Yours sincerely,
John Bennet

Mrs Bennet to Mrs Gardiner

Longbourn, Hertfordshire,
October 8

Sister, Lizzy is too busy to write herself, but I wanted to tell you the wonderful news: she is to marry Mr Darcy.

I knew how it would be as soon as I saw them together at the assembly. I said to Mr Bennet, 'You mark my words, we'll have Lizzy at Pemberley before the year is out.' Such a charming man! So handsome, so tall! A house in town, ten thousand a year! How rich and great Elizabeth will be! What pin money, what jewels and carriages she will have!

But I must go. The gentlemen are coming to luncheon and I must speak to Cook. We are having venison and fish and six sauces. A man like Mr Darcy will have French chefs, I am sure, and I am not about to let him think that we cannot cook in Hertfordshire. I intend to give him a luncheon the like of which he has never eaten before.

Your sister,
Janet

Miss Mary Bennet to Miss Lucy Sotherton

Longbourn, Hertfordshire,
October 9

Most noble Friend,

It has been a week of proposals. Mr Bingley has proposed to Jane, Mr Darcy has proposed to Elizabeth and Mama has proposed to move to Pemberley after the wedding.

I was surprised that Mr Bingley offered for Jane because he seemed eager to leave Netherfield last year, and as for Mr Darcy, he has never looked twice at Elizabeth in his life, except to find fault with her and to say that she was only tolerable. I have read much about the fickleness of women, and indeed I have made many extracts on the subject, but it has become clear to me that men are the fickle sex.

I am beginning to lose my faith in extracts.

Your dolorous sister of the bosom,
Mary

Miss Elizabeth Bennet to Mrs Gardiner

Longbourn, Hertfordshire,
October 10

I would have thanked you before, my dear aunt, as I ought to have done, for your long, kind, satisfactory detail of particulars; but to say the truth, I was too cross to write. You supposed more than really existed. But *now* suppose as much as you choose; give loose to your fancy, indulge your imagination in every possible flight which the subject will afford, and unless you believe me actually married, you cannot greatly err. You must write again very soon, and praise him a great deal more than you did in your last. I thank you, again and again, for not going to the Lakes. How could I be so silly as to wish it! Your idea of the ponies is delightful. We will go round the Park every day. I am the happiest creature in the world. Perhaps other people have said so before, but not one with such justice. I am happier even than Jane; she only smiles, I laugh. Mr Darcy sends you all the love in the world that he can spare from me. You are all to come to Pemberley at Christmas.

Your loving niece,
Lizzy

Mr Darcy to Lady Catherine de Bourgh

Netherfield Park, Hertfordshire,
October 10

Lady Catherine, I am sure you will want to wish me happy. I have asked Miss Elizabeth Bennet to marry me, and she has done me the great honour of saying yes.

Your nephew,
Fitzwilliam Darcy

Mr Darcy to Miss Georgiana Darcy

Netherfield Park, Hertfordshire,
October 10

My dear sister,

I know you will be delighted to hear that Elizabeth Bennet and I are to marry. I will tell you everything when I see you next.

Your loving brother,
Fitzwilliam

Miss Georgiana Darcy to Mr Darcy

Darcy House, London, October 11

Oh, dear brother, I cannot tell you how delighted I am! I have always wanted a sister, and Elizabeth is the very one I would have chosen. I do so hope she will love me as much as I already love her.

When you told me you wanted to introduce me to her in Derbyshire, I suspected you were in love with her; indeed, I suspected it even before that, for you had a look about you whenever her name was mentioned. No one who did not know you as I do would have noticed it, but I hoped then that you might have found someone to make you happy. I know how difficult you are to please—oh dear! that did not come out as it should!—but there are so many women who court you for your name instead of yourself and you see through them at once. I am beginning to know something of it myself, and although last year I could not see through it, I believe that I now know the difference between honest interest and self-interest. At least I hope so.

But Elizabeth is not like that. She is warm and kind and *genuine*. I do not know how else to explain it. She was so good to me in Derbyshire. She persevered in talking to me, even though I was so shy I could do nothing but murmur in monosyllables. I wanted to make a good impression on her, as I could tell at once that you were full of admiration for her—your eyes soften when you look at her, you know, and the expression of boredom you frequently wear completely disappears—and I was so afraid of saying something foolish that I could scarcely say anything at all. Then I worried that she would think me a fool, but she made such an effort to put me at my ease that I soon felt much more comfortable.

But I think it was when we stayed beyond the half hour, and you then asked me to join you in inviting her to dinner, that I was sure she was special to you. And I was so pleased, even though I was alarmed at the thought of being your hostess on such an important occasion, for you know I do not want to ever let you down again in any way.

That is why I decided to receive her in the salon. The windows there, you know, are my favourite, opening as they do right down to the ground. I was so afraid of doing wrong that I was tongue-tied when she arrived, but I saw by her expression that she did not think any the worse of me for it. I am glad she was so forgiving, for you know I did not perform my duties as hostess very well. Having given orders in the kitchen the night before and having sent to the hot-houses for the best fruits, I froze when they were brought in, and if not for Mrs Annesley, I would not have remembered what to do. You will think me a sad case, I am sure! I am only glad you were not there to see my embarrassment. I was very glad when you came in to play the host, and I felt such happiness when I saw your eyes go to Elizabeth. I was glad for you and glad for me, selfishly, because I felt from the first that I could easily love such a sister.

She was so good to me when Caroline began to talk about the militia. I wanted the ground to open up and swallow me. I could not lift my eyes from the carpet. I knew that Caroline wanted to pain Elizabeth, for she had not been able to resist laughing at the Bennets when we were playing our duets or singing together, and saying that they all ran after the officers. She could not have known how she was wounding me when she mentioned them. Elizabeth's collected behaviour, however, soon calmed me and I was able to raise my eyes again.

I was hoping to see more of her, and I was very sorry when her uncle had to return suddenly, taking her with him.

And here, dear brother, I have a confession to make. It has troubled me for some time but I cannot have secrets from you. I know what it was that took you to town. You handed me one of my guardian's letters in a hurry, without first removing the page that was for you alone. I also know why you helped in the way you did. I suspected it at the time, and I hoped to hear that I would have a sister months ago, but, however, I am very glad to learn that I am to have one now, especially as it is the right one.

Do you think we might go shopping together when she is in town? It would be such fun to do the things that sisters do. Elizabeth, I know, has four sisters of her own, but I am persuaded that she is kind enough to indulge me, if you will permit it. I am so happy I feel as if I could write another four pages, but I cannot end the letter without asking when the wedding is to be.

Your loving sister,
Georgiana

Lady Catherine de Bourgh to Mr Darcy

Rosings Park, Kent, October 12

Fitzwilliam,

I do not call you nephew, for you are no longer a nephew of mine. I am shocked and astonished that you could stoop to offer your hand to a person of such low breeding. It is a stain on the honour and credit of the name of Darcy. She will bring you nothing but degradation and embarrassment, and she will reduce your house to a place of impertinence and vulgarity. Your children will be wild and undisciplined, and your daughters will run off with stable hands. Your sons will become attorneys. You will never be received by any of your acquaintance. You will be disgraced in the eyes of the world, a figure of contempt. You will bitterly regret this day. You will remember that I warned you of the consequences of such a disastrous act, but by then it will be too late. I will not end this letter by wishing you happiness, for no happiness can follow such a blighted union.

Lady Catherine de Bourgh

Miss Anne de Bourgh to Miss Georgiana Darcy

Rosings Park, Kent, October 12

Dear coz,

We have just heard the news. Mama had a letter from Fitzwilliam, telling us of his betrothal. It is such a relief, I am overjoyed and I wish Fitzwilliam and Elizabeth every happiness!

Mama, on the other hand, is not overjoyed, and I am keeping out of her way. I sent a message downstairs to say that I was not well and I intend to keep to my room all day. I hear from my maid that the Collinses have thought it expedient to visit Mrs Collins's family in Hertfordshire and I am not surprised. Mama is livid. She has had three of the maids and two of the footmen in tears this morning, upset by her complaining about anything and nothing. She has written a letter to my aunt in Cumbria, telling her she must write to Fitzwilliam and forbid the match. It will do no good, I am sure my aunt is too sensible to take any notice, but it has gone some way to relieve Mama's feelings. She further relieved them by writing to Fitzwilliam and telling him he would disgrace his name, his family and indeed everything else if he married Elizabeth. However, I am sure he will be too happy to care for anything Mama might say.

I intend to remain in my room for two or three days and I have had the foresight to bring my pencils and paints, my needlework and my novels with me.

Do you think Henry will be home for the wedding? If so, I hope he might call on us here at Rosings, though I would not blame him if he stayed away. I wish we might attend the wedding, but Mama is so angry that she has declared she will not go and so there is no hope of that—unless she changes her mind, so that she can stand up when the vicar asks if any man can show any cause why they may not be joined together, and say that yes, she knows of a just cause, that Elizabeth would pollute the shades of Pemberley! Oh dear, I wish that thought had not occurred to me, for I now find myself wondering if it might happen. I will have nightmares about it, I am sure; or, even worse, that Mama might stand up and say that he was promised to me.

I will not think of it. I will think of church bells and white satin and flowers instead. You must tell me all about it; I rely on you, Georgiana.

Your dear coz,
Anne

Mrs Bennet to Mrs Gardiner

Longbourn, Hertfordshire,
October 15

My dear sister,

Were there ever such times! Jane to marry Mr Bingley, Lizzy to marry Mr Darcy! We are coming to London to shop for wedding clothes and we will be with you on the eighteenth. Poor Lydia had no time to shop for her clothes, but I mean to make up for it with Lizzy and Jane. I will not let anyone say that my girls did not have the best dresses for their wedding. Speaking of Lydia, I have told her to write to her sister and beg her husband's help for poor Wickham.

He has been very hard done by and I am sure that Lizzy's husband would be glad to be of use to him. Who better than his own brother-in-law to assist him? I am sure he deserves it, for never a handsomer young man lived.

Now, if I can only get Mary and Kitty married, my happiness will be complete. Mr Darcy's cousin, Colonel Fitzwilliam, will be standing up with him, and I think he might do for one or other of them. Then there is Mr Bingley's younger brother, who is to stand up with *him*. To be sure, the Bingley fortune comes from trade, but Mr Bingley and his sisters are very genteel, and I am sure the rest of the family is just the same.

We will stay with you until Monday.

Your sister,
Janet

Miss Mary Bennet to Miss Lucy Sotherton

Longbourn, Hertfordshire,
October 16

Most noble Friend,

This has been a doleful time for the cause of Learned Women. One of my sisters is already married, and now two more of my sisters are betrothed. Although I never had any hope of Lydia, and very little of Elizabeth, I did think, in time, that my sister Jane might abandon the path of frivolity and walk the highway of learning. But alas! It is not to be. Now Kitty and I are the only two girls remaining unspoken for. Kitty says she will never find a husband if Papa keeps her chained to Longbourn. I applauded her attempt at imagery; however, as we were at my aunt Philips's house at the time, her metaphor of being chained to Longbourn was not well chosen. When I pointed this out, Mama said, 'Oh, Mary, do be quiet,' but Mr Shackleton agreed with me.

He told me I looked charming in my new gown and asked me to dance with him. When I demurred, he reminded me that dancing was a healthful exercise and said that, in point of fact, he thought it more beneficial than playing the pianoforte, for that exercises only the fingers and dancing exercises the entire body.

I was much struck by his comment and I have decided that I should dance more often. Once my sisters have left the neighbourhood, I will no doubt be called upon to display true elegance and erudition, in the physical as well as the mental arts.

As Mr Shackleton led me back to my seat, I overheard my aunt Philips saying that we had had three weddings, and would no doubt soon have another one.

I cannot think what she means, unless she was referring to Kitty, who sat next to Mr Haydock all evening. He is visiting his cousins and means to spend some weeks in the neighbourhood, though what he can have to talk to Kitty about I do not know.

Your fellow traveller through this vale of vice,
Mary

Miss Kitty Bennet to Miss Eleanor Sotherton

Longbourn, Hertfordshire,
October 17

Dearest Ellie,

It is not fair, Mama is to go to London tomorrow with my sisters Jane and Elizabeth, but she will not take me. I do not see why I should not go to London, for I am sure that my attendant's gown is just as important as their bridal gowns, or at any rate, nearly so. But I am to be left behind with Mary.

We have had a new visitor to the neighbourhood: Mr Haydock, the vicar of Kympton. I met him at my aunt Philips's house. You may be sure I let him know what I thought of him for stealing poor Wickham's living from him, but Mr Haydock just looked down his nose and pretended not to know what I was talking about, then tried to say that Wickham had not deserved the living, and then laughed at me when I told him he was an odious man and that I would not speak to him. And he is odious, though admittedly very handsome. It is a good thing Lydia was not here, or she would have been very severe on him.

Mama says that, now my older sisters are getting married, I must hurry up and find a husband for myself. Mr Darcy's cousins will be at the wedding and Mama says I must try to catch one of them. I am sure I will do my best. They are all very rich and if they are handsome as well, I think I would like to marry one of them. Lydia got a husband by running away with him and Jane got one by going to stay with him and Lizzy got one by nursing her sister devotedly. But as I believe Papa would track me down if I ran away with anyone, and as I cannot invite myself into someone else's house, and as I have no sister to nurse, then unless Mary should happen to be taken ill, I do not know how it is to be done.

I said so to Mr Haydock, but he only laughed at me.

I saw that he was to be no help and so I suggested to Mary that she should visit Cumbria and endeavour to catch a cold there, but she said she could not catch a cold to order, and when I said that she should pretend to have a cold, she said that he who walketh in vice does so ne'er so often as something or other, and then looked pleased with herself and said she must remember to tell it to Mr Shackleton. I do not know why she does not marry him and have done with it, but she says she will never marry, she is a follower of the goddess Athena. She has asked Mama to buy her an owl. Mama said she had better have a new dress instead and make herself agreeable to all the rich gentlemen who are certain to be at Mr Darcy's wedding.

Lots of love and kisses,
Kitty

Mrs Lydia Wickham to Miss Elizabeth Bennet

Newcastle, October 23

My dear Lizzy,

I wish you joy. If you love Mr Darcy half as well as I do my dear Wickham, you must be very happy. It is a great comfort to have you so rich, and when you have nothing else to do, I hope you will think of us. I am sure Wickham would like a place at court very much, and I do not think we shall have quite money enough to live upon without some help. Any place would do, of about three or four hundred a year; but, however, do not speak to Mr Darcy about it, if you had rather not.

Your sister,
Lydia

Miss Georgiana Darcy to Miss Anne de Bourgh

Netherfield Park, Hertfordshire,
October 29

My dear Anne,

I write this to you in the carriage on my way back to London from Netherfield Park. You made me promise to tell you all about the wedding and I have now the leisure to do so. I travelled to Hertfordshire on Saturday and my guardian escorted me. I must confess I thought of you for most of the journey, and how you would have liked to be sitting with him in the carriage; I do so sincerely hope he comes to see you soon. We stopped for lunch at an inn and arrived at Netherfield Park in time for dinner. Caroline was there, saying how happy she was, but although I do not like to think ill of people, I believe she was not really happy. I overheard her once, as I entered the room, saying something spiteful about Elizabeth to her sister; however, perhaps I misheard. I hope so.

I spent the next few days getting to know all of my future sisters, as well as Elizabeth's parents, and the time passed very quickly.

We all retired early the night before the wedding and woke to mist, but it soon lifted and by the time we had finished breakfast it had cleared away completely. Fitzwilliam seemed very nervous and so did Mr Bingley. It was up to my guardian to distract their thoughts and occupy them until it was time to leave.

I dressed with great care, as you can imagine, given that I was to be an attendant. My dress was very elegant, white muslin with ribbon trim and white flowers in my hair. Elizabeth and Jane looked beautiful. They were dressed in white silk, but Jane's dress had a round neck whilst Elizabeth's had a square neck, the one trimmed with ribbon and the other with lace. They wore veiled bonnets and carried bouquets of roses, from which Kitty had removed the thorns. I believe she enjoyed the day as much as I did, for she was an attendant, too. She had the idea of decorating the lich-gate with flowers, and they smelled lovely as we passed underneath.

The ceremony was so beautiful that I almost cried, although I must confess I had an anxious moment when the vicar asked if anyone knew of any reason . . . I could only think of you saying that your mama might turn up and halt the wedding, and I glanced towards the door once or twice, expecting to see her there. But it all went well. Mary played the organ—I believe it must have several keys missing, for it sounded very odd—and then all too soon the ceremony was over and we all went back to Longbourn for the wedding breakfast.

Mrs Bennet introduced Kitty and Mary to my guardian and remarked on how handsome they were looking, and said what a pity it was that all his brothers had not attended the wedding. And I could only think how I wished you were there, and that your mama would say that you were looking handsome to him. There was a great deal of eating and drinking, and one of Charlotte Collins's little brothers kept saying that when he was a man he would drink as many bottles of wine as he wanted, and Mrs Bennet said that he shouldn't, and he replied that he should, and so it went on— until Mrs Bennet espied Mr Bingley's brother, Mr Ned Bingley, who stood up with his brother, and introduced him to Kitty and Mary.

Mr Ned Bingley is very different to his brother, but I like him. He is very honest and says what he thinks. He did not flatter me or praise me and I liked that. I am afraid that a great many men give me compliments because they know I am an heiress. Miss Bingley tried to introduce him to Miss King, saying that she had inherited ten thousand pounds, but he said he had no wish to live off his wife.

He does not have a great deal of charm, but I have experience enough to know that charm is dangerous and not worth a great deal.

He asked me about myself, and he was interested to learn that I was Fitzwilliam's sister, but more because I was the sister of his brother's friend than because I was a great heiress. Somehow his straightforwardness made it easier for me to talk to him and I asked him about himself. He is engaged in trade, and although I should have been horrified, I found that instead I was interested. He owns a number of shops in the north and he said that if ever I find myself in Yorkshire, I should tell Charles and then Charles will tell him and he will show me round one of the shops himself.

I was also introduced to Mr Bingley's mother. Anne, what can I say? I have never met anyone like her. She frightened me at first because she was so different to anyone I knew, and she was so very unlike Caroline and Louisa. But she had a good heart and I saw her wiping away a tear as Jane and Charles left the church. I believe she will by this time have returned north with her son Mr Ned Bingley.

Elizabeth and my brother left for the Lake District at about the same time. Elizabeth looked radiant. There is no other word to describe it—she positively glowed. Her eyes were sparkling with happiness and I have never seen my brother look more proud or happy. I hope I may be so lucky when I marry.

By this time they will be on their way to the Lake District, where they are to visit the Fitzwilliam cousins and tour the lakes before returning to Derbyshire. Elizabeth is looking forward to meeting Ullswater. I am glad Ullswater is more staid now and does not jump up at people as she used to, though I think that Elizabeth would only laugh and not shout at her and say she should be confined to the stables.

I will soon be back in London but I will be spending Christmas at Pemberley with my brother and sister. My sister! How good that sounds!

I hope your mama has recovered from her ill humour by then, and we might all be there together.

Your loving coz,
Georgiana

↞ NOVEMBER ↠

Mrs Elizabeth Darcy to Mrs Gardiner

Fitzwater Park, Cumbria,
November 4

My dear aunt,

You will see from the address on this letter that at last I am touring the Lakes, and it has been well worth the wait. I thought nothing could be better than our wedding, which was perfect, but the week since then has been even better. Every day brings me new knowledge of my husband and the knowledge draws me closer to him. I am more in love with him than ever and I know my husband to be violently in love with me.

How you will smile as you read that phrase, and how you teased me when I used it last year, saying that Bingley was violently in love with Jane. But if you could see me now, then you would not tease me, I am convinced, for you would be forced to acknowledge the truth of it. I have proof of my dear husband's uncommon love and affection every day. I believe I am the happiest woman alive. And this is before I have even taken up residence at Pemberley!

But you will want to know more about our wedding trip. We set out after the wedding breakfast, travelling for some way with Jane and Charles and seeing the sights together, alternating an hour or two in the carriage with an hour or two of walking through new and pleasant countryside or visiting some place of interest.

We stopped overnight along the way, once at an inn and the rest of the time with my husband's friends. They were very pleased to see us and welcomed us into their homes. When we had travelled as far north as Yorkshire, Jane and Charles left us, going on to see Charles's family. I know that Jane was feeling apprehensive about meeting the rest of his family, but I have had a letter from her this morning and she says with relief that they made her very welcome and that she likes them very much. This will not surprise you, for when did Jane ever dislike anyone? But I believe, from what she has said, that they are good people, and more like Charles than Caroline.

My husband—you will be hearing that phrase a great deal in this letter, for I am very much enjoying writing it!—my husband and I then travelled on to Cumbria, stopping to enjoy the scenery whenever a particularly splendid view offered itself. We took advantage of the fine weather and often made a picnic in some picturesque location, enjoying being just the two of us.

Today we arrived at Fitzwater Park. Colonel Fitzwilliam was here to greet us, having travelled more quickly, and it was good to see a familiar face in the midst of so many unfamiliar ones. He has a large family. His mother made me very welcome, but his father was more reticent, merely looking down his nose at me and saying, 'Harrumph!' It was no worse than I expected from an earl, and it was a good deal better than I was prepared for. At least he did not tell me I was polluting the shades of his ancestral home. I cannot really be surprised at his attitude, since he obviously expected his nephew to marry a young woman with an old name, at least, and very possibly with a title. What interested me was my husband's reaction. He was not in the least put out. There was no hint or suggestion in his face, voice or manner that he agreed with his uncle; indeed, he wore an expression of quiet pride and happiness whenever he looked at me. It is wonderful to see how it transforms his face, that smile. I cannot decide which I like most: his haughty expression, which, it must be admitted—though not to him!—is decidedly attractive, or his softer expression, which is merely decidedly handsome!

He introduced me to his cousins and they were all more or less agreeable. Peter was out walking with one of his friends, but another five cousins were indoors. I will not trouble you with all their names here; suffice it to say that I liked all of them at least a little, and I liked Maud very much. I expected to like her, because Georgiana had already told me something of her kindness, but how often does it happen that a person we think we will like turns out to disgust us in some way? But Maud was lively, sensible and amusing. She has two very well behaved children and Darcy is their godfather.

It was a revelation to me to see him allowing the children to pull his coat tails and play with his watch, with never a cross expression or a word of impatience. I had never considered him in such a light before, but I believe that as well as making an excellent husband he will also make a very good father.

You see, aunt, I can find no fault with him. How long this will last I do not know, but I beg you will indulge me in this one letter and then I promise not to boast of his many perfections again. It must make you very tired; indeed, you are probably running over the lines with a quick eye and a sigh even now! And so I will tell you more of Cumbria.

The scenery is even more dramatic than it was in Derbyshire, with mountains whose sides are clothed in the colours of autumn and whose tops are hidden in the clouds. The walking here is invigorating and the scenery breathtaking.

Fitzwater Park is even larger than Rosings and more imposing.

It is in an elevated position with grounds that stretch down to the lake. There is boating on the lake whenever the weather is suitable, I am told, and we hope to go sailing tomorrow. I have also been promised a view of Aira Force waterfall, which drops sixty-five feet and is said to be very splendid. I will write and tell you more when I have seen all the sights.

Your loving niece,
Lizzy

Mrs Jane Bingley to Mrs Elizabeth Darcy

Netherfield Park, Hertfordshire,
November 17

My dear Lizzy will forgive me for saying that she was quite wrong when she thought that she and Mr Darcy would be the happiest people alive, for I am convinced that that honour goes to Charles and myself. I cannot believe there was ever a time when I did not know him, for he is as necessary to me as breathing. I sought to be happy when I thought all hope had gone, but I could never concentrate or take pleasure in anything, all I could do was school myself to pretend. But now, how different everything is! I knew as soon as I met him that Charles was just what a young man ought to be: sensible, good-humoured and lively, with easy manners and good breeding. Now that I have him as my husband I have everything I could wish for.

Our visit to Yorkshire was interesting but I am glad to be back home—or where, for a time at least, we are making our home—at Netherfield Park. I like the house very well, I always have, but I must confess, Lizzy, that it is already proving to be too close to Longbourn.

When we returned from Yorkshire, we found Lydia and Wickham at Longbourn. They had overstayed their welcome, however, and Papa had given them a strong hint to be gone. They had ignored this hint, but when we returned they found it expedient to act upon it and in short, Lizzy, they came here. Fortunately, Wickham was called back north yesterday and they have left us now, but I dare say they will be here again before very long. They are finding it very difficult to manage on what little money they have. Lydia has never been good at economising and I am afraid they live beyond their means.

I hope it is not unkind of me to say that I am glad they have gone, for just at this moment I would rather not have guests. Charles and I are establishing our life together and it is not very convenient, particularly as Mama visits Netherfield every day. When she cannot get the horses for the carriage, she walks. I dare say the exercise is doing her good, and I think it is of benefit to Mary, for Mama must have company and either Kitty or Mary, or both, always accompany her. But for my part I could wish for rather more time to ourselves and rather less time with my family.

Charles bears it very well, even though he has already been persuaded to help Lydia and Wickham, and I fear that Lydia means to write to you, too. He says they are no trouble and that he is delighted to have them here, and he remarks that I was good to his family and that he has every intention of being equally good to mine.

Though his family are not what I am used to, I confess I like them. His mother is an affectionate woman who sincerely dotes on her children, and his brother Ned is very courteous. He reminds me of my uncle Gardiner: a man of business, and energetic in pursuit of it, but with good manners and good breeding besides. The little ones are lively and playful; in short I feel myself to be very fortunate.

You will be pleased to know that Mary studies less than formerly, which I think is a good thing. Mr Shackleton has persuaded her that too much study is bad for the brain.

Kitty has become closer to Maria Lucas in Lydia's absence. Away from Lydia, she is becoming more sensible and is far better company.

I am not the only one to think so. The rector of Kympton, Mark Haydock, has been spending some time in the neighbourhood and he seems to find Kitty's company amusing. I have caught him once or twice looking at her with an air of benevolent indulgence. For her part, I believe that Kitty has a liking for him, or will have, once she forgives him for taking Wickham's living; for of course she has heard the story from Lydia, in a very partial form. Certainly she seems to want his good opinion, and as he is a sensible man, I have high hopes of his attentions being good for her.

Charlotte and Mr Collins were here for a short visit earlier in the week but have now returned home. We were invited to a party at Lucas Lodge in their honour and we accepted. Lady Lucas could talk of nothing but Charlotte's interesting condition and Mama talked over her about Mr Darcy. I think Mama is growing bored, now that three of her daughters are married, and when Mary and Kitty marry, I think that it might be better if Charles and I were no longer in the neighbourhood, for she will have a great deal of leisure and will be here even oftener than at present.

After Christmas we intend to look about us for another house. Charles has long wanted to buy an estate, and as Netherfield Park is entailed on Frederick, it would not be possible to buy it, even if he wanted to. But I think he has a mind to move farther north, perhaps into Cheshire, and I am in agreement. The lease on Netherfield runs out next September and we hope to have found our new home by then.

Whether the Sothertons will move back to Meryton, who can say? It will depend on Mr Sotherton, and whether he has conquered his propensities for fast living. Frederick, at least, it appears, has been saved, for Susan writes that he has mended his ways. I am glad. I always liked him and felt he was good at heart. I would like them to return to Meryton and I know that Kitty and Mary would value Ellie and Lucy's company.

But that is for another time, indeed, another year, and there are many things to look forward to before that. Will you come to us for Christmas? I am longing to see you again.

Your loving sister,
Jane

Mrs Elizabeth Darcy to Mrs Jane Bingley

Pemberley, Derbyshire,
November 22

Dearest Jane,

I can see that we will have to perpetually argue about who is the happiest, because I cannot forego my own claim. Is not marriage wonderful? I cannot think how I managed before! Everything about life is so much better now. Our visit to the Lake District was wonderful and even the travelling was not tedious. Cumbria was very striking—beauty on an impressive scale—and the Fitzwilliam family were very grand but for the most part they were friendly.

We will not be able to join you for Christmas, as we will be holding a house party here, and of course you must come to us. Do say you will. Mama writes to me every day, dropping hints about visiting, and if she has a firm invitation for Christmas, I believe it will protect us from an impromptu visit before then. I have invited Charlotte as well, but she is not inclined to travel, with her olive branch so near to being delivered.

I have persuaded Fitzwilliam to invite his aunt Lady Catherine. I cannot say that I particularly want her here, but the rift must be healed sometime so it might as well be now. My resentment, once incurred, does not last forever, you see, though I am relying on you to rescue me from her if the occasion demands!

But do not let the thought of her prevent you coming to us. I am longing to show you Pemberley and I am growing to love it more every day. Fitzwilliam says that I must redecorate it if I wish but I prefer to leave it as it is. Everything is in good taste, and besides, it reminds me of my first visit here with my aunt and uncle. I can scarcely believe it was less than a year ago.

Fitzwilliam loves it even more than I do. He enjoyed our time in the Lakes but even then I could tell he was longing to return. He was eager to show me all his favourite spots in the house and garden and he wanted to introduce me to all his neighbours. We have been dining out every evening and so far I have met eleven of the principal families of the neighbourhood. I hope to meet more when we host our first dinner party next week.

Their welcome to me has been varied. Some of them have been warm and friendly, showing an interest in Hertfordshire; indeed, the Braithwaites know the Lucases—it seems that they all met at St. James's. But others look down on me shockingly. My dear husband left his conversation to give me his support last night when Mrs Yates drew her skirts away from me as though I were contaminated and asked me pointedly, 'Who are your people?' But I understood her malice easily enough, as her unmarried daughter was by her side, and I was not to be intimidated by the likes of a Mrs Yates, you may be sure. It is a good thing I have some irritations to put up with, or else my life would be in danger of being too perfect!

Lydia has already written to me, saying that Wickham would like a place at court and asking me to speak to Fitzwilliam about it. I have no intention of asking my husband to help Wickham any further, but I sent Lydia some money; otherwise I fear she will bankrupt the shopkeepers in her town before she is done.

It is interesting to hear that Kitty likes Mark Haydock. I think

I will invite her to stay on at Pemberley when the rest of our guests leave after Christmas so that she can see more of him. Kympton is not too far away and she will be company for Georgiana. Georgiana is still very shy, although growing less so, and she would benefit from Kitty's lively spirits, as Kitty would benefit from Georgiana's elegance and poise. The two of them will complement each other very well.

But now I must go, for if there is anything I like more than writing to you, dear Jane, it is spending time with my husband and being the mistress of Pemberley. For all its grandeur, it is home—as anywhere would be home that held my dear Mr Darcy.

Fondest wishes from your loving sister,

Mrs Elizabeth Darcy

ABOUT THE AUTHOR

Amanda Grange was born in Yorkshire, England, and spent her teenage years reading Jane Austen and Georgette Heyer whilst also finding time to study music at Nottingham University. She has had more than twenty novels published, including six Jane Austen retellings that look at events from the heroes' points of view. *Woman* magazine said of *Mr. Darcy's Diary*, "Lots of fun, this is the tale behind the alpha male," whilst *The Washington Post* called *Mr. Knightley's Diary* "affectionate." *The Historical Novels Review* made *Captain Wentworth's Diary* an Editors' Choice, remarking, "Amanda Grange has taken on the challenge of reworking a much-loved romance and succeeds brilliantly." *AustenBlog* declared that *Colonel Brandon's Diary* was "the best book yet in her series of heroes' diaries," whilst Austenprose declared *Henry Tilney's Diary* to be a Top 10 Austen read of 2011. Her paranormal sequel to *Pride and Prejudice—Mr. Darcy, Vampyre*—was nominated for the Jane Austen Awards. Amanda Grange now lives in Cheshire, England. You can find out more at her website, www.amandagrange.com.